PRAISE FOR SHARON SHINN AND *ARCHANGEL*:

"Taut, inventive, often mesmerizing, with a splendid pair of predestined lovers."

—*Kirkus Reviews*

"Displaying sure command of characterization and vividly imagined settings, Shinn absorbs us in the story . . . an entertaining SF-fantasy blend that should please fans of both genres."

—*Booklist*

"Excellent world building, charming characterizations and a sweet plot . . . a garden of earthly delights."

—*Locus*

"The spellbinding Ms. Shinn writes with elegant imagination and a steely grace, bringing a remarkable freshness that will command a wide audience."

—*Romantic Times*

"Shinn has created an enchanting world . . . I recommend this [book] without reservation."

—*The Charlotte Observer*

NOW, SHARON SHINN RETURNS TO THE COMPELLING WORLD OF SAMARIA IN AN EXTRAORDINARY NOVEL OF ANGELS AND MORTALS, MUSIC AND MYSTERY, SCIENCE AND FAITH . . .

Ace Books by Sharon Shinn

THE SHAPE-CHANGER'S WIFE
ARCHANGEL
JOVAH'S ANGEL

Jovah's Angel

Sharon Shinn

ACE BOOKS, NEW YORK

This book is an Ace original edition,
and has never been previously published.

JOVAH'S ANGEL

An Ace Book / published by arrangement with
the author

PRINTING HISTORY
Ace edition / May 1997

Cover art by John Jude Palencar.

For information address: The Berkley Publishing Group,
200 Madison Avenue, New York, NY 10016.

The Putnam Berkley World Wide Web site address is
http://www.berkley.com/berkley

ISBN: 0-441-00404-0

ACE®
Ace Books are published by The Berkley Publishing Group,
200 Madison Avenue, New York, NY 10016.
ACE and the "A" design are trademarks
belonging to Charter Communications, Inc.

PRINTED IN THE UNITED STATES OF AMERICA

10 9 8 7 6 5 4 3 2 1

CAST OF CHARACTERS

In Bethel

Alleluia, the new Archangel
Delilah, the fallen Archangel
Levi, Delilah's husband
Dinah, Samuel, Asher, Timothy — angels of the Eyrie
Gideon Fairwen, a Semorran merchant
Rebekah, the last oracle of Mount Sinai
Daniel, an Edori engineer living in Velora
Caleb Augustus, an engineer living in Luminaux
Noah, an Edori engineer, Caleb's best friend
Thomas, Sheba, Martha, Laban — members of the Edori tribe living near Luminaux
Joseph, proprietor of a singing establishment in Luminaux
Hope Wellin, Alleluia's mother
Deborah, a young girl living in Chahiela

In Jordana

Micah, the leader of the host of Cedar Hills
Job, the oracle of Mount Egypt
Marco, an Edori engineer living in Breven

In Gaza

Jerusha, the leader of the host of Monteverde
Mary, the oracle of Mount Sudan
Aaron Lesh, Emmanuel Garone — Manadavvi leaders

JOVAH'S ANGEL

PROLOGUE

Everyone had said it was a bad idea to fly back that night. For one thing, they had all had too much wine, and the Archangel herself was no exception. For another, the storm, which had been brutal for the entire weekend, had only let up marginally; there was still enough power in one of those gusts of wind to slap a walking man off his feet. Jovah only knew what one blast of that wind could do to an angel flying high above the earth in the unprotected frozen streams of air.

But it was impossible to tell Delilah anything. "I am safer flying back to the Eyrie than you are walking across the room," she scoffed to Gideon Fairwen, whose guest she had been for the past two days. It was to celebrate his daughter's summer wedding to one of the Manadavvi landholders that Delilah and half the angels from her hold had been sojourning in Semorrah until all of them, quite frankly, were sick of the self-satisfied pomp. "I will be held in the hands of the god himself."

"But surely—tomorrow morning—when the storms have abated somewhat and the sun is out . . ." Gideon protested. Truth to tell, he did not want to be the one to send a drunken Archangel to her doom on a moonless night, though he was not averse to having fifteen fewer mouths to feed at his breakfast table the following morning. Weddings were an expensive business, not that he begrudged a penny, not if it meant securing trading rights with some of the wealthier Manadavvi. And entertaining angels was always such a strain, though it was said throughout Samaria that Delilah required nothing more than good companionship and free-flowing wine to be content. "Better for everyone if you stay the night," he said.

One or two of her angels had added their voices to his, decrying the lateness of the hour and the distance to be flown. But her husband, Levi, as reckless as she, said, "Oh, don't be such cowards, it's only a four-hour flight," and laughed at all of them. It was his laugh that decided Delilah, for she loved the way he laughed, with his head thrown back and his blue eyes glinting through half-closed lids. He was always challenging her to something, daring her to back down; but she had never backed down once from any proposition he made her in the three years they had been married.

"Settled, then," she said briskly and glanced around the room to get the silent acquiescence of her attendant angels. She turned back to her host. "Gideon, you will send our belongings by cart in the morning, will you not? Thank you. It has been a most enjoyable stay."

Within minutes, the whole cadre was outside, on the roof of Fairwen's magnificent palace overlooking the bridge that tied the city to the Jordana shore. Besides Levi, there were two other mortals among the visitors from the Eyrie, and it had to be decided which angels would transport them for the first leg of the long flight. Delilah would carry Levi, of course; no question about that. He was six inches taller than she and a good seventy pounds heavier, but angels possessed, in addition to their fabulous wings, an amazing physical strength. It was one of the few points on which Levi conceded Delilah's superiority—reveled in it, in fact—her ability to carry him in her arms as she flew above the world.

So they assembled on the rooftop in the lashing dark, feeling the wind half lift them from their feet and laughing at its dizzy power. "Race to the Eyrie!" someone called out, but Delilah unexpectedly showed a grain of caution.

"No—stick together," she said. "We want to be close in case someone comes to grief in this storm."

They laughed at her but casually agreed, and then they all launched themselves at once in a feathery explosion of speed and flight. Once in the air, it was impossible to stay too close together, for with wingspans topping twelve feet, they all required a great deal of room in which to maneuver. Still, they fell into an informal pattern, Delilah in the lead, and Dinah began singing one of the pretty folk songs popular in the southern farmlands. The rest of them took it up, adding harmony and descant, changing the lyrics to suit themselves, and laughing because they knew—they all knew—it was tantamount to sacrilege to be aloft and singing anything except a prayer to Jovah. They were angels; they were supposed to carry the petitions of mortals to the ears of their god, and he heard them better the higher they flew. They were not supposed to be singing of broken hearts and vengeful love as they swept across the heavens so high their wingtips almost brushed Jovah's face.

In the lead, Levi, lying cozily in Delilah's arms, was the next one to offer a song, breaking into a tavern ditty of dubious lyrics. He had a fine, strong baritone which carried well to the angels following, and the rest of them happily responded with the appropriate chorus after he finished the verse. In the third stanza, he began making up lyrics, each set more bawdy than the last, causing Delilah to laugh so hard she almost lost her hold on him. He flung his arms around her neck in mock alarm, wrapping his fingers in her dense black curls and pleading for salvation.

"If I did drop you, you would deserve it," she told him. "Don't think I didn't see you flirting with the bride's sister—what was her name?—the tall girl with the bad hair."

"Laura—Logan—Lowbrow—some L name," he said with a groan. "She was such a bore. I only talked with her because Fairwen seemed so fond of her and it seemed a politic move. Can never be too friendly with the river merchants, so you've always told me—"

"With the river *merchants*, I think I said, not their daughters—"

"Isn't it the same thing?" he said, and turned his face in to nuzzle at the slim white column of her throat. She giggled and tossed her head back, then threatened to drop him again.

And so the first two hours of their flight passed, and morning began to make its tentative streaks across the horizon behind them. Before them the sky was still black, blacker than it should be for what was almost dawn, but then, the fist of night was still clenched around the storm clouds of the past two days. As they flew higher, to clear the currents over the northern edge of the Sinai Mountains, that fist shook that handful of cloud like a child would shake a toy, and sent the whole sky tumbling down around them.

Or so it seemed. One of the younger angels shrieked. All of them felt the familiar air boil insanely about them, smash them together, throw them apart, bat them from side to side till they were spun in circles. Now there was a confusion of shouting, names called out, cries to "Glide! Glide on your wings!" from someone who thought he'd mastered the knack of flying in a gale. Another upthrust of wind scattered them like litter across the alleyway of the sky; and then a sudden, deadly vacuum opened beneath them like a pit, and they all fell into it.

They landed in a tangle of feathers and feet, some on top of each other, some yards away. Instantly there was an outburst of sound—piteous wailing, sharp questions, a quick inventory of casualties. Samuel, the most senior of the angels in this troupe (and one who, by his own admission, should have known better than to embark on this midnight flight), was the first to find his feet and move from body to body, ascertaining injuries and their extent. Despite the weeping and the consternation, he was relieved to find most of the travelers relatively whole. Dinah appeared to have broken her leg, and Asher seemed dazed and stricken, but even the mortals had survived the crash landing fairly well, though both their escorts confessed to having dropped their burdens somewhere during the hazardous descent, try though they did to hang on.

Delilah, the one Samuel had looked for first, was the one he found last—and the first one whose condition caused his heartbeat to quicken with apprehension. She lay on her side in a hazard of boulders, her right wing bent crazily beneath her, her left stretched behind her like a sail spread for drying. Her eyes were closed but she was alive, for she cried out softly like a child praying for succor. She did not appear to be conscious or at least aware; and only the continuous whimper betrayed that she was still, momentarily at least, breathing.

Levi lay in her arms—she of all the angels had not let go her charge—but he lay even more quietly than she. Even from a distance, Samuel could guess the worst: The angelico was dead.

"Jovah be merciful," Samuel whispered, and though he whispered, every other angel heard him, and ceased his own lamentations, and grew afraid. "He is dead and she disabled. What will become of us if the Archangel cannot fly again?"

It was more than a week before news of the disaster made its way around Samaria, and that because Delilah herself refused to allow anyone to speak of it. They had brought her, dizzy and in great pain, home to the Eyrie, risking the flight because they feared she would die if they attempted to carry her in by cart. It was through sheer indomitable will that she resisted the comforting descent into oblivion, where neither physical nor emotional anguish could follow. Instead, she fought to stay alive, conscious, in control. No one outside the Eyrie was to know *anything*, she decreed; not until she knew. Not until she was positive that her wing was irrevocably broken, that she could not be repaired, that all hope was gone.

She did not speak of Levi, and no one mentioned his name to her. It was fascinating and a little frightening to watch this playful, lighthearted girl—she was only twenty-five, after all; everyone remembered her as such a delightful, wayward child—summon up all her resources of strength to deal with every simultaneous disaster that could befall her. Grieving was not a luxury she had at the moment; survival was the issue. Could her wing be healed? If not, essentially her life was over.

For a week, the secret held; then somehow—no one ever knew who broke the silence or how the rumor spread—everyone in Samaria learned that storms had capsized the Archangel, and disaster was in the offing. Well-wishers and curiosity-seekers converged on the mountain hold, though they were barred from ascending the great stone stairs that led to the angel quarters. Angels from the other two holds were not so easily turned away, however, and they swooped in from above to demand answers and predictions. Could the Archangel be saved? Would she live? Would she fly again?

Could she possibly continue her reign as Archangel if she had been damaged for life?

These were not questions that could be answered in a week, although the prospects from the outset looked grim. Physicians were brought in from all over Samaria—from the wealthy Manadavvi enclaves, from the sophisticated river cities, from Luminaux, where the best of everything could be found—and none of them could offer the Archangel hope. The wing had been broken close to the great joint that connected it to musculature in her back; some essential artery or sinew or nerve path had been severed, and not all their limited science could deduce how to reknit the cut connection. She could not, of her own volition, unfurl that wing; she could not feel an anxious finger sliding down the mesh of feather and skin. Thus with men who had broken their spines—their legs, their feet, became useless; these limbs could not be animated by the will of the man who owned them. Thus with the Archangel's wing.

But if Delilah could not fly—if Delilah could not soar through the heavens, lifting her magnificent voice in prayer to Jovah—if she could not quickly be summoned to any troubled spot in the whole of Samaria—how could she serve the god or his diverse children? How could she intercede for them, guide them, ask the god to chastise them? How could she be Archangel?

Of course, she could not. But who would be Archangel in her place?

Two months after Delilah's fall, the two living oracles of Samaria met in the abandoned holy place of Mount Sinai to ask the god that very question. They were even more solemn than they might ordinarily have been, being forced to approach the god with such a question. No oracle had ever had to go to Jovah to ask him to name an Archangel while the Archangel still lived, and this was a grave and grievous task. But the fear in their bones went deeper still, for they were not sure Jovah would answer their questions or listen to their petitions.

These two months had seen an unprecedented surge in violent weather from northwestern Gaza all the way to the lower coastline of Jordana. Along the coasts, hurricanes sprayed venomous water into the marine cities, leveling a few of them, rendering one or two unlivable. In the deserts near Breven, continuous rain had turned the sandy miles into virtually impassable swampland; and nowhere were farmers assured of receiving appropriate amounts of rain for their specific crops. The angels, who had always successfully petitioned Jovah for more snow, less rain, gentler winds, these days sang to him in vain. If he listened, he did not care. If he answered, it was with more storm. They had no certainty that he would view this new request with any more interest.

The oracles had chosen to meet at Mount Sinai not only because it was midway between their own retreats but because it was the oldest and most venerable seat of holy power on Samaria. Here the original settlers had first communicated with their god; here were the archives (in texts now mostly unreadable) that described those earliest encounters among divinity, angel and mortal. Here, they hoped, Jovah might still pay attention to the crises of his people.

They arrived almost simultaneously, young Mary from Gaza and ancient Job from Jordana, and together entered the cool, echoing stone hallways of Mount Sinai. Rebekah had died a year ago and no one had come forward to replace her, and the remaining oracles were at a loss. Their own callings had become clear to them in unmistakable visions, but if anyone in all of Samaria was dreaming of the honor of becoming oracle, no one had stepped up to claim the position. They had each asked Jovah for guidance, but he had failed to respond to either one.

Ghostly gaslight from eternally burning sources lit their way through the pale granite corridors, and they followed the familiar turnings to the central chamber, where they could summon the god. Here, a glowing blue plate was set into the stone wall with a rolling chair even now placed casually before it; this was where the oracle would sit to commune with the god. They could almost believe Rebekah had just this moment stepped away from her seat there to stretch her stocky legs; both of them wished she was here now to consult with them.

"Mary, would you care to lift our petition to the god?" was Job's formal invitation, but he was the elder and this was delicate work, and so she yielded the place to him. He sat with a certain reverence before the pulsing screen, running his hands experimentally over the strange hieroglyphics on the shelf before him. When he touched a symbol, it would appear on the face of the blue plate, forming words in a language so old only the oracles could learn it; and when the god responded, he did so in the same forgotten tongue. They called this bright screen the "interface," though it was a word that had little meaning to them. So did the oracles before them name the device, and the oracles before them, back to the founding of Samaria.

Job worked slowly, as he always did, because this alien language did not come easily to him and he did not want to err. He constructed his first message, a simple greeting, merely to confirm that Jovah was awake and ready to hear petitions. He was relieved beyond measure when the reply came quickly back in navy letters laid against the glowing screen.

The second part of the message was complex and had to be carefully worded, so he read it aloud to Mary before touching the key that would signal to Jovah that his thought was complete. "The Archangel Delilah has been irretrievably injured and can no longer fly in your exalted service," he quoted. "It grieves us to say we believe a new Archangel must be chosen, so that all your wishes may be promptly carried out. Are we correct? Must a new Archangel be selected?" Mary nodded, and Job sent the message to Jovah.

There was a long pause before the interface wavered and reformed, new letters marching across its screen. "If the Archangel cannot fly, she cannot be Archangel" was the uncompromising response. "She cannot serve."

They had expected it, but it was a blow nonetheless; and they were already mentally recasting the phrasing to soften its impact on Delilah. Jovah was not, though they did not like to spread this information, the most sympathetic of gods in his direct dealings with the oracles.

"Who then should be Archangel in her place?" Job typed laboriously onto the screen. "Jerusha is leader of the host at Monteverde, and very capable. Micah leads the host at Cedar Hills, and he has the trust of all the merchants and landowners. Both are young, able to serve the seventeen years that remain of Delilah's term."

He had barely sent the message when the screen wriggled and Jovah's answer appeared starkly before them. They read the name once, twice, silently, then looked at each other in astonishment.

"The angel Alleluia, daughter of the angel Jude and the mortal woman Hope?" Mary said aloud. "Can he truly mean that? Is he sure?"

"I can scarcely ask the god if he is *certain*," Job replied with grim sarcasm. "And he has well and truly named her—that is her father and that is certainly her mother."

"But she is—no one knows her, not the river merchants or the Manadavvi—even the angels . . ."

"She is scholarly, certainly, and reclusive," Job said, as if defending Alleluia, as if he was not as shocked by Jovah's choice as Mary was. "But her knowledge of Samarian ways is no doubt extensive—"

"Job, we are in a *crisis* here!" Mary cried, striking her hands together in frustration. "Every day a fresh storm breaks across the Jordana deserts, and the oceans along the southern coasts are fierce with waves. The Bethel farmers are crying for succor, which Manadavvi landowners can give them, but at a price no one can afford. Half of Breven is turning into some kind of factory as they build more and more of those machines—and who is to regulate the merchants? Who is to stop the storms? Who is—the angel Alleluia! Who will listen to her?"

"Jovah, perhaps," was Job's simple reply. "He must have chosen her for a reason."

Mary tossed her hands in the air, a gesture of despair. "There is no reason in Samaria anymore," she said. "No reason in Jovah's ways, no reason at all."

"Trust in the god," Job said. "We have no choice."

"Ask him again," she urged. "Make certain—"

He splayed his hand in a gesture of futility, but complied, to ease his own troubled mind as far as possible. "Confirming: the angel Alleluia of the Eyrie, daughter of the angel Jude and the woman Hope?"

"Yes," came Jovah's answer, as quickly as his last reply. "Name her Archangel immediately."

Job looked soberly at Mary. "So speaks the god," he said formally. "We must carry the news at once to the angels."

Mary took a deep breath and expelled it on a hopeless sigh. "Then we must," she said. "To the Eyrie first, I suppose, since we are here. I do not want to be present when Delilah hears the news."

"I feel sorry for her," Job said softly.

"Delilah? Yes, except that she brought it on herself—"

"For Alleya," Job corrected. Mary looked startled to hear him use the shortened name by which people addressed Alleluia; it did not seem a formal enough address for one who would soon be Archangel. "She is no more fit for this job than a mortal girl fresh from the northern foothills."

But his words gave them both pause, for, more than a century ago, just such a girl had come to power as the bride of the Archangel Gabriel, and she had not done so ill.

Mary sighed again. "So perhaps there is hope after all," she said. "Jovah defend us in our hour of need."

"Amen."

They stood—suddenly both inexpressibly weary—and made their way back out of the flickering gray tunnels. They felt, if possible, even more anxious than they had been going in, for no one would like their news, and no one would think their problems were on the way to being solved. What could they do? They could not gainsay the god. He had knowledge beyond their own; his inscrutable choices were always wise over the reckoning of centuries.

So they left, and climbed slowly down the mountain, and forgot, or did not realize, that they had failed to shut down the interface screen that linked the mortals of Mount Sinai with their god. And they did not see, because the message appeared an hour or two after they departed, that the god had more words for them, written in a tongue that only they would understand. Just two words, straightforward and plain, but no one was there to read them; and even if anyone had wandered by chance into this most holy of places, almost no one would have been able to decipher the god's arcane request.

Chapter One

Caleb Augustus stood on the mountaintop with his hands folded across his chest and prayed one last time that his theories of aerodynamics and meteorology were sound. Then he took a running start, unfurled his arms, and leapt off the point of the low mountain. For a few fateful seconds he sank rapidly; then the air caught under the great leather wings strapped to his arms, and he was lofted above his former perch. He laughed aloud. He couldn't help it. He was flying, impossible but true—he was *flying!*

It didn't last long, though longer than he expected. Two vagrant currents caught him almost playfully; he could feel the breezes curl, then shred apart under his outstretched limbs. He knew from past experience that pumping his arms furiously did almost nothing to increase his altitude or slow his eventual descent, so he concentrated on keeping his shoulders level, his wrists high, catching the breezes as they swirled him in one direction, then another. Like a bark boat in a shallow stream. Wherever the element took him, he would go.

It took him, and fairly unceremoniously, to the rocky ground a few hundred yards from his jumping-off point. One minute he was gliding along, coasting like a hawk above its prey, the next he was tumbling gracelessly through the empty layers of air to land in a painful heap on the stony ground. But this he had learned about from experience, too, and he had taken care to pad his chest and his knees and his head with soft wads of clothing. He rolled awkwardly to his knees and climbed to his feet—and then spread his wings again and laughed out loud once more.

"I was *flying*, Noah, you should have seen it!" he shouted. "Give me five years and I'll figure it out. I swear, I'll be the first mortal on Samaria to take wing alongside the angels."

There was boundless joy in that thought, and it sustained him through the long, tedious process of disassembling his wings, carefully unrolling the soft, stretched leather from the light wood frame and just as carefully loosening the myriad joints of the frame and collapsing it into one small bundle. A long trip and two hours of preparation beforehand, five minutes of flight, then two hours of cleanup afterward; most men would call that a small return for such a great investment. But then, Caleb reminded himself, they weren't visionaries, creative geniuses, scientists like him. They might have pleasures that lasted a little longer, but surely none that were more intense.

And another two hours on the road back home. Someday, he promised himself, he would fly back to Luminaux, coast lazily in on his great stretched wings, and set the city agape—if anything could elicit such a reaction from the Luminauzi, which he rather doubted. Someday—but for now he had to settle for loading his bundles into a rented cart hitched behind a borrowed horse, and plod back to the city at a rate that was almost wrenchingly tedious compared to the pace he longed to set.

Early winter dusk was wrapping itself across the far horizon as he first spotted the faint azure haze that signaled the approach to Luminaux. The city was illuminated with a combination of gaslight, candlelight and the new marvel, electricity. Indoors, these lights were a reasonable white, but outdoors the residents of the Blue City filtered everything through tinted glass to give the entire public arena a somewhat aqueous glow. Even by day, Luminaux flaunted a similar color, since it was built of sapphire granite and cobalt mica and overrun with phlox and delphinium. There was no place like it anywhere in Samaria, and Caleb loved to come home to it by night.

Once inside the city gates, it took him nearly another hour to dispose of the horse and the cart and store his experimental wings. By then he was famished. He strode west from the city till he reached the Edori camp, maybe a hundred patched tents clustered around a third as many fires, but no one there had seen Noah.

"When will he be back? Do you know where he went?" he asked a cluster of teenagers who were sitting on the farthest edge of the campground, playing some dice game or using that as a plausible excuse to engage in the inevitable rituals of courtship. Caleb had learned long ago that, in an Edori enclave, it was unnecessary to look for friends or relatives of the man you were hunting up; everyone in the group was equally likely to know the business of every other clansman.

"I think he went to town," one of the girls answered, as if "town" were a foreign place hundreds of miles away, not a collection of buildings she could see clearly from where she sat. "About an hour ago."

"Do you know where in town?" Caleb asked patiently.

"There's a place. There's a singer there," one of the boys volunteered. "He's been going there almost every night."

"I remember him raving about some new soprano," Caleb said with a smile. "You don't happen to remember just where she's performing?"

"It's named after an angel," the girl said helpfully. "Cherub. Something like that."

Caleb could not help laughing. "Well. Thanks. I'll go try to find him. If you see him before the night's over, tell him I was looking for him. I'm Caleb."

They smiled and nodded and benignly watched him go. He set off back toward the lights of the city, shaking his head very slightly. Odd group, the Edori. They would welcome any stranger into their midst with the utmost friendliness, incurious and unalarmed; he could as easily have stayed all night at the encampment awaiting Noah's return, been offered food and drink and a place to sleep by any of a dozen total strangers. No wonder they were a dying race, nearly herded into slavery and extinction 150 years ago and, now, crowded out of their nomad life by an aggressive, expanding population that had no patience for their unhurried ways. He liked them, but he knew he could never live such an undirected life.

Under the blue streetlights he paused to get his bearings. Luminaux boasted more nightclubs and symphony halls than any other city in Samaria—there was no such thing as a separate entertainment district, so no telling where Noah's new singer might be. Something to do with angels. What could the girl have been talking about?

But two blocks of aimless walking led him by fortunate chance to his destination—a low, dark building with lightless windows and a door curtained over with black velvet. Guarding the door was a glass statue of an angel lit from within by a turquoise flame. Her crystal hands held a triangular pennant, white letters embroidered on a blue serge field, and the single word spelled "Seraph."

Must be the place, Caleb said to himself, smiling, and pushed through the soft door to enter.

Inside, there was scarcely more light. Faint blue bulbs outlined a narrow stage at the far end of the room and traced the aisles between tables and doorways. Candles provided a touch more light at each table, but Caleb noted that the seated patrons leaned close together to get a better look at each other's faces. Servers made their way cautiously through the dark thicket of chairs and bodies, balancing trays and memorizing their steps between stations.

Someone was on stage, playing tentative-sounding chords on a magnificently tuned dulcimer. Must be the interim entertainment, Caleb thought, since it sounded more like background music than a headline performer. He had no musical ability himself, but it was impossible to live in Samaria and not acquire, effortlessly almost, discriminating taste and the ability to judge talent. Music flowed through Luminaux like electricity through the wire; it provided more wattage than the Gabriel Dam on the Galilee River. Luminaux would as soon paint itself crimson as forego its music—and this idle performer was not the one people had crowded into Seraph to see.

For the place was quite full, every table taken and two or three dozen patrons leaning against the uneven walls or standing by the stage in small, excited groups. It would be hard to find Noah in this shadowy place, peering past groups of strangers to search for the familiar face. Caleb eased his feet forward onto the dark pathways and made his way almost by feel from table to table, scrutinizing all the patrons as he passed.

He had traversed maybe three densely packed rows when he came across a small table jammed up against the east wall with an angled view of the stage and only one patron seated there. He could tell it was a man but couldn't see his face, so he said "Noah?" in a low voice and waited for a response.

"Yes, who—Caleb! Where did you come from? Are you with anyone? Have a seat!"

Caleb laughed and sat down. "I came looking for you. A couple kids back at the camp said you might be here. Once again, I commend the Edori on their group intellect, the ability to sense the actions and emotions of one of their tribe even though separated by a geographic distance that can transcend hundreds of miles—"

The grin was hard to see in the dark but unmistakable in the voice. "I probably told someone where I was going. Why were you looking for me?"

"You said it couldn't be done—"

"No! You didn't get those damn wings to fly!"

"Yes—I, even I—lowly mortal that I am."

"I don't believe it, not *fly*. You glided, am I right? You jumped off a mountain, came down, swirled around in the thermals a little, but you weren't self-propelled. You didn't have control, you didn't get distance. You weren't flying. Am I right?"

Caleb waggled his hands dismissively; a technicality merely. "I was airborne, that's what counts. I got the start, I got the *germ* of flight. Okay, so it lasted maybe ten minutes—"

"See, it has something to do with thrust. Liftoff. You don't have power—and you don't have the fuel source to supply you with power if you do figure out how much power you need."

"Power—why are you so insane about a power source? Birds don't have any special thrust engine, angels don't—they have wings, they get lift. Why should I need some outside boost?"

"They have wings that have more strength, flexibility and rapidity than your poor little mortal arms can generate—and it has something to do with body weight, I'm convinced. Birds have those light bones."

"Well, angels weigh as much as mortals do—more, most of

them, because of that muscle mass—and it doesn't seem to slow them down."

"I know. There's just something to the formula we haven't worked out yet."

"But we will."

"Hell, yes. If not us, nobody."

A soft-footed waitress startled them both by materializing out of the inky darkness. "Would you like something to drink?"

Caleb glanced at Noah's glass. "Wine? The house drink. Whatever. And can I get something to eat? I'm starving."

She took his order and as silently disappeared. "So was it wonderful?" Noah demanded. "This pseudo-flight. This almost-flying."

"It was—" Caleb spread his hands. "Someday I'm going to meet an angel that I actually trust, and I'm going to have the nerve to ask him to carry me from Luminaux to the Eyrie or somewhere, and I'm going to know what it's actually like—but this came as close to fabulous as anything I've ever experienced. Like drifting down a river, except there's nothing, not even water under you. Like levitating. Except you can *feel* the air. It *is* like the river; it pushes and gives with an actual pressure. I felt—" He laughed. Caleb was not a religious man, paid no respects to the god, but it was truly how he had felt. "I felt like I was in Jovah's hands. And they were ghostly but substantial."

"You'll let me try them, of course."

"Of course. If you'll take me for a ride in your monster machine."

Noah laughed, with an edge of rue. He had, for as many years as Caleb had labored over his wings, struggled to build a self-propelled land vehicle. He had succeeded, more or less, but even he admitted that his large, awkward, noisy, smelly result was not an ideal means of transportation.

"We'll take a trip," he promised. "I need to see how it holds up over distance. We can go out to Breven or maybe up to Semorrah. Make it a vacation."

"Pick your day," Caleb said. "Sounds like fun."

The waitress brought Caleb's food and a bottle of wine, and he ate quickly. He was famished, the day's exertions having taken a physical toll. "So tell me," he said around mouthfuls, "this is the place you've been raving about? With the singer?"

"You'll rave, too, when you hear her."

"I'm not much of a connoisseur."

"You don't need to be. And once you meet her—"

"Oho! This has progressed, then."

"A few nights ago I introduced myself. I didn't realize—but wait till you see her for yourself. Anyway, she's been fairly friendly. More than I would have expected."

"Tired of all that fawning from the elite Luminauzi intellectual circle, she falls for the simple good-heartedness of the earnest Edori boy."

Noah laughed self-consciously. "Something like that. She's been knocked around a bit, is the impression I get. Acts sort of tough and worldly, but—oh, you know. Everyone longs for a place of quiet and ease. Anyway, that's how I read it. If you stay long enough, you'll get to meet her. She'll come over to the table after her last set. At least, she has the past couple nights. Well, this week."

"I'll stay," Caleb said, inwardly marveling. Noah was usually so offhand and cheerful about his numerous affairs, as all the Edori were. It was unlike him to seem so serious about a woman. "What's her name?"

There was, or seemed to be, a moment of hesitation before Noah answered. "Lilah."

"And I take it she's not Edori?"

The faintest laugh. "No."

"I can hardly wait, then."

He did not have to. Even as he spoke, the dulcimer player finished his piece and rose to his feet. An odd sound ran through the crowd—more truly, it seemed as though an excited silence fell over the audience, creating a static charge. Wineglasses stopped clinking. Rustling ceased. Every listener faced the front of the room. A heightened light seemed suddenly to focus on the stage.

There the back curtains parted as if swept back by invisible hands, revealing the silhouette of a single figure standing mostly in the shadows. Little could be seen of her face, though in the uncertain light she appeared young; her pale oval face was framed by a mass of dark curls. She had her arms crossed high upon her chest, each hand resting on the opposite shoulder in an almost suppliant attitude. She was dressed in flowing robes that, because of her unmoving stance, fell around her like the marble gown of a statue. Behind her, folded tightly back, angel wings made their peculiar and beautiful rise and curve. She looked like nothing so much as an effigy upon a tomb, an eternal prayer to Jovah for mercy.

Caleb glanced sharply at his friend. "She's an angel? Or is that just an affectation for this place?"

Noah motioned him to silence, not answering, not taking his eyes off the performer. Caleb swung his attention back to the stage. Lilah had taken a step forward and swept her arms before her, palms upward, in another gesture of entreaty. From somewhere out of sight came the plaintive, disembodied sound of a single flute playing a melancholy scale.

It was hard to tell exactly when the singer joined her voice to the flute's, for surely they exhaled two or five or seven notes in flawless unison, till the woman's voice broke free of the pipe's and climbed above it in a series of minor intervals. Her song was wordless, her voice as pure and uninflected as the silver flute, and the overall effect was absolutely unearthly. Caleb felt his heart twist with an inexplicable malaise, and he was swept by a wave of deep and unutterable regret for all the missed opportunities of his life, all the friends lost and years too easily wasted. It was a gentle sadness without the slightest hint of bitterness, but he was shocked at its thoroughness. As the eerie voice soared higher, its sweetness thinning till it almost faded, he took a long, unsteady breath. So might a man feel who had spent the night sobbing over vanished love.

Simultaneously, both voices trailed to a breathless silence. There was no motion, no sound, from the stricken crowd. The singer, who had bowed her head as she finished her song, raised her chin and took a step forward to the edge of the stage. She surveyed the audience for a moment—and, unbelievably, laughed.

"Welcome once again to the unique entertainment you have come to expect here at Seraph," she said, and in the dulcet voice was the unmistakable taint of sarcasm. She tossed her hair back and flicked her eyes around the room, assessing the expressions of her audience. Many, Caleb guessed, surely looked as he did—

like coma victims coming to in a much stranger world than they remembered leaving. This was not the persona one would have expected of a woman with such a celestial voice. "I'm Lilah, I'm the one you came to hear, even if you don't know it yet. Don't bother writing down your requests, I just sing whatever I feel like. If I don't sing what you came to hear—well, feel free to come back tomorrow night and every other night until I've satisfied you all.

"Boys?" she added, without a pause or change of tone, and suddenly a hidden band broke into a fast-paced melody that Caleb found vaguely familiar. Some popular tune of the day; no doubt he'd heard it on some street corner or in a crowded tavern. When Lilah's voice came swooping down on the opening words of the first verse, he suddenly remembered that he liked the song immensely—it was his favorite; he had never heard anything he liked better. Not until he felt the sting in his palms did he realize he was clapping with the rhythm, as was everyone in the room. Had he known the lyrics, he would have been singing along.

"Who *is* she?" he found time to whisper to Noah between the end of this song and the start of the next, but Noah merely waved at him again and did not trouble to answer. And it did not matter. Lilah had begun singing again, something a little slower this time but just as upbeat, and actually, nothing at all mattered. Caleb grinned foolishly and let his heart be uplifted.

The concert continued well into the night, the mood of the crowd shifting as rapidly as the tone of Lilah's songs—although, after her opening number she stayed mostly in the cheerful range of emotions. In fact, from time to time she dipped straight into rowdy, not to say risqué, and more than once her listeners were on their feet, stamping their heels, pounding their hands together, and echoing choruses back at her as she teased them from the stage. It was an exhausting performance, even for the audience; when she at last bowed good night after her third riotous encore, Caleb finally noticed that he was sore, tired, and filmed with sweat all the way to his hairline.

"Does she sing like that every night?" he asked, dropping into his seat with a sigh of exhaustion. "How does she have the strength?"

"Every night that I've been here," Noah replied, sinking

down beside his friend. "And I think it's harder on us than on her. She doesn't even seem tired at the end. Like she could do the whole set over and not notice the effort."

Caleb drained his wine (forgotten for this hour or two) and then his goblet of water. "So tell me," he said, "who *is* this woman? She can manipulate a crowd of Luminauzi socialites as easily as a child can charm his uncle. I consider myself pretty immune to persuasion, but I was dancing in my chair along with the rest of them."

"Well . . ." Noah said hesitantly, "she's an angel."

Caleb nodded. "So I gathered. No one but an angel could sing like that. What's she doing *here*? Kicked out of Cedar Hills for inappropriate behavior? Because you have to admit she crossed the line once or twice."

"Didn't seem to bother you at the time," Noah said sharply.

Caleb's eyes widened at the swift partisanship. "All right, then, let's just say I've never heard an angel sing the one about the woman with the three lovers. And I can't imagine that Micah would be happy to know that one of his host is performing tavern songs for the masses down in the Blue City."

"She's not from Cedar Hills," Noah said almost grudgingly. "Anyway—if that's what she wants to sing—it must get tiresome, doing all those endless masses and those dreary requiems."

"You still haven't answered the question."

"So what was the question?"

"Who is she? And why is she here?"

"Ask her."

"You don't know?"

"I think you'll figure it out when you meet her."

Caleb took a breath, let it go on a sigh instead of another question. "Right. Well, then. Another bottle of wine? Looks like we'll be here for the evening."

But the crowd began emptying out sooner than he expected, and within twenty minutes of Lilah's last number, Seraph was almost empty. Checking the time, Caleb realized that it was later than he had thought; she had sung for nearly two hours, and the time had just melted away. Noah took advantage of the unoccupied tables to snag an extra chair, and asked the waitress for another wineglass and a plate of cheese and fruit.

"She'll be hungry," he said to Caleb.

"I would be."

Despite these preparations, Caleb harbored a secret doubt that Lilah would actually join them. She seemed too rarefied to settle even briefly among the ranks of men; it would be like holding a conversation with a fire. Or with an angel, more accurately. Something he had never done.

But there she was, a graceful shape against the patchy darkness of the bar. She wended her way through the clustered tables and pushed-back chairs as delicately as if she were stepping a path in a rose garden. Still she carried her great wings tightly behind her, as if they were bound back; their feathered edges trailed on the floor behind her, and she seemed not to care that they swept through spilled ale and scattered crumbs.

"Food and wine—I knew I could count on you," she said by way of greeting, dropping into the empty chair with a deliberate crumpling motion. "Those fools think I can cavort up there all night without rest or sustenance. I'm utterly famished."

"You were marvelous, of course," Noah said.

She laughed and quickly ate a bite of cheese. "Bar songs," she said mockingly. "A child could sing them and bring the house down."

"You don't have to sing bar songs," Caleb said. "I think they'd listen to serious music even more happily. For myself, I preferred the first piece you did, though it nearly broke my heart."

She turned wide, black, marveling eyes on him—as if astonished that he had dared to speak, or possibly as if she had not realized until this moment that there was someone else at the table. Up close she had a rich, dark beauty, white skin laid hauntingly against velvet black hair. Her wings repeated the same chiaroscuro motif, each blindingly white feather edged in shadow-black. "And what are *your* credentials for determining the proper musical mix to provide for the discriminating Luminauzi audience?" she asked. "You own a music hall, perhaps? You are yourself a musician? You have another venue to offer me where songs of spirituality and mysticism will be greeted with sober acclaim?"

Amazing; she could do with her speaking voice what she could do when she sang, and that was whip up any emotion she wanted in anyone who listened. But Caleb was stubborn, and on guard against her now. He would not allow himself to be derided. "You must have been to Giordano's and La Breva," he said coolly. "They offer music on the classical scale, and they're always packed to overflowing. Anyway, I think you could sing anything you chose to here, and people would come to listen. You have an awesome voice."

"Thank you," she said, still taunting him. "And I sing what I choose to sing, anyway. So don't pity me for my song selection. I choose what makes me happy."

Clearly untrue; anyone less happy than Lilah, even on brief acquaintance, would be hard to locate. The full red mouth fell of its own accord into a pout more sad than sullen; there was a troubled weariness deep in her dark eyes that even the mockery could not disguise. "Well, what you sing seems to please your audience, at any rate," Caleb said quietly. "I have never enjoyed a concert more."

"Thank you," she said again. "Do please return sometime."

It was at this point that Noah intervened to make introductions. "Lilah, this is my friend Caleb. The engineer I told you about."

"Oh, yes, the one who builds flying machines," she said, turning her gaze back to Caleb. "Tell me, how does the project go?"

Caleb was suddenly acutely aware of her own folded wings, held rigidly behind her as if they were not part of her. Most angels he had observed carried their wings like bequests handed to them personally by the god; they could not lavish them with enough attention.

"Not as well as I would like," he said with a smile. "Noah tells me I am only gliding, not truly flying. He's right, I need some sort of engine, but then you have all sorts of fuel problems—which could be dangerous, especially combustible fuel, and I can't see how you'd get electricity if you're airborne. But I enjoyed the gliding."

"That's all we talk about," Noah said, and Caleb sensed in him an eagerness to change the subject. "Motors. Fuel. Propulsion. Locomotion. I've told you about my land vehicle, of course—"

"I believe I could build it myself," Lilah murmured.

"Caleb and I want to take it for a long drive to see how well it holds up. We're thinking about Semorrah. Or Breven. Actually, I may have business in Breven fairly soon."

"What business?" Caleb asked.

"Mmm, it's pretty speculative. Shipbuilding."

"You don't know a damn thing about boats!"

"Motorized. Or part-motorized. Get them through the windless days. For long voyages."

"I'd have thought that problem was worked out long ago."

"New project. Well, as I say, it's iffy right now. But if I need to go to Breven, that would be the perfect test."

"Sure, get us stranded somewhere in the Jordana deserts, no water, no food, no horses to carry us to anything resembling civilization—"

"We can have followers. I'll have some of the kids from the campsite come behind us on horseback. If we break down, they'll be along in a day or two to rescue us. Would that make you feel safer?"

"Infinitely."

"Sounds like fun," Lilah said. "When do we go?"

Noah's successive emotions of shock, delight and cautious disbelief were easy to read. "You'd like to come? Really? Caleb's right, it could be a horrific trip."

"With not much to show for it at journey's end," Caleb added. "Breven's a smelly, squalid, miserable city. Ever been there?"

"Oh, yes," Lilah said with a secret smile.

Noah addressed Caleb. "Well, you can blame the likes of you and me for Breven's nastiness today," he said. "If it weren't for the engineers and the scientists and the relentless inventors experimenting with power and coal—"

"Truly. We made the engines, we made the factories, we made the Jansai into the happy little industrialists they are today. And I still say, on with progress. But that doesn't erase the fact that Breven's an ugly place with no charm to recommend it, and if it wasn't for the sake of the journey I wouldn't agree to go at all."

"You didn't answer me," Lilah said, and her wonderful voice was plaintive. "Will you take me?"

Noah looked at her helplessly. "If you want to go, we'd be overjoyed to have you," he said. "But I don't imagine the trip will be much fun."

She shrugged. The hunched bells of her wings rose and settled with her shoulders. "It's a change," she said. "I can't tell you how I crave—something different."

"What about your job?" Caleb asked. "Will they let you leave? I imagine a trip to Breven would take five days at least, each way."

She smiled at him. The first smile she'd bestowed on him. Even resisting her, he felt the brilliance of that smile scissor through him, slitting his flesh from brow to heel. "I'm not worried about finding employment," she said very gently. "I'm worried about finding entertainment. I think this would be fun."

Caleb spread his hands. "Then you're invited."

"If we go," Noah amended. "I won't know for a while."

"We'll go, anyway. We'll find a reason."

"Well, we'll see. If it's not Breven, we'll go somewhere. We can vote."

"Semorrah," Caleb suggested.

"Gaza," Noah said.

"Somewhere in Bethel. I know—Velora," Caleb said. "It's supposed to be a little Luminaux."

But Lilah had turned her face away and Noah looked suddenly grave. "Not Velora," the Edori said gently. "We'll think of something."

So the fallen angel had ties to Velora, and not happy ones, either. Not that Caleb hadn't already figured that out. Not that he hadn't realized, very early into the conversation, just who this angel was.

He did not have time either to apologize or pretend ignorance. They were joined at that moment by a slim, sleek, well-dressed man who dripped all over with gold and arrogance. He was attired with Luminaux elegance, but Caleb sized him up instantly as transplanted Jansai—one of the cutthroat, capitalistic ex-slavers from Breven who had flourished in the young industrial age of Samaria.

"I see you gentlemen are enjoying yourselves," the man said civilly enough, but something in the smooth voice instantly roused Caleb's antagonism. "Something more I can get you before you leave? I'm afraid Lilah won't be able to visit with you much longer. She needs her rest to maintain her voice."

The man stood directly behind the angel, and so he did not see the scornful smile that crossed her face; but she did not contradict him or even appear annoyed. Noah, on the other hand, contained his irritation only with an obvious effort.

"I wouldn't want to keep her if she's ready to go," the Edori said.

But she was already on her feet. "Oh, I must. Joseph—this is Joseph, by the way, he owns this delightful establishment—is kind enough to look after me, and he knows I would stay out all night carousing if someone didn't fetch me at the proper time."

"Carousing seems a little strong," Caleb remarked.

She smiled maliciously. "But I do like it."

Joseph had draped his arm across the angel's shoulders, carelessly brushing his elbow against the heavy feathers of her wings. She seemed, but perhaps it was Caleb's imagination, to shudder ever so slightly as he touched her, squeezing the ball of her shoulder with his thick, well-manicured hands. Caleb remembered suddenly, information gleaned from some source he could not recall now, that angels hated having their wings touched, except in the most intimate circumstances, and sometimes not even then. Perhaps that was all her momentary distaste signified.

"Will you be singing tomorrow night?" Noah asked, coming to his feet. Caleb stood also.

"No reason not to," she said. "It's what I live for, after all."

"Then I'll probably be here tomorrow night. To see you."

"Good," she said, but over her shoulder; Joseph had turned the angel and begun walking her away. "I'll come by afterward to share a drink with you. Caleb—it was divine meeting you. I'm sure we'll become best friends on our journey."

The two men stood silently for a few moments, watching the entwined figures fade into the room's shadows. Caleb glanced at Noah. "I don't suppose you want another drink," he said.

Noah nodded. "I do, but not here. Let's go."

So it was to be a late night, after all. They left, then spent ten minutes walking the glowing streets of Luminaux, trying to agree on a tavern. They settled finally on Blue Sky, one of the few places with good food, no music, and service around the clock. They sat, and Noah ordered more wine. Caleb settled for coffee.

"You're fishing in troubled waters," he observed, after a long moment in which neither spoke. "Be careful you don't go tumbling in headlong and drown."

Noah laughed shortly. "Wouldn't be hard to do," he said. "She's a siren. She could lure any man to his doom."

"You know who she is, of course," Caleb said.

Noah nodded. "The Archangel. She doesn't answer to her name, though. Won't talk about it at all."

"Former Archangel," Caleb corrected gently. "And I don't know that I blame her."

"I keep thinking—I keep wondering—what exactly got broken. How the injury happened. Why it hasn't been fixed."

"Well, she fell from the sky—"

"I mean, there's so many things that we know now that we didn't know ten or even five years ago. Look at the Gabriel Dam. Ten years ago, people would have said it couldn't be built. Now it supplies power to half the towns in southern Bethel and Jordana."

"What does that have to do with Delilah?"

"There must be a way to fix her wing. What is it that's broken? Can't it be replaced? I know every medical expert in the country went to her after she fell, but maybe she should go to the scientists instead. They would look at the problem differently."

"Suggest it to her," Caleb said, though he didn't think she'd be particularly receptive. "You're a scientist."

Noah raised his dark eyes to his friend's face. "I thought maybe you could help her," he said.

"Me? Why me?"

"You're the specialist in building new wings."

That caught Caleb totally by surprise, although, adding it up swiftly, he realized that Noah had been pointed toward this proposal the whole night. It actually made sense, if he wasn't the one expected to produce miracles.

"I've built stationary wings—gliders—you described them yourself," he said gently. "They're complex and mobile, yes, but not independently powered. An angel's wing—it must operate like an arm, on a series of muscles and bones. What do you think I could do?"

"You could look. You could think about it. I'd work with you. It's just that I have to try. If she'll let me. I have to see if I can help her. Caleb, there's no piece of machinery existing today that you and I couldn't build by scratch and probably improve on, and the human body, you've said it yourself, is just a complicated piece of machinery. Surely there's something we can do. If she'll let us."

"I don't know that she'll ever trust anyone enough to let him experiment on her," Caleb said. "She's wearing heavy armor, Noah. She's not going to let a lot of people through."

"She'll get to know us, she'll trust us, and we'll take it from there," Noah replied.

"If she's interested—" Caleb began, then paused.

"Then you'll try?"

"I'll try. If she'll agree." He had only met the angel once but Caleb was fairly certain she wouldn't be interested in their speculative, exploratory help. He did not say so to Noah.

The Edori nodded, smiled, and seemed to grow visibly happier in a matter of seconds. He sipped his wine, then looked up at his friend. "And I was right, wasn't I?" he asked.

"About what?"

"Her voice. You loved her voice, didn't you?"

"She sings as if her soul were in flames," Caleb said soberly. "I have never heard a voice like that in my life."

"They say the new Archangel can't come close to her—in voice quality, I mean, I have no idea how she performs her other duties. They say the new girl—"

"Her name is Alleluia," Caleb interjected mildly.

"They say her singing is just ordinary, compared to Delilah's."

"Well," said Caleb, "I would imagine that would be true no matter who they had picked. But they must have had their reasons for choosing her, even if she can't sing."

"Still, she was the second choice," Noah pointed out. Clearly he would champion Delilah against all comers.

"And she must know it," Caleb said. "It must make things very hard for her. I wonder what she's like."

Chapter Two

The Archangel Alleluia sat in one of the locked, soundproofed music rooms that lined the lower level of the Eyrie, and wondered why this was always the setting when she received bad news. Perhaps it was because, seeking solitude or silence, she often retreated to one of these rooms where, by custom, no one was supposed to interrupt. Perhaps it was because, lately, there was nothing but bad news.

Today she had gone to one of the music rooms for a short respite from the squabbles of her daily life and to listen to one of the minor recordings left behind by the first angelica, Hagar. These recordings were a marvel of lost technology, providing perfect renditions of some of the most difficult masses sung by the most accomplished of the early settlers. The angel hold at Monteverde was equipped with similar rooms where the masses could be played and learned by angels planning to perform at the Gloria or some other function. (The machines at Windy Point had been destroyed 150 years ago and could not be replicated at Cedar Hills.) How to make the recordings, and how to build the listening equipment, were bits of knowledge lost hundreds of years ago when the early colonists made the decision to abandon the benefits of science—abandoning, at the same time, its destructive potential. And so future generations were bequeathed odd remnants of equipment that operated in what was to them a completely mysterious manner.

It stood to reason that present-day mortals and angels would have no idea how to repair such machinery should it break down, and that was today's catastrophe. There were twenty music rooms at the Eyrie, and the equipment in all but two of them had, in the past few months, completely ceased to function. None of the angels who poked and prodded at the unfamiliar dials could cause the divine music to once more come soaring from the hidden speakers. The singers were effectively silenced; and one more joy was lost to Alleya.

Still, there had been two machines that continued to work—until today. While Alleya was listening to the Bardel requiem in C minor, the soprano solo abruptly halted in mid-ecstasy. No fizzle, no static, just sudden and complete silence. Alleya had crossed to the wall of knobs and switches and cautiously fiddled with one or two, but she knew it was hopeless. The machine was broken, and she did not have the skills to repair it. Perhaps no one did.

With the air of one acquiescing to utter defeat, she spread her hands and allowed herself to sink slowly to the floor. Her shapeless blue tunic puddled around her; her wings spread and flattened against the stone tiles. She drew her knees up, crossed her arms upon them, and rested her head upon her forearms. It was very tempting to just completely give up.

She had been in this very room three months ago when the first wave of bad news hit—although it might be inadequate to label as "bad news" the message that had completely and miserably reordered her life. The oracles Job and Mary had been ushered in by Samuel, who had temporarily taken charge of the Eyrie while Delilah lay immobile. They all looked grave beyond imagining; Alleya could only think that Delilah had died.

"Alleya," Samuel had said in an unwontedly kind voice. He was a serious, thoughtful man who did not give much rein to the softer emotions. "May we talk with you?"

She had brushed futilely at her hair (no doubt a mess) and wished she had taken more time with her appearance that morning. It was not often she was asked to converse with the oracles. "Of course. I was just practicing. Here, let me turn the music off—"

She was as nervous as if she knew what they had come for,

but in fact, exalted company always made her a little uneasy. "It doesn't matter," Job had said, stilling her with a motion of his hand. "Hagar's voice is always welcome."

So she turned and faced them, feeling strangely penitent, although she couldn't imagine what she had done to earn their displeasure. No one spoke for almost a minute, and she realized with a shock that the oracles and even Samuel seemed almost as embarrassed as she.

"Has something happened to Delilah?" she asked finally, just to break the silence. "I mean—something else—"

Job shook his head. "The Archangel remains as she has been," he said unhelpfully. "And that is—broken and irreparable. Jovah has decreed that a new Archangel must be chosen."

Alleya felt a rush of pity for the beautiful, fiery Delilah, so different from herself. Delilah had had it all, achieved the pinnacle and gloried in it; and now she would have nothing.

"Does she know?"

"She has just been told."

"Did she—what did she say?"

"She was calmer than I expected," Samuel answered. "The news did not come as a surprise. But I think she will be wretched soon enough. We must take care to treat her very gently."

Alleya nodded. No one spoke again for a minute or two. Hagar's inexpressibly sad voice rose and fell behind them, lending the whole episode an air of sweet tragedy.

"Of course, a new Archangel must be installed immediately," Job continued. "It is Jovah's will."

"That will be very difficult for Delilah," Alleya said.

"Difficult for the new Archangel," Mary murmured.

"We have been to Jovah and asked for his choice," Job went on. "And he has surprised us all by naming . . . you."

It was a good twenty seconds before his words sank in, and even then, they did not make sense. Alleya found herself staring at the older oracle, whose lined, intelligent face and sober mien did not appear to lend themselves easily to a joke of this magnitude. "Jovah said—what?" she asked, her voice completely choked.

"He chose you to be Archangel in Delilah's stead," Samuel said.

She swung her gaze around to his face. Samuel she knew

would not make a mockery of her this way. "That's not possible," she said faintly.

"It seems unlikely, on the face of it," Job conceded. "But we asked more than once. He named the angel Alleluia, daughter of Jude and Hope. You are the only angel who answers to that description."

"But I—don't you see?—I'm not trained for this, I don't have the skills for this—I'm—surely I'm the last angel the god would choose for such an honor."

"Jovah has his reasons for every decision he makes," Job said piously. "Even when those reasons are not clear to us—"

"Yes, but—*I* can't be Archangel!" she said desperately. "I can't deal with the Manadavvi and control the river merchants and keep an eye on the Jansai—or, Jovah save me—lead the Gloria in front of all those people—"

Mary and Job exchanged sharp glances. Alleya fell silent. "Interesting," Job murmured. "Those are of course some of the duties of the Archangel. But there are more. You can, I assume, do a weather intercession as well as the next angel?"

Now Alleya threw a panicky look at Samuel and crossed her arms stubbornly across her breast. "I suppose so," she said.

"In fact, did not three angels fly to the mine compound near Hagar's Tooth, praying for the rain to stop, but to no avail? And did you not fly there once, and sing one prayer, causing the clouds to part and the rain to dissipate?"

She did not answer, so Samuel spoke for her. "You did, Alleya. And that was not the only time."

"Luck," she whispered. "The right time. The storms were ready to pass, anyway."

"The god hears you," Mary said. "And where the god pays attention, can mortals and angels fail to listen?"

"Easily," Alleya responded. "I am not an intercessor with the god. I am not a mediator among men. I am—Samuel, tell them. I live here, I do the work I am asked to do—there is nothing about me that would cause the god to single me out. Ask him again. He has chosen wrong."

But they would not listen. To all her protests, they replied, "Jovah has spoken" or "The god has called your name," and nothing Alleya could say would induce them to change their minds. "We must make the announcement to the angels," Job said finally, weary of arguing with her, and led the small procession from the music room toward the broad common plateau, where most of the other angels were gathered. Alleya trailed helplessly behind them, still protesting but not aloud, for basic human instinct told her that she would make herself look irretrievably ridiculous if she was caught bemoaning her new estate in front of all her peers.

And so the announcement was made, and Alleya's bewilderment was mirrored on the faces of all the other residents of the Eyrie, and those who looked at her did so with marveling, disbelieving faces. Others turned away to share their amazement with their neighbors. Alleya kept her eyes averted but not cast downward—no, she looked slightly above the rest of them at the rosy beige stone of the Eyrie walls. And she thought, *This is the worst day of my entire life.*

Nor had it rapidly improved. Job and Mary stayed two more days at the Eyrie, holding private discussions with Alleya to go over some of her duties as Archangel, things she would be expected to do, things she would be expected to know. Samuel had kindly explained to her what he knew of political alliances throughout Samaria, the relationship between the Manadavvi, the river merchants, the Jansai—and now, the growing group of independent and increasingly wealthy landowners who owned either massive farming concerns or some of the southern mines.

"But I am not a politician," he apologized. "If you could talk to Delilah, you would get much better advice from her."

But there would be no help available from the deposed Archangel. Everyone had counseled Alleya to wait a few days, maybe a few weeks, before approaching Delilah with a mixture of regret, supplication and camaraderie—"I am so sorry that things happened this way, but since they did, won't you help me as I know you can?"

And Alleya, who had dreaded the meeting, had gratefully put it off another day, and another. It was not that she and Delilah had been hostile in the old days, when everything was as it should be—they'd just had very little to do with each other. Well, they were so different—Delilah so outgoing and sure of herself, brilliant at maneuvering people, gifted with a luminous beauty and an extraordinary voice. And Alleluia, shy, reserved and scholarly, owning a voice that was no more than pretty, and hopeless at managing people. They'd had no particular reason to be friends.

But they could be allies, or so Alleya hoped during her first two uneasy weeks as Archangel. But that last shred of solace evaporated one morning when Samuel brought the bad news (yes, she was in the music room) that Delilah had vanished in the night. She had informed no one, taken nothing, just removed herself from the Eyrie in bitter stealth.

It would not be hard to track her, if they attempted to do so. Everyone in Samaria knew her face, knew her voice, knew her story. But Samuel was certain they would not need to search for her. "She'll let us know where she is," he said a dozen times. "She's a reckless girl, but she's not that heedless. She knows we may have need of her."

And indeed, ten days later, Delilah did send a courier with a message that she could be found in Luminaux if anyone had reason to contact her. She did not give an address, though, and Alleya sometimes doubted if even the Luminaux location was correct, but it did not matter. Delilah was gone, and effectively out of reach for help with day-to-day problems; and those mounted with each passing week. Alleya had not wanted to be Archangel, and she was not enjoying a single day of it.

And now even the old angels had failed her, the musicians who had laid down these tracks six and a half centuries ago. She had to be note-perfect on at least one Gloria-quality mass within four and a half months, and she had been rehearsing diligently during whatever free time she could find. But if she could not listen and could not learn, she could not possibly give a creditable performance at what would be the most public event of her life.

She ground her forehead against her crossed arms and fought back the urge to cry. She almost succumbed, but in a matter of minutes she had managed to force back the tears and come steadily to her feet as if she were in complete control. It was a small victory, but a victory nonetheless, and Alleya savored it; for she'd had precious few triumphs in the past three months. Even a little one would do.

* * *

She had scarcely set foot outside the room when Samuel approached her. She was sure, from the expression on his face, that she would not want to hear the news he brought. She was right.

"Visitors, awaiting you in the small breakfast hall," he said.

"Visitors from where?"

"Gaza. It is Aaron Lesh and Emmanuel Garone of the Manadavvi. They do not look pleased."

"When have they ever?" Alleya said lightly, but she frowned as she spoke. She had dealt very little with the Manadavvi since she'd been named Archangel—mostly, she felt, because they had decided she was too insignificant to bother with. Of all the mixed races and social strata on Samaria, the Manadavvi were the highest and the most self-sufficient. Consisting of a few fabulously wealthy and tightly guarded families, the Manadavvi owned the most productive farmland on the continent. These huge tracts of land, which lined the upper northeast coastline of Gaza, for centuries had been farmed by dependent workers in an almost feudal arrangement, with the Manadavvi as oath-holders. Some of that had changed back in the Archangel Gabriel's time, for he had fought to get rights and autonomy for the Gaza serfs; but lately, with the onset of primitive industrialization, conditions for the tenant farmers had steadily worsened. Efficient machinery was beginning to replace humans in the great work of planting and harvesting the Manadavvi estates, and the humans who had lived for generations servicing the same land were finding themselves without homes or employment.

Alleya had not found time to address this problem.

"Did they say—?" she began.

Samuel shook his head. "Only the Archangel is good enough for them to speak to."

Alleya actually grinned. "Would you like to participate? Come along to give me a little added consequence?"

"If it would please you."

"I need any help you can offer," she said frankly. "Please ask someone to bring refreshments to the breakfast hall. I need to do what I can to improve my appearance. I'll be there in ten minutes."

There was a moment's pause. "Make it twenty," Samuel said. Alleya was surprised into a laugh. Even though it was not entirely a joke. From her first wretched day as Archangel, Samuel had been her most consistent ally, unobtrusive, helpful, informative and kind. If he thought she should appear her best for her high-brow visitors, he was no doubt right.

"Twenty," she agreed. "I'll do what I can."

As swiftly as she could, she negotiated the tunnels of the Eyrie warren, all carved from the rich, warm stone that made the Velo Mountains the most beautiful in Samaria. She no longer made the automatic turning toward her own small room, the chamber she had lived in since she was a child, but instead went straight to the larger apartment that had been Delilah's. Alleya was wholly uncomfortable there, despite its many amenities. She still felt like an intruder—worse, an imposter. Though the room now contained her own furniture, and the closets were filled with her own clothing, she felt as if she were usurping somebody else's life.

And she didn't even want to.

Inside the room, she dashed to the full-length mirror to take inventory. Face smudged, clothes wrinkled, hair a disaster. Make it thirty minutes. She had read somewhere that only unimportant people would jump to do another's bidding; people of consequence made others wait for them. Promptness had always seemed to her more a matter of courtesy than consequence, but for the moment Alleya was willing to subscribe to the theory. She should not shame herself before the Manadavvi.

Therefore, she washed her face quickly and applied the lightest of cosmetics, then attired herself in the sky-blue gown that matched her eyes and suited her coloring best. She was never able to do much with her hair, a fine, shoulder-length butter-blond that resisted any styling, so she just brushed it vigorously and tied it back with a matching ribbon. For jewelry, she wore only the bracelets that all angels wore—in her case, sapphire fleur-de-lis set in a gold band. The sapphires identified her as an angel of the Eyrie; the pattern was one she had chosen when she first arrived at this hold. Most angels wore designs that identified their lineage, but Alleya had no close blood ties to anyone at the Eyrie.

When she was done, she eyed the whole picture once more in the glass. She looked grave and tidy; that would have to do. Now if she could manage to avoid being flustered or intimidated, she should be fine. She hoped Samuel was already in the breakfast hall.

He was, and he and the Manadavvi men were sipping what seemed to be a fruit drink. Alleya came through the doorway slowly (though she had practically run down the hallways to get here) and nodded at everyone coolly. That was the other thing she tried to remember: The power belongs to the one who listens first.

The two Manadavvi crossed the room to stand before her, making infinitesimal bows. "Angela," they said, using the courtesy title in low, well-bred voices. "Good of you to see us so soon."

She glanced at the tray of food and drink that lay on a nearby table. "You have been taken care of? Is there anything I can send for?"

"No, we have been well looked after."

"Thank you, angela."

"And your journey? Was it cold traveling this time of year?"

"We kept ourselves warm, thank you."

"The weather? It still holds good across the Gaza border? I have not heard reports of a new storm in some weeks."

"The weather has been excellent, angela."

From the corner of her eye, she saw Samuel smile slightly. This was, then, the correct way to open the conversation, with genteel trivialities. Alleya was not sure how much longer she could sustain it, but she was damned if she would ask them what they came for. Let them make the awkward transition.

She poured herself a glass of what the others were drinking, and found it to be really excellent unfermented grape juice. Possibly a gift from the Manadavvi, because it certainly wasn't a traditional Eyrie offering. "Do you plan to stay overnight? We have room here for guests, of course, or Samuel could recommend one of the better inns in Velora."

"Thank you, angela, our accommodations have been seen to."

"This is a wonderful drink. Of such quality that I would venture to guess it came from Manadavvi vineyards."

"Indeed, angela, Emmanuel brought two cases for your exclusive use. Despite the storms, last year was an excellent year for grapes, and we wished to share the bounty with you."

"I greatly appreciate it. Samuel, you have tried it?"

"Indeed, Alleya, and found it most superior."

His use of her nickname had to have been deliberate; Samuel never committed social solecisms. She thought quickly. Ah—yes. Proving to the visitors that he was on intimate terms with the Archangel, and thus a party to be reckoned with. Automatically giving his voice more weight, if he should choose to speak. She smiled at him.

"Perhaps you should reserve a bottle or two for yourself," she said. "I'm sure there's enough to share."

"I was hoping you would say that," he said, returning her smile.

This byplay finally proved enough for the Manadavvi, who almost visibly shifted into a businesslike mode. "It is about vineyards and their harvests that we have come to talk to you," said Aaron Lesh. He was a young, round-bodied man who appeared to have lived easily and well, though his ice-blue eyes belied any impression of softness. By contrast, Emmanuel was tall, spare, older and absolutely ruthless, in a civil and efficient way. They made an odd pair, until you remembered that the common denominator for all Manadavvi was acquiring wealth and keeping it.

Alleya contrived to look solicitous. "There is a hazard to your vineyard? The storms have caused flooding? Or—some insect infestation, perhaps? I know little about crops—"

"There is no threat to the growing of the product," said Emmanuel, "but in the selling. In the shipping. In taking it to a viable market."

On the instant, Alleya realized what the visit was about and that her own moral ground was much higher than theirs. Betraying nothing, she kept an inquiring and respectful expression on her face. "Yes? You are having trouble with the markets?"

Aaron seemed exasperated. "Not with the markets—with the shipping," he said. "The market is there. Semorrah, Castelana, all the river cities—they could consume practically every bottle of wine we produce, and funnel the rest to Breven. The river cities are the key, you know, to our distribution network."

"Not just for wine, but for grain, fresh produce and dried meat," Emmanuel cut in smoothly. "Only a fraction of our harvests do we sell direct. Almost everything goes through the river merchants."

"And you have come here—why? You suspect some deception on the part of the Semorran buyers? You think they are treating you unfairly? Offering you an insufficient price?"

Emmanuel looked annoyed. "We have no quarrel with the merchants," he said. "It is getting to the merchants that is the problem."

Alleya spread her hands. "I don't understand. What problem?"

Aaron took up the attack again. "The Galilee River has always served as the conduit between Gaza and the river cities—" he began.

"And the storms have flooded the river? Made it impassable?"

Emmanuel gave her a sharp look; he was beginning to suspect that she was being deliberately obstructive. Aaron plunged on, unheeding. "No—well, yes, there has been a little danger to the rivercraft because of higher waters, but that is not really our problem. We just deliver the merchandise to the banks."

"And *that*, angela, is the heart of the trouble," Emmanuel interrupted again. "We always used to take our wagonloads to the highest point of the river, just south of the Plain of Sharon, and the merchants' boats would meet us there. But now—the land along that portion of the river is no longer available for open commerce. We have had to reroute our wagons fifty miles farther south, causing delays and some accidents as the drivers try to find the best passageway—costing money, angela, costing money."

"The northern portion of the river is no longer open for commerce . . ." Alleya repeated slowly. She chose to let Aaron complete the sentence.

"Because it has become a protected area for Edori," he burst out.

Alleya looked at him thoughtfully. "It was my understanding," she said slowly, "that it had been agreed upon by a council of angels, merchants, Edori and other citizens that it was in the best interests of all the people of Samaria to create sanctuaries for the Edori. Were you not consulted? Did you not agree?"

It was the most inflammatory issue that Samaria had dealt with in half a century, and had been painfully settled only last year; and literally no one wanted to see the arguments reopened. The nomadic Edori tribes, who had for centuries wandered where they would, had found, with the growth of urban areas and the shrinking of the open land, fewer and fewer parts of Samaria available to them. In the past twenty years, the number of Edori had dwindled alarmingly—with many moving to the cities and even to the farmlands, it was true, but many more just dying off from inability to sustain their traditional life. In a bitter and passionate series of conferences last year, a delegation of statesmen from all classes of Samaria had agreed that the only way to save the Edori was to grant them possession of a few wild tracts of land. Getting the council to agree to such a step had been hard enough; choosing the sites had been nearly impossible.

"Absolutely—the only thing to be done—everyone knows that," Aaron said hastily. "We want sanctuaries as much as the next man does. But not quite there, do you see? Fifteen miles down the river—or even on the Jordana side of the Galilee—"

"But all these sites were carefully chosen by the same council, if I recall correctly . . ." Alleya said, again slowly, again as if uncertain of her facts. Which she was not. She may not have been involved in this particular affair, but she was a voracious reader and she remembered everything; it was her one real skill. "Everyone agreed to them. Even the Manadavvi."

"That was before we realized quite how it would affect the shipping patterns—"

"But you must have studied the proposals—"

"Angela. We did not," Emmanuel put in. He was very fond of taking control, cutting right to the heart. "As Aaron says, we have no interest in seeing the Edori dispossessed. Far from it. But moved, perhaps. Downriver? Across the bank? I believe Edori can live anywhere. What difference would a few miles make to them?"

"The east side of the Galilee River floods ten times more often than the west side," Alleya said, softly and immediately. "Fifteen miles farther down the river—even twenty miles—the land is so rocky that you could not pitch two tents side by side. Hardly ideal living conditions."

"Hardly ideal traveling conditions," Emmanuel retorted. "Those rocky ways make it difficult for wagons to pass, and we have lost more than one shipment as drivers tried to negotiate unfriendly pathways."

"That is a hazard," Alleya said sympathetically. "But if these are pathways you will be using for years to come, it might be worth the investment to build roads that your wagons can more easily traverse. So you have less risk of loss and injury."

A brief expression of hatred tightened Emmanuel's lean features. "The cost," he said gently. "The manpower."

"Come now, you have manpower,"Alleya said. "I believe there are any number of idle tenant farmers who could be usefully employed in digging you a reasonable road to the river."

"But the *cost*," Aaron complained impatiently. "You can't realize—"

Alleya spread her hands again. "Charge more for your wine and your vegetables," she said. "Isn't that how a merchant always covers his expenses? Besides," she added, smiling good-humoredly, as if they were all in on a joke, "I happen to know your new harvesting equipment is saving you a fortune in labor costs and actual produce recovery. Half again as much yield in some crops, because the machinery is so efficient—isn't that right? So surely you can afford a little extra outlay, one-time only, to build your necessary roads. It's a business expense, is it not, gentlemen?"

She kept her expression mild and reasonable as she waited for them to refute her. They could not, of course. She saw a frown take shape on Aaron's face as he gradually realized she had too many points in her favor; Emmanuel was, as usual, way ahead of him.

The last person she expected to hear from at this juncture was Samuel, but now he spoke up. "There is another solution, if you're so set on shipping from the northernmost point of the river," he said.

Aaron swung quickly his way; Emmanuel eyed him more warily. "What is it?" asked the younger man.

"Freight your merchandise through the Edori territory, and

pay them a passage fee," Samuel proposed. "Don't you think that would work, Alleya?"

It was all Alleya could do to keep from laughing aloud. It was sensible, charming, and completely unpalatable to the Manadavvi. "I think the Edori would be quite interested," she said. "They probably wouldn't charge much, you know. The Edori have no head for business."

"Pay the *Edori* so I can take my wagons across their land?" Aaron exclaimed. "I'd rather walk it all the way to the ferry at Semorrah!"

"Well, that's your choice, too," Alleya said smoothly. "Actually, I think you have any number of solutions to consider. All workable. Go back. Talk to the others. I'm sure you'll find that one or the other of these suggestions will be acceptable to everyone."

After that, it was barely three minutes before the Manadavvi made the briefest of farewells and exited without a backward look. Just as well. They were scarcely out of sight before Alleya and Samuel began laughing so hard that they could not speak. Alleya felt the tears come to her eyes, and still she could not repress the hysteria.

"No head for *business*—" Samuel choked out once, and that set her off again. She was blinded by laughing; she didn't see him approach, and so his hug of congratulations caught her completely by surprise. But she welcomed it. She thought she deserved it. Her second victory of the day, and this one actually worth recording.

But there were still setbacks to contend with—namely, the failure of the music machine. Late in the afternoon, Alleya set out for Velora to see if, by chance, anyone there could give her advice.

Velora was a bustling, happy, cosmopolitan town nestled up to the foot of the imposing Velo mountain from which the Eyrie had been carved. The city had sprung up centuries ago specifically to accommodate the angels and the petitioners who visited them there, so it possessed a welcome, friendly air and a multitude of amenities. It was often compared to Luminaux (though it had no real hope of eclipsing that fabled city), and everyone who visited Velora fell in love with it.

Years past, the only drawback to Velora was that there was no easy way to ascend from the city to the angel hold on the mountaintop, for the steep cliffs were impassable. Angels habitually ferried petitioners up to the hold—or, more often, glided down to the city limits to hear what their visitors had to say.

But no longer. Nearly seventy-five years ago, the angels had approved a project to cut a massive series of shelves into the face of the mountain—steps shallow enough for a child to climb, but broad enough for a man to lie on comfortably with his head pillowed on the next stair up. The project was wildly popular with the merchants and the common folk of Bethel, who turned to the Eyrie when they sought divine intervention. The angels also were overwhelmingly in favor of the change, because for more than seventy years the Eyrie had been the only one of the three angel holds that was almost completely inaccessible.

Before that, only Monteverde in Gaza had been in easy reach of any petitioner who wished to speak directly to an angel. Windy Point, the hold that served Jordana, had been clawed from an inhospitable mountain range so bleak that no small community could gain a foothold close enough to cater to the hold's inhabitants. But the Archangel Gabriel had destroyed Windy Point 150 years ago—or asked Jovah to do so, and the god had complied. When the new angel hold, Cedar Hills, had been laid out in milder southern Jordana, its architects had followed the Monteverde plan. Thus a mortal merely had to walk up to the angel compound, request in hand, to receive a hearing.

Not wanting to appear so much more aloof than their brethren, the Eyrie angels backed the plan to terrace the mountain with a stairway to their doors. Velora merchants, always quick to capitalize on an opportunity, instantly set up carts and tiny storefronts along the serried rise, the result being that the climb up the mountain was a colorful adventure. Sweet hot cinnamon rolls, bright red headscarves, flashing jewelry bearing exotic designs edged in sapphires—these, anything, could be purchased on the slow ascent. It was the most sought-after real estate in Velora.

Although she could fly from the mountaintop to the city proper in about a minute, Alleya almost always chose to walk down. Back in her (so often rued) days of anonymity, she had derived a childlike pleasure from shopping through the splendid array of finery. Now that she was Archangel, and owed to her constituents some attentions, Alleya had found that her frequent treks down the great stairway gave her an opportunity to talk informally with the merchants, the petitioners, the buyers and the artisans, who thronged up and down the steps. Everyone always seemed pleased to see her—which, genuine or not, was a rare enough occurrence that she always enjoyed it. Her pleasures were not so great that she could afford to throw the simplest ones away.

So, right after the sun slipped past its highest point, Alleya headed for the great stairway and made a roundabout descent. Though the weather was cold, the terraced marketplace was as busy as ever. "Angela! Angela!" voices called to her, pitched to carry above the murmuring of the crowd. Sometimes all that was required was a wave of recognition in return; sometimes nothing would do but that she must stop at some gaily striped booth and sample a new batch of candy or try on the finest lace gloves. Invariably, gifts were pressed upon her, which she had learned to graciously accept. Every broker wanted to be able to brag to his customer, "Well, the Archangel has a set of these, and she loves them." The advantages to them outweighed their slight cost, and her embarrassment.

An hour later, sporting a gauzy new scarf worked in gold and silver, and munching a pastry from a bagful of goodies, Alleya stepped off the last stair and into the quieter region of Velora proper. Here, the real business of the town was done; merchants counted the inventory in their warehouses, and musicians taught students in a hundred schools. Brokers made deals, restaurateurs laid out their plates, and jewelers held dignified consultations with their most discriminating clients.

Alleya moved much more quickly once she had gained level ground, making her way to a small, crowded shop on the south edge of town. Hanging unevenly over the seamed wooden door, a worn sign simply offered "Repairs." Alleya peeked through the glass, but no one appeared to be at work in the shop. She opened the door and went inside, anyway.

The place was a marvel of odd scents and unfamiliar objects, all jumbled together—metal, leather, oil, grease, and the hot smell and bursting spark of untamed electricity. Alleya stood in the center of the small, crowded space and did a slow pirouette, but she could not have described a use for any of the devices hanging on the walls or scattered across the floor. Some of the great mysteries of progress.

She had rung a small doorbell when she entered, and it was only a matter of moments before she was joined by the owner of the shop. "Angela!" he greeted her, bounding out from an uncovered doorway and hurrying over to shake her hand. "It has been some time since I have seen you here."

"Hello, Daniel," she said, smiling up at him. He was a big, strongly built Edori, with the characteristic dark coloring in eyes, skin and hair. Like most Edori she had met, he was outgoing, eager to please, prone to digression and fascinated by anything mechanical. He was known as *the* man to go to if you needed a watch fixed or a newfangled piece of equipment fine-tuned, but his shop had never been particularly successful, financially speaking. Alleluia repressed a smile. No head for business. "How has everything been with you?"

"Good, good, couldn't ask for a better year." Daniel beamed. "You've heard of the new steam-powered water systems that all the mighty-mighties have to install in their homes these days? Regular well water is not good enough for them—it has to be free-flowing water, it has to be hot, it has to be available in half the rooms of the house. So! Wonderful for me! Half the steam valves stick after two months, and if the hoses aren't connected just right—I can't tell you the tiny, *tiny* things that go wrong with these little contraptions, and the allali customers don't have the first idea how to fix them." He glanced at her guiltily after using the uncomplimentary Edori term for rich, idle city dweller, then went on with his story.

"And of course, once they've had the advantages of hot, ready water they simply can't go back to their old lives, so the steam systems have to be fixed *right now*. It takes me, believe it, five minutes to put everything in order again. I can charge them what I like! I have fixed every steam system in Velora at least once, and I've been called as far away as Semorrah—although that one was a little more complicated, a big system and it had a number of flaws. But I fixed it. I showed one of their houseboys how it was done, so they'll never need to bother me again. I don't understand how something so easy can seem so impossible."

Alleya smiled at him again. "It seems impossible to me," she said. "I'd be bathing in cold water my whole life if someone didn't install these things for me."

He laughed and threw his hands apart. "But then, you find it easy to fly—and me? I couldn't fly if the fate of the Edori rested on my back. So Yovah put us all here to accomplish different things, yes? And fixing little valves and engines is my task."

It always gave her a start to hear the Edori call the god by their version of his name. It was so easy for her to forget that not everyone viewed Jovah exactly as she did. And what she had heard of the Edori religion shocked her enough to keep her from investigating more closely.

"I have something I wish you could fix for me, but I don't think you can," she said. "I've asked you about it before."

"Ah, yes—those ancient machines that play music from Hagar's time," Daniel said instantly. His failures were rare enough that he remembered them all. "I looked, but—"

"Now another one has broken. Only one is left," Alleya said sadly. "I came to ask you—if you cannot help me, do you know someone who might? In Luminaux, perhaps, or even Breven. Although I have always thought you were the best."

He laughed; no competitive spirit here. "There is always someone better, no matter what your skill," he said comfortably. "Think! What are your great talents? There is someone else just as good somewhere in Samaria. It does not pay to be too vain."

She was still trying to think of her most promising abilities. A mind for detail. An abiding faith in her god. These did not seem to make her unique. "I'm not vain," she said, smiling.

"No, you're modest" was Daniel's unexpected rejoinder. "But that's not so bad, either. Angela, I may have a name that will help you. There is a man in Luminaux, another Edori, but he might not be the one, either. He has a friend whose name escapes me—they are said to be the best engineers in the country, though—how do I put it?—somewhat erratic. They are inventors, not good solid repairmen like me." His laugh boomed out again. "They were both involved in the Gabriel Dam project—in fact, I think this friend was the chief engineer who took over when things were beginning to look like they would not go so well. He is credited with saving the project, if I'm thinking of the right man. Were I you, he is the one I would contact."

"But you don't know his name?" she said gently.

Daniel grinned. "Well, Noah's the name of his Edori friend, and you can find any Edori in Luminaux by going down to the campsite."

"Will he know your name? Can I tell him you sent me?"

"Angela, it is an honor to be asked to do a service for the Archangel, even among the Edori," he said. "He will not need coaxing."

She could not help another answering smile. "I keep forgetting."

"Better a little vain than too modest," he admonished. "I said there were repairmen as good as me. I did not say my talents were only passable."

"I said nothing derogatory about my talents."

"Name them for me!" he exclaimed. "List your great charms and mightiest strengths!"

No angel would have talked to Alleya this way, and no common mortal either; still, it was hard to be offended when he seemed so earnest. "I remember things—details, books I've read—I can put them all together and get a good picture," she said a little haltingly. "That's really it, except for ordinary angel things like flying and singing."

"You can stop the rain," he said. "You can blow away the storms."

"Again, any angel can."

"Not so well as you. Yovah has never failed to hear you. Is that not something you should lay proud claim to?"

It terrified Alleya when people continued to say that; for, in this crazy climate, with thunder and gale piling up across the continent, how long could she be sure the god would be pleased by her voice? "He hears me now," she said, her voice low. "Once he heard every angel. He may not listen to me much longer."

"He will," Daniel said solemnly. "Do not doubt him."

"How can you be so sure?"

"He must hear one of you. Or we will all be lost."

Chapter Three

Caleb had spent most of the day running copper pipes through the four stories of Vincent Hammad's house. It was a job any laborer could do, and so he had told the silversmith, but Hammad had said he knew the difference between an item handcrafted from start to finish by the master and an inferior piece in which a student had sloppily followed his teacher's design. Besides, Hammad could afford to pay the price for Caleb's services, whether the task was menial or inventive, and anyway, Caleb didn't mind a little simple honest toil now and then. So he took care with the pipes, and laid them exactly where they should go, and soldered them at the joints with slow precision. When he finally got to constructing the housing for the steam unit, he would be able to rest secure in the knowledge that none of the pipes would blow under the whoosh of sudden pressure.

By the time he left at sunset, he was tired with the self-satisfied weariness that comes after hard work on a worthwhile project. Walking unhurriedly home, he paused at a street vendor's to buy a paper cup of hot chocolate, and he had finished it by the time he passed a meat-seller's fire on the next corner. He dropped the cup into the flames, exchanged nods with the vendor, and continued on his way home.

He lived in three rooms over a bakery, a small apartment filled with light and the luscious scent of rising yeast. In the three years he had lived there, he didn't think a single day had gone by that he had not paused, morning or night, to buy a loaf or a pastry from the proprietor or one of her five daughters. "If you sleep by water, you dream of water" his mother had used to say (for she had grown up a stone's throw from the Galilee River). If you slept by a bakery, you ate bread, and never tired of it.

Tonight the friendly, gray-haired woman wrapped his rolls for him with a knowing smile. "You've got company upstairs," she said. "I told her you usually came back about this time, but that sometimes you don't, but she said she would wait. I left her on the landing outside your door."

Since the landing was really a lacework iron balcony, the waiting quarters were not especially cramped; but Caleb was expecting no visitors. "Company?" he repeated. "Who?"

"She didn't give her name." The baker leaned forward to whisper. "But she's an angel."

He knew only one angel. "Dark-haired? Beautiful?"

"That would be her."

"Hunh. Wonder what— How long has she been here? Did you feed her? Maybe I should get a couple extra rolls."

"Twenty minutes or so. And she bought her own rolls."

He grinned and left the bakery, taking the sturdy metal stairs two at a time. At the top of the landing, leaning against the railing with her folded wings toward him, Lilah waited. She must have heard his feet clattering on the stairs, but she did not face him until he spoke.

"Ah, the beautiful, mysterious stranger that has long been foretold," Caleb greeted her. "Great messenger of light, how may I serve you?"

Now she slowly turned around to survey him. "And I thought I was sarcastic," she observed. "But you outdo me."

"I doubt that," he said, unlocking the door. He had, more as an experiment than from any fear that someone would steal his meager belongings, outfitted the door with a complex mechanical baffle that even Noah had been unable to untangle. "Come right in. If I'd known you were going to be here, I would have brought you some beer."

"I've already refreshed myself, thank you very much," she said, following him inside. "I drink very lightly before a performance." She met his quizzical look with a bland smile. "And sometimes more heavily than I ought to afterward, but only sometimes."

"I've never seen you in a drunken stupor," he said. "So I believe you. Are you hungry? I have rolls and I believe I have some shrunken oranges. I wasn't expecting company, you see."

"Not hungry, thanks. Though I'll sit down if that's all right."

"Please do."

She looked cautiously around the big open room as if she was not sure where it was safe to sit. Caleb tended to be tidier than most men he knew, though by no means fanatical about it, so the room was clean enough but a little cluttered. Scattered everywhere were bits of engines, partial valves, ripped sketches of electrical diagrams, and models of possible projects. The furniture was functional but not particularly decorative and relatively sparse. None of it was designed to accommodate angel wings. After a moment's consideration, Lilah settled herself on a wide, low stool and continued surveying the apartment.

"But how utterly cozy," she said. "How can you drag yourself away every morning?"

He grinned and sat down on a chair nearby. "Ah, I'm a busy man. Many clients, many projects. No temptation at all to loll around in my perfect surroundings."

"Well, they certainly suit you."

She glanced around again, and he studied her. In the three weeks since he had met her, he'd had only a few conversations with Lilah, and all of them had been slightly edgy, lightly ironic. It was impossible not to be drawn to the former Archangel, for she had a challenging charm, but Caleb always felt wary in her presence. As if there was more going on behind her smiles and her teasing than he could fathom.

"So tell me," he said. "No doubt you've been perishing of curiosity this past month, wondering how I live, but surely that wasn't a lure strong enough to draw you here tonight. So why have you come?"

She glanced at him with those night-dark eyes, and gave him a sidelong smile. "Perhaps I thought you would invite me to dinner."

He raised his brows. "I never eat dinner" was his automatic response. "Just bread and fruit. Of course I'm willing to share."

Now she laughed. "That's almost certainly a lie," she observed, "but I won't take offense since that's not why I'm here."

"Well?"

Again the coy look, assessing him. "Joseph wanted me to ask you if you'd be willing to take on a job at Seraph. Something about sound. Improving the acoustics, I think, though perhaps he was talking about some kind of system to amplify the music. I didn't entirely understand it. I find all this mechanical talk appallingly boring."

"Sound isn't really my field—I'm more into motion," Caleb said. "But I know a little about acoustics. As for amplifying music, there are a few men working on it, but they haven't quite figured it out yet. There's not much we know about sound—it travels, of course, and it can be conducted, but not easily broadened—"

"Really," she interrupted. "I don't have much interest. Talk to Joseph, see exactly what he wants."

He watched her a minute, trying to see behind the perfect skin that lay so luminously over the bones of her face. "And why ask me?" he said.

"You're supposed to be the resident genius."

"I mean, as opposed to Noah. His reputation equals mine."

"Ah, well, Noah," she said, casting her eyes toward the ceiling with a small smile. "I think perhaps Joseph might be a little jealous if Noah spent all his days *and* all his nights at Seraph. He thinks that Noah distracts me, you see."

It had been a subject of much speculation between Caleb and his far more interested Edori friend: Exactly what was the relationship between the angel and the owner of the bar? She could not be attracted to him; Joseph was the sort of man who grew only less appetizing on greater acquaintance. Noah favored the dark idea that Joseph had some kind of malevolent hold on Lilah, refusing to release her from unwary promises given in the past. Caleb's own theory was that she was seeking a life as wretched as she could stand, to divert her from an interior pain that he would guess was nearly unbearable. He had chosen not to voice this opinion to Noah.

"And does Noah distract you?" he asked pleasantly.

She smiled. "I find him quite endearing. So sweet, you know. I didn't believe such purity really existed."

Caleb snorted. "He's not quite an innocent, you know. The Edori—"

She waved a hand impatiently. "Oh, spare me the tales of Edori promiscuity. That's not what I'm talking about. He has an uncorrupted heart. So few people do. And they're never men."

"Thank you on behalf of my sex."

She laughed at him. "I don't think you're corrupt, exactly," she said. "But you're not pure-hearted. You're a little cynical about people in general. The worst never surprises you, though you're always delighted by the best. You take what comes, enjoy what you can and shrug off the rest."

It was an eerily accurate reading from someone who was virtually a stranger—and a self-absorbed stranger at that. But he remembered hearing, somewhere, in some forgotten conversation, that Delilah had been the best ever at reading other people, identifying their motives and using their foibles against them. The new Archangel apparently did not have this skill.

"And won't Joseph be jealous of me if I'm there all day and all night?" he asked abruptly. "I come to hear you almost as often as Noah."

"Oh, no. You don't worry him. I told him you don't like me."

He raised his eyebrows. "Did you? For the sake of expediency, or because you think it's true?"

She was smiling that covert smile again. "Oh, it's true. You think I'm—untrustworthy. You think I'm merely flirting with your friend. You think I have a capacity for wounding people—and that I like to do it."

He replied just as candidly. "I think you've been hurt enough to figure other people deserve a little pain. Spread it around a little."

"You see what I mean? Noah would never say a thing like that to me. He's not cruel enough."

"Would Joseph?"

"He's not clever enough."

"I don't pretend to be clever and don't wish to be cruel. I

don't dislike you. I don't entirely trust you. I do wonder how you deal with all that misery unless you can find ways to channel it someplace."

Her dark eyes mocked him. "Misery?" she repeated.

"If my hands and eyes failed me and I could no longer do the work I love—yet my mind remained active, inventing things I could never actually put together—I think it might make me a wretched man. I know who you are, Delilah. Noah knows. I would imagine everyone who sees you knows. It's a hard secret to keep."

She sat up straighter, a little flare of anger washing color across her face. "If I had wanted to be secretive, I would have hidden myself in Hagar's retreat and shunned the company of mortals," she said haughtily. "I would not have climbed on stage to sing with a voice that everyone in Samaria recognizes. Naturally people know me. But few of them choose to taunt me with my past."

"I wasn't taunting you," he said softly. "And you know it. You read me right, but I believe I understand you well enough. I have no wish to make my best friend jealous merely to provide you diversion. If Joseph is so interested in having me wire up something in his place, tell him I'll see what I can do—as long as Noah does the job with me. Would that satisfy him, do you think? Would it satisfy you?"

She stared at him a long moment, flags of fury flying across her cheeks. But, give her credit, she did not refute the accusation. He thought that, as a change from Joseph's oiliness and Noah's purity, she might find his forthright astringency a refreshing change. He couldn't help it; a warm smile escaped him, and he shook his head.

"Come on," he said, rising to his feet and holding his hand out to her. "I will buy you dinner. I'm hungry after all."

She waited a mutinous moment. "If you think you're safe with me," she said. "If you're sure you won't succumb to my wiles."

"I'm sure," he said, earning another quick look of resentment. But then, surprising him, she laughed gracefully and acquiesced. She allowed him to pull her upright and usher her from the apartment. Caleb paused to lock the door behind them, wondering what in the god's name he was going to tell Noah about this evening.

Later, Caleb would date his friendship with the fallen Archangel from that evening—not the dinner itself, though he enjoyed it immensely, but from that swift, honest conversation in his apartment beforehand. Over the meal, they laughed and talked like old friends, Delilah favoring him with her wicked and dead-on views of the most prominent civil leaders of Luminaux and, when he knew them, the men and women who dominated the rest of Samarian society. Reviewing the conversation later, he was surprised to remember that he had done more than his share of talking, mostly under her gentle ironic prodding. So that she had learned more of him than he had of her, except that she was exceedingly pleasant company when she chose to be.

Though it was hard to imagine falling in love with her. She could dazzle anyone, he had no doubt, but love was a different matter. It would be like attempting to embrace a star, dizzyingly above you in a winter sky. He did not aspire so high.

Noah, he was convinced, had no such trouble imagining that fate, though he never spoke of the state of his heart. When the two men talked of Delilah, which was often, they spoke in more general terms.

"I wonder if she finds it strange, the company she keeps these days," Noah once said. They were, of course, at the back table in Seraph, nursing their third or fourth glass of wine. Delilah had just finished her last set and had been called to a table of Semorran visitors—wealthy young women, or so it appeared, vacationing here on their parents' money. "She used to be first among angels. She arranged dinner parties for the Manadavvi, and the river merchants bribed her with expensive presents. Now, the shopkeepers and the wine sellers call her by name, and the little girls who would have been afraid to touch her hem insist that she sit with them and taste their wine."

"And those she has chosen as friends don't seem too promising, either," Caleb responded. "Me, a rootless inventor, and you, one of the godless Edori."

"Hardly godless," Noah murmured.

"By the angels' criteria you are. An Archangel and an Edori—now, that's a strange pairing."

"Not so strange," Noah said. "There was just such a pairing not so long ago."

True enough; though the marriage of the Archangel Gabriel and the Edori slave woman Rachel was hardly the ordinary fabric of divine life. "Well, a hundred and fifty years," Caleb drawled. "I don't believe the two races have even *spoken* since."

Noah smiled faintly and lifted his glass. "Here's to improving harmony between the mortal and the angelic," he said. "I stand ready to do my part."

But that was as far as the talk went; Caleb wondered how deep the dreams had gone. It didn't help matters that he and Noah had accepted Joseph's job offer (which had nothing to do with sound, in fact, and everything to do with improved lighting), which took them to Seraph on a daily basis. Delilah was never there during the days (apparently she was a late riser; they never once saw her before the sun went down). Still, her presence informed the place like a perfume, and all the modifications they were doing were specifically designed to focus more attention on her while she stood upon the stage.

Delilah was never there, but Joseph was never absent, and the two men grew heartily sick of him before the first day was over. He liked to watch them work, offered ridiculous suggestions, and shared with them details of some of the shrewd business deals he had made in the past. More than once he offered to set them up with "a nice girl, she's friendly, she likes Edori" or "a beautiful brunette, a Jansai princess. Her mother and father guarded her too long, as the Jansai do with their women, and now she wants to learn about what she missed."

"Do you think Delilah knows?" Noah asked once after they had declined the offers with enough force to send their employer from the room. "I think he's actually housing prostitutes, maybe in this building. Do you think we should tell her?"

Caleb thought again of the expression that always crossed Delilah's face when Joseph came anywhere near her—a mixture of revulsion, relief and mental obliteration. As if she were thinking, *This is as bad as it gets. No worse.* "She knows," he said.

"I think we should tell her."

Caleb shrugged. "You do it, then."

"Well, she'd leave him then, don't you think?"

And Caleb thought, as he often did, *You may love her, but you don't know her nearly as well as I do.* Then again, perhaps that was why Noah loved her.

It was impossible to tell how Delilah viewed Noah. She seemed to treat him as she would any infatuated schoolboy, with a mixture of affection and mockery. She was never unkind to him, but she was never particularly genuine with him, either. But something—his devotion, that innocence she found so attractive—drew her to him night after night when she could have been pleasing Joseph much better by mingling with the wealthy and powerful patrons of the establishment. If Noah was at Seraph, sooner or later she would come to his table, if only briefly, and exchange a few words and a smile. Caleb had observed no one else to whom she paid the same degree of attention.

One night in particular stood out as typical of the strange, troubled relationship. It was several hours past midnight and Caleb was longing for his bed. But Noah had insisted they stay just another five minutes, just another ten, till Delilah made her ritual appearance. When she finally made her circuitous way to their table, she refused to sit, but stood with her hands folded on a chair back, chatting idly.

"I hate this time of year, don't you?" she asked. "It's dark and it's cold. By the time I wake up, it seems there are only two or three hours of sunlight left."

"You should try getting out and enjoying the beauties of the season," Noah suggested. "I'll take you walking some day. We'll look for the birds that have come south for the winter, and watch for ice on the river."

She laughed and flicked her gaze to Caleb. "Now, that's a proposition I haven't heard since my teenage years," she said. "I never believed in any of that let's-look-for-baby-deer routine, but somehow I think our good-hearted Edori would really take me on a nature walk."

"Probably do you good," Caleb responded. "Noah can identify trees and shrubs for you, too. He knows everything about plant life—what'll cure you, what'll kill you. He'd probably even find the herb that would sweeten your disposition."

"Ah, I don't want sweetening, I want amnesia," Delilah said. "I'd be the nicest girl you ever could imagine if only you could"—she paused and lifted one hand to give it an indeterminate wave—"clean out some of these dreary thoughts in my head."

"For that you need science, not medicine," Caleb told her. "You must have heard how dangerous electricity is. A stray current can lance right through you, erase everything in your brain." He glanced around. "We've got a few loose wires here. Would you like to try it?"

"Caleb!" Noah exclaimed, but Delilah merely laughed.

"I'll keep it in mind," she promised. "If things ever get too grim."

"I would hope, before they got *that* bad, that you'd try a few other remedies first," Noah said.

Now she gave him her attention, and a smile that was genuinely sweet. "Don't worry about me, kind Edori," she said. "Suffering is the only true gauge we have."

"Of what?" Noah demanded, but she did not answer. Joseph, who had been exchanging pleasantries with three men at a nearby table, had just then appeared at Delilah's side.

"And what did you think of the concert tonight?" he asked, lacing his massive fingers through Delilah's small ones. Her hand, lost in his, looked like a doll's. "Lilah's voice pleased you?"

"As always," Caleb replied. "We are both addicted."

"We are all addicted," Joseph said. He tucked his free hand under the angel's chin and gave her a quick kiss on the mouth. Caleb felt Noah go rigid beside him; his own muscles tensed, though it was hardly the first time they had seen the Jansai kiss Delilah. She, as usual, made no move to draw away, showed no expression that could be read without liberal speculation. Casually, when Joseph dropped his hand, she turned away and picked up Noah's wineglass from the table.

"I'm so thirsty," she murmured. "Thank you, of course."

And she took one swallow and set the glass back down. But Caleb could not help thinking that she wanted the drink to wash away the kiss, and sipped from Noah's glass because his touch had alchemized the wine into something purer. Fanciful, of course, but Delilah inspired fanciful thoughts. There was nothing about her that was mundane.

That Noah had seen the gesture as something entirely different was evident by the smile on his face; he thought she honored him by drinking from his goblet, setting her lips to the rim where he had placed his own mouth. A kiss across glass, so he read it—and who was to say that he was not right instead, or in addition? She was as complex as the mysterious flame that ran through their wires and switches. They would always be guessing with mistresses such as these.

And so they spent their days and most of their nights at Seraph, although Caleb simply had to break away from time to time. For one thing, he had other jobs in the city to complete; for another, he was not by nature happy to be pinned to one place.

"You should have been born Edori—you're wanderer enough for it," Noah told him one night when, for a change of scene, they had decided to have their evening meal at the Edori campsite west of town. Caleb recognized only two or three of the ten people seated on mats and rough stools around their cooking fire, though Noah seemed in some vague way to be related to them all. That was the Edori way; anyone was welcome at any tent, at any campfire, and young boys Noah had never once mentioned would approach him casually and call him "brother." If it didn't get too suffocating, Caleb supposed, such intimacy might have a certain appeal.

"And getting itchy feet—itchier by the day," he agreed. He hitched his stool closer to the fire. Even in the warm southern provinces, winter made the night chilly. "When is that trip we're supposed to take in your machine? What have you been calling it—the Beast? That would break up the dull routine very nicely."

One of the older Edori men looked up from his stew. "Is that the trip to Breven?" he asked. "To meet with Marco?"

Noah nodded, not seeming to mind this intrusion into a private conversation. "Yes, Thomas, but not for another two or three weeks," he said. "That's when all the other Edori will be arriving in Breven, and we'll get a better idea of numbers."

Caleb was bewildered. "But what are you saying?"

"I told you—I have a client interested in motorized boats."

"*Edori* clients? But where are they going? Edori don't travel by water."

Thomas laid aside his plate with the air of one preparing to enter a deep philosophical discussion. "Only way to get where they're going is by boat," he said softly.

"But—" Caleb began, and then stopped. "Oh, surely not," he said. "They can't believe you can build a motorboat that will take them all the way to Ysral."

"If not Ysral, where?" the old man said. "If not now, when? The hills and valleys of Samaria are closing against the Edori. Once there was not a mountain, not a river, not a desert that we could not cross, not a stone we did not recognize, for we had been to the place where it was chipped from the ground. The Edori lived everywhere. And now—"

"Now," a much younger man joined in passionately, "we are herded together in sanctuaries that no farmer and no Jansai would think it worth his time to spit on. Are we expected to farm these havens? Mine them? Merely to camp there, living off the rocky land that cannot even sustain its wildlife? These are not sanctuaries, my friend, no matter what the allali call them. They are living cemeteries. The Edori have been sent there to die."

"But Ysral—" Caleb started.

"It is far," Thomas conceded. "We do not know how far. But the Edori have traveled great distances before, and endured hardship to get there, and with Yovah's guidance arrived safely. We can make it to Ysral and our new life."

"But no one has ever *been* to Ysral—or at least, returned to tell of it!" Caleb exclaimed. "There are no maps—you have no idea what hazards lie in your path as you cross the ocean, what storms may beset you, or how many days you will be on the journey. You do not even have any proof the place *exists*—you could sail on for eternity, till your sailors die and your food runs out and your boat rots beneath your feet."

"Which is why the motorized boat has met with such enthusiasm among the Edori," Noah murmured. "It is much faster than a vessel which relies on wind or manpower, and it is never becalmed."

"It is still dashed to the ocean floor in a storm."

"Possibly, but a power source independent of wind and waves will make it easier to control in a gale."

"What do you know of it? You've never gone to sea in your life."

"No, but so the sailors have told me. Why are you so skeptical? I thought you'd be excited. A whole new problem—a whole new puzzle."

"Well, and, certainly, if the project was to design a motorboat to allow fishermen to go a few extra miles off the Jordana coast, I'd say yes, great idea, let me help. But this is—This is like my designing a pair of wings and telling a boy he can fly to Mount Sinai with them. I know he can't."

"He could, if you could just perfect your design," Noah said with a smile. "It is the invention that is at fault, not the destination."

"Possibly—but you cannot even be sure of your destination!"

"It has been told to us by descendants of those who have been to Ysral and returned," Thomas said. "They have described the beautiful land and its sumptuous fruits, the water sweet as honey—"

"I know, I know," Caleb interrupted, "and nothing but harmony there as the Edori live in peace among their brothers. The Edori have talked of a homeland in Ysral since before the days of slavery under Raphael. But those are myths—legends—those tales are from so long ago that you cannot remember which father first told it to his son. How can you be sure those journeys were actually made—to and from Ysral? There is no proof. There are no mementoes ferried back across the ocean. There are only stories."

"How do we know that Yovah exists and that he carried us to Samaria in his own cupped hands more than six centuries ago?" Thomas asked gently. "We have no proof that he guards us, that he listens to our prayers—"

"Especially lately," muttered someone in shadow on the other side of the fire.

"Don't start a theological discussion with me," Caleb warned. "I am not a man with much religious faith. That is the wrong parallel to draw."

"No faith?" Thomas asked, clearly incredulous.

"Don't start," Noah murmured. "Truly—"

"But where exactly is your faith uncertain?" Thomas asked,

unheeding. "Surely you believe that Yovah dwells in the heavens above us, ready always to hear our petitions and respond to our needs?"

Caleb took a deep breath and expelled it. "Where is the proof of that?" he asked finally. "How do we know he is there?"

Thomas gestured. "The rains, the winds—"

"They come as they will. We have studied this, a little. When water evaporates into a cooler air mass, it condenses. In a laboratory, you get mist on your glass. Over a continent, you get rain."

"But the control of the rain! The dispersion of the storms! When the angels fly aloft and sing their prayers, causing the clouds to part—"

"The clouds will eventually part no matter what. Sun and storm make a pattern we can forecast even when we cannot alter it. And," Caleb added, nodding toward the shadowy form who had spoken earlier, "if the angels ever had any ability to influence weather, they appear to have lost it now."

"Not the Archangel," said a woman sitting to his left. Both Caleb and Noah looked sharply her way; Caleb was the first to realize that she referred to the woman who had replaced Delilah at the Eyrie.

"They do say Yovah listens to her when he hears no one else," another Edori agreed. "But still there are storms."

Thomas continued addressing Caleb. "And still you do not believe?"

"I am not that impressed by weather."

"What of the other manifestations? The thunder and the lightning bolts that the god throws down when men have misbehaved or failed to honor him?"

Caleb spread his hands. "What thunder? What lightning? Have you personally witnessed this?"

"In the time of Rachel and Gabriel—"

"Rachel and Gabriel! A hundred and fifty years ago!"

"Yovah sent lightning twice in the space of a few days. Once to bring down the Galo Mountain when the Gloria was not sung on the appointed day. And once to destroy Windy Point, when Gabriel asked him to level that evil place."

"Were you there?" Caleb asked quietly. "Did you see this? Did anyone you know see this?"

"The tale has been told by the fathers of our fathers' fathers, who were there and saw it. And they told their sons, who told theirs, who told theirs."

"A story," Caleb said simply. "A legend."

"Then why is the Galo mountain burned black with marks that will not wash out after more than a century of rain? Why is the ground below Windy Point covered with smashed boulders that appear to have been flung from a great height? What destroyed these places, if not the god?"

"Anything," Caleb replied. "A stone that fell from the sky. Such a stone fell twenty years ago, causing the whole plain north of the Heldoras to light up like fire."

"But that stone left a crater half the size of the Plain of Sharon," Noah pointed out. "Not jagged rocks as sharp as cut glass."

"Well, then, there are other explanations. If in fact lightning smote the mountains, why not just plain old lightning? There's plenty of that. Who said every bolt had to be generated by the god?"

"Well, no, not every bolt, but these were documented—"

"Not well enough for me," Caleb said.

Thomas continued to regard him steadily, more with amazement than ire. "So," he said. "you are truly an atheist. Then how do you account for us being here at all—living on Samaria—brought here by what device if not by Yovah himself?"

Caleb grinned. "Now, that's a mystery that puzzles me every time I open my mind to it," he admitted. "The Librera says Jovah carried us here in his cupped palms, over a great distance, from a far place filled with violence and hatred. But how did he do that? How did he pick us? *Why* did he pick us? Although the why is not nearly as compelling as the how. In his cupped hands? What does that mean? If I chose to carry something over a great distance, I would find a box or a bucket or a container of some sort. Say I were going to move a colony of ants from Gaza to Breven. I wouldn't want to carry them in my *hands*. They'd never make the trip safely. Hands must be a metaphor in this context, but a metaphor for what? And what exactly is meant by a great distance? The distance from Samaria to the stars that we see above us—how far is that? We can't even guess how to measure that sort of space. Perhaps it was no more than the width of the ocean. Perhaps Jovah carried us *away* from Ysral, a place of violence and hatred—"

That, of course, was going too far; half-a-dozen Edori voices rose in protest. Caleb laughed and flung his hands up for peace.

"Anyway, you see, these are the questions that vex me when my thoughts turn to Jovah and the origin of the race," he said. "I am a man of science. I question everything. And so far, religion has not provided me with any answers I like."

Thomas turned to Noah and patted him on the shoulder, while gesturing back toward Caleb. "Be sure and guard this one very closely," he said in a kind voice. "His way is hard, and he is likely to stumble."

Noah was grinning. "I do what I can for him. He's fairly hopeless. A good mind, you know, but somewhat disordered."

"I am not the only one who thinks this way," Caleb pointed out. "The more we know of science, the more we question about god."

"Questions are good," Thomas said. "I hope you find your answer. There is only one, but it may take you your lifetime to discover."

"Well," Noah interjected, "there's one answer he hasn't given us yet, and that's whether he'll help build the boat. Yes? No? Let me think about it a day or two?"

"I think it's crazy," Caleb said. "But I understand your desire. I'll help, if the offer's still open."

"Yes!" Noah exclaimed, knocking his fists together in a gesture of victory. "I knew you couldn't resist the challenge."

"You need me," Caleb said. "You're not smart enough to design such a project on your own."

With a yelp of protest, Noah lunged for his friend and wrestled him to the ground. They rolled clumsily from side to side, bumping into bodies and kicking apart the fire. Around them was the sound of Edori laughter and the smell of disturbed ashes. Caleb was laughing too hard to put up much of a struggle, but he eventually managed to fight himself to a sitting position, with Noah's hands still clamped around his neck. It was a raucous end to a pleasurable day, and he found himself preferring it to another night at Seraph. When Noah released him, one of the Edori brought them each another mug of ale, and they continued drinking companionably well into the night.

Thus, Caleb was not at his best the next day, more tired than he should have been and dragging from the effects of the alcohol. He put in a good day's work (not at Seraph this week; one of the music schools wanted him to design a machine that would automatically strike hammers against their collection of bells), and figured he would make an early evening of it at his own place for a change.

It was a regime he followed for three days running, and he was surprised at how pleased his body was at the early nights and extra hours of sleep. He was not surprised, the evening of that third day, when one of the baker's daughters told him he had company awaiting him on the balcony outside his door.

"It's an angel lady," she said, her voice lowered, as if those bright wings endowed the beings with enhanced hearing as well as flight and beauty.

"No doubt," Caleb said a little wryly. "Why don't you— I'll take some of those sweet rolls as well, while I'm here. Since it looks like I'll be entertaining."

The girl put four sticky buns into a bag. "She's very beautiful," she offered. "I didn't know you knew any angels."

"Well, I know one."

"She didn't give me her name, and when I asked what I should tell you, she said, 'Tell him it's the Archangel.' "

Caleb laughed, although it struck him as odd that Delilah would so name herself before this young girl—before anyone, actually. It was a title she seldom laid claim to.

"Thanks for the advance warning," he said, and left the shop to take the iron steps two at a time. But when he arrived at the top of the landing, he received a profound shock: The slim blond angel standing motionless before him was not Delilah. It was no one he had ever seen before in his life.

Chapter Four

Alleluia had left the Eyrie with a sense of relief. So many of her days seemed hedged about with difficult decisions, deep uncertainties, tasks to be performed that she had somehow overlooked. Now at least, however unsuccessful her mission might prove to be, she was taking action, and this made her feel somehow stronger. She was a woman with purpose, on a mission, with a goal.

Even better—she was escaping. She had always loved the Eyrie, ever since she first went there to live—loved its glowing rosy walls, its endless labyrinth of rooms, the color and motion and sound that made it such a vivid place. Especially the sound, for the Eyrie was alive with music. Night and day, singers gathered in two- and three-person shifts to sing from the open room built at the highest point of the hold—so, night and day, the air was flavored with the sweetest of music, the heart was soothed by the most harmonious of sounds. Every singer in the hold took his or her turn in the duets and small chorales; it was one of the details for which the Eyrie was famous.

But sometimes—and it was almost sacrilege in a land devoted to the principle of harmony—sometimes Alleya found herself longing for a moment or two of silence. An hour, perhaps; indeed, she would not complain at a day's worth of stopped music. It was one of the reasons she so often took refuge in the soundproofed music rooms; there she could have complete quiet for as long as she desired.

Now, of course, that angelic harmony was the least of the noises to assault her. More likely, it was a merchant's angry voice or the sound of someone calling her name on a note of panic. Doors slamming. Arguments. She longed for a cool, still place where no one spoke for hours at a time.

In fact, that was one of the reasons she had decided to make Mount Sinai her first stop, although she had perfectly legitimate reasons for going there, too. Knowledge of past history had served her so well in her dealings with the Manadavvi that she thought general research might give her more ammunition in future debates.

It was Samuel who had suggested that Mount Sinai might offer other treasures as well, for it was the first site to be opened by the oracles when the colonists arrived on Samaria. It was generally held to have the most complete library of texts brought by those early settlers. But those manuscripts, as Alleya pointed out, were in a language long since discarded by the Samarians.

"But isn't that the language the oracles still use?" Samuel asked. "When they're speaking with the god?"

She had stared at him, for of course he was right. "And they must learn it somehow," she added for him. "So there must be—what? Grammar books? Manuals? Dictionaries?"

"Something," he agreed. "If you look, you'll find something. Or you can always ask Job or Mary how they learned and if they'll teach you."

They had looked at each other a long time, weighing that. Then—"Nooo," they said in unison, and they both laughed. Alleya had so far managed to steer pretty much clear of the oracles; she didn't need one more set of people telling her what to do.

So on a cold, brilliant day she left for Mount Sinai, the first stop on a trip to Luminaux to look for an electrician who could bring her music machines back to life. It sounded very productive and necessary—not at all like she was fleeing to a place of silence and peace.

It took only a few hours of easy flying to cover the 150 miles to the mountainous slopes that housed the oracle's retreat. As she stepped inside the cool, gray tunnel that led to the interior of Mount Sinai, Alleya was filled with a sense of absolute calm. Her heartbeat slowed; she felt the blood flow more contentedly in her veins. Her mind cleared, washing away debris and static she had not even been aware of. Even her wings felt lighter.

As she stepped—tiptoed—through the wide tunnels, the only sounds were the whisper of her wings across the stone and the tiny tap of her careful footfalls. Like the Eyrie, Mount Sinai was perpetually lit with muted gaslight, but here the effect was of silver coolness, witchlight against a lifting mist. Alleya liked the dreamy effect, remote and soothing, in keeping with everything else about this place.

She passed quickly through the first rooms she came to, the public foyers and the smaller conference rooms. She had spent a few days here when she was quite young, and she'd never come back, but she remembered the layout fairly well. Down that hallway, the sleeping rooms and the kitchens; down that one, the oracle's private chambers. But here, at the center of the maze, were the rooms where the mystic's true work was done: the archives, where all knowledge was kept, and the central chamber where the glowing blue plate provided an interface with the god.

Alleya had meant to go directly to the archives, but the eerie blue light on that glass screen drew her across the room almost against her will. Not touching anything, she spread her fingers and suspended her open hands over the knobs and buttons that the oracles pressed when they wished to communicate with Jovah. Job, she remembered, had called it a keyboard. He had touched his fingers to three of its symbols, and the lights and letters on the screen had instantly rippled and rearranged themselves. It was the most awesome thing Alleya had ever seen.

The pictures on the screen now were unmoving, unreadable, navy-colored hieroglyphics against the celestial background. If she could memorize them, Alleya thought, and if she could indeed find some grammar book to teach her the old tongue, she might be able to decipher whatever message the god was sending now to an empty room. She smiled at the thought. Jovah knew better than to communicate with someone who wasn't there.

And better than to try to communicate with someone who could not reply. Resolutely she turned her back on the mesmerizing display and slipped into the huge room that opened off the central one. This one was darker than all the others, and bigger, so that it took her eyes a moment to adjust. It was just as she remembered: piles of leatherbound books lining every wall, additional volumes more coherently arranged on wood shelves that reached almost to the high, sloped ceiling, maps attached by hooks to the stone walls, and locked metal cases holding who knew what treasures or secrets.

She remembered the last time she had been here, nearly twenty years ago, holding her mother's hand and too fascinated to be frightened (as she should have been). "What's that place? What's that map? Is it Samaria? Can I go look at it?" she had asked, and her mother told her to be quiet just as the oracle Rebekah told her No. (No what? No, it was not Samaria? No, she could not look at it? In any case, she did not go any closer. Rebekah found what she was rummaging for in that back room, and they had all returned to the god's chamber.)

Now she could go as close as she liked and examine the pictures on the wall. For there were three maps, she saw as she went deeper into the room—one she could see from the doorway and two that came into view only after she stepped inside. She went to the far wall to examine the one that had first caught her eye.

It was not Samaria, that was certain—it did not look like any place at all. It was merely a series of dots, and clusters of dots, with white lines hand-drawn at various locations connecting dots so that they formed fanciful faces and shapes. Alleya traced the designs with her finger. This one looked like a horse; this one like a flower in full bloom. A broken red line made an erratic path from one corner of the map diagonally to the other, almost as if someone were laying a course between the dots and faces. She could not even begin to guess what such a map might be recording; perhaps it was something else entirely. In any case, it was so old that the paper was brown and the red of the pathway had faded to a muddy color.

The hangings on the other wall looked more like maps to her—and one might even be Samaria. It was oddly proportioned, though, as if the continent had been laid across a globe and stretched and pulled to make it fit some unfamiliar contours. The

Galilee River was sketched in, as were some of the major mountain ranges, but the land was not divided into the three provinces as it was in every modern map. So! Perhaps these were the rough dimensions of Samaria as the settlers had first seen it, hastily outlined and inaccurately represented, but essentially a plot of the homeland they would create. It must be as old as the history of the angels. It made Alleya shiver to look at it.

The other was far more detailed, a map of continents and oceans with every river, lake, mountain, desert and city shaded in and named. Idly reading over the foreign words, Alleya was startled to find, here and there, names she partially recognized: Jordan, Galilee, Bethlehem. Could this be a depiction of the place the settlers had come from? Alleya brushed her finger across the faded coastlines, the gray seas, and felt another chill spider walk down her back.

But she was not here to look at pictures hundreds of years old, maps that could tell her nothing. Books—now, books could tell stories with morals she needed to learn. If she could find the right books.

She sorted through the shelves and piles for a good hour, opening dusty covers and scanning incomprehensible pages, looking for names or phrases that sounded familiar. At first she made a stack of possibilities—anything that mentioned Hagar or Uriel, the first Archangel, often enough to seem like a record of their time period—but these began piling up so quickly she realized she would need another qualifier. And the task was beginning to look hopeless, for, as Alleya scanned the pages, she saw that almost none of the words were in current usage; she would have to look up each one, laboriously, individually—assuming she could actually find a dictionary. It could take years to translate a single chapter, and she did not think she had anywhere near that much time.

Until what? she thought, for the idea that there was a deadline approaching made her uneasy. *Don't have much time until what?*

So it looked hopeless, but a certain stubbornness made her keep combing the shelves, anyway. Chance and her random browsing brought her a most fortunate find just as she was about to give up completely. It was a massive leatherbound book that she found on the floor, lying on top of two smaller books. The flyleaf of the biggest volume was inscribed by hand and signed by the oracle Josiah:

"I, Josiah, in the fifth year of the glorious reign of the Archangel Gabriel, have, at the direction of the Archangel, begun a translation of the earliest accounts of the settlers' arrival in Samaria. It is the Archangel's fear that we will lose the ability to read those early records as we lose all touch with that ancient language and as we forget the stories that have been told to us by our fathers and their fathers. Thus I set down in the modern tongue the words written in the lost language, choosing for my text the first volume of the historian Paul, known for his keenness in observation as well as his accuracy . . ."

There was more in the same vein, but Alleya skipped it to skim through the handwritten manuscript itself. Josiah had laid out the book in an unusual style, with a page of the old language facing a page of the modern version, so that the knowledgeable reader could interpret controversial passages of the original text for himself. Indeed, in several places he had inscribed question marks and possible alternative definitions in brackets next to a vague word in his translation. Just in flipping through the pages, Alleya found two instances where he had written yet another word in the margin, attributing it to "Ezekiel" or "Jezebel." The other two oracles of his time, Alleya presumed; who else would know the ancient writing?

It couldn't have been better. It was as if Gabriel had anticipated her need and fulfilled it; no wonder they said he had been the greatest Archangel of all time. Alleya was filled with equal parts excitement and awe, but she took a moment to glance at the other two books in Josiah's little pile. One was completely unreadable—possibly the original text from which Josiah had been translating. The other—ah, another discovery, as good as the first.

This was not exactly a dictionary but a book of phrases written in the original language and translated to one that seemed very close to the modern Samarian version. It too was handwritten, with an inscription on the opening page from someone identified only as the oracle of Gaza during the reign of Michael. Well, there had been more than one Archangel named Michael, so it was impossible to place the oracle in a specific time frame, but it scarcely mattered when the seer had lived as long as he or she had taken the time to set down important knowledge in writing.

Alleya looked more closely at the lines of text and their explanations. Even the quasi-modern interpretations, though put in familiar words, made very little sense to her. "Is the genealogical program loaded?" "Is there sufficient memory left?" "Are there records that need to be purged?" Paging back to the introduction, Alleya received yet another jolt, for here the oracle had written, "Instructions for the novice upon first beginning to interface with the god." These were the words and phrases used by the oracles when they spoke to Jovah through the glowing screen. These were words only the holy people should see, and Alleya closed the book quickly.

And then, after a moment's thought, she opened it again. She was Archangel; she was desperate; and in her own way she communicated with the god all the time. This had been left to her, almost deliberately, it seemed, by the great men and women of the past. She would be foolish to leave it behind if it could help her learn what she needed to know. It was a bequest, and she would not forgo or abuse it.

She took another minute or two to look around, but she knew she had found what she came for. So she slipped the books into her leather carrying sack and slung the strap over her shoulder.

Entering the main chamber as she left the archives, Alleya could not resist one more glance at the interface. The next time she was here, perhaps, she would be able to read the dark words on the glowing screen, though she would not do anything so intemperate as to respond.

She turned to go, paused, and turned back, narrowing her eyes against the distance that separated her from the blue screen. She could not be sure, but she thought the hieroglyphics on the interface now were different from those that had appeared when she first stepped into the chamber. She crossed the room to stand once more before the screen, trying to remember exactly what those other letters had looked like. Well, there had been fewer of them, that much she remembered; the screen was now crowded with symbols, numbers, a pattern of pinpoints. That was not what had been displayed when she first walked in.

And then, causing her backbone to melt into her knees, the screen dissolved and shifted even as she watched it. She gasped; her hand flew to her mouth, but she stayed frozen in place as the letters wriggled and re-formed. Two short words only, but invested with a silent urgency, for each letter was several inches high and each word filled half the screen. It must mean something, something tremendous or terrible, but Alleya had no idea what.

Who was the god addressing and what was he asking? What was so pressing that he must offer his thoughts to an empty room, or did he hope that some learned stranger would happen through and see the message on his screen?

Or did he somehow know Alleya was standing there watching—and was he directing his message at her?

Leaving Mount Sinai, Alleya was in a state of some perturbation, so she was not paying complete attention during the early stages of her flight southeast toward Luminaux. She therefore barely noticed the sudden drop in temperature as she crossed the Galilee River, and the first strong gust of wind caught her almost totally off-guard. She had been flying lower than usual, out of sheer laziness, and the force of the wind knocked her sideways and dangerously low to the ground before she pumped her wings furiously enough to regain the necessary altitude—

Where she began to be more alert. The icy currents swirling into the warmer southern air were sure signs of trouble, and she was not surprised, a few miles later, to find herself heading directly into a pelting rainstorm. The central regions of Samaria had received more than their share of rain in past months, although recent reports had indicated the weather was under control. But even from her vantage point far above, Alleya could see the ground was marshy; stands of trees stood drooping in unnatural pools of water, and fresh rivulets made rippling patterns around rocks and boulders that used to rest idly on dry ground. Clearly, rain was not welcome again here today. No one had asked her for a weather intercession—but she was here, and it was one of the few things she was truly good at.

She increased the pace of her wingbeats, angling upward

through the dense wet masses of clouds. She was aiming for the still sun-drenched sky above the storm, but she climbed and climbed through the heavy air and never broke free to daylight. The clouds were thicker than she had ever seen them, piled on top of each other in impenetrable profusion.

Very well; she could sing in the storm. She slowed the sweeping rhythm of her wings, feeling the feathers curl and drag as they passed through the sodden air. All she needed was enough motion to hold her in place, although the air itself was so liquid she almost felt she could float in it as she could in a river. She lifted her arms above her head in a gesture of supplication; then, closing her eyes, she began to sing.

Her voice was sweet and thin as drifting campfire smoke; she always pictured its spiraling sparkle wending its way toward the god like a trail of vapor. Odd people had been moved by her voice. Poets, madwomen, autistic children, angels who cared for no singers but themselves—these were the people who crouched at her feet when she offered prayers to Jovah. Most others merely listened, and nodded, and went on their way, unaffected.

But Jovah heard her. He always had. Almost, she could follow the disintegrating mist of her song as it glittered through the lowering clouds and arced through the layer of sunlight somewhere above her, then skittered past the coruscating stars straight to Jovah's ears. Like the lunatics and mystics, he heard her; her voice caught his wandering attention. She felt him start, as if he had been touched unexpectedly on the cheek, and then relax again as he realized it was only Alleya asking for a simple favor. *Yes, of course, happy to do what you ask*, she imagined him saying; and as she thought it, the air around her began to shift and lighten.

She stayed aloft another thirty minutes or so, hovering where she had prayed, and feeling the clouds shred away beneath her wings. It was a glorious feeling to petition the god and have the god respond. No matter how often she tried it, Alleya was gratified beyond measure when she succeeded. She strove hard not to be vain about her ability, for, after all, any angel could do the same, but she could not shake the secret belief that her voice pleased Jovah when other voices angered him, or bored him, or made no imprint upon his indifference; and it was indeed a marvelous thing to be one who could charm the god.

When it was clear that the storm had ended—even now a few shards of sunlight were slicing through the clouds—Alleya shifted her weight, dropped a few hundred feet and began flying more purposefully toward southern Jordana. She had wanted to reach Luminaux tonight, but realized that she might have delayed too long, for she had one more stop to make before she could complete her journey. She needed to make a visit of strategic importance to the angel hold at Cedar Hills.

There were many who considered Cedar Hills the best of the angel holds, but for Alleya's taste, it did not have quite the majesty of the Eyrie or the quaintness of Monteverde. Built on an open, level plan, it seemed to her much more of a peasant village than a seat of divine power—which had been exactly the intention when it was built. However, the small houses, pretty shops and scattered angel dormitories seemed more like a campus for music students than a place where people gathered to confer about the god. Alleya landed gracefully in the well-trimmed patch of green, set aside specifically for angels to come to rest, and glanced about her at the bustling activity of the city center.

Micah, the leader of the Cedar Hills host, might be anywhere—if he was even here. She first tried the central compound, a four-level boxy stone building where most of the important functions of the angels were held—public meals, rehearsals, hearings with petitioners. He was as likely to be there as anywhere.

In fact, he was just leaving the building as Alleya approached it, and he came directly to her side as soon as he saw her.

"Well, this is an honor, angela," he said, surprised but gracious. "What brings you to our humble hold?"

"Travel to Luminaux, mostly, and a desire to stay in touch," she replied. "It seems I am rarely in Cedar Hills these days."

"Well, you have much to occupy you in Velora," Micah observed, leading her to a low, inviting building wrapped in the aromas of bread and coffee. "Let's have something to eat, shall we, and catch up on events?"

He got them seated in a private room, ordered tea and cakes, and proceeded to regale her with tales of Cedar Hills, lightly told. Alleya listened, trying to decide if he seemed nervous or merely guarded. The third time he mentioned the Manadavvi Aaron Lesh, she realized he was uncertain about broaching a delicate topic.

"So the Manadavvi have been here," she said directly. "What were they asking for? Special favors for their distributors, or for you to use your influence on me?"

He smiled ruefully and stirred his tea. "Both, actually. And in fact, it wasn't the Manadavvi here, though it may as well have been. It was old Esau Heiver from Breven—one of the Jansai industrialists who deals with the Manadavvi."

"Buying or selling?"

"Both. Buying raw material, selling finished products. You want luxury, angela, you go to Breven. You think you find it in the Manadavvi homes and the Semorran palaces, but they manufacture it in Breven. Unbelievable things—the silks they are weaving in those new factories are softer than a baby's cheek. And the gold—they are making plates and cups and furniture from gold faster than the Bethel miners can dig the stuff up. You should fly up there for a day just to look at what they're making."

"Thank you, I avoid Breven whenever possible. I find the Jansai hard to love."

"As do we all."

"So why was Esau here? Complaining about the shipping problems along the river? I had a little dispute about that myself."

"No, I think he's entirely willing to let the Manadavvi solve their own problems. What the Jansai are unhappy about are the restrictions on child labor—they don't want to give up the children. And, perhaps, in a few instances, they have a point. Children have smaller fingers, can reach into some of those wretched machines with more ease than adults can—but I have an innate distaste for the whole picture, those little bodies slaving away in those metallic coffins—"

"What did you tell him?"

Micah gave her his easy smile. He was a pleasant and likable fellow, but just a little lazy; Alleya did not always trust him to hold the moral line. "I told him I would discuss the situation with the Archangel, for I was sure you would have strong views."

Alleya brushed a hand through her hair. It felt tangled and wind-blown, and no doubt looked worse. "Oh, I do," she sighed.

"I think the children should all be in school or playing happily on their lawns, but we both know there are too many children who have no access to either."

"Sometimes the children are the only family members able to work in the cities," Micah said softly. "Just the other day, a family came here. The father had worked in one of those factories. Lost a leg when some big wheel came crashing down on him. The mother—pregnant again. Four children already in the family. What can they do? He can't farm. She has weaving and sewing skills, but with the factories working at top efficiency, the cost of a simple handmade garment is two or three times the price of one of those silk gowns. The children could work in some of those factories—although, give them credit, these parents were looking for something better. But many parents choose that option—and they weren't so happy when those age restrictions went into effect, either."

Alleya nodded. "So what did you do? With the family?"

"Oh, gave the woman a job sewing feast-day outfits for the angels. I can't bring myself to wear factory-made clothes."

"That was a good solution."

"Yes, but I don't have that many jobs to offer. And it's an issue that needs to be addressed. You and I both know that unless we enforce the laws, there will be violations—and I don't have the manpower to patrol the factories of Breven every day."

Alleya combed her fingers through her hair again. "Well, then. Let's amend the laws. What do the Jansai respect above anything else?"

"Money," Micah answered without hesitation.

The Archangel nodded. "Exactly. Tell them they can employ child labor—but at double the rate of an adult worker, and for half the time. So that a child who works a half day receives a full day's salary. And that it must be documented. And that children who are short-changed should report it, and the errant factory owners will be fined. Everybody gets what they want, and those who abuse the system are exposed. No black market, no incentive to lie."

Micah's brows rose, and he smiled. "I like it," he said. "What about the age restriction?"

"Keep it at ten, for now. Let's see how many violations we have."

"You realize, of course, it will ultimately send a wave of fury through the Manadavvi. Since costs will go up, prices will go up, and the Manadavvi are the buyers—"

"Cost of doing business," Alleya said, smiling faintly. "If their prices go up enough, then women like your new seamstress will become marketable again, as expenses even out. Perhaps I don't have a head for business. It doesn't seem so bad to me."

"You just don't like the Manadavvi," Micah said. "It doesn't trouble you if they are unhappy."

She was surprised into a laugh. "How insightful," she said. "I am one of the common people, you know. I have their interests more at heart."

"Well, and there are more of them," Micah said lightly. "So we should all be watching out for their interests."

She wasn't sure he meant it, but it sounded good, anyway. "Have you had other crises?" she asked. "What about weather? As I came across the Galilee, I flew through a rainstorm. Have there been problems?"

"The Galilee? Just south of Castelana?" he asked. She nodded, and he continued, "It never stops raining there. I have been there—I've sent my angels over—the clouds lift for a day or two, then they come piling back. Sometimes they don't lift at all. I'm worried about flooding down on the southern plains—all those croplands . . ."

They discussed storm systems for another twenty minutes, during which Alleya grew increasingly uneasy. In Bethel, the weather had stabilized during the past three months (*since she had become Archangel*, she thought, though she did not say it aloud), and she had not gotten many reports of exceptional turmoil in the other provinces. But here Micah was calmly telling her of the continuing gales sweeping from Breven to the river on an almost regular basis, of small towns given up and two mines abandoned because the wet ground gave way.

"But I was not aware that problems were so severe," she broke in. "I thought—things have been calm enough in Bethel . . ."

Micah shrugged. "It no longer seems so bad. This has been

the way of things for, oh, ten or twelve months now. So now, instead of a northern desert and a southern farmland, we have northern farmland and a southern marsh. We will adjust."

Alleya was a little distraught. "But—Micah, don't you see?—the change in the weather is only part of the problem. What's alarming is that the angels cannot stop it. Does Jovah not hear our prayers asking for the storms to cease? If Jovah had decreed that it was time for Samaria to be remade—desert into farmland, as you say, farmland into swamp—I would abide by his commands. But to lose the ability to whisper in his ear—"

"Maybe he has made his decree," Micah interrupted. "Maybe he has not told us so, but he has decided to change our world. How do you know this is not what he wants?"

She stared back at him, for the thought had literally never crossed her mind. Could Micah be right? Every muscle in her body tensed in denial. "I don't think so," she said, her voice almost a whisper. "I don't believe it. Because I hear him—he hears me. If he truly wanted to flood us all, he would not respond when any one of us prayed."

Micah shrugged, then gave her a quick smile. "I bend more than you do, angela," he said. "I take what the god sends, and I deal with the events handed to me. I don't fight what I cannot control. Tell me how to turn back the rains, and I will. But if Jovah has made up his mind, I do not see that we can reverse his decision."

She was quiet for a long time, wondering if Micah spoke the truth, wondering if Jovah indeed had drawn so far away from his people that he would not care that their world turned upside down. "I suppose we could ask him," she said very softly. "I suppose—perhaps the oracles could put the question to him."

"He answers the oracles in roundabout ways," Micah responded. "I have never gotten a reply that made much sense to me when I went to Job. But there would be no harm in asking. You have other questions to put to the god, I know."

That caused Alleya to look at him sharply. "I? What do I have to ask him?"

Now Micah was smiling broadly, seeming without effort to put aside the solemnness of the last exchange. "Why, who will sing beside you at the Gloria, of course," he said. "That is coming up in a few short months, you know."

"Who will sing—but all the angels, of course."

Micah laughed, genuinely amused. "Alleya, you must have been to dozens of Glorias in your life! You know they are always led by the angelica—or the angelico, in your case—your husband, dear girl."

"My *husband*!" she exclaimed. "But I don't have—I don't even—" She felt her cheeks heat and her words tangle, so she fell abruptly silent.

"Exactly my point! You must know that Jovah always picks the one the Archangel will marry. The Archangel goes to his oracle and asks the god to make his selection, always a mortal, of course—"

"I realize that," she snapped. "I just didn't— This is impossible. In the next four months? To find a husband? There is too much else to do."

Now Micah was sobering; his mood changes seemed to be instant and complete. "As far as I know, this is one tradition the god has never forsaken," he said. "If you expect him to hear you at the Gloria, you need to sing it with your chosen angelico at your side. It will not be so bad—they say the god always chooses for you a mate ideally suited. But it must be done soon, Alleya. You should go to Job while you are here."

"It is proving to be a strange journey, all in all," she murmured.

"What?"

"Nothing. I had intended to go to Luminaux first. But maybe you're right. Maybe I should travel to Mount Egypt and ask Job these difficult questions."

Micah rose to his feet and Alleya followed suit. He was smiling again. "Well, they say the god always hears you," he said. "Perhaps this time he will give you answers you like."

CHAPTER FIVE

So Alleya spent the night in Cedar Hills instead of traveling on to Luminaux that evening as she had intended. She found, to her surprise, that she missed the sound of constant singing in the angel hold, especially when she woke late in the night and found sleep difficult to recapture. She was not eager to fly to Mount Egypt and ask Job to seek a husband for her. The dry, withered, formal man did not seem to her to be an ideal matchmaker. Still, he was the senior oracle; she owed him some honor.

Micah had taken pains to make her visit pleasant, and so she left the next morning feeling relatively refreshed. She had never been sure Micah liked her, and she still was not sure, but perhaps it was just as he said. He accepted whatever was sent his way, be it storm, scandal or Archangel, and he dealt with each as best he could.

The skies were cloudy but dropped no rain as she completed the short flight to Mount Egypt, where she arrived close to noon. Like Sinai, Egypt was hollowed out of a deep tunnel in a fairly steep mountain range; and like Sinai, it was eternally lit, serenely quiet and meticulously maintained. Unlike Sinai, however, Egypt was alive with whispering activity, for Alleya was sure she counted a dozen acolytes scurrying about their tasks as she was ushered from the public reception area to the private chambers.

The inner sanctum of Mount Egypt was laid out much like

the one in Bethel, down to the glowing blue glass plate set into the far wall. Job was standing before it, as if he had just now risen to welcome her; the pale phosphorescent light behind him outlined his frail body with an odd, almost liquid glow.

"Angela," he greeted her, moving forward to take her hand. His fingers felt as light as cat's bones. He seemed indescribably old. Alleya had a brief moment of panic as she thought he could easily die—any day now—and Samaria would be down to one oracle. As the Eyrie was down to one music machine. Truly, it seemed everything in her world was falling apart at once.

He was still speaking. "An unlooked-for pleasure to see you," he said. "I hope it is not trouble that brings you to my door."

"Not exactly," she said. "Or at least, no new trouble."

He ushered her to a low sofa pushed against one wall, and they both sat. "So," he said, "you think I may have new answers."

She made an indecisive motion with her hands. "I was just at Cedar Hills, discussing things with Micah. Apparently weather patterns in Jordana are worse than I had realized—whole tracts of land, even small towns, have been abandoned to flooding and other disasters. I expressed shock that the god no longer hears the angels when they ask him to divert the rain. Micah, on the other hand, suggested that the god has decided to change the face of Samaria. And I wanted to know—Is there a way you could find out? Could you ask Jovah? Because if he is deliberately sending storm and flood to Samaria, I do not want to keep praying for sun."

Job pondered a moment, his wrinkled face showing no expression except contemplation. "Well, Micah," he said at last, on something like a sigh. "He does not trouble to look for hard explanations."

Which was rather an enigmatic reply. "Then you do not believe that is what Jovah intends?" Alleya asked. "Because my heart says such a thing is not possible. But my heart has been wrong before."

"After six centuries of graciousness, it seems unlikely that Jovah would abandon us now," Job said. "How could we have offended him? We sing the Gloria every year. The priests travel the country, blessing all newborn babies and giving them the Kiss of the god." He automatically touched his hand to the crystal node embedded high in his right arm. Such a Kiss Alleya also wore, as did everyone on Samaria who had been dedicated to the god. Jovah continued: "The angels pray daily, asking for his attentions. We live as we have always lived."

"Things have changed," she said softly. "The cities. The factories. This new—what do they call it—electricity? It is a strange, alien power, and perhaps Jovah does not like it. Perhaps this is his way of showing his displeasure with our new devotion to science."

"It is a possibility," Job acknowledged.

"The Librera teaches us that technology destroyed our ancestors," Alleya went on. "Perhaps it is not technology itself that destroyed them, but Jovah's anger with their technology."

"It is hard to know," he said.

"Well, couldn't you *ask* him?" Alleya said with a touch of impatience. "Ask why he has sent so much rain. Ask if he is angry with us, and why. If he tells us he is appalled at our new science, then—"

"Then you will convince the Manadavvi and the Jansai and the Luminauzi to give it up?" Job asked. She could not tell if it was sarcasm in his voice or just weariness. "I doubt anyone would be equal to that task, angela."

It was true; the whole country would rise in revolt if she attempted to turn them away from the giddy glimpse of the future. "Ask him, anyway," she said. "For we should know."

He hesitated, and she suddenly remembered Micah's words: *The god answers the oracles in roundabout ways.* It seemed fairly clear that Job was reluctant to carry out this task. "If you can," she added. "I do not know how such a question is worded, or what you are allowed to ask."

He rose abruptly to his feet. "Come. We will see what he will tell us. These days Jovah has been less communicative than usual, and his replies are not always easy to decipher. But perhaps—"

He did not finish the sentence. She followed him to the radiant screen of the interface, no doubt feeling an inappropriate little thrill at the thought of actually watching an oracle speak to the god. Job seated himself in a sturdy wheeled chair before the screen and carefully played his fingers over the hieroglyphs on the keyboard. Symbols appeared in cobalt letters across the screen as he typed. When he was done, he tapped a square green key on the left margin of the keyboard. The letters disappeared.

She knew she should not interrupt him, for this was holy work, but she couldn't stop herself. "What did you ask him? What did you say?"

"I asked him if he had decided, in his wisdom, to send Samaria many rainstorms this year."

"And he said?"

"He has not replied yet."

But within seconds, the screen flickered and new letters formed. Job read them over slowly, seeming to translate them with difficulty. A frown gathered his wrinkles more tightly around his eyes.

"What has he said?" Alleya demanded.

"He says, 'I do not send the storms.' "

"He does not—" Alleya's face contracted into a matching frown. "Well, but he sends the storms away. Ask him that. Perhaps the rain clouds gather of their own accord, but Jovah can scatter them."

Again the interplay of mortal words and divine ones. Job nodded. "Yes, he says he can disperse a storm if he is asked to do so."

"But—" Alleya experienced a spasm of frustration. If this was always what it was like to communicate with the god, no wonder the oracles dedicated their lives to the job. It appeared to take forever to get a simple question answered. "But lately he has been asked to disperse many storms, and he has not. Has he chosen to ignore the prayers of the angels?"

The god said he answered the prayers when the prayers were put to him in such a way that he could answer.

"What does that mean?" she asked the oracle.

"I have no idea."

"Does he mean he answers the prayers of certain angels?"

The god said he answered prayers whenever he understood them.

"This makes very little sense to me," Alleya said nervously. "Do you know what he means?"

"Sometimes it is hard to tell exactly what the god intends to say."

"Does he wish us to accept the rain?" she said. "Ask him that. Does he want to see Samaria flooded?"

No, the god said. He had no desire for flood.

"Then how can we phrase our prayers so that he will hear them and understand?" Alleya asked.

Job typed in the question and then sat a long time, staring at the reply. Alleya waited maybe a minute before she demanded, "Well? What does he advise?"

Job lifted his hands from the keyboard in a gesture of resignation. "He tells us to ask the son of Jeremiah."

"*Who*?"

"The son of Jeremiah."

"Which Jeremiah? There must be dozens."

Job turned his head to look at her. Even his eyes appeared faded almost to the point of transparency. She felt another wash of fear. "He does not amplify. Just 'the son of Jeremiah,' no 'Jeremiah, son of Efram' or 'Jeremiah of upper Gaza.' In the past, such vague references often have referred to a great figure from the past, but—I can think of no historical Jeremiahs so significant that Jovah would expect us to recognize them simply by their names."

"Can you ask the god to identify this man a little more closely? What is this son's name?"

Job requested more information from the god, but he shook his head when the answer came back. "He just says it again. The son of Jeremiah. Perhaps he does not know the name."

"Perhaps there is no one. Perhaps it means nothing."

"We should ask him something else. Maybe he will give us a more helpful answer."

Alleya smiled briefly. "All right. This question of technology. Is he angry at us for our development of science?"

"But if he says he is not sending the storms, he could not be using them to punish us for science."

"Ask him, anyway."

She was not sure how Job phrased the question, but Jovah's

reply was somewhat baffling. "Science is not evil if you can control it," the god said.

"Doesn't sound like he's angry," Alleya observed. "Ask him how we can control what we create with science."

The instant the letters flickered on the screen, Job sat back in his chair with a little exclamation of annoyance. Alleya had never seen him display even that much emotion before. "What?" she asked, though she thought she could guess.

Job pointed at the screen and read: " 'Ask the son of Jeremiah.' "

"Let's change the subject completely," Alleya said. "Micah sent me here with another question to ask the god."

"As you see, he is not being particularly helpful today," Job said a little grimly. "But I am happy to do whatever I can for you."

Normally she would have been shy about such a question, but the last few interchanges had thrown this whole matter into a different light. Now it was not a personal issue. "Micah says I must have an angelico to sing beside me at the Gloria," she said. "And that Jovah will choose him. Ask him if he has such a man in mind for me."

Job gave her another quick, sideways glance as if, under different circumstances, he would have liked to discuss that a little more minutely. But now he merely nodded, spelled out his question and pressed the square key on the left.

"Who should be angelico to the Archangel Alleluia?" he murmured as he watched the letters disappear.

When the blue text re-formed on the screen, even Alleya was familiar enough with the shape of the symbols to know what the answer was. "The son of Jeremiah," she said softly. "Holy one, I believe the god has no answers for us today."

Job wheeled slowly around to face her. Hard to tell from that solemn face, but his mood seemed both baffled and grave. "Or we must look everywhere to find this man," he said. "For he has every answer we need."

She left Mount Egypt later than she wished, because Job insisted on feeding her, and the acolytes served very reverently. It was a quick flight to Luminaux, but once she arrived in the Blue

City, everything seemed to slow down. Well, at least that was the case at the Edori quarters where no one seemed familiar with the concept of haste. As she approached the camp, she was greeted pleasantly by a group of young mothers who appeared to be taking a dozen children into the city for an afternoon of recreation.

"I'm looking for someone—not an Edori man, but a friend of an Edori man—and I thought someone here could help me," she said.

"What is his name?" one of the women asked.

"I don't know his name. His friend's name is Noah."

"Oh! Noah! He's not here, but he should be back tonight sometime. Although maybe not till late. Well, sometimes he doesn't come back at all, but tomorrow, then."

"Is there somewhere I could look for him? Does he work in the city?"

The women exchanged frowning glances. "He did have a job in the city but I think it's finished," another one said. "Did he get another job? I think so."

"For the music school, wasn't it?"

"No, that was months ago! Where has your head been?"

"Well, he was excited about that job."

"He's excited about every job."

"Well, if he's not at the music school," Alleya said pleasantly, "is there somewhere else he might be?"

"He could be anywhere, really," the first woman said. "Wait for him. I'm sure he'll be back tonight or tomorrow. Someone will be glad to give you dinner and a place to sleep."

Surely no one could seriously expect the Archangel to fly hundreds of miles merely to sleep on a cot in a crowded Edori tent. But not one of the women wore a smirk of irony; they all continued to smile in the most friendly way. "We've room at my tent," the youngest said helpfully. "Although the baby still cries in the night."

They did not recognize her. That was the only explanation. For all her dislike of her position, it was still a shock to be found unfamiliar. "Thank you, no," she said as politely as she could. "I'd much rather sleep in a bed in town. But if you don't mind, I'll just continue on into the camp and see if someone else might be able to help me."

"Thomas," suggested the first woman. "He often eats at Noah's campfire. He might know more."

"Thank you," Alleya repeated, and parted from them.

The campsite, which she wandered around in for a good thirty minutes, was overrun with dark-haired children and women, but fanatically clean and well-organized. Alleya supposed that they systematically buried their garbage or removed it and made everyone adhere to strict standards of personal hygiene. She could discern no order at all in how the tents were erected and where the campfires were built, and every adult in passing seemed equally likely to correct or comfort an errant child. No doubt she just happened to catch smiling faces and laughing interchanges, but the Edori she noticed looked universally happy and at ease.

She only had to ask once for Thomas, because the cheerful woman she accosted patted a young boy on the cheek and said he'd take her right to Thomas's tent. "He should be there," she said. "His leg's bothering him, so he's been staying in the past few days."

And indeed, when her fleet-footed guide (running twenty paces ahead of her and chanting "Thomas, Thomas, Thomas") showed her to the designated tent, the man she sought was already standing outside awaiting her. He looked to be in his late sixties, weathered and tired, but like the others he had a smile of welcome on his face and seemed prepared to offer Alleya a lifetime home.

"Good afternoon," he greeted her. "Are you looking for me?"

"One of your friends, actually," she began, but before she could go on he spoke again.

"Have you had a long flight? Would you like water or wine? Here, these chairs don't look very sturdy, but I made them myself and they will hold even a fat man." He laughed.

She smiled, but briefly. "A short trip, and I'm not thirsty *or* tired, but I understand your leg is painful—"

"Yes, and it's a good thing to sit in the sunlight and be lazy at my age," he said, sinking down into one of the chairs. Perforce, Alleya followed suit, arranging her wings behind her as best she could. "Rest while you can, that's my motto. Rest while you can.

There is always plenty of work awaiting you when you rise again."

"All I want to know," she said, "is where I can find a man called Noah, so I can find a friend of his and offer him a job."

"Noah's in town working at the house of—the singer, what's his name? He's considered very fashionable now, but I don't care much for the overtrained voices myself. I prefer simple tunes and some harp music now and then. You say you have a job for Noah?"

"For his friend, actually, though I don't know his friend's name. He was recommended to me by one of the Edori in Velora—Daniel, maybe you know him—"

"Of course! Daniel of the Calasinsas! A gifted man with his hands, very gifted. No patience at all with animals, but with machines—I never saw anyone more painstaking."

"Yes, well, I have a machine that can't be fixed and Daniel suggested that this friend of Noah's might be able to help me."

"Caleb? If he can't fix it, it's broken forever."

"So if you could tell me where Noah— Wait. You know his friend? What did you say his name was?"

"Caleb Augustus. He was out here the other night. A brilliant mind for engineering, but too much doubt in his soul. Not enough faith. He'll come to believe some day, though."

She had no interest, at the moment, in any man's soul. "It's his engineering talents I'm desperate for," she said. "Do you know where I can reach him? Where he works or where he lives?"

She had a fair idea of how the Edori operated by now, so she was braced for a vague reply like "in the city" or "my friend Ebenezer might know where he once spent the night." Therefore she was delighted when the old man replied at once, "Oh yes. He has rooms above a bakery on Fortune Street. But his hours may be strange. I think he comes and goes as he pleases."

"Would that we all could," Alleya said lightly, rising to her feet. "Thank you so much for your help."

He had not recognized her either, she realized as she wound her way out of the camp—carefully, so as not to be trampled on by any of the careering children—and took off for the city. Not so odd, perhaps—the Edori had never had much formal interaction with the angels. Unlike other mortals, the Edori never felt compelled to call on the angels for aid; they had their own prayers, which they addressed directly to the god, and their own ceremonies for worshipping Jovah. They even had an annual Gathering in which all the scattered tribes came together for a week of celebration, and during which they offered prayers to Jovah for safety in the coming year.

Still, they had never entirely divorced themselves from the grandest Samarian ritual of all, the Gloria. For this event, held at the spring equinox on the broad, flat Plain of Sharon, people from all over Samaria gathered together to lift their voices to Jovah in song. It was a ritual as old as their society, performed first by the original settlers who had traveled here to escape their own world of violence and dissent. Because they had come from a place of such hatred, the colonists had vowed to make harmony their guiding commandment here in their new community—harmony among all people, at all times. So they had made a covenant with Jovah: They would gather every year to sing the Gloria, and among the singers would be angels, Edori, Manadavvi, Jansai, farmers, miners—representatives of every province and clan of Samaria. If the Gloria was not sung by sundown of the chosen day, the god would send a thunderbolt to destroy the Galo Mountain. If, three days after this, the Gloria still had not been sung, Jovah would send lightning to annihilate Semorrah, the principal river city. If it was not sung three days after that, he would destroy the world.

It had almost happened once, back in the time of Rachel and Gabriel. Sundown had thrown its gaudy colors over the hushed plain where only silence had greeted the god's listening ear. In that time, a few lunatics had come to doubt the existence of the god, and this was their way to challenge him. They had wanted proof, and he had given it to them in full measure, leveling the mountain that had once been one of the highest in Samaria. Today there was little left except charred rock and a ragged gap in the mountains circling the Plain of Sharon.

And if she, the Archangel Alleluia, did not sing a mass with the son of Jeremiah at her side, the same thing could happen again this spring—the same thing or worse. That was a pleasant thought to take with her into the luminescent city where she was just now arriving.

The people of Bethel had a saying: If you cannot be happy in Luminaux, you have forgotten joy. Alleya thought it was probably true. Even anxious, impatient, weighted with worries and baffled by responsibilities, she felt a smile settle over face as her feet touched those marbled blue cobblestones. There was such vibrancy in the air, such a sense of expectation and promise. Snatches of music curled around her head as she walked a few speculative blocks, looking for Fortune Street. Stately harps, laughing flutes, twinned voices in spiraling arabesques—the potential dissonances swirled gloriously together like melted ore. So too with the veritable feast of aromas—baking bread, spilled wine, cooking meat, delicate perfume—they blended together into one delicious scent. And everywhere there was color, motion, light, activity. The city itself seemed like a live thing in a celebratory mood.

She eventually had to ask for directions, which were gaily given, and she finally made her way through the throngs of people downtown to the somewhat quieter residential district where Fortune Street was located. The bakery was not hard to find, and the young girl working behind the counter greeted her with a smile. Alleya resisted the urge to buy a dozen loaves of bread and eat them, one right after the other.

"I'm looking for someone I believe lives here," she said. "His name is Caleb Augustus."

The girl nodded. "Yes, angela. He rents the rooms upstairs, but he's not here right now."

"Will he be back soon, do you think?"

"Well, maybe. Sometimes he doesn't return until late, after the bakery's closed. Last two nights, he was here right at sundown."

It was probably an hour until that time; so Alleya had a wait ahead of her. But she could pass some of that time securing a hotel room. Samuel had suggested she stay with one of the wealthy merchants who liked to keep on cozy terms with the angels, but she'd decided she would rather be on her own for a night or two. No politicking, no forced graciousness. The prospect was actually heady.

"I'll come back in an hour or so then," she told the girl. "If you see him before I return, could you tell him to wait for me? I would like to see him."

The girl was nodding. "Surely, angela. Who shall I say is looking for him?"

It was unlike Alleya to feel such a spurt of temper, but it had been just a little irritating to go the whole day incognito. "Tell him I'm the Archangel," she said shortly, and left without another word.

She was somewhat placated when, at an elegant but unpretentious hotel a few blocks away, the manager instantly came forward to offer her his finest room. Like the girl in the bakery, he used merely the ritual courtesy title of angela; unlike the girl, he clearly knew whom he was addressing. The room he showed her to was high-ceilinged and pretty and obviously designed to accommodate angelic guests: The temperature was cool (because angels flew so much at cold, high altitudes, their bodies burned at a higher rate than mortals), and the chairs offered cutaway backs that would not restrict the great feathered wings. She flashed her sapphire wristlets at him, for all charges she incurred would automatically be paid by her hold. He nodded and left the room.

Alleya took a few moments to enjoy the view from her window, wash her face and attempt to untangle her hair before she ventured back outside into the vivid sunset. Something else they said in southern Bethel: Every sunset in Luminaux is more brilliant than the last. Something else Alleya had never had a reason to question.

Caleb had not arrived at Fortune Street when she returned, but Alleya accepted the girl's offer to await him on the balcony. The view here was just as good as the one from her room, and she leaned on the railing to watch the sun-shot sky turn from vermilion to indigo. The splendid display made the wait seem short, but she was more than ready to proceed by the time she heard footsteps running lightly up the metal stairs. She turned her back to the embers of the sunset and waited for the engineer to appear.

Chapter Six

For a moment, Caleb could feel himself staring like a half-wit. He experienced a momentary thrill of danger, as if a vision stood before him, as if one of the fabled Librera angels had come to demand from him some impossible service for the glorification of the god. She looked, in fact, like the personification of one of those mythic angels, with her pure yellow hair, her perfect oval face, her flowing white tunic and her fanned lace wings. The fading glow of the sunset haloed her hair with gold, edged her wings in scarlet. He would not have been surprised had she opened her mouth and begun reciting prayers in the old tongue, invocations that would wield such power that he would, against his will, fall to his knees in supplication.

When she did speak—mundane words in a familiar language—he was so unprepared that he missed the sense of her opening remark. "I'm sorry," he said, embarrassed. "What did you say?"

A quizzical look now made the solemn face look a little more human. "I said, I didn't mean to startle you. I thought that girl would have told you I was here."

"Oh, she did. But she didn't say it was you. I mean, she said it was an angel and I was expecting someone else. . . . I'm sorry. I'm not usually so incoherent."

She smiled briefly and unexpectedly, an expression that gave her face an immediate quaint charm. "I'm not used to having such an effect," she said. "You needn't apologize."

He smiled back. "I'm Caleb Augustus. Is that who you were looking for?"

"Yes. I'm Alleluia, but no one calls me that."

"I would not be so familiar, angela."

"No, I meant—" She paused and shook her head, as if it was beyond her capabilities to explain. "It's such an odd name."

"Is it? I think it's beautiful. As if there was much rejoicing when you were born."

Now the quizzical look altered to something a little more sardonic. "Not exactly," she said dryly, and then instantly changed the subject. "I came here because I heard you were an engineer with a special gift, and I have need of that gift."

"I hope it is something I can help you with, then," he said. All of a sudden he remembered his manners. "I'm sorry! I shouldn't keep you waiting out here! Come in, I'll give you something to drink and one of these rolls. They're really very good."

He opened the door quickly, before she could demur (as she seemed about to do), and then thought he might have acted rashly. His place had been more of a mess in the past, but it was not at its best even so; he would have preferred the Archangel to see his habitation in a more pristine state.

But, "Too late," he said aloud, and led the way in. She seemed amused rather than appalled as she stepped inside and glanced around the tangle of furniture and machine parts that constituted his main living quarters. "I'd like to say that it usually looks better than this, but—"

"Someone cleans my rooms for me, or they would look much like this," she assured him. "Only yours is more interesting." She walked to a rotary arrangement of metal blades and spun them slowly with her fingers. "For instance, what does this do?"

"It's supposed to cool the air," he said. "But it doesn't. When you move it with your fingers, see, it creates a soft breeze."

"I can scarcely feel it."

"Right. Spinning it with your fingers doesn't make it move fast enough. Plus, who wants to stand there pushing it around for hours? The idea is to make it move on its own. But so far, every motor I've built generates too much heat. No net gain of cool air. I'm still working on it."

She shook her head. "Where do you come up with such ideas?"

He tapped his forehead. "They just appear in there fully formed. Like dreams."

"Whispered to you by the god."

He shrugged. "Well, maybe. So, would you like something to drink? To eat?"

She seemed to debate a moment. "Yes, I believe I would. People have been feeding me all day, you see, more or less against my will, but I'm starting to feel a little hungry again. Can I sit on this?" She had moved to the backless stool that Delilah had used on her first visit. Obviously the only piece of furniture in the place that would accommodate an angel.

"Certainly. I'll be back in a second."

In the tiny kitchen, he poured juice and arranged the rolls on a tray, then carried it back to Alleluia. "This is the only food I have, so I hope you're not *too* hungry."

"This is perfect. Thank you."

He sank into a far more comfortable chair a few feet away and surveyed her. Even close up and after a few minutes of conversation, she still looked to him like one of those first angels set on Samaria, handcrafted by Jovah with extreme and loving attention. He voiced the thought that appeared (just like his inventions) fully formed in his head. "I believe I would have picked you for Archangel, too."

She paused with a roll halfway to her mouth, looking even more amused now. "Would you? I was Jovah's second choice, and most would say a bad one."

"I can't imagine why."

She tilted her head a little to one side to examine him. "You know nothing about why Jovah chooses his Archangels or what the role entails, do you?"

"Very little," he admitted. "I am going on looks alone."

That surprised her, for her eyes widened briefly; then an expression of cool poise settled over her face again. "I'll take that as a compliment," she said. "But looks have absolutely nothing to do with it."

"I would guess the job is half negotiating with mortals and half praying to the god," he said. "Which part do you feel unsuited for?"

Again, the flicker of the eyes; she was not used to such plain speaking. "I am unused to dealing with powerful and stubborn men who know very definitely what they want," she said carefully. "I do not have the—charm—that Delilah had. I do not know how to persuade people that they're wrong without alienating them. Which Delilah was very good at. But I am fairly stubborn. And I'm learning."

He sipped his drink. "And your singing?"

She smiled again. His imagination, surely, that the smile lit the room. "Some people like it," she said modestly. "And the god hears me. So you could say I meet that requirement."

"I enjoy a beautiful voice," he said. "Some day perhaps I can hear yours."

"Come to the Gloria," was her instant response. "Or—I forgot—you are not a religious man, are you?"

Now it was his turn to be surprised. "Not particularly," he said. "But who told you that?"

"A man by the name of Thomas, down at the Edori camp. He said you were lacking in faith." Her eyes were focused on his right arm, on the black lump that once had been the Kiss of the god. "And I see he was right. How did that happen?"

Automatically, his hand went to the smooth marble nodule in his arm, dead now, carrying no messages to the god. On Alleluia's bare arm he could see her living Kiss. "Like everyone else, I was dedicated to the god when I was born. My parents were—Well, my mother was as devout as anyone, I suppose, but my father was a questioner. Questioned everything—got it from *his* father, whose grandmother was—well, it's a long story. But he got it honestly. My father pioneered some of the research into electricity that has galvanized the world we live in today, although he didn't know nearly what we know now. Anyway, we worked together on an early project in which we hadn't yet learned how to direct that power. And it's a deadly power."

He paused a moment. He couldn't remember the last time he had told this story. When he told Noah, perhaps. "And it went amuck. Killed my father, almost killed me. I saw the flame arc across my body like candlelight passing over a wall. The Kiss in my arm sizzled—and exploded. I cannot describe how agonizing . . . And my father was dead. And the fire was gone."

Alleluia took a deep breath. "But you could have—I don't know that it's ever happened before, but you could have had the Kiss replaced. I know priests—"

"I didn't want to," he interrupted gently. "What could be the point of being dedicated to a god who would let my father die?"

She watched him narrowly. "Death is always sad and rimmed with grief. But all men die. That is not a reason to forsake the god. That is a reason to trust him and love him, for it is to his arms you will be remanded when you too pass from this world."

He made a conciliatory gesture with his hands. "It is true that all men die, and that death is a ridiculous reason to hate anything," he acknowledged. "But I lost my faith at that moment, and I never regained it. I began to question, and I did not find answers. Not with a god. I found them in science."

She said softly, "But it was science that killed your father, and not Jovah. Why would you still trust *it*?"

He smiled crookedly. "Maybe I don't trust it. Maybe I want to tame it so I can understand what it did."

"So who was your great-great-grandmother?" she asked.

He laughed at her quick, pouncing change of subject. "She was the lost daughter of Nathaniel," he said. "Or have you never heard of her?"

She actually clapped her hands together like a schoolgirl. "The wicked Tamar!" she exclaimed. "Of course I have heard of her. Nathaniel and Magdalena were the only two angels ever allowed to intermarry by a special dispensation of the god. They had six daughters, five of them angels of spectacular voices and great sweetness of disposition. And then they had Tamar, who was born without wings and proved to be a great trial to them. Or so the histories say. Didn't she— I thought she died when she was very young, in some ill-fated boating accident or some disaster riding a horse."

"No, she disappeared when she was in her early twenties, and they didn't see her again until Nathaniel was dying. At least, this is how the family history records it. Apparently they'd known she was alive all this time, because her Kiss was still active, and every once in a while they would have one of the oracles ask the god to track her. They say her mother, Magdalena, fainted when Tamar walked into the room—although whether from mortification or affection one hardly knows. I tend to vote for mortification. They say Magdalena was a silly woman."

"So, you're descended from the first angels of Cedar Hills," Alleluia said. "I would not have thought it."

"It's a very distant connection," he said. "And, as you see, I've moved pretty far down a different road. I don't trade much on my family background, but you did ask."

"Well, I don't trade on mine at all," she said, and then, as if afraid he would follow up on that opening, briskly turned to business. "But I didn't come here to swap tales of our ancestors. I came to offer you a job, if you'd be interested."

"Anything that has sent you searching for me all the way from the Eyrie would have to be unusual enough to interest me," he said. "Who told you to look for me, by the way?"

"An Edori engineer named Daniel who lives in Velora. Who told me to look for your friend Noah, who would direct me to you. It was a little more tortuous than I anticipated, but now that I've found you—"

"I'm eager to hear about this job."

"Have you ever been to the Eyrie or Monteverde?"

"No."

"Then you haven't seen the machine I'm talking about. It's leftover technology from the original settlers, and it plays music—recordings of the masses sung by Hagar and some of the first angels. We have no idea how they made the recordings or how the equipment works, but there are—oh, three hundred masses and other pieces available to us. Except most of the machines at the Eyrie have failed in the past few months. Now there is only one operational, and my guess is that it too will break very soon. And I wondered if you might be able to fix one of them."

He was wholly intrigued. "What powers these machines?"

"Powers them?"

"Makes them go. Supplies their energy." She looked completely baffled, so he tried to explain. "Every inanimate object that acquires force, energy or motion has to have it supplied by an outside source," he said. "For instance, that fan blade over there. You can move it with your finger or I can build a motor that turns it, but that motor is activated by electricity. All the factories in Breven are run on steam heat, but they require fire to create the steam which is compressed in a box until it whooshes out with tremendous force." He flung his hands apart to illustrate. "Now, perhaps our ancestors knew of other sources of power, but to date, this is all we have—manual labor, steam and electricity."

"What creates the electricity?" she asked. "It seems to come from nowhere."

He smiled. "Mostly it comes from falling water," he explained. "The Gabriel Dam on the Galilee River, for instance. Millions of gallons of water pass over it every day, and that motion creates another motion in equipment we have set up—" He paused; there was no simple way to explain this, and he didn't think she really wanted a lesson in hydroelectricity. "Think of the falling water as substituting for the energy you would supply if you pushed something very hard. Motion can always be translated into power."

"I don't think we have anything like that at the Eyrie," Alleluia said. "I don't know what makes the machines work. I was hoping you would."

"I'd love to look at them, in any case. I've never seen any of the settlers' technology. It must be fascinating."

"I worry about that. This sudden leap forward into science. I don't know that we were meant to discover—electricity—and falling water—and factories. Science is what sent the colonists from their home world to Samaria, you know—science and all its destructive power. Who knows that our scientific discoveries will not inevitably start us down the road that led them to disharmony and death?"

"Science is not evil! Name a single evil thing it has done."

She turned one hand palm up in her lap. "Chased the Edori from their homes," she said. "Created great stinking factories in Breven and the mining towns. I believe science is changing the face of Samaria, Caleb Augustus, making the villages cities and the farms wastelands. I wonder how we will turn back to a simpler way of life."

"Why is it better because it is simpler?"

"Why is it better because it is more complex?" she countered. "What has electricity given you except sharper lighting and mass production? Those factories have completely changed the structure of buying, selling and making original goods. Is that a benefit? It does not seem so to me."

"We are in the early days of science," Caleb argued. "From the things we discover today we will learn amazing things. Travel, for instance. My friend Noah has already built this—contraption—a self-propelled vehicle that covers the ground two or three times faster than a man on horse. Someday maybe we shall build machines that can fly! We will—"

"Fly! Why should you want to do that?"

He laughed at her. "Because I can't! Because I know it is possible, and I want to know how it is done."

"To what end? To get from Luminaux to the Manadavvi compounds in two days instead of ten? Why is haste so desirable? Why make the world revolve that much faster?"

He smiled and shook his head. "I can't explain. Maybe there are no benefits, or maybe the disadvantages outweigh the advantages. I still want to do it. I want to discover what can be done. I want to make things, build things, expand things, speed things up. I want to know how things *work*. It's a fever in me. And I happen to think what I can create will make life better for some people."

"And people like me who fear progress are all to be scorned for their timidity and their lack of vision."

"Not at all," he said seriously. "It is people like you who make people like me justify ourselves. And that is no bad thing, either."

"In any case, I have no right to be moralizing," she said with a sigh. "Since I came here specifically to exploit your talents. It is just that—sometimes I wonder. Where we are going, and what we will regret once we get there."

"We will always regret something," he responded. "I would rather rue what I did than what I failed to do."

Alleluia smiled, seemingly with an effort. "Certainly that is an optimistic way to approach it," she said. "So! You will come look at my machines?"

"Yes, as soon as I can. I have a job here that will take me another three or four days. Can you wait that long?"

"I am at your mercy," she said lightly. "Since you appear to be the only man in Samaria who can help me. Come when you can."

He took a deep breath and braced his hands on his knees. How did one invite the Archangel to dinner? "That settled," he said, "can I offer you another service? May I take you out for something to eat? Luminaux is an inexhaustible banquet, so they say. I know a number of restaurants a stranger might not be familiar with—"

She hesitated, then smiled. "I appreciate the offer," she said, "but I have one more task in Luminaux, and perhaps I should concentrate on that."

"What is it? Maybe I can help."

"I believe—we have been told—that Delilah is living here somewhere. She has scarcely communicated with any of the angels since she left the Eyrie, and I just want to know if she is well." Alleluia shrugged. "Not that I think she is particularly interested in seeing me, or any of us, for that matter. But—just to find out."

"As it happens . . ." Caleb said slowly, "I know where she is."

She looked at him sharply. "You do? Someplace disreputable?"

"Now why would you say that?" he marveled.

She flushed. "I'm sorry. It's just that— Delilah always lived at the extreme edges. I am only guessing, but if she feels cast out from the angels, I would expect her to embrace the worst that the mortal lifestyle has to offer. I'm sorry if I wrong her."

"I was thinking you must have known her very well."

Alleluia shook her head. "Watched from a distance. Delilah was the kind who thrived on being at the absolute center of the world. And she was the best at balancing all those opposing forces. But if that excitement has been taken away from her— Well . . . I imagine she must be thriving on something else."

Caleb rose to his feet. "Let me show you," he said. "I don't think you'll like it, but it sounds like you won't be surprised."

* * *

They arrived at Seraph about an hour before Delilah was scheduled to perform. For reasons it was hard to analyze, Caleb was glad that Noah would not be here this evening, for he was away on a weeklong trip to a mining town near the Corinni Mountains. He ushered Alleluia to a table more centrally located than the one he was accustomed to taking; no one would automatically look for him there. It had the added advantage of being equidistant from the strings of lights outlining the walls and stage. Thus they sat in a pleasant semidarkness where they were unlikely to attract much attention.

"The food is fairly good," Caleb said. "We sometimes come here every night of the week."

"We?"

"My friend Noah and I. The Edori who was supposed to direct you to me."

"Is it the food that draws you or the company?"

"Noah has become very friendly with Delilah. She calls herself Lilah here, by the way, but I imagine everyone knows who she is."

He thought he had skated through that one successfully, but Alleluia instantly asked, "And have you become very friendly with her, too?"

"I'm friendly with everyone," he said, and let it go at that.

She ordered a light meal, skipped the wine, and looked around her with the close attention she seemed to give to everything. She was the only angel in the place, but the rest of the clientele was fairly upscale, if young. Just the sort of rich, bored, jaded socialites who would get a kick out of seeing a fallen Archangel sing for their entertainment. Alleluia offered no comment.

"When does the show begin?" she asked.

"Soon. Are you sure you don't want wine?"

"I'm sure."

They ate the last part of their meal in virtual silence. Though she was pleasant and responded any time he essayed a remark, Caleb sensed Alleluia growing tense or at least very focused, and he eventually gave up all attempts at conversation. She continued to watch the people and listen to the musician playing the dulcimer, and betrayed no signs of impatience.

It was later than usual, and all their dinner debris had been cleared away, when Delilah finally took the stage. Thanks to all the work Caleb and Noah had done, these days her entrance was most dramatic. All the lights in the room went out, sending a gasp through the crowd. Slowly, filtering down from above like a single directed ray of sunshine, one narrow spotlight came to life. From the darkness on the stage it shaped a shadow—bowed head, sculpted wings, praying hands—until, gradually growing stronger, it painted the whole angel in a brilliant, iridescent light. As the light grew brighter, the angel lifted her dark head, spread her clasped hands, and seemed to be bathed in the white radiance of absolution.

As always, she began with that unearthly, heartbreaking croon, a prayer for mercy, perhaps, or a requiem for a lost soul. Or both. As many times as he had heard it, Caleb was always moved by that first eerie song, driven to the edge of grief but comforted by the incredible richness of Delilah's magnificent voice.

He glanced at Alleluia to see her reaction. Even in the near-total darkness, he could make out the pale oval of her face turned toward the stage, and the stony expression that had settled across her cheeks. Her eyes were narrowed and her lips were very slightly pursed, as if she were judging a contest and had to concentrate closely. With something like shock, he realized that she was not impressed. What could she think was missing from Delilah's voice? What memories could she compare it to, that she would think this performance was in any way inferior?

He was still watching Alleluia when Delilah made her abrupt, unnerving switch to one of the bawdiest ballads Caleb had ever heard her sing. The Archangel's eyes widened a little, but she looked neither surprised nor censorious. In fact, a faint smile touched her lips and she shook her head so slightly that the motion was almost undetectable. Caleb was oddly relieved.

They did not speak for the duration of the concert but, like the other patrons, sat mesmerized by the angel's performance. Caleb wondered if Delilah somehow knew who was in the audience and was doing her best to be outrageous, for every song she offered was rowdy or tasteless or both, and her grimaces and gestures were suggestively in keeping with the lyrics. No one else in the audience seemed disapproving; maybe it was just his table-mate who made Caleb more than ordinarily sensitive to Delilah's selections.

When the performance ended nearly ninety minutes later, the house lights went down with a crash of cymbals and rose again to thunderous applause, by which time the stage was deserted. Caleb instantly fixed his attention on Alleluia, noting that she was clapping her hands politely and watching the stage as if she expected an encore.

"Is that the end of it?" she asked, turning to Caleb.

"Yes. She'll come out into the audience shortly, at least she usually does, but she won't sing again tonight. I imagine a performance like that must be fairly exhausting."

"Oh, I don't know," Alleluia said idly. "It takes at least as much energy to sing one of the high masses, and the range is more difficult, and the music far more intricate. And Delilah used to come away from singing a mass even more charged up than she was before she started. She feeds on her own energy, you know. Nothing seems to drain her."

"So what did you think?" he asked, because he really couldn't tell.

"Well, it's certainly a waste of the most beautiful voice of our generation," she said flatly, "but I'd rather see her sing this sort of thing than not sing at all. Delilah would die if she didn't sing."

Not at all the answer Caleb would have expected from the Archangel—until he had met this particular Archangel. "That's generous," he said. She appeared surprised.

"Ah, angela, it's good of you to grace us with your presence," came a voice behind them, and suddenly the unctuous Joseph was at their table. "Did you enjoy the performance? Lilah is superb, is she not?"

"Unequalled," Alleluia agreed. "You are fortunate to have her."

He smiled his oily smile. "We make each other's fortunes," he said. "I provide her an unmatched venue, she provides a certain talent. The key to a profitable business relationship."

"Yes," Alleluia said. "Well."

He leaned closer, till his face was inches from the angel's.

Alleluia held her position, but her cool eyes narrowed. "Do you sing, angela?" he asked suddenly. "How's your voice?"

Caleb actually caught his breath. In Samaria, where musical ability was almost universal, it was the rudest question that could be asked of anyone, most particularly an angel. Joseph apparently did not intend it as an insult, however; he waited eagerly for an answer.

"I sing as well as any angel, I suppose," was Alleluia's dry reply. "Why do you ask?"

He gestured toward the stage. "I'm the only club owner in Luminaux who has an angel singing for him full-time. So far, I haven't encouraged the appearance of guest artists, because who could compete with an angel? But when I saw you here, I thought—Ah! Another angel! That's who! What a coup for Seraph to have two angels singing. Even better, she's dark and you're fair—"

"I really don't think so," Alleluia interrupted with some force. "Thank you all the same."

"It wouldn't have to be for more than a few nights," Joseph persisted. "And not tonight—I'd like to have a little time to advertise it—but day after tomorrow, say, for three nights running."

"I'm not interested in performing for you, sir."

"The pay is good," he coaxed. "And the exposure—After this, you could get a job wherever you liked."

She stared at him helplessly for a moment. Caleb struggled to contain a laugh. Clearly the Jansai had no idea who he was soliciting. "The job that I have takes all my time as it is," Alleluia finally managed to reply. "I'm not looking for more work."

"One night?" he asked. "Sing for me one night?"

"Alleya never sings in public except to pray," said a cool, rich voice behind them, and Delilah's dark shadow fell over their small table. *Alleya.* Caleb quickly committed the name to memory. "Don't importune her, Joseph. You'll only make her nervous."

"Think about it," he urged Alleluia one more time. "Let me know if you change your mind."

Alleluia spread her hands, but before she could answer, he had left. The Archangel shook her head. "Well, I have to admire his ambition, but he is a little overbearing."

"Still, I like the idea of you standing on stage beside me, singing your sweet prayers and calming down the crowd once I've riled them up," said Delilah, collapsing into one of the empty chairs at their table. "People would think they'd sinned and been forgiven once they came to one of our concerts."

"Oh, I think they're much happier just having sinned," said Alleluia. Her eyes were fixed on Delilah's face and her whole posture was wary. "But I can see why they'd enjoy your performance."

"Can you now?" Delilah said lightly. "I must say, I was shocked when I saw you in the audience. I didn't think you'd stoop this low just to indulge your vulgar curiosity."

"Maybe all of us have vulgar tendencies," Alleluia responded. "Under the right circumstances."

Delilah laughed out loud. "Well! Not quite the meek, self-effacing Alleya I left behind—has it been a lifetime ago? How do you flourish in your new role, angela? Are you enjoying yourself?"

Alleya chose to take the question seriously. "Not at all," she said. "Not a day goes by that I don't wish it was you there instead of me—I and everyone who is forced to deal with me, I might add, though no one has been rude enough to say it to my face."

"Just flatter them and pretend to listen to their ideas," Delilah advised her airily. "It's all they want, a chance to say what's on their minds. Then go on doing what you were doing before."

"They seem to want more than that," Alleya said quietly. "The Manadavvi want to eliminate the Edori sanctuaries—or at least relocate them. And the Jansai—"

A quick frown pulled Delilah's brows down. "The sanctuaries! That's impossible. It took months—"

"Well, they have withdrawn their proposal for the moment, but I expect them to come back with another."

"Which sanctuary? Ah, the one at the Galo, right? They fought that one from the beginning."

"They're complaining about portage costs, but I told them they could pay the Edori for passage rights, and they didn't like that any better."

Delilah grinned. "A good answer, though. Don't let them harass you. The Manadavvi will exploit every weakness, but they're too cowardly to disobey you outright. They have too much respect for authority."

"If you have any suggestions for dealing with them—"

It was the wrong thing to say. Delilah, who had for a few moments seemed natural and engrossed, instantly grew affected and indifferent. "I! I have no interest in these political squabbles. I am the deposed Archangel, my dear. I don't have much wisdom to offer."

"I know that's not true," Alleya said softly. "It would help me a great deal to know that if I needed advice, I could come to you."

Delilah laughed. "Well, yes, and it would help me a great deal to know that if I prayed hard enough, Jovah would give me my life back. But he won't and you can't and so there's not much else we can do for each other." She came fluidly to her feet, her black-edged wingtips making a graceful sweep across the floor as she stood. "It's always a treat to see you, of course, and I do hope you'll come back and visit, but don't be asking me questions about troubles in the realm. And I won't expect you to sing 'The Ballad of Hairy Mary' with me. Do we have a bargain?"

Alleluia looked up at her gravely. "I didn't come here to make you unhappy," she said. "I wanted to see if you were all right, if you—"

"All right! I'm fine! I'm well! I'm delighted to be here! Life could not be better for me in any respect! Does that satisfy you? Go back to the Eyrie, angela, and sing your heart out in praises to the glorious god. Don't trouble yourself over me, and I won't worry about you. Thanks so much for coming to my concert. And I'll talk to you some other time."

And giving them a mocking half-curtsey, she spun on her heel and stalked away. Even angry and flustered, she moved with unconscious grace, and they were not the only two who watched her till she disappeared.

Then Caleb turned back to Alleluia, whose gaze was bent to her folded hands. "That didn't go so well," he commented.

Alleluia moved her head indecisively from side to side. "About as well as I expected," she said. "Better, maybe. I wasn't sure she'd talk to me at all."

"I've never seen her like that," Caleb said. "Sarcastic and flippant, yes, but never so—"

Alleluia looked up. "Hurt."

"I was going to say 'angry.' "

She nodded. "But mostly hurt. I don't know how you mend someone who is so badly broken."

"Is it just that she can't fly?" he asked.

She smiled briefly. "You're the one who wants to invent wings," she said. "How would you feel if you once could fly and then those wings were taken away from you?"

"Devastated," he admitted. "But I don't think it would make me bitter enough to hate myself."

She nodded. "Probably not. You'd invent something else to occupy your time. But with Delilah . . . it's not just the flying. It's the fact that, unable to fly, she is unable to be Archangel. She is—ordinary. Not even an angel. Mortal. Delilah has a kind of brilliance that can't be turned down. And if it doesn't shine outward, it glares inward and burns everything else away."

"So what will happen to her?" he asked.

Alleluia smiled sadly. "You're the one who's supposed to be so talented," she said. "Why don't you try to fix her wing?"

Clearly she wasn't serious, but Caleb said, "I've thought about it. I've been afraid to bring it up, because—well—"

"Because she makes everything hard. Do you think you could really help her?"

"I don't know. Probably not. I'd be willing to try."

"I'd be grateful for that much—just trying."

He smiled at Alleluia, more warmly than he intended. "Then I'll see if I can convince her to let me examine her wing," he said. "I would like to earn your gratitude."

She may have flushed; it may have been a shadow from a passing waitress. "You'll earn it soon enough if you repair my music machines," she said.

"I'll be in Velora by the end of next week."

Five days later, Caleb left Luminaux and headed northwest toward the Eyrie. Although the days had been busy and the nights full of companionship, the hours had seemed to crawl by. He could not remember the last time he had been so impatient to begin a trip—or see again someone he had just met.

When Noah returned, Caleb told him of his new commission, and the two engineers theorized about possible problems in the equipment, although Noah did not seem to be giving his full attention to the discussion. Abruptly he asked, "What was she like? I can't believe you're going off so quickly to help her."

Caleb was completely astonished. "Why not? I can't believe you aren't begging me to let you come along."

"To help the *Archangel*? How I could I be so disloyal?"

"Disloyal—" And only then did Caleb realize that Noah was angry on Delilah's account, and could accept no other angel in her place. "She was very nice," he said, which immediately seemed inadequate. "She was serious and she seemed kind and she doesn't particularly want to be Archangel. She appeared genuinely worried about Delilah. And she wasn't offended by any of Delilah's songs."

Noah tossed him an indignant look, and Caleb realized his attempts to describe Alleluia were woefully weak. "She's a usurper," the Edori said. "And I cannot believe you are so interested in currying favor among the allali that you would take on a commission like this."

Caleb waited a moment to let his flash of anger die. "If Delilah cannot be Archangel, someone must be," he said gently. "I don't believe this girl wants the job. It's a hard one, and she's not suited for it, but she was chosen, and she's doing the best she can. It's unfair of you to hate her for something that is not her fault. I don't think Delilah hates her. Why don't you ask her?"

Noah's answer was defiant. "I will."

But Delilah, when questioned about Alleluia that night after her concert, merely threw her hands in the air and laughed gaily. All her passion of the other evening was gone; this night she seemed as lighthearted as a child.

"Alleya," she said. "Such an odd girl. Most angels are pretty sure of themselves—arrogant, even—but Alleya would always hang back, let others talk, completely trample her. She always hated to be singled out for any attention, and I never saw her volunteer a word in groups of more than five people. But you couldn't help but like her. She would do anything in the world you asked of her, and she knows things—facts and stories and details nobody else remembers. She's kind of come into her own lately, gotten a little more poise—which is good. She'll need every ounce of self-possession she can muster up."

She shook her head, still thinking, then turned to Caleb and laughed. "Remember the other night when Joseph was trying to convince her to sing? It was ludicrous. She hates to perform. She doesn't mind singing in front of people if it's a mass or one of the sacred rituals, but anything else—forget it. She can't do it. I don't know how she'll lead the Gloria in front of thousands of people, although maybe she won't find that so hard since it is, after all, sung to Jovah. But I promise you this: She won't find it easy."

"You sound like you know her pretty well," Caleb said, although Alleluia had said that was not the case.

Delilah shrugged. "Well, any time you live among a small group of people in a place no larger than the Eyrie, you form an opinion of everybody. But I don't know her well. I don't know that anyone does. Maybe it's hard to make friends among people who've known each other from birth unless you were born there, too."

"What?" said Caleb.

"She was born in some godless little town in southern Bethel and didn't come to the Eyrie for years and years. I don't think her mother was an angel-seeker, but she—"

"A what?" Noah interrupted.

Caleb grinned. Even he had heard this term. "An angel-seeker," he repeated. "A woman who purposely—ah—dallies with angels in order to become pregnant with a little cherub."

"What's so wonderful about having an angel child?"

Delilah gave him a mock scandalized look. "The status—the prestige—the thought of living in a hold for the rest of your life without having to do another day's work. Believe me, more than one woman has made it her life's goal to seduce an angel and bear his child."

"But not all an angel's offspring are also angels," Caleb said.

"Oh no. Not by a lot. Which is why there are so many unclaimed children in the cities by the holds, because the mothers will sometimes abandon their mortal children. We try to curb the practice, but—well, since we want the angel children, too, we aren't on any particularly high moral ground."

"So most angel-seekers instantly bring their little winged infants to the holds," Caleb prompted. "But in Alleluia's case—"

"Alleya's mother didn't bring her to the Eyrie till she was, I don't know, ten or twelve years old."

"Why not?"

"Who knows? I never asked Alleya. She's five or six years older than me and, as I've said, we were never close. But I think it must have been hard on her, coming in at ten years of age to such a strange environment. She never really did fit in."

"And how do you think she'll fit in now that she's Archangel?" Caleb asked.

Instantly, Delilah's face grew impassive. She picked up her drink and took a long swallow. "Now," she said deliberately, "I have no interest in her at all."

Traveling on a borrowed horse, it took Caleb seven days to cross southern Bethel from Luminaux to Velora. Winter made the countryside seem shadowy and drab, especially around the mining towns, where even from miles away the burnt-metal residue of the refineries thickened and grayed the air. *And this is progress, and I have wrought it*, he thought. Still, he could not be entirely sorry. In fact, he couldn't help thinking how much faster and better his journey to Breven would be when he and Noah (and perhaps Delilah) rode in the Edori's powered vehicle across the tedious desert.

He liked Velora, though; he had never been to the cheerful little town crowded up against the Velo Mountains. No Luminaux, of course, but by no means shabby. He wondered if it would be acceptable to bring a gift to the Archangel, and once the idea was in his head, he couldn't shake it loose. So he spent an hour or so on the chilly ascent to the Eyrie, dawdling at merchants' shops and wondering what might be appropriate. In the end he settled on a hair clip of gold filigree that she, with her tangled yellow hair, could probably use. It was not so expensive as to embarrass her; another point in its favor.

He completed the climb and found himself on a wide stone walkway that led to a broad plateau. There were dozens of people ahead of him, either waiting in patient boredom or stating their cases to two angels and one mortal who appeared to be prioritizing petitions. Caleb was tempted to push his way to the head of the line and announce, "I was *invited* here, take me immediately to the Archangel," but his innate courtesy prevailed. He waited his turn, listening in untutored appreciation to the breathtaking voices singing somewhere nearby in flawless harmony. If the machines were broken, it must be live music—and why would you want machines if you had singers like that to listen to?

When he finally had a chance to give his name, he was gratified to see quick interest light the face of the older male angel who was helping him. "She'll be glad to see *you*," was the instant response. "I can't get free here for a moment or two, but if you don't mind finding your own way, I can tell you where she is."

"That suits me," Caleb said, and listened closely to the directions. From what he could see of the tunnels opening off the plateau, the Eyrie was a maze and easy to get lost in. But the instructions seemed clear. He thanked the angel and ducked into the warmth of the nearest corridor.

A few turns, a few steps down, another corridor, a row of identical doors. Caleb went to the one that had been specified and knocked loudly. There was no answer, but the angel had warned him there might not be ("If she has the music loud enough, she won't hear you. Just go on in. She never locks the door"). So he knocked a second time and, without waiting for a response, turned the handle and entered.

To find the angel Alleluia sitting in a heap in the middle of the floor, her arms wrapped around her updrawn legs, her great wings bowed around her shoulders, crying as if her heart were broken.

CHAPTER SEVEN

Alleya had returned to the Eyrie to find that she had been missed—which was not quite as pleasant as it might have been. Reports had come in from northern Jordana the day she left: Residents were concerned about continuous heavy snowfalls that had made all the roads impassable. Meanwhile, rain was the problem over the lower half of the Plain of Sharon, causing the Galilee River to rise, the Edori sanctuary to flood, the river cities to feel imperiled and the farmers along both borders to worry about damage to their crops.

"But that's not the worst of it," she was told. (The worst of it, she had already privately decided, was the fact that three of the younger angels had chosen to convey all this information to her within minutes of her return, having clearly formed a concerned committee in her absence.) The speaker just now was the impetuous and dramatic-looking Asher, a dark-haired, sloe-eyed angel whom all the mortal girls were mad for.

"What could possibly be worse?" she asked.

He missed the irony. "The Manadavvi think it is happening on purpose—that you, that we, that somehow angels have engineered all this rain, to punish them for daring to question you about the Edori sanctuary."

Now her attention sharpened; that indeed was pretty bad. "How do you know this?" she demanded. She did not think

Aaron or Emmanuel had had time to return to the Eyrie with complaints during the time she'd been away.

Dinah spoke up next. Like Asher, she was dark and intense; together, the two were usually a volatile mix. "We were in Gaza while you were gone, and while we were there, some of the Manadavvi came back from the river, telling stories of the floods. They had been trying to get a shipment to Semorrah, and lost two boatloads when the riverbank gave way. They were really angry—"

"And they were afraid," Asher interjected.

Alleya touched each of them with her glance. "And did you fly out to the plain? Was it storming?"

"Of course we went immediately," Asher said with some indignation. "And we prayed for hours. The storm did not lift. It did not even seem to lighten."

"How long has it been raining there?"

"By now, probably five days without ceasing," Dinah said. "Before that, intermittently."

Alleya spread her hands. "Why weren't we told of this? Aaron Lesh and Emmanuel Garone were here not long ago, and they seemed eager enough to bring up other problems."

The three angels exchanged glances. Timothy, a fair-haired, good-looking but petulant young male, spoke next. "Maybe they were afraid to say anything to your face," he suggested. "But they blame the angels."

"Who blames the angels? For what?" Alleya said impatiently.

"For the storms. They think we're sending them."

"That's ridiculous. Why would we do that?"

"To punish them. They weren't very clear about it, but there was talk—"

"From whom? Did any of the Manadavvi actually take one of you aside and say, 'Why are you angels sending us all the rain? What have we done to you?' " Her own words gave her pause—just so did she sometimes word her mental supplications to Jovah.

"Well, no," Dinah said, glancing sideways at Asher.

"But you were consorting with some of the Manadavvi servants, and they repeated the gossip to you. Is that it?" Alleya asked.

Asher said defiantly, "I heard it from more than one person, and they all seemed convinced that we were sending the rain. That we meant something by it."

"But when you went to sing prayers—"

"Well, we weren't successful. They think maybe we didn't try."

"And when we told them you were gone," Dinah said softly, "they didn't believe us."

Alleya flung her hands out. "But it makes no sense! What could we possibly have to gain by flooding out the Manadavvi and the river merchants? Why would it occur to us to do so?"

"Emmanuel Garone claims that angels threatened to do it in the past," Timothy said solemnly. "When the Manadavvi were difficult."

Alleya threw him a startled look. "Well! Someone's been reading his history books," she said. "I wouldn't have expected a threat that old to still frighten anyone."

"You mean, an angel actually made such a threat?" Dinah asked. "Who?"

"The Archangel Gabriel, in fact," Alleya said. "Back when *he* was feuding with the Manadavvi. As it seems all Archangels must eventually do."

"What are you going to do?" Dinah asked.

"Fly to the Plain of Sharon, obviously, and see if the god will heed me. Although I would like a little time to rest my wings and change my clothes."

The three younger angels traded looks again, making Alleya suspicious. "What?" she demanded. "What are you thinking?"

Asher tilted his chin in the air, a pose that made him look even more than ordinarily striking. "We were thinking—you should let the rains continue just a little longer. How dare they say such things about the angels! And we have heard how they came here days ago, questioning the sanctuary treaties and looking for more special privileges. We think the Manadavvi have flouted the Archangel's authority too long—yes, and the river merchants as well. It is no bad thing to make them worry a while. Perhaps then they will show us a little more deference."

Jovah save me from the young and righteous was Alleya's first thought. She closed her eyes briefly and wondered how Delilah would handle this. With a jest and a mocking remark that would be so cleverly worded it would instantly deflate Asher's whole arrogant argument. But she was not Delilah.

"One of the luxuries the Archangel does not have is spitefulness," she said, her voice gentle but the words barbed. "Any misuse of power, whether active or passive, is shocking and inadmissible. I would no more deliberately allow the river to flood than I would pray for the god to loose thunderbolts on the Manadavvi compounds. We want harmony, not vengeance."

"Justice!" Asher burst out.

Alleya smiled faintly. "It is not justice when your only motive is to make someone else sorry," she said. "I believe that you tried to disperse the rains. I hope I am able to succeed. If I am not, the Manadavvi will really believe the worst of us, and then I think we will have a true crisis on our hands. I do not wish the Manadavvi to actively turn against us."

"Of course you will be able to stop the rains," Dinah said, her voice suddenly uncertain. "Why would you not?"

"Why were you unsuccessful?" Alleya asked with a shrug. "Jovah does not hear all of us, which is a frightening thing to me. It makes me wonder if someday he will no longer hear me."

Now they all wore matching looks of apprehension, as if it had never occurred to them that she, too, might one day be fallible. Alleya could not decide if that comforted or appalled her. "Angela," Dinah asked, "why does Jovah continue to send the rain?"

"And the snow, and the drought, depending on where you are," Alleya added. "I don't know. I'm sure he has his reasons, but they are at present unclear to me."

She had escaped as quickly as she could to seek the solitude of her bedchamber. It seemed like more than three days since she had left, and she wanted nothing so much as to rest, relax, gossip with Samuel (*Guess where I found Delilah!*) and read the books she had borrowed from Mount Sinai. But she had spoken truly to her little trio of avengers. She could not in good conscience let the rains fall and make no effort to stop them.

So, late that afternoon, she set out again, this time for the Plain of Sharon. It was almost nightfall by the time she arrived, and a sullen sunset offered just a faint tainted light to see by. She always found it an impressive, sobering sight: the shattered black peak of Mount Galo breaking the ring of mountains that enclosed the plain. The god's finger had touched the world, electrifying it the way Caleb's mysterious fire had electrified his body, leaving behind a seared mark and the memory of tremendous power. She would have given much to have been present the night the god blazed down in wrath. She thought that her awe would have far outweighed her terror.

Because of the rain, she had flown in low, and now she spiraled upward over the broken mountain. The air was treacly, clinging to her wings with actual malice; she had to fight her way higher to get as far above the storm as possible. Even after she cleared the worst of the rain, the air about her felt dense and unforgiving, and she had a curious sense that all acoustical properties had been deadened. Usually, this far above the earth, the air currents felt alive; even before she started singing, she would hear the echoes of her wingbeats batted from star to star. She could sense that Jovah was listening, just waiting for her voice, and that he knew before she started to sing just what she was going to pray for.

But tonight she had no such illusion of an eager listener. Instead it seemed as if she were in a close room whose walls were covered with padding—it was as if, no matter how loud a sound she chose to make, the noise would be muffled by invisible quilted walls. Her imagination, surely; the wet, clogged air was coloring all her perceptions.

She slowed her wingbeats to hovering speed, clasped her hands and began singing. Her voice seemed to linger too long in the air around her, the new notes piling on top of the old ones in tumbled disharmony. She was in a net of her own music, a sticky web of her tangled prayers, and she knew this was not a song that was ascending to Jovah.

She drove her wings down twice, hard, gaining altitude, then settled into a slow flight pattern that made a gigantic circle over the plain. As she flew, she offered her prayer again, and again each word lay on the air where she sang it, neither rising nor disintegrating. She sang the prayer again, trailing it behind her like a banner, each note so solid and distinct that she could almost read the music, staff and score. Again she circled, still singing, adding another layer of music, and another, till she had laid a coil of prayers high over the ruined peak of the Galo Mountain. And not a single note overlapped another; every word was clear, pronounced on its perfect pitch; and suddenly it seemed that Jovah was able to understand what, for hours, she had been saying. For she felt the air around her shift and she heard the dull continuity of the falling rain skip and falter; and she saw her golden song literally unfurl as it lifted itself to Jovah.

And she slowly descended through the unraveling clouds, and she was afraid, because next time she might not guess how to arrange her prayer so that the god heard it; and clearly he was beginning to have trouble now hearing even the Archangel.

She returned to the Eyrie late the next day, having stopped overnight in a small town in northern Jordana, to pray for the cessation of snow there the following morning. This intercession was much more straightforward than the one over the Galo Mountain, and she flew home feeling slightly comforted. But only slightly.

All still was not well at the Eyrie, for the river merchants had sent a politely worded letter asking her to meet them in Semorrah at her earliest convenience. They were not specific about their concerns, but she could guess what they were: the portage rights that the Manadavvi had asked about, and the fear of flooding because of the long rains.

"You go," she told Samuel, reading him the letter. It was signed by Gideon Fairwen, long-standing president of the merchants' guild and the richest man in Samaria aside from the Manadavvi. "Tell them I'm too busy to come."

"They'll be insulted."

"Well, it will be a measure of just how seriously I view their complaint. They should know by now that I've stopped the rains over the Galo, so that should answer that question—and I can't bear any more whining about the damned Edori sanctuary. So you go. If they have any other problems they want to discuss with me, tell them to come here."

He smiled. "I'll bring them back with me."

She smiled in return. "And take Asher. He's looking for a fight. But keep him more or less under control."

So Samuel left with Asher in tow, and they were gone three

days. Which passed in relative, welcome quiet. Alleya used that time to begin study on the books she had borrowed from Mount Sinai, although the reading went slowly. In many places, the translator had guessed at a word or a phrase, labeling it with a question mark and enclosing it in a bracket. She was a little disappointed that the history book glossed over the mechanics of the settlers' arrival on Samaria, merely explaining it as a "miracle wrought by Jovah," although she had never heard it described in any more explicit terms.

The first chapter seemed to be little more than a list of the names and genealogies of the colonists—with a mysterious notation that all this information had been "fed" to Jovah. She was fascinated to learn, however, that there had not been perfect harmony among these original Samarians, and that a small splinter group led by Victor and Amos Edor had refused to conform to the basic governmental patterns that the others had voted in.

"The Edori!" she murmured. "Descended directly from the first malcontents. I wonder who else knows that?"

The second chapter, however, made her sit up straight in her chair and read as fast as her eyes would take in the words.

"Now, even before Jovah had set his children onto the land of Samaria, he had seen that it was ravaged by storm. In the southern portions of the chosen land, rain followed rain followed rain, and in the north, snow followed snow. Elsewhere the land was dry and offered no water, not for bathing, not for drinking, not for raising crops. And Jovah said, 'We must remake this land in the ways that are pleasing to us.'

"And for this reason, and for other reasons, Jovah set about creating the angels. He drew aside men of science and whispered instructions into their ears while they slept. Then, for twenty days, he watched his children as they labored on their new land. From the twelve hundred that he had set down on Samaria, he chose fifty. These fifty and the men of science he drew apart from the rest; and following Jovah's instructions, the men of science practiced their crafts of <*biology*?> and <*genetics*?> and grafted wings onto the backs of the fifty mortals. And thus were angels created."

Alleluia looked up, wide-eyed with shock. The angels had been created by men? Specifically to control the weather? This was not the way the Librera, the holy book, recorded the birth of the angels. She had no need to look the passage up, but she did so anyway, fetching her leatherbound copy of the Librera and opening it to the first chapter, which described the arrival on Samaria. As she remembered: "Then Jovah created the angels to watch over all the peoples of Samaria and ensure harmony throughout the realm." Nothing about weather.

Nothing about the continent being uninhabitable without intercessions by the angels.

Nothing about men of science practicing their diabolical magic. In fact, the Librera only mentioned technology in the most scornful of passages, leading the modern reader to assume that all the colonists had abhorred science and all its gifts and trappings.

And yet scientists, under the guidance of the god, had made men into angels.

She continued reading, although her brain felt disordered and she was not sure she would make much sense of the next few pages.

"Then Jovah took the angels aside and said to them, 'These are the prayers I will teach you. You will sing these words when you wish for storm, these words when you wish for sunshine, these words when your crops fail and you need <*freeze-dried*? *frozen*?> seed grain. My supplies are virtually limitless; they will be available for centuries, so ask for what you need.'

"Then Jovah said to the angels, 'Here are more prayers that I will teach you. When your people are swept with plague, sing these prayers and I will send you <*anti-something*? *medicines*? word unclear> to heal them. When the women miscarry and the men turn to sport instead of love, I will send you manna to make the wives again seem attractive to their husbands, if you will sing these words.'

"Then Jovah said to the angels, 'I have set my <*satellites*? word unclear—maybe means *ears*> above you close to the earth so that I can hear you any time you pray. But if my <*satellites*> ever fail, I have set <*ears*???> in the Corinni Mountains and in the Plain of Sharon and in <???*Arrand*? not a place on any maps>, and these shall carry your words to me instead.' "

Alleya read the last paragraph three times, hoping it might

make more sense, but it did not. If these satellites were devices that amplified the angels' voices and helped carry them to Jovah's ears, perhaps they had failed; perhaps that was why Jovah was having so much trouble hearing them now. But what had he put in the Corinni Mountains and at the Plain of Sharon that would facilitate the angels' prayers—and where exactly (for these were both fairly broad geographical areas) were these mysterious objects located? And how in the world would she recognize them even if she came across them?

She read a bit farther, but the history offered no new revelations, at least in this chapter. Just as well, she thought, laying the book aside and massaging the back of her head. What little she had learned so far had clarified nothing and shaken some of her profoundest beliefs; and she was not sure she had the strength right now to endure any more surprises.

Samuel returned grim-faced and weary; Asher seemed even more fired up than he had been about the Manadavvi situation.

"They blame the angels for the storms," the older man said. "They think it is some plot to bring them to heel, and they are very angry."

Asher struck a pose, imitating Gideon Fairwen. " 'What have we done to earn the anger of the angels? We live as we have always lived, do business with the men we have always dealt with. Why would the angels turn against us?' The man makes me sick."

"Did they believe what they were saying, or do you think this is a conspiracy with the Manadavvi to give them an excuse to flout us?" Alleya asked Samuel.

"Hard to tell. But they did seem angry."

"But surely they noticed that the rains had stopped."

"Yes, after a week of rain. And the river had already risen."

"So what did they want from us? An apology? A concession? Why did they call us there?"

"To tell us not to think they can be controlled by such tactics," Asher said scornfully. "To warn us that they will rebel if we continue tampering with the weather."

"To remind us that mortals and angels agree to work in harmony, and once the harmony has been disrupted, it is impossible to restore," Samuel said more soberly.

"Yes, well, very effective if we were in fact trying to punish them," Alleya said sharply. "But since we are not—a vexing complication. I cannot afford to have the merchants and the Manadavvi in mutiny. What has Jerusha said about any of this?" she continued, turning to Asher. Jerusha was the leader of the angel host in Monteverde. "You were in Gaza recently. Did you see her?"

"We did not stop by Monteverde. I could go now—"

Alleya shook her head. "I'll go. Maybe she'll have some advice."

But Jerusha, when consulted on the following day, gestured in her characteristic short, dismissive way and shook her head. "I know there is unrest among the Manadavvi," she said. "There always is. It irks them that, powerful as they are, they are not all-powerful. They are always seeking the rift in the fabric of Samaria."

Jerusha was small, dark and unemotional; her movements were precise and her mind analytical. Still, Alleya thought, the situation called for a little more worry. "Have they complained to you?"

"Incessantly. Since the rains started. We have done what we could. We have been able to shift some of the smaller storms. But none of our prayers seems to have a lasting effect."

"Why?" Alleya demanded in frustration. "Why can Jovah not hear us?"

Jerusha shrugged. "Or why does he choose not to? There is a purpose in everything he does."

"He says," Alleya responded slowly, "that he is not punishing us. That he answers us when he is able."

"When did he say this?" Jerusha asked.

Alleya waved a hand to denote a southerly direction. "I saw Job a while ago. We asked the god questions that he answered in the most circuitous manner."

Jerusha smiled faintly. "As he answers everything. And did he tell you how to stop the storms and the flooding?"

"He told us to seek help from the son of Jeremiah," Alleya said dryly. "Which was not at all illuminating."

"Who is Jeremiah?"

"Precisely."

"It was the name of the Archangel Gabriel's father," Jerusha said. "But he lived hundreds of years ago."

Alleya lifted her head consideringly. "Job said it might be a reference to a historical figure," she said. "And did not Gabriel have three sons?"

"Yes, all dead for a century or more."

"Well, their sons or their sons . . . The records must be somewhere. In the Eyrie, no doubt."

"Jovah keeps such records," Jerusha reminded her. "The oracles record such information for him when they list the names of those who have been dedicated by the priests." Unconsciously, her hand went to the Kiss in her right arm. "So Jovah knows the name of every man's son."

"Yes, well, Jovah chose not to be more specific last time I asked him, so I think I would first try another set of records," Alleya said with some asperity. "But I thank you for the thought. I will see what I can discover about Gabriel's progeny."

So, back at the Eyrie, Alleya found her way to the archives and researched the lives of the children of Gabriel and Rachel. Indeed, they had had three sons, and each of those sons had had a number of children, but the records were vague about the family members who were not angelic or in some other way illustrious. For instance, very little was said about the second son's second daughter, who apparently eloped with some Edori nomad at a young age and could have had any number of children. The Edori as a rule did not dedicate their children, so Jovah was unlikely to have kept track of these particular offspring; and who knew how many of *them* had had children and which of them might be the very man Jovah desired?

Alleya rubbed a dusty hand across her forehead, leaving a track of dirt. *Think clearly*, she admonished herself. *Jovah would not have singled out someone of whose existence he was unaware. He asked for the son of Jeremiah, thus he knows of such a man, thus the man has been dedicated. It does not matter if Gabriel had a hundred untracked Edori grandchildren or great-grandchildren; the designated son of Jeremiah would not be among them.*

Although that still did not tell her who this mysterious man was, or where he could be found.

And could she really spend the next few weeks of her life trying to reconstruct Gabriel's family tree? Perhaps she indeed must return to one of the oracles and ask for guidance.

It was a day of petty frustrations, for a series of other annoying problems cropped up. No one had signed up to sing the harmonic for the noon hour, for instance, so at the last minute Alleya and Dinah scrambled to the open stone grotto at the top level of the compound and offered a few unrehearsed melodies. Their voices did not blend particularly well, especially when they had not practiced their numbers, so Alleya was unsatisfied with the result—and displeased that such a long-standing tradition had almost been so casually broken.

When Timothy and one of the mortal girls relieved them an hour later, to sing a much smoother requiem, Alleya instantly turned to Dinah. "As of this minute, I'm putting you in charge of this," she said. "The singers for the harmonics are to be scheduled at least one day in advance from now on. And if no one has signed up for the shift, you have the authority to conscript anyone you choose and sing the other half of the duet yourself."

Dinah looked as if she could not decide if the commission pleased or annoyed her. Alleya added, "Thank you," somewhat abruptly, and the younger angel smiled. "I will not fail you, angela," she said, and that seemed to take care of that.

But then one of the cooks complained about meat from a Velora vendor, and the vendor insisted on seeing the Archangel personally to defend himself, and a committee of farmers who had traveled all the way from middle Jordana wanted to discuss the encroachment of the Jansai traders onto property they had always considered theirs. The voices seemed to rise around her in an indecipherable babble; she felt a low grade of panic set in, and found herself deferring or delegating as many decisions as she could. The Jordana contingent she promised to meet with in the morning; the cook she fobbed off on one of the older mortal women who had lived in the Eyrie for decades. Before one more person could catch her eye or tap on her shoulder, Alleya escaped down the lower tunnels to the last remaining music room.

Where she slipped in a recording of simple love songs performed by the divine Hagar, the single disc in the whole collection that did not feature sacred music. She stood in the middle of the room and closed her eyes, imagining all her stress and worry draining away, through her spread fingertips, through her toes, rising through the top of her head unimpeded by her tangled hair. She pictured herself growing lighter, translucent, weightless, insubstantial enough to be buoyed two feet above the floor by the music. She felt her wings shirr, and her muscles melted lovingly across her bones.

Then the music abruptly stopped.

As if she actually had been dropped from a low height onto the stone floor, Alleya felt her head snap backward and her spine jar into place. Fresh panic rose through her throat; her cheeks cooled with anxiety. She quickly crossed to the panel of knobs set into the wall and began twisting and turning the dials. *Not this machine, too, not the last one, not the only one* . . . When the soaring music suddenly erupted again, rescued by who knew what combination of prods and pushes, Alleya was so relieved that her whole body went slack. Her legs could not support the weight of her body, so she let herself crumble slowly to the floor. She drew her knees up for a place to rest her heavy head; she wrapped her wings around herself for comfort; and she gave in to the overmastering impulse to sob.

At which point the door opened and Caleb Augustus walked in, and stopped to stare at her in blank astonishment.

Chapter Eight

Alleya scrambled to her feet, catching her shoes in her pooled tunic and almost pitching headlong back to the floor. Caleb hurried forward to grab her arm but she jerked away, hot with mortification. She could feel the heat rising to her brows, the stickiness of tears drying down her face; she had never felt more completely at a disadvantage.

"Angela, are you—?" he began, but she interrupted before he could complete his sentence.

"What are you doing here?" she demanded, running ineffectual hands through her hair, down her skirts. "How could you just walk in without knocking, without permission—?"

"The angel sent me here, he said you would be glad to see me—"

"*What* angel?"

A tentative grin crossed the visitor's face. "Well, he seemed to recognize my name and I didn't ask him his," he said a little whimsically. "He said you would want to see me right away."

She turned her back on him, endeavoring to compose herself. Her breath still caught raggedly in her throat. It would not take much to start her crying again, and she *would not* do it in front of this man. In front of anyone. "I wanted to see you, but under more controlled circumstances," she said as levelly as she could. "Excuse me. I will be myself in a moment."

He walked around her to come face to face again. "But won't

you tell me what's wrong?" he coaxed. "I can't stand to see you crying and not be able to help."

She laughed shakily. "I think my problems are insoluble," she said, "ranging as they do from great to small. Today just featured too many in succession. I don't ordinarily give in to them like this, however."

"It's reassuring to know you do."

"Reassuring? In what possible way?"

He was smiling. He had a marvelously inviting smile, filled with complicity and sympathy; if she was not careful, she would find herself telling him every thought in her head. "It makes you seem more human. More approachable. I find you just a little intimidating, you know."

She laughed in sheer disbelief. "Me? Intimidating? Most people are more likely to find me—obscure. Insignificant."

He surveyed her with a closeness that once again made the blush rise. "Maybe intimidating was the wrong word. You seem remote, hard to reach, as if you were standing in a marble chamber very high above the world and the rest of us called out to you in voices that you heard only distantly, if at all. It makes me feel as if I were addressing a painting of an angel and not a real person. But when I come in to see you crying—well, then, you're right down on the trampled earth with the rest of us."

Her flush intensified, partly to be told such a thing, partly because she was unnerved at how well he had described the way she often felt. But: "I wish I could find that high, quiet chamber today," she said a little tartly. "Believe me, I would hide myself there and never come back down."

"And so what are the problems great and small that have reduced you to tears?" he asked. "Maybe I can help."

"Oh, let me see. A quarrel between the cook and the butcher, a delegation of unhappy Jordana farmers, threats from the river merchants, complaints from the Manadavvi, rebellion among my angels—and, just now, my last music machine seemed to break. That was the final disaster, I think, the mishap that pushed me to the edge. A minor problem in comparison with the rest, but—"

"It seems to be working now," he said, swinging around to

examine the equipment with careful fingers. "What a beautiful song. Who is this singing?"

"Hagar. The first angelica. Her voice could make the most mundane music seem sublime. They say that Rachel had a voice as brilliant as Hagar's, but of course we no longer know how to record singers—and anyway, I don't believe it. No one else could sing like this."

"How was it recorded? May I see?"

So she stopped the music and extracted the small silver disk. It was completely featureless except for its shape and color; it bore no ridges or markings. Caleb turned it toward the light to watch the reflection glitter along its surfaces, front and back.

"Amazing," he said. "I don't even know what this material is."

"Do you think you can figure out how the equipment works?"

"I don't know. Not if it's as foreign as this."

"What kind of tools do you need?"

He pointed to his shoulder; he was, she realized, wearing a bulky backpack. "Brought them all with me. Should I start with this machine, or one of the machines that is already broken?"

"One of the broken ones!" she answered swiftly, and he laughed. "Well, but as long as this one is still working—"

"I understand perfectly. Show me where I should begin."

For the next hour, Alleya watched the engineer dissect one of the failed machines. It would not have been, ordinarily, the sort of pastime she enjoyed, for she had no aptitude for electronics—or interest in them, either. But there was something about Caleb Augustus and his complete absorption in his task that made her feel a certain sympathetic kinship. Just so did she feel when she was lost in the labyrinth of a melody or keeping her balance on the rippling arpeggio of a duet. He could not have appeared more entranced.

While he was too engrossed to notice her, she studied him. He looked like nothing so much as a farmer's eldest son, dressed up (but only slightly) for market day in the biggest town for a hundred miles. He was a little bigger than the average man but not brawny; his features were strong and intelligent. His sandy hair was cut close enough to stay out of his way but with no special attention to fashion; though his clothes were clean, they showed much wear. He was a man who liked to be comfortable, she decided, but who rarely worried that he would be otherwise. He looked as though he found the world nearly always a welcoming place. Not surprising; she was glad to have him here. She imagined most people were pleased to see him.

She was even able to restrain her impatience to know what he learned, so she did not bombard him with questions about how well his task was going. In fact, she just sat there, leaning one shoulder against the wall, and watched him. He had pried off the glass and metal faceplate that guarded the inner workings of the player, and exposed a whole range of wires and circuits that would have sent her into instant despair. He had only looked more intrigued, and had begun to cautiously poke at each gleaming joint and intersection.

Now and then he murmured aloud, though she had no illusions that he was addressing her. "Well, if *that's* a moving part, what's moving it? Although—I don't see why this one should have to move, and it seems to—and where the hell is the power coming from?"

He had extracted the oddest array of tools from his pack, and with these he slowly began disassembling the machine. She bit back an automatic protest ("Don't, you'll break it!"); what more harm could he possibly do? But she could not resist one question. "Do you think you'll be able to put it back together?"

"Uh-huh," he said abstractedly, still completely focused on his work. "But I don't know if I'll be able to put it back so it works."

"Is there anything I can get you?"

"Some water would be nice."

"For the machine?"

At that he did give her his attention, flashing her a quick grin. "No, for me."

She was embarrassed, but how could she know what a piece of equipment might require? "Would you rather have wine? Tea? Juice?"

"Whatever's handiest," he said, and went back to his work.

So she fetched him a snack tray—wine, water and pastries—

returning to find dozens of unidentifiable parts arranged precisely on a white rag laid on the floor. The hole in the wall had become deep enough for Caleb to insert his head.

"How about some kind of light?" he asked, not even withdrawing his head when he heard her enter. "I can't see everything in here."

"You mean a candle?"

"Is that all you've got?"

"We don't have any electric-powered lights."

"Well—make it an oil lamp, then. I don't want wax falling anywhere inside here."

So then she left to find him a lamp with a glass shade, but the shade was green and he asked if she could find something clear. Because the color made it difficult to ascertain which wire was which. So she left again, returning with the requested item.

"It'll have to do," he said, fitting the shade over the brass casing. "Can you stand here and hold it for me? No, a little higher. The light has to shine in. Yes, that's right. Hold still."

So she stood there another hour, motionlessly as possible, and thought that this was the pleasantest hour of the day that she had passed so far. It didn't seem to occur to Caleb Augustus that this particular brand of menial labor ranked far below the general run of responsibilities that fell to the Archangel, and obviously she could have assigned someone else the task.

But she liked watching him work.

It was quite late in the day by the time he laid aside his last tool, pulled himself gingerly from the cavern he had excavated, and shook his head. Alleya set the lamp down and rubbed her arm.

"Well?" she asked. "Can you fix it?"

"I don't know," he said. "I can tell what's wrong, I think, but I don't know if I can compensate for it."

Her heart sank; she had been convinced he could help her. "So what's wrong?"

He held up a small cylinder, about the size of his little finger. "As far as I can tell, this is the power source of the machine. I've never seen anything like it. I can't imagine how it works, but somehow it seems to hold stored energy. And when the machine is turned on, this little item releases enough energy to make all the parts go around. But all the energy seems to have been drained away. Therefore, no moving parts. No music."

"So can't you just—do something else to make the things move?"

"That's what I've been trying to determine. But it's a very delicate balance in here. My wires are thick and clumsy things next to theirs—like a rope compared to a length of thread. I could rig a motor that would generate the power you need, but I don't know if I could conduct that power inside the machine without hopelessly tangling up everything inside. Plus—my motor would be fuel-generated, and create fumes and noise, and so you wouldn't want it in the room. Can't really appreciate the sound of Hagar singing when she's competing with a motor making all kinds of racket."

Alleya felt blank. "But then—you're saying—there's nothing you can do?"

"Well, I can try to set up a motor in the hallway, say, and run the wires in, and see if I can generate the juice. You'd have to be careful not to dislodge anything—not trip over anything—and you'd still probably hear some of the noise from the hall."

"The rooms are acoustically perfect," she said automatically. "They deaden all outside noise."

"Well, you wouldn't be able to close the door all the way."

"Ah."

"And if *that* worked—Have you ever considered having the entire hold wired for electricity?"

She just looked at him for a moment. It was as if he'd asked her if she had ever considered pulling out all her wing feathers, one by one. "It's not—it never crossed my mind one way or the other."

"Well, there would be a lot of advantages," he said. "You could get rid of your gaslight, for one thing. That's always a danger, you know, gas. It can kill a man in a few minutes."

"So can electricity," she answered with asperity, then remembered his father, and wished she hadn't.

But he grinned. "Right. Power is always inherently dangerous. You pick your devils, I suppose. But if you wired for electricity, you could do all sorts of things, not just with lighting. You could have powered lifts to haul items up the mountain, just for instance. One of the Semorrah merchants is having a friend of mine outfit his vaults with electronic locks that can only be opened by himself."

"Well," Alleya began dubiously, "you know I'm not convinced that widespread technology is always a benefit."

He held up the silver music disk as if it were something incalculably precious. "If we understood the principles behind this little gadget, and if we understood how this entire piece of equipment operated, think what you could do then! You could record your *own* music! These disks are, what, six hundred years old? Hasn't there been other splendid music written in the past six centuries? But you have no way to record it for other generations to hear, do you? It's all"—he waved his hands—"passed on from one generation to the next. Oral history."

"Well, there are ways to write the music down so that you can learn it without having heard it performed—"

He shrugged; clearly an inferior method. "But you don't get that nuance, do you? You don't get to hear the quality of the singer's voice."

"Well, no," Alleya admitted.

"If we could understand this technology"—he turned again to admire the disemboweled machine—"we could record your voice. Delilah's. Think of the possibilities! You wouldn't even have to attend the Gloria in person. You could record your mass some day when the weather was good and all your best singers were in attendance, then set up your machine in the middle of the Plain of Sharon, hit a button—and suddenly, all the music of the angels would come pouring out."

Alleya was shocked to her soul. "You couldn't do that!"

"No," he confessed. "Not only do I not know how to record the music, we have a very hazy understanding of how sound is transmitted in the first place. It travels, of course, like a rock ricocheting off a canyon wall, but—"

"I meant, even if the technology existed, you couldn't have—a *machine* singing the prayers to Jovah!"

That stopped him from a digression into the nature of noise. "What? Why not? I would think it would be a tremendous savings of time and effort."

"But time and individual effort is what the Gloria is all

about!" she exclaimed. "It's not just the music—it's what the music represents. All the people of Samaria coming together in harmony, working in concert, proving to the god that they are living in peace. Even *if* he could be fooled by some mechanical reproduction of those voices—even *if* that were so, the very thought of such a thing is sacrilegious. Is blasphemy. The idea of the Gloria is not to trick the god. The idea of the Gloria is to keep men from falling into war and destruction."

Her vehemence had pulled him up short. Now he gave her a slow smile and shook his head. "I'm sorry, I didn't mean to rouse such passion," he said. "You forget you're not talking to a god-fearing man. I don't tend to think of the divine aspects of things."

"And you forget you're talking to the Archangel," she said tartly. "Jovah is always present in my thoughts."

"I'm constantly amazed at how convinced people like you can be—angels, and most of the Edori, and many other men," he said. "You don't even question. You don't even wonder. You merely say, 'Jovah is there,' and that is the end to it. No doubt or speculation."

Alleya spread her hands. How could she possibly explain? "I don't understand how you can doubt," she said. "There is proof every day of his existence."

"Proof? I see no thunderbolts, no strikes of lightning. I hear no majestic voice speaking to us from above. I do not—forgive me, angela, but I do not—see him answering the angels' prayers. I would think, these days more than ever, you would have disbelievers in your ranks."

"There are disbelievers, although generally not among the angels," she answered quietly. "And yes, these days Jovah seems deaf to the angels—some of the angels, some of the time. But not deaf to me. I hear him listening to my voice, as you hear a mortal man in the same room listening to your conversation even if he does not reply. The silence is not empty silence. And he responds to my prayers."

"I understand you dissipated the storms over the Galo Mountain when no other angel from Monteverde or the Eyrie could do it."

"Jovah chose to heed me. And even if he had not, I would

not have doubted his existence. I have witnessed too many other miracles."

He smiled a little sadly. "I admire your faith, but I have no desire to copy it. I will be a doubter to the end."

She smiled back, lifting her hands in benediction. "Jovah will watch over you nonetheless," she said.

He glanced around at the mess he had made on the floor. "I need to put all this back together—but, if you don't mind, I'd rather leave it till I've seen what I can do with a motor. It might take me a day or two to rig what I need. Will that be a problem?"

Her eyes traced the same circuit across the scattered coils and parts. "I don't think so. No one comes into these rooms anymore since the equipment failed. We can leave a note on the door. Nothing will be disturbed."

"Good. I'll be back in the morning if I can scrounge up a motor."

"You know about the Edori Daniel in Velora?"

"That's the first place I intend to go."

"And do you have accommodations in the city? Or would you like me to see what might be available here?"

"I'd prefer the city, thank you. But I was wondering—"

"Yes?"

He seemed to speak with unwonted formality; perhaps, for a change, he was the one who was embarrassed. "If your duties permit, I would like to have dinner with you tonight. I enjoyed our last meal tremendously."

She had thousands of domestic details to attend to, and she was half-promised to Samuel for the evening meal, but suddenly she could not bear the thought of denying herself one brief opportunity to escape. "Oh, yes, that would be lovely," she said, before she had time to think about it too long.

"Can you go now?"

"I need an hour or so to take care of some things. We could meet in Velora, if you like."

"Any place you'd recommend?"

"There's a place you might like called Obadiah's. The food's good and it's quiet enough to talk. There's music, of course—I don't believe there's a single restaurant in Velora that doesn't offer some kind of music—but it's mostly background noise. Does that sound all right?"

He smiled warmly. Really, he had the most attractive smile. "In an hour and a half?"

"I'll be there."

Over dinner, the talk almost instantly reverted to religion. "What I would most like to know," said Caleb, "is how Jovah brought us here. How he chose Samaria, yes, but more than that, how he carried out the actual mechanics."

Alleya laughed. Tonight she had relaxed her usual rules of personal conduct and agreed to a glass of wine. She had rarely indulged in alcohol before she became Archangel, and never since then, because she felt her abilities were already insufficient to her task; being rendered tipsy would in no way improve her chances of succeeding at her job. But. Tonight. One glass of wine.

"A miracle wrought by Jovah," she agreed. "I know. The Librera is very unspecific. Even the old history books are not clear on how the miracle was accomplished."

"So how do you think it was done?"

"I think he wrapped his fingers around us and carried us here."

"Through space? From another world? How far? How far away do you think the nearest star is? I think the distance is unimaginable. How long did it take? A minute? A year? A century?"

"What does it matter how long it took? It happened. We are here. That is all the evidence you need."

"No, it is not all the evidence I need," he retorted, smiling. "I want diagrams and distances and facts."

"They don't seem to be available. I have found some old texts—translations of histories written shortly after Samaria was settled—and even there very little is explained. Maybe they were translated so long after the event that the translators didn't have words for what the colonists experienced. Or maybe no one understood how Jovah transported us."

She smiled. "I have found an old reference to two contentious brothers named Victor and Amos Edor," she continued. "They left the original group of settlers and refused to join the new communities, and took their wives and children with them. So it seems that from the very beginning, the Edori did not behave like the rest of us."

"And they still don't believe like the rest of you."

"They worship Jovah, as we do. Though they name him differently."

"They believe that Jovah watches over all of Samaria, and listens to anyone's prayer, not just the angels'," Caleb said.

"The angels believe Jovah hears everyone but that he hears the angels more clearly."

"And the Edori think that Jovah is only one god of many—the only god who watches over Samaria, perhaps, but not the only god in the universe. They say that for every other world, a god has been chosen—that if you were to travel to some other planet, for instance, it would not be Jovah you prayed to but—who knows?—Novah or Shovah or Carovah." He had started seriously enough, but ended on a laugh as he made his little rhymes.

Alleya was half shocked and half fascinated. "Do they truly? But then do they feel there is no coherent force in the whole universe, just all these independent godlings? Who ensures harmony? Who keeps the gods from feuding?"

"They say there is a god greater than all these lesser ones. They call him the nameless one, and they say he protects the universe."

"So this nameless one, I suppose, instructed Jovah to carry us from the old world to the new one. Does that mean Jovah once watched over that old world—and then abandoned it?"

"I never asked the Edori that. A good question! Of course, if everything we have learned is true, it is a world that deserved to be abandoned by its god."

But she felt a stricken look tighten the skin on her face. "And how did those who were left behind learn that their god had abandoned them?" she asked in a low voice. "Did he cease answering their prayers? Turn his face from them? Allow them to be slowly destroyed by storm and flood?"

"More good questions," Caleb said gently. "But you say that Jovah still hears you."

"So far," she said. "So far."

She took another sip of her wine, but it fell to a hollow place in her stomach. She could see that her distress was having its effect on Caleb, for he visibly searched for another topic of conversation.

"After you left us in Luminaux," he said, "I asked Delilah to tell me what she knew of you."

Alleya made an effort and smiled. "I would be interested to know what she said."

"Oh, mostly what you had told me yourself—that you were quiet and kept to yourself and did not like to perform for others. But she also mentioned that you were not born at the Eyrie, that you came here when you were ten or twelve. And I found myself wondering where you had been before then. And why your parents did not bring you to the hold sooner."

A little laugh escaped her; no one had asked her this story for fifteen or more years. "Well. You've heard about angel-seekers, of course."

"Yes."

"Well, my mother was not that sort. My mother—she is difficult to describe. A very focused, dedicated, unsentimental woman who has devoted her life to others. She was not chasing down handsome angels in Velora or Cedar Hills. She was overseeing a community for the blind and the deaf in a small town on Bethel's western coast. That's what she still does. Anyway, about thirty years ago, violent illness spread through the community. My mother ran up the plague flag, and an angel responded. He prayed for medicines, which Jovah delivered, and he stayed a day or two to make sure everyone began to recover. By the time he left, apparently, my mother was already pregnant with me."

"That's a fairly dry tale," he commented. "Did she fall in love with him? Was she heartbroken? Did she ever see him again?"

"You have to understand, my mother is a fairly dry woman. I have asked her those questions many times myself. She never gave any satisfactory answers. As far as I know, he's the only man she ever made love to, for while I lived with her, she had no lovers. Why him? Why then? Did he seduce her? Did she seduce him? Did their Kisses light when they first saw each other, as is said to be the case when true lovers meet? She never told me."

"Do you know who he is? Perhaps you could ask him."

"His name was Jude. He was from Monteverde, and he died before I came to the Eyrie. I never had the courage to ask any of the older Monteverde angels what they knew of him."

"So. You were mysteriously conceived, and born in a remote village. But surely, once your mother realized that her child was in fact an angel—"

"She would have instantly taken me to a hold?"

"Yes."

Alleya shook her head. "Ah, not my mother. She was too busy. She had too many others to care for. And she needed me there."

"But—surely—one of the others—they must have noticed that you were an angel child and realized that you should be among your people."

Alleya smiled. "They were blind."

He threw his head back, startled. "So they did not know you were an angel?" he asked slowly.

"They knew. The blind learn by touch, and so all of them had felt the feathers of my wings. They knew I was an angel. But they had been isolated all their lives. They didn't know the conventions that govern an angel's life."

"Not all of them were blind, you said. Some were deaf."

She nodded. "Yes—and they, too, had lived apart even from mortals most of their lives. It didn't occur to them that I did not belong there. Besides, they had their reasons for wanting me to stay."

"Which were?"

She smiled again. "That they could hear me. Even those who were stone deaf since birth. When I sang, they could hear my voice. It was the most marvelous thing that had ever happened to them—you could see it in their faces. I sang, and they heard music. I have never had an audience so appreciative. Not even Jovah."

He leaned forward, fascinated. "They could hear you? Clearly enough to make out words?"

"Well, you have to understand, many of them did not know

words becaus they had never heard words spoken. But they could hear my music, and a sort of—I guess it sounded like a croon to them. To people who could hear nothing at all, even something so formless was miraculous. I used to sing to them for hours.

"And there were some," she continued, "especially those who had lost their hearing when they were older—after some accident or a fever—they could distinguish words when I sang. I was even able to teach some of them more words. They don't speak well, of course, but they can communicate."

"I'm awestruck," Caleb said. "I've never heard of such a thing."

"Well, so you can see why my mother wanted to keep me around."

"The question now is why she ever let you go."

"I don't believe she would have of her own free will. But one summer we were visited by a new band of traders—these were Jansai, and most of our other traders had been Edori. The leader of this group started questioning my mother very closely about me, how old I was, who my father was, how much time I spent in the holds and how much time with her. I think her fear was that he would go to the Archangel and trade his information about me for money or special privileges."

"And your mother was afraid that you would be taken away from her and never allowed to see her again."

"Oh, no. She was afraid the angels would come looking for me—and insist that she come with me to a hold. She did not want to leave Chahiela, you see. So instead of taking me to the Eyrie, she took me to Mount Sinai to ask the oracle Rebekah for her advice."

"I'm sure that was an interesting experience. Were you afraid?"

"Of Rebekah? Not at first. She was very old, you know. She died a few years ago. I was overwhelmed by Sinai, though—all those tunnels and that inexplicable interface. I remember trying to peer into one of the rooms off the main chamber—and she scolded me for not sitting quietly. She obviously had not had much experience with children."

"So she told your mother you should be taken to the Eyrie."

"Yes, but my mother would not take me. So Rebekah summoned one of the angels to come fetch me, and my mother went home."

"Before you had left?"

"Yes."

"Leaving you alone with Rebekah?"

"Yes. Although I really spent most of those three days with the acolytes. I had no idea what was happening to me, where I was going, why. It was a dreary time."

"I can imagine! It seems very heartless, all in all."

"I told you, my mother is an unsentimental woman. She could not keep me, so she took me where I was supposed to be, and didn't fret about it."

"And how often did you see her after that?"

"Oh, I always go back to Chahiela for a week or two a couple of times a year. When I was very young, one of the angels would take me. When I was old enough, of course, I flew by myself. Everyone is always happy to see me, and I sing for them, teach some of the children new words. But it seems like a strange world to me now. There are many new inhabitants that I don't know. And it is impossible to feel close to my mother. So I no longer look forward to the visits. It no longer feels like a place where I belong."

"And the Eyrie?" he asked, watching her closely. "Does it feel like a place where you belong?"

She smiled somewhat sadly. "You know the answer to that."

"Where, then? What would feel like home to you?"

She raised a hand to brush it through her hair. She was not sure she was enjoying this part of the conversation any more than she had enjoyed the part about Edori beliefs. "Maybe someday I will feel at home in a place, maybe with a person," she said. "And you? Where do you feel most comfortable?"

He shrugged. "I could live anywhere, I imagine. All I need is access to technology and an interesting project to divert me, and I'm reasonably content."

She made the effort and smiled. "A project like wiring the Eyrie for electricity."

He smiled back. "Wiring the Plain of Sharon for sound."

"Oh yes! Recording the angels' music."

"Learning to fly."

She shook her head. "You will die still wanting to accomplish impossible things."

"Better than to die wishing I had not wasted my life."

"I envy you a little," she said. "Knowing what you want."

"You'll know it when you come upon it," he said. "Everybody does."

It was the longest, most satisfying meal Alleya remembered sitting down to in the past year—maybe five years. Maybe ever. She was sorry when she realized they had to go: The waiters were clearing away dishes from the other tables, all empty, and the quiet, pretty background music had stopped some time ago.

"I think it's past midnight," she said, appalled.

Caleb laughed. "Well past," he said. "Time for all good angels to be sleeping soundly in their beds."

She left him on the cold, empty streets of Velora and made the short flight to the sleepy compound high above the city. Even at this hour, sweet harmonic voices drifted through the stone warren, singing melodies of peace and contentment. As always, Alleya tried to identify the performers. Timothy, she thought, and a mortal girl who had just given birth to an angel child. The name escaped her at the moment. She retreated to her room, did the most cursory washing up and tumbled into bed. She was asleep in minutes.

The next two days, she left Caleb pretty much to his own devices as he scoured the city and set up a temporary workshop in the music room. She checked on him periodically and made sure someone brought him food, but her own time was fully occupied with visiting petitioners and residents who brought her domestic problems. And there was nothing she could do to speed Caleb's progress, anyway.

The afternoon of the third day, he came looking for her. She was conferring with two Luminaux merchants who were eager to set up a trading arrangement with all the angel holds, when Caleb practically came bounding into the room.

"It's not perfect, but I think you'll—oh, I'm sorry. They just said you were in here—"

Alleya could not help smiling. He looked flushed with eagerness and obviously had good news. "I'll be done here in twenty minutes or so," she said. "I'll come to you."

So she agreed rather hastily to the merchants' request and ushered them as politely as she could to the exit at the grand stairway, then hurried down to the music rooms to see what Caleb had wrought.

A low drone, interrupted at close intervals by a metallic coughing, guided her toward the chamber he had set up as his headquarters. Over that unattractive noise the magnificently twinned voices of Hagar and Uriel rose and fell in the Uvalde mass. The odor of hot oil drifted greasily back. Rounding the final turn in the corridor, Alleya paused at the sight that greeted her—a squat black contraption of wires, valves and mysterious protrusions sitting outside the open door of the music room. The singing apparently came from the repaired equipment. The chugging and whining and fuel smell came from Caleb's machine.

But it did seem to be working.

Alleya stepped inside the room to find Caleb still tinkering with the faceplate on the wall. "Have you really achieved this miracle?" she asked, and her voice brought him instantly around.

He was beaming. He had streaks of dirt across his face and his forearms, and he looked like a little boy who had just discovered spiders. "I think so, yes," he said, very excited. "Come in, come in. When you close the door, you can hardly hear the motor running outside—"

He actually took her by the hand to pull her in, shutting the door behind her. The thick cords along the floor kept the door from closing completely, but most of the outside noise was blocked out. In contrast, the sublime duet seemed to grow louder, purer. Alleya shut her eyes briefly, following the intricate ascent of the music. Caleb seemed not to notice he had lost some of her attention.

"I had to jimmy this wire, and the casing doesn't fit properly, but that doesn't seem to matter. As long as you keep the motor supplied with fuel and you're willing to put up with its byproducts, you can run your machines. Actually, I think it's strong enough to power two of the machines at once, but if you wanted juice for more than that, you'd need another motor."

Alleya opened her eyes. "What kind of fuel does it require?"

"It's a special kind of oil. Daniel can supply more when it runs out."

"How does the motor work? How do I turn it off and on? Where does this special fuel go in?"

"Here, I'll show you. It's simple, really."

So he led her back into the hallway and showed her the switches and the fuel intake valve and told her what she should not touch. She nodded because it really didn't seem all that complicated. She motioned him back inside the soundproofed room and closed the door again so they could talk without shouting.

"So you think you understand it?" he asked.

"It seems clear enough," she said. "But if the motor breaks down when you're gone—"

Caleb grinned. "Daniel can fix it if there's a problem. The motor itself is pretty straightforward. The trick was converting its power to the machine's power."

"But you did it."

He couldn't help showing how pleased he was with himself. "I did, didn't I? I wasn't sure I could."

"I can't tell you how profoundly grateful I am. Now, tell me what I owe you, and be assured I'll recommend you to all my friends."

He looked blank for a moment, as if he had forgotten that this was a skill he could be paid for, and then grinned sheepishly. "I'll send you a bill," he said. "It will take me a little time to figure time and parts. I—it will be expensive, I'm afraid—"

She laughed. "Worth it. Charge what you will."

"And will you celebrate with me tonight? After I clean up, of course."

She knew a moment's extreme temptation, but she could not escape tonight's schedule. "I would. I can't. I have burghers from Semorrah and Castelana meeting me for dinner, and they're none too happy with me as it is. I can't abandon them a second time to Samuel."

He looked as disappointed as she felt, which was a comfort, though he made an effort to hide it. "Well, then. When you have your next insoluble project. Think of me, and I'll be glad to help. With anything."

"I'll keep that in mind. Or if I'm in Luminaux again for any reason—to see Delilah or whatever . . ."

"Yes," he said quickly. "Let me know. We'll—we'll have dinner or something."

They both fell silent, she at least feeling awkward and stupid, he looking as if he had much more to say but could not frame the words. Outside, the motor churned out its ragged heartbeat; inside, Uriel's deep voice modulated into the minor key of a sorrowful plea for mercy. Why was it so difficult to say a simple goodbye?

"Well, then," she said, and held out her hand. "Till Luminaux, or later. And send me that bill."

"I enjoyed working with you, angela," he said, closing his hand over hers and holding it rather tightly. "I look forward to my next opportunity to serve you."

She disentangled herself quickly, mostly because the warm, comforting clasp of his hand gave her so much pleasure. At the door, she turned back briefly. "Goodbye, Caleb Augustus," she said formally, then hurried down the hallway as fast as she could go.

It was not till the next morning, when she returned to the music room, that she found his gift, wrapped in a scrap of blue silk and left on top of one of the silver music disks, where she would be sure to see it. With it was a plain piece of paper on which "Alleya" had been carefully hand lettered. Unwrapping the silk, Alleya exclaimed at the pretty gold hair clip adorned with a single sapphire. She could not resist setting it at once into her hair, where it seemed to instantly restore a certain order to the usual unruliness.

Although she should not accept such a present, of course.

Although people were frequently bringing gifts of thanks to the Archangel and, indeed, any angel who had helped them.

Although, technically, he was the one who had helped her.

But she knew she would keep the gift, anyway.

Just to prove to herself that the miracle was still intact, that the magic had not evaporated overnight, she turned the ignition on the motor, flipped the switches on, and inserted Hagar's secular music into the player. Delirious music instantly burst through the hidden speakers, filling the room with brilliance. Alleya closed her eyes, giving over all her other senses to the music, and swayed slightly to the slow, hypnotic beat. If she could sing like this, if anybody alive could sing like this . . .

Suddenly her eyes snapped open and she read again her name written in Caleb's hand. It was the first time he had addressed her as anything except "angela." She had not even been sure he remembered that her name was Alleluia. Who had given him this name, and why did it give her such a strange shiver, as though an intimate hand had passed over the inner feathers of her wings? She folded the paper into tiny squares, turned off the music, shut down the motor, and left the music rooms to address the urgent problems of the day.

Chapter Nine

Caleb stood silent for a good two minutes, staring at the monstrous vehicle that Noah had named the Beast. It was one of the unsightliest constructions he'd ever seen, and, in the course of his career, he had built more than his share of ugly but functional machines. This one blended the worst characteristics of anything Caleb had ever cobbled together: It was big. It was noisy. It was cumbersome. It produced a fearsome odor. And in no way did it appear to be something he'd care to entrust his person to if he had any notion of comfort over a long journey.

"Isn't it beautiful?" Noah enthused. "What I particularly like is the framework above the passenger compartment where we can hang a tarp if it starts to rain."

"As it's likely to, since the rain never ceases in Samaria," Caleb responded somewhat absently.

"The steering principle isn't difficult, but there's sort of a trick to it. I figure you and I will take turns actually driving. I don't think Delilah will want to do too much of the manual labor—"

Caleb wrested his fascinated gaze from contemplation of the Beast and asked, "Is she really coming with us?"

Noah nodded. "Oh yes. I asked her again last night, just to be sure. I thought she might change her mind, but— Anyway, I don't think she'll be doing any of the actual piloting. But you and I can split that up."

"Oh, gladly." Caleb finally found the willpower to move and began a slow circuit around the vehicle. It was as big as two Edori tents back to back and rested on a frame supported by six metal wheels. Each wheel was set with serrated spikes ("to dig into the ground in any terrain and keep the vehicle steady," Noah had informed him). The front two wheels were on a cumbersome axle that could be turned from left to right, guided by a two-handled steering mechanism in what Noah referred to as the driver's compartment. It took, Caleb surmised, a certain amount of physical strength to operate the two handles in tandem. Although there was a dilapidated barstool bolted down in the compartment, Caleb didn't fool himself that the driver would be sitting down much. Mostly he'd be on his feet, hauling on the handles and swearing loudly.

The unfortunate passengers were confined to an area about the size of an average kitchen table, where two small leather sofas had also been secured in place. There was very little room for their feet or personal belongings, although they could see out the open framework of the car to view the passing countryside. It was doubtful they'd be able to amuse themselves with idle talk, since the motor, situated in the back third of the contraption, made a commotion so loud as to drown out even the most determined conversationalist.

The motor was powered by steam generated by any kind of fuel the driver could scare up—firewood, coal, oil—and though there was a fuel storage container built into the vehicle, Noah had confessed that it wouldn't hold enough of anything to take the Beast more than fifty or sixty miles.

"So I figure we'll be stopping for firewood pretty often," he said. "Which is why I configured the stove to burn anything. Who knows what we'll come across for fuel?"

"Who knows, indeed?" Caleb echoed. "Maybe if we get desperate, we can burn our clothes."

Noah grinned. "They wouldn't take us very far."

"Do you have to stop every time you refuel?"

"If you're using oil, probably. But for wood and coal—see,

the stove is close enough to the passenger compartment for the riders to feed in more fuel."

"Oh, delightful," Caleb said. "I'm sure that's the job Delilah will want to volunteer for."

"Well, I figured you and I—"

"Could take care of that part when we weren't driving. I guessed that. But tell me, how were you planning to make this fabulous journey if I hadn't agreed to go with you? Since clearly the Beast is a two-man operation."

Noah grinned again. "Well, I would have bribed one of the *mikele* to come with me," he said, using the Edori word that meant young boy. "He could have handled the refueling part, though I wouldn't have let him drive. But once you said you'd go—"

"A little free slave labor."

"Hey. All in the interests of scientific advancement. So what do you think? Are you impressed?"

"Dumbfounded," Caleb said. "It's the ugliest thing I've ever seen. And the noisiest—"

"You're just jealous," Noah replied, unruffled. "Because you couldn't even begin to know how to put the whole thing together."

"Wouldn't have wasted my time on it."

"Yeah, gone off and tried to make angel wings instead. That's something that'll get you far, trying to learn to fly."

They bantered a bit more as Caleb continued to inspect the car. He had to admit, Noah had done an excellent job of selecting and fitting his materials, considering they were all cannibalized from other projects and never intended for use in a self-propelled motorized land vehicle. He asked a few more questions about parts and fuel and climbed throughout the interior to get a feel for the inside dimensions, but Noah was right: Caleb could not have improved on this particular project.

"So when do we leave?" he asked, descending cautiously. He could see already that getting in and out of the high compartment would take a certain amount of practice, at least to accomplish gracefully.

"I figure it will take us five days to get there. So maybe we should allow a week. In case of breakdowns or mishaps, you know."

"Oh, I know."

"The Edori conference is in twelve days. So we should leave early next week to allow plenty of time."

"Have you got a route mapped out?"

"More or less. The difficulty is finding a way that offers water and fuel for the whole trip. I also want to stay away from the main roads, because I don't think we'd be popular company. So we'll be camping most of the way."

Caleb nodded. "How often do you have to add water?"

"About as often as you add fuel."

"That could be a problem. Unless you follow the coastline."

Noah shook his head. "Seawater's a last resort. The minerals clog up the steam lines. But in an emergency it will work."

"Can we carry water with us?"

"Some. But once we run out of water—"

Caleb smiled swiftly. "We'll have Delilah pray for rain."

A quick frown crossed Noah's dark face; then he decided to ignore the joke. "I've got half-a-dozen Edori who've agreed to follow us with extra horses. They've got my map—plus, it won't be hard to follow our tracks. They'll only be a day or two behind us. Worst case, we wait for them and go on by horse."

"Sounds as workable as it can get," Caleb observed. "I'm almost looking forward to it."

"Hey, it'll be the adventure of your dull life," Noah said.

"That's right. I keep forgetting that you're doing me a favor by letting me come with you."

They spent some more time discussing what food items they could bring (what there might be room for) and looking over the map Noah had drawn. Most of the land around Breven had always been a desert, but the recent storms had created marshy ponds in half-a-dozen previously dry gullies. Winter never came harshly to this quarter of Samaria, so they would be dealing with mud, not slicks of ice. "We should be all right," Caleb decided, then shrugged. "If not—still a grand idea."

"Dinner tonight at Seraph?" Noah asked as Caleb gathered up his backpack and prepared to go.

"Can't. I've been gone too long and I have too much to do. Maybe later in the week."

"All right. Till then."

And as Caleb left for the short hike from the camp into Luminaux, he reflected wryly that Noah had not once asked him about his visit to the Eyrie. He wouldn't have expected him to inquire after the health of the Archangel, but he had thought that Noah would be interested enough in the foreign technology to want to hear about that part of his visit at least. But apparently not.

Just as well. Caleb did not particularly feel like talking about it.

Half of his return trip he had spent castigating himself for the foolish, romantic gesture of leaving a gift for Alleluia; the other half of the trip he had spent wondering what plausible excuse he might have for returning to the Eyrie in the near future. None came immediately to mind. Surely something would occur to him.

Because she had seemed to enjoy spending time with him. That could not have been his imagination; she had laughed and talked and told him secrets about her life, and she was clearly a woman who did not do so lightly. They had nothing in common, of course—neither interests, nor attitudes, nor desires, and certainly not faith—but something about her appealed to him so mightily that he could not force her from his mind.

So he would find something urgent to do in Velora as soon as he returned from Breven, and after that, well, he would see.

He had gone straight to the Edori camp upon his return—not just to return the horse, which he had borrowed from Thomas, but to check in with Noah about the trip to Breven. And to talk about the wondrous systems inside the angels' music machines.

Or not, as it turned out.

He made it to the outskirts of Luminaux just as the natural light began to fade and the far more magical, artificial light of the city began to work its azure charm. The woman who ran the bakery had collected a pile of mail for him—three commissions from Luminaux merchants, an inquiry from a large farming conglomerate just across the river, a note from his mother, a sealed packet containing the final payment on a very expensive wiring job he'd done two months ago.

"Here," he said with a smile, handing most of the money over to his landlady. "I never seem to keep it long."

She took it, but wistfully tried to hand it back. "You're paid up through this month," she said.

"For next month. I'll be traveling, and I don't know when I'll be back."

"You're always good for your rent," she said, but she accepted the money this time. "I've had many who weren't nearly as reliable."

"Ah, you love me while I'm solvent," he said, heading out the door. "You won't say such kind things about me when I've lost all my commissions." Her laughter followed him out.

Upstairs, he spent a few minutes sorting out clean clothes from dirty and deciding which of the offered projects he cared to accept. Tomorrow he needed to check back with a couple of his most recent clients to see if they had any questions or problems with their installations. He also needed to lay in more groceries, take in a pair of boots to be resoled and gather up supplies for the trip to Breven.

And, sometime tomorrow or the next day, he needed to find an hour to have a private conversation with the angel Delilah. He had made a promise to another angel, and whether or not she had been serious when she made the request, the promise was one he intended to keep.

At the Grammercy House, the specialty of the day was a grilled fish concoction that looked inedible but was, in fact, delicious. Caleb, who was not a connoisseur, wondered what was in the sauce and the seasonings, but decided to ask neither the waiter nor Delilah, both of whom could probably tell him. Some things, he had learned, lost their appeal when investigated too closely.

"Nice place," he said, looking around. The white velvet curtains had been drawn against the midafternoon sun and the whole room exuded an air of hushed, dark calm. All the patrons spoke in low, indistinguishable voices; the servers moved soundlessly between tables.

"You haven't been here before?" Delilah asked.

He shook his head. "I'm more of the beer-and-sausage type of guy. Tavern food. This is a little upscale for me. I'm not entirely sure how I'm supposed to behave."

"But you fake it so well."

Delilah had agreed to meet him for a late lunch ("What I consider breakfast," she had drawled) without hesitation. Perhaps she thought he was interested, at last, in flirting with her. Perhaps men were always asking her out for meals. She was dressed in somewhat unflattering black, which richened the shadows of her hair but drained the color from her face. She looked as if she'd been sleeping until a few minutes ago. Caleb, who liked to be up with the dawn, could not imagine such slothfulness.

"I would guess you've tried every restaurant in Luminaux," he said.

"Well," she replied, "the classier ones."

"Where do you rank Seraph?" he asked.

She laughed. "Oh, at the lower end. Not the sort of place I would frequent if I didn't have a job there."

He studied her. "It can't be that you're singing for the money."

"Well, the so-refined Joseph does pay me. But I'm not there for the financial advantage—I go for the entertainment value."

"But you're the entertainment."

"Let me rephrase. I go there for its value in distracting me. You can't, after all, sleep all day, every day. It's a way to fill the hours."

The words were bitter but the tone was light. Self-mockery on display at an early hour. This would be no easier than any conversation with Delilah ever was.

"Well, there's the trip to Breven," he remarked. "That should fill a few days. A couple weeks, actually, between the trip there and back. Though it's likely to become tedious in its own way."

"I like a little variety in my tedium. I'm looking forward to it."

"Have you seen Noah's Beast?"

"His what?"

"The Beast. The—vehicle he's built to take us to Breven."

"No, but I'm sure it's awful. From what he's said. He's very proud of it, though, so I'm going to try not to laugh at it."

"It's more than awful. It's noisy and it smells like a factory, and it'll take two strong men to guide it all the way to Breven."

"Good thing you're coming with us, then."

"Oh, I'm sure Noah could find one of his Edori brethren who'd be just as useful as I would."

"He doesn't seem to think so. It's always Caleb-this and Caleb-that, and 'Anything I can't handle, Caleb can.' Really, it makes me see you in quite a different light. Up till now, I'd always thought you were rather ordinary."

"Well, it's gratifying to be so highly thought of."

"I don't think he'd make the trip without you."

"And of course we're both counting on your help, as well," Caleb added with a grin. "We thought you might like to help steer from time to time, and maybe gather firewood at the rest stops."

Delilah smiled beatifically. "Clearly you were amusing yourselves with idle chatter. No one would bring me along to perform manual labor. It's obvious I'm too delicate."

"My private opinion is that you could wrestle yourself free from a pack of wild dogs, but it's true that we figure you'll be mostly decorative," Caleb said. "I, in fact, have a hard time believing you're really going to come with us."

"Of course I am. The appeal of the novel, you know."

"It'll be uncomfortable," he warned. "Cramped quarters. Lousy food. And that constant smell."

"Are you afraid I'll be complaining all the time?" she asked. "I'll be so stoic, you'll hardly know me."

Caleb gave an exaggerated sigh of relief. "Well, that's the promise I was hoping for."

"And is that why you invited me to lunch?"

"Oh, no," he said. "I had a question to ask you."

"I'm all agog."

He took another bite of his fish before continuing. "Tell me," he said. "If someone wanted a favor from you which you would probably refuse, how should he approach you?"

Sudden interest brightened her eyes. "First, he should take

me to a fabulously expensive restaurant and ply me with exotic wines."

Caleb smiled. "It's too early in the day for wine. For me. You, of course, can drink when you like."

"No, I try not to drink before a performance," she said regretfully. "My voice is my one remaining vanity, so I try not to abuse it."

"So how can I win you over, then? They have some tempting desserts on the menu—"

She laughed. "We'll see how hungry I am when I finish my meal. What is this favor you want from me?"

"It *would* be a favor to me," he said seriously, leaning across the table to make his pitch. "I'm like a kid who can't rest till he's tasted every kind of candy in the store. I see a scientific challenge, and I have to try to solve it. I can't think of anything else. I have to know if I can fix it, or design it, or improve it. It's like a fever."

"Well, I don't have many scientific challenges lying around awaiting solutions," she said. "So I can't guess—"

"Your wing," he said. "I'd like a chance to look at it and see if I can come up with a way to repair it."

She grew statue-still, statue-silent. It was as if the hollows and planes of her face were instantly recarved, recast into lines of suffering and grief. He imagined that even her heartbeat, for a moment, squeezed to a stop.

"Maybe I can't do anything to help you," he went on, when it was clear she would say nothing. "But I've built a lot of electrical systems—and the body is, in its way, an electrical circuit, with energy running along the muscles and the nerves. Maybe I can—"

"No," she said, and the word was said in the ugliest tone he had ever heard her use.

"I know it is difficult to contemplate hope again," he went on. "I know you have been looked at by almost every doctor and surgeon in Samaria. But I'm not—"

"No," she said again, and her voice was a little stronger.

"But I'm not a doctor. I'm an engineer," he finished. "And I would be approaching the problem from a whole different angle."

"No," she said. "How many times do I have to say it? No, no, no. I have been through that too often to endure it again."

"If I can help you," he said, "how can you refuse me?"

"Because you can't help me! No one can help me! I am broken beyond repair, don't you see that? Jovah realized it instantly! He cast me aside because I could no longer serve him. He knew long before the doctors and the surgeons and the other angels were willing to give up hope. He knew, and he abandoned me—"

She stopped abruptly, made a visible effort to control her unsteady voice. She shook her head and put her hands up before her as if to fend off accusations. "I know it is not your intention," she said clearly, "to be cruel. But it is cruel to ask me to try again. I cannot do it."

"I hope you don't expect me to travel all the way to Breven with you, eyeing you and wondering."

"If you must. Add it to the tribulations of the trip."

Caleb shook his head and played his trump card. He had figured the conversation would go roughly this way. It was why he had, earlier, allowed her to rhapsodize about his value to Noah. "I won't make the trip unless you'll agree to the examination."

"What?"

"I'm sorry. It means that much to me. If you won't let me examine your wing, I won't go to Breven with you and Noah."

"That's ridiculous," she snapped. "One thing has nothing to do with the other. Besides, you have to go. Noah needs you."

"He'll find somebody else."

"You know that's not true. You're the only one he trusts. You're the only one who can actually help him."

"I won't go unless you consent to the examination."

She rose to her feet. Even with her wings folded tightly back, she was an impressive sight, all flashing dark eyes and divine indignation. "Then we will go without you," she said. "And may Jovah forget your name."

She swept from the restaurant, nearly trampling a few unwary souls who happened to be in her way. Caleb calmly watched her go; he had more or less expected their meeting to end this way. He liked the curse, though; it was not one he had heard before. He rubbed the shattered black Kiss on his arm, and murmured, "But he already has."

* * *

Noah was distressed to learn that his two closest friends had quarreled "and at such a time! Couldn't you have waited till we got back from Breven?"

"You told me weeks ago you wanted me to look at her wing. And now you're saying that I brought it up?"

"Well, no, but—well, yes, right at this time. What if she decides not to come with us? Because of what you said?"

"The trip will be easier, then," Caleb said callously. "But she'll come. She's too desperate to get away. And she'll let us look at her wing, too."

"Because you've put her in a dreadful position—"

"She'll survive the examination. And maybe we'll do her some good."

Noah muttered but stopped arguing, although he still seemed unhappy with Caleb's timing and his methods. But three days before they were scheduled to leave for Breven, the two men were admitted to Delilah's opulent apartment (paid for, Caleb surmised, by the oily Joseph) to see if they had the skills to repair the broken wing of the fallen Archangel. Noah had negotiated the permission; Caleb didn't ask what he bargained with.

Caleb brought every tool, wire and recharger he possessed, so he was loaded down with baggage. Noah carried almost as much. Delilah herself admitted them at the door, cool and wordless, and gestured for them to follow her down a gilded hallway. There appeared to be no servants in the place, though Caleb supposed that was just for this occasion; he pictured Delilah surrounded by maids, hairstylists, footmen and cooks. Today, however, she would want privacy.

The room they were shown to seemed to be a music salon, for it was furnished with a few delicate chairs, a long wooden bench covered with a quilted cushion, a harp, a dulcimer and a painted metal stand holding a variety of flutes. Caleb wondered which of these instruments, if any, Delilah played. Except for its luxurious appointments, which seemed very much in character, the apartment held no traces of Delilah at all. It looked like a lovingly designed cage built to hold an exotic butterfly—crafted with her in mind, but taking into account none of her true desires.

Three huge gauze-draped windows provided abundant sunlight, one of Noah's requirements. All the furniture except the quilted bench had been pushed flush against the walls; the bench had been placed squarely in the middle of the open space. Another requirement, room to work.

"Is this the way you wanted it?" Delilah asked in a neutral voice.

"Yes, it's perfect," Noah said quickly. "Thank you."

She gave him a heavy, unreadable look which made his face tighten, then looked away. She perched on the bench as lightly as that butterfly, as if she might, when startled, burst instantly into flight. Her face was turned toward the nearest window and her eyes were half-closed, as if she were, for the last time in her life, enjoying the caress of sunlight upon her cheek.

Well, enough of this. "Everything's fine," Caleb said briskly. "Noah, could you draw those curtains back all the way? Delilah, we need you to lie facedown on the bench and spread your wings as far as they will go."

Now she gave Caleb the look, weighty and unfathomable, but he merely nodded to confirm his instructions. Without another word, she rolled gracefully into position, pillowing her chin on her clasped hands and unfurling her wings. Her left wing unfolded like a cloud teased open by the wind, but her right wing fell awkwardly from her shoulder to the floor, and lay there, bent and motionless.

Caleb moved to her left side and Noah joined him. The broad wing appeared to spring from a narrow band of cartilage set just in from the shoulder blade. Inches from the joint, the cartilage branched into a wide, springy web of tissue and sinew, the framework of the entire wing. Feathers were overlaid in a careful, interlaced pattern on both sides of this network, hiding the complex weave of muscle, tendon and vein.

"Can you operate your wings independently?" Caleb asked.

"Yes," was the terse reply.

"Flex your left wing for me. Slowly. Just a little bit."

The great wing lifted a few inches, settled, lifted again. Caleb watched the faint ripple run along the length of the framework. He placed his fingers lightly along the thickest cords at her shoulder blade. She shivered but did not protest.

"Again," he said. "More slowly."

This time he felt it as the muscle bunched and responded, sending its signals through three main branches that led to the upper edge of the wing's framework, the lower edge, and a middle line. He carefully pushed away the feathers along this central pathway, tracing the route by feel, by eye, as it arched and straightened and tapered out only at the ragged edge of the feathered wingtip.

"See it?" he said to Noah. "I think that's the main operative muscle. It carries the most weight and the bulk of the energy."

"What about the top and bottom muscles?" Noah asked. "Peripheral wing control? Auxiliary power?"

"A little of both. Maybe the wing's too heavy to be moved by one muscle alone."

Caleb slowly traced the route of the main muscle again with his index finger. The extended wing was so long he could not stand in one place and reach from end to end, but had to walk a few paces as he followed his path. "You can feel that, can't you?" he asked Delilah.

"Of course I can."

"All the way? Everywhere my finger touches?"

"Yes."

"How about this?" And he traced a similar path along the top edge of her wing.

"Yes. Not as distinctly."

"And this?" The bottom edge.

"Yes."

Caleb glanced at Noah and nodded. The men repositioned themselves on the right side of Delilah's body, over the broken wing. The downy mass was just as broad, just as delicate as the left wing, but there was a curious, lifeless quality to the spill of feathers on this side of the angel's body. There was no jagged rip in the muscles or the tissue, no improper joint where the wing appeared to have been folded roughly back, no way to tell by looking just where the problem lay. But clearly no will of the angel's animated the wing; it lay there like something apart from her, responsive to no touch and no instruction.

"You still have some control over this wing, don't you?" Caleb asked. "For instance, you can fold it back, move it out of your way."

"Yes."

"Show me."

As she lifted the wing slowly, twice, and let it fall, Caleb laid his hand gently on the cartilage and muscle mass at the edge of the shoulder blade. As with the left wing, he could feel the energy surge and pulse through the covered nerves; the problem did not lie here.

"Can you feel my hand?"

"Yes."

"I'm going to move my fingers down the middle of your wing. Tell me when you can no longer feel my touch."

Slowly, once again pushing the sleek feathers aside as he progressed, he ran his fingertips along the main line of muscle and nerve. He had traveled maybe eight inches from the base at her shoulder when she said, "There."

He paused, his fingers searching out any infinitesimal knot under the central cord. There was nothing. "Here? You feel nothing from this point on?"

"That's right."

He backed his fingers up half an inch. "But here you still feel me?"

"Yes."

He slid his fingertips forward again, seeking a break, a mass, something to account for the loss of feeling. All was smooth, even, untroubled. The break was undetectable to the touch. He nodded to Noah, standing at the top edge of Delilah's wing while he stood at the bottom edge.

"Test the upper perimeter," he said. Noah ran his hand with loving delicacy along the entire ridge of the upper framework, from base to wingtip. "What about that?" Caleb asked Delilah. "Could you feel that?"

"Yes."

"The whole way?"

"Yes."

"All right. Now I'm going to test the bottom edge. Tell me when you can no longer feel my fingers."

But he traced the web from backbone to feather's edge and she never once stopped him. "So those nerves are in place, top and bottom," Caleb murmured to himself. "It's just that central line—"

"The one that carries all the weight," Noah interjected.

"That broke. One line to fix."

Noah looked at him. Caleb nodded. One line to fix, but how?

"All right, now I'm going to do a couple of tests," Caleb said. Every time he spoke, he was addressing the back of Delilah's head. She never once looked at him or appeared to be anything but barely tolerating the proceedings. "Let me know if this hurts—or if you feel anything."

She nodded her dark head. Caleb went to his bags and dug out a small device consisting of a wheel, a pump, a jumble of wires and a set of small metal pincers. He handed the bulk of the device to Noah, then carefully attached the pincers to the angel's wing, along the central muscle past the point where she had any feeling.

"Does that hurt? Can you feel that?"

"No."

"All right. What we're going to do now is give you a little jolt of electricity. It could be a little painful, but it's not dangerous. It will feel—oh, no worse than running your finger through a candle flame. Are you ready?"

"Yes."

Caleb nodded to Noah, who had settled the base of the device on the floor. Caleb positioned himself over the spread wing, one palm flat on either side of the pincers, to check by feel the level of current in the angel's wing. Noah pumped the plunger rapidly about a dozen times, causing the wheel to fly into a silver blur.

"Ready?" the Edori asked.

"Ready."

Noah pumped one more time, then flipped a switch which opened a line of electricity through the short wires. Caleb saw the faint spark as the fire flicked against the angel's feathers—and the whole wing shuddered once, violently, lifting three inches into the air and falling back to the floor.

Caleb looked sharply at Delilah's head. "Did you feel that?" he demanded.

She was looking away. She had not even seen her wing's response. "No. Was that what was supposed to hurt so much?"

Now Caleb's eyes locked onto Noah's shocked gaze. "Again," he said. "I want to replicate."

"But you saw—"

"Do it again."

So Noah, his face set and strained, again pumped the wheel into a frenzy and released a quick charge into the wires. Again, the great wing spasmed and lifted, then fell to the floor, unable to sustain its weight. Again, there was no reaction from Delilah. Again, Caleb felt the power leap across his hands as they lay spread along that broken central nerve. He knew what the problem was, all right. He just didn't know how to fix it.

They stayed at Delilah's for another hour, probing the complex web of her wing structure with their array of tools. They learned nothing they had not known with the conclusion of the first test. When they declared themselves finished and began repacking their equipment, Delilah calmly came to her feet and smoothed her hair and clothes back into place.

"I hope you gentlemen had a pleasant time," she said. "I assume from your sober faces that you have no glorious news for me."

"Not at this time," Caleb said. "But we have ideas."

She gave him a stately nod. "Which of course I would like to hear about at some future date. You cannot imagine my excitement."

"Delilah—" Noah said, a note of protest in his voice.

She smiled at him briefly. "It's not important," she told him. "It was a matter of indignity only. No expectation and no pain. But it would please me if neither of you came to Seraph for the next two days. I need time to compose myself."

And without another word, she left the room. Noah looked after her with longing and despair. Caleb more practically finished their packing.

That night, the two men met again over an Edori campfire, where those who had joined them showed only puzzlement at their conversation.

"The muscle is intact," Caleb said. He had made a few

sketches that afternoon, and now he and Noah pored over them. "It responds to stimulus. But the nerves themselves have been severed—"

"And can provide no stimulus," Noah finished.

"If we had a power source—" Caleb said, brooding. "If there was a way to wire her for power—say, a small generator strapped to her chest, run off the motion of her left wing—"

"Too complex," Noah objected, shaking his head. "And too chancy. There are times an angel's wings scarcely move, as they just hover above the ground. She would run out of power, come tumbling down—"

"And I'm not sure the wingbeat offers enough energy, in any case," Caleb said. "Well, then, a fuel-based source? Although all available fuels are noxious and unreliable, I would think, for airborne travel—"

"Plus, Caleb, think of the wiring involved! If a single connection got dislodged in flight, she'd plummet—"

"I know. I know. But it seems so obvious. So simple. If we could find a way to stimulate the muscle, a self-contained power pack . . ."

"Well, there is no way. She was right. It is better not to flirt with hope."

"But there is a way," Caleb said slowly. "I saw it just the other day at the Eyrie. Unfortunately, it no longer works."

"What are you talking about?"

Caleb shook his head, held up his left hand with his smallest finger extended. "A power supply device no bigger than this. An object that stores energy for centuries, apparently. At the angel holds, these were used to supply energy for the music machines. But their power has all been drained. How was it gathered in the first place? And how much power can such a small thing generate? *That's* what we need to fix Delilah's wing. A self-contained power source that's small and infallible. Then she could fly again."

Noah was staring at him, amazed and hopeless. "But Caleb, we don't have such a thing. We don't know how to make one. She'll never fly again."

Caleb returned the stare, a certain sternness in his own gaze. "We can try," he said. "We're scientists, or have you forgotten? We've invented stranger things."

"But nothing more dangerous," Noah said softly. "Nothing more fraught with pain."

Caleb hesitated, shrugged helplessly, and finally nodded. But his mind went back to the problem again that night, and other nights, and he could not always tear his thoughts away.

Chapter Ten

Although Noah had been despairingly pessimistic about the chances, Delilah seemed to have forgiven both men by the time they all set out three days later on their great adventure to Breven. Caleb had avoided Seraph in the interim, since that's what the angel had requested, but Noah had only been able to stay away for one night before returning. In great relief, he reported that Delilah had joined him for a drink and behaved more or less normally.

"Of course she did," Caleb said with a certain cynicism. "She can't afford to hate us forever."

"I don't see why not. I would, if I were her."

"We divert her. She needs us. I told you she'd come around."

Caleb had been less sanguine about the possibility of Delilah joining them at the Edori camp at an early hour in the morning, which was the time the men had chosen for departure. But this time he was the one pleasantly surprised as, before dawn had completely banished the darkness, Delilah came riding into camp in a horse-drawn gig driven by a city ostler. She was dressed in some shapeless cotton tunic and leggings, as befitted a day of uncomfortable travel, and she had only a modest number of bags stacked behind her in the cart—another surprise. Caleb had been sure she could not travel without every stitch of clothing she owned and dozens of pieces of luggage.

"The best of the morning to you!" he said in greeting, coming over to lift her from the high seat. She permitted him to swing her down, though she easily could have jumped to the ground, and she even smiled at him in her usual sideways fashion. "I confess I was sure we'd have to drag you wailing from your bed."

"Why, no," she drawled. "I was so excited I failed to sleep at all. Where do you want my valises? I packed as lightly as I could."

"You packed excellently. Here, I'll get them."

It took only one trip to carry all her belongings over to the Beast, which was rumbling mightily as the motor chugged away at idle. Noah was still loading their own supplies of food, water, fuel and clothing, and it was becoming clear that the passengers would be cozying up with their own suitcases, but all in all, Caleb didn't think they'd done a bad job of organizing. Delilah had even thought to bring her own canteen of water.

"I thought you might refuse to allow me to wipe my face or wash my hair if we didn't have enough drinking water," she said when she saw Caleb's approving look. She had to raise her voice a bit to be heard over the rumble of the motor. "So I brought my own. You can't have any, unless we're stranded in the desert dying of thirst, and then I imagine it might be in my best interests to keep you alive."

"Something to keep in mind," Caleb said easily. "What are my incentives for treating *you* well?"

She laughed at him. "Picture yourself explaining my death at your hands to—Alleluia, for instance, or any of the angels. I think that should be incentive enough."

He grinned, not at her mockery but at her high spirits. Starting out on this trip, she was about as happy as he had ever seen her. "Right as always," he said. "I'll try to remember to feed and cosset you."

"I'll pamper you, if Caleb doesn't," Noah said, coming around from the side of the vehicle. "I think we're all finished here. Are you two ready to go?"

"Ready and looking forward to it," Caleb said promptly. "Angela, can I help you in?"

Her gaze flickered to Noah and then back to Caleb. "Certainly," she said, accepting Caleb's hand. "Give me a moment to arrange myself on the—seat. I'll try to get my wings out of the way."

She climbed daintily into the high carriage and picked her way over the bulked luggage. Caleb turned to Noah. "Do you want to take the first turn, or shall I?"

"I think I'd better," Noah said. "In case it does actually explode in my face."

"The motor's more likely to explode, and we're closer to that," Caleb observed. "Coward."

Noah grinned. "Climb in. It's the ride of your life."

Within five minutes, they were all aboard. A circle of giggling, excited Edori mikele had gathered to see them off, and they all broke into shrieks of laughter when Noah slammed the switch into forward and the Beast lurched forth with a roaring bellow. Caleb waved at the small crowd; Delilah blew kisses. One of the boys shouted something at them which was completely indistinguishable over the noise of the engine. With a slow, ragged motion, Noah hauled the vehicle into a quarter turn to clear the edges of the camp, then pointed its nose in a northeasterly direction. They were on their way to Breven.

The first few miles passed without incident as they all got used to the motion and noise of the self-propelled car. Once clear of the camp, Noah opened up the throttle, increasing the noise level along with the speed. Caleb judged that at its fastest, the Beast covered between fifteen and twenty miles in an hour, which impressed him. He was less impressed by the attendant inconveniences—for one thing, the heat generated by the motor was fierce enough to be felt by the passengers. For another, random sparks and cinders were constantly flying out to land against their clothes, their hair, their skin, Delilah's feathers. For another, when the car slowed for a hill or some other obstruction, the wind created by its forward motion was lost, and the smell of oily fuel became overpowering.

Still, they were moving, and more or less consistently, in the direction they had chosen. And it was a beautiful day, and a grand experiment. Delilah sat facing Caleb, and never once complained or protested. Indeed, she said almost nothing (since conversation was limited by one's willingness to shout), but sat there with a curiously serene smile on her face, watching the scenery crawl past. Nothing like the view she would have from the air, Caleb guessed, when every tree and every boulder must look tiny, flat and unreal; but still, a change from Luminaux. Delilah seemed like the kind of woman who would die fairly quickly if her life offered no variety.

It took them only a few hours to make it to their first landmark, the Galilee River. Noah and Caleb had decided a few days before that their best hope of crossing Samaria's biggest river was to take the Beast across the Gabriel Dam. For the most part, ordinary travelers were not encouraged to consider the dam a bridge that they could cross at will—there were fords and bridges at intervals up and down the river that divided Bethel from Jordana. But most of those structures were comparatively frail and narrow, and might be unable to support the weight of something as massive as the Beast. Besides, no one at the Gabriel Dam was likely to deny Caleb the right to cross any time he chose.

"Caleb built this dam," Noah told Delilah as they pulled up on the Bethel side and climbed down to the ground just for the pleasure of watching the great sluice of water pouring through its ordained slots.

"Really? All by himself?" was her reply.

Caleb grinned. "Not even close. Actually, I had nothing to do with the construction. I just designed the hydroelectrics."

"Which were the whole point of the dam," Noah pointed out.

"Well, certainly I was useful," Caleb said modestly.

Three of the engineers who were permanently stationed at the dam had spotted the travelers and now approached at a run. Pointing and whistling, they circled the Beast and bombarded the men with questions. Caleb had worked closely with all three engineers, and Noah knew them at least by sight.

"What a comedown!" one of them said to Caleb, gesturing back at the stately, massive dam. "From that—to this!"

Caleb shook his head. "Not mine. I'm just along for the ride."

"Better not ride too far!" one of the others cautioned. "This is going to knock itself apart in about five more miles!"

"Come with us!" Noah retorted. "Show us you're smart enough to put it back together!"

Caleb drew closer to the first engineer and gestured to the cascading water. "Any problems?"

The man shook his head. "The usual small things. She runs like a dream. I hear falling water in my sleep."

"How long are you posted here?"

"Another eight months. Then, I think I'll be heading up to Gaza."

"What's in Gaza?"

"You haven't heard? They're planning a dam at the head of the Jonah River. Construction starts late this year."

"The Jonah? Must be a Manadavvi project."

"It is. It'll power the whole damn coastline. You looking for work? Engineer in charge is Rafe Coburn. He'd hire you any day."

"Tempting," Caleb said, though he was in no way tempted. One project as magnificent, as possessive, as completely demanding as the Gabriel Dam was enough to last him a lifetime. "But I have a lot of other things I want to do."

The man slapped him on the arm and laughed. "Nah," he said. "Do it again till you get it right."

After spending fifteen minutes or so exchanging news and insults, the travelers climbed back into the Beast and roared across the wide concrete expanse of the dam. The metal cleats of the wheels made a horrific screeching sound on the hard surface, audible even over the relentless motor, but otherwise they crossed without incident. Soon enough they were back on soft, forgiving soil, waving goodbye to the men behind them.

Delilah leaned forward to offer her first unsolicited comment. "This actually feels pleasant, after the bridge," she said into Caleb's ear. "Do you suppose anything will make us appreciate the noise?"

Caleb laughed and shook his head.

A little after noon, they made their first scheduled stop at a small stream that had been marked on Noah's map. Everyone was put to work, the men doing the heavy labor of hauling water and searching for firewood, Delilah assigned the less grueling task of laying out a meal.

The angel surprised them with a few courtly additions to the meal: fruit she had picked while they worked, and powdered sweeteners for their fresh water. Even the dried meat tasted good on this first stop. They were all buoyed up with excitement and hungrier than they had imagined.

"My turn to drive," Caleb said when they rose to their feet and prepared to move on. "Any little tricks you'd care to share with me before I discover them for myself?"

"She turns right easier than she turns left," Noah said. "When you're going left, allow for a long, slow curve, so start a few yards back from where you think you should. I already showed you how to brake and throttle. That's about all there is to it."

"All right. Let's refuel, and we'll be on our way."

It was an entirely different experience, Caleb discovered, driving the Beast. First, his seat was significantly higher than the passengers', giving him a more lordly view of the countryside. Second, there was something deeply satisfying about being in control of all this raw, stupid power, forcing it to bend to his will, creating motion and direction out of fire and steam and metal. It was more of a physical workout than he'd anticipated, because the throttle and the brake each were operated by pedals that required him to throw his whole body weight behind both feet; and turning the car in either direction demanded all the strength in his arms and his back. He learned quickly enough (as Noah surely had) that his best course was the straightaway, rolling over any minor obstructions that didn't look likely to tilt the Beast over on its side, and that the only good reason to vary his speed was to come to a complete emergency halt. Those rules digested, he thoroughly enjoyed himself, jouncing along on his unsprung seat like a kid riding pillion on his father's horse. He felt like king of the world. It was the most fun he'd had since flying.

Still, after a few hours, it became somewhat tedious; it was hard to imagine how well this would wear over four or five days. He was glad for a break a couple of hours after his shift started—gladder still when they reached their scheduled campsite for the evening, and he was able to bring the Beast to a halt.

He cut the motor, and the silence pressed against his eardrums with an actual, palpable weight. In fact, for a moment it did not seem like silence at all, but a muted roaring, as if he were hearing the Beast from a great and puzzling distance. He shook his head slightly as if to dispel the illusion, and he heard Noah laugh behind him. He turned with a smile.

"We'll all be deaf before the trip is over," the Edori remarked.

Delilah was rubbing her left ear. "I thought it was just me. You sound like you're far away."

"You'll be fine in a few minutes," Noah told her.

Indeed, during the bustle of preparing camp, Caleb found the sensation gradually fading. Since there was still an hour or two of daylight left, he and Noah fetched water and fuel so they could start out immediately in the morning; again, Delilah prepared the meal. Caleb would never have imagined the angel to be the happily domestic type, but she seemed quite cheerful as she watched the fire and heated bread in the coals.

She had another surprise in store for them at this meal. Light as her baggage was, she'd managed to tuck in a single bottle of wine, and after they'd eaten, she poured it into their three metal camp cups. "Here's to a successful first day of our journey," she said, lifting her cup in a toast. "It was more fun than I dreamed it would be."

Caleb grinned, but Noah seemed worried that she was being ironic. "I hope it hasn't been too grueling," he said anxiously.

She gave him a brilliant smile. "No, it's wonderful," she assured him.

There was not enough wine in a single bottle to make the three of them drunk, but something had lifted their spirits to a pitch of high silliness. Delilah started singing some of her cabaret songs, and clapped her hands when Caleb came in on the choruses (he knew them all by now). Noah didn't join in till Delilah switched to a sweet country ballad that Caleb didn't know. He was surprised to hear Noah add a tenor harmony to the second verse—even more surprised by the rich, mellow tones of his friend's voice. Delilah, he noticed, showed no such amazement, leading him to suspect that she had heard Noah sing before—privately.

"I didn't know you were a singer, Noah," he said when the song ended. "You could be on the stage right alongside Delilah."

Noah grinned. "No, I usually reserve my performances for the sacred ceremonies. If you had come to the Gathering last year—as you were invited to—you'd have heard me then."

"Well, I'm impressed," Caleb said frankly. "But then, I don't know much about music."

"Sing something else for us," Delilah urged the Edori. "What was that one you sang the other day that I liked so much?"

"Oh, 'Susannah's Tale.' But it's sad."

"Isn't that the kind of song you sing over a campfire late at night after a long hard day of travel? Songs of lost love and redemption?"

"Now you've got me curious," Caleb said. "You'll have to sing it."

"All right, all right."

It was a bittersweet song, telling the story of the Edori woman Susannah, stolen from her lover by an Archangel when the god told him she was his chosen bride. In fact, the lyrics were not particularly mournful, but the melody had been written in such a grieving key, and the singer's voice was so effective, that Caleb truly felt himself beginning to grow a little depressed. Well, a tale of heartbreak and forbidden romance was likely to stir in any man memories of his own personal tragedies, his own unattainable desires. Caleb fixed his eyes on Delilah's motionless wings, outlined by the smoldering fire, and thought about another angel with whom he reasonably had no connection at all.

As Noah ended his song on a long, low note, Delilah chimed in an interval above and then swung into her own sweet, woeful lament. This one concerned a lost child traveling from city to city looking for her father. If Caleb believed that such banal lyrics would have moved him, he was wrong, for, again, he felt his heart squeeze down with misery and sorrow—but perhaps it was not the song itself, but the marvelous, manipulative power of the singer herself. Hard to remember that this was the same woman who could belt out eight verses of the most vulgar ditty imaginable, and with equal conviction. Hard to know whether the laughing or the melancholy face was the true one.

This time, as Delilah finished, Noah laid his voice under hers for a note or two, then glided into another song. At last, relief. This one was livelier, though hardly light, another love song but one with a happy ending. Delilah added a whimsical, swirling descant to his chorus, a flurry of notes and shifting harmonies that left Caleb breathless; he couldn't wait for the second verse to end so he could hear that combination of voices again. When they finished, he applauded.

"More! More!" he called out.

Delilah laughed. "Sing with us, won't you?"

"I can't compete at this level."

"Oh, sing with us," Noah urged. "We're just entertaining ourselves."

"I'd much rather listen," Caleb said. "You can't believe how much I'm enjoying myself."

So they sang another hour at least, changing songs, changing moods, with a fluidity that amazed Caleb. The longer he listened, the more convinced he became that this was not the first time Noah and Delilah had wrapped their voices around each other with such sensuous pleasure, and the more certain he was that they had performed a second, more intimate duet. They read each other's cues too easily, they understood that secret language of the eyes and hands that only lovers used. But Noah had said nothing of this to Caleb. When had it transpired? And wasn't it clear to everyone—even the Edori, and most certainly the angel—that such a liaison could only end in heartache for one of them at least? As the evening wore on, Caleb listened ever more soberly to the songs of longing and despair, and realized that the performers were singing about themselves.

The next day passed much as the first one had, except that the trip was made a little more wretched by a slow, inexorable rain. Cold, fat drops startled the travelers awake, and they hastily rose and prepared to leave. Noah moved every single piece of luggage in the passenger compartment to retrieve a huge tarpaulin folded under one of the sofas. He and Caleb lashed this to the upper framework of the vehicle, creating a close, dark, but somewhat protected cavern for the two passengers. The tarp stretched most of the way over the navigator's seat, but their route took them straight into the angled spray of the rain.

"Driver's going to get wet," Noah called out to Caleb over

the sound of the motor and the low grumble of thunder. "You want to drive first or second?"

"I'm not afraid of rain," Caleb shouted back. "I'll go first. Maybe it'll clear up."

But it didn't, and when they switched places at noon, Noah drove on in pretty much the same downpour Caleb had faced. Caleb was pleasantly surprised, however, to find how cozy the passengers' compartment was, especially since the heat from the indefatigable churning of the engine poured through the whole damp cave. His wet clothes started to dry a little, or at least seemed less chilly, and he grinned at a somewhat bedraggled Delilah.

"Well, if this is the worst of it, it's not so bad," he said. "Of course, who knows what's in store tomorrow."

"Hail," the angel said pessimistically. She gestured at their sagging roof. "I don't think this will be much protection then."

"At least we don't have to worry about finding water today."

"I think it's raining like this all over middle and eastern Jordana," she said. "We won't have to worry about water for the rest of the trip."

If that was true—and it probably was—their real concern became how to move the heavy Beast over the endless miles of wet desert sand. Back at the Edori camp, Noah and Caleb had discussed this more than once. The Beast weighed perhaps two thousand pounds—and was made no lighter by the addition of three passengers—and it could easily be mired in the treacherous sand of the former desert. Mired forever.

It was Thomas who had suggested they follow one of the old Jansai trading routes that hundreds of years ago had led travelers in and out of Breven. There were three principal roads, he said, one going straight north along the coastline, one straight south, and one that looped around the southern edge of the Caitana Mountains and headed due west toward Castelana.

"They were paved when they were built, but they haven't been maintained for a hundred years or more," Thomas had said. "Still, I'd guess the old roads would hold you up better than the swampland that the desert has become. You wouldn't want to take a horse down those roads today, or even a man, because they're nothing but chunks of rock and sudden gaps, but your vehicle, there, with those wheels—"

"Built for that kind of terrain," Noah had replied. "But Thomas, I never heard of these roads before. When were they built?"

"When Breven was in its heyday," had been the reply of another Edori, a man so old he looked as though he might actually remember those long-ago days. "That was—oh, sometime before Michael was Archangel. Before the river cities became the trading center for Samaria. Caravans were coming in and out of Breven every hour, but they had trouble crossing the desert. That's why the Jansai built the roads."

"Breven fell from grace a little after Gabriel began his reign," Thomas finished. "Not so much commerce passing through Breven. But then they started building up the shipyards, and that took away from the caravans, too. So nobody uses the roads anymore. They're in terrible shape. But I think they'd serve you."

"I never heard of these roads before," Noah repeated. "How do you know about them?"

Thomas gave him a wintry smile. "Because when I was a boy, the Edori did not live settled in campsites like any allali merchant. We traveled every season, every moon cycle, as an Edori should. We knew every mile and every footprint to be found in Samaria. Even now I could tell you of hills and valleys and hidden rivers that you would never find, seeking on your own. No one knows where they are, except Edori. And even the Edori are forgetting."

Caleb had never heard of the roads either, but he believed Thomas when he said he could draw them a map. And they had planned their route so that, in the middle of their third day and about halfway through their journey, they intersected one of the abandoned roadways built by Samaria's greatest traders more than two centuries ago.

At this point, they were still traveling through relatively gentle countryside, all winter-brown shrubbery and hardy trees that thrived in the flat plain between the straggling Caitanas and the bunched Heldoras. Thomas had warned them that the road was so overgrown by grass and weeds that it would be hard to see, "but I think you'll know it when you run across it." He was right:

About an hour past noon, as they chugged along in their usual style, all three riders felt a sudden jolt and jumble as the big cleated wheels bit into a hard, broad surface.

"This may be it," Noah called back to the passengers. "Let's get out and check."

They all piled out, though Delilah did very little to help ascertain what, exactly, they had stumbled across. Noah and Caleb fell into squats and began digging through the matted dead grass to find what kind of texture lay beneath, and how wide a swath it offered. They dug up a few clusters of grainy black rock wrapped in a hardened solution that looked much like the cement of the Gabriel Dam; and, casting from side to side, they determined that this had been spread into a roadway that was nearly twenty feet across.

"Plenty wide," Noah said, standing upright and wiping his hands on his trousers. "Probably allowed enough room for travelers to pass in opposite directions."

Caleb nodded. He was still studying the ground, trying to find any visual clues that would reveal the location of the buried road. "Going to be hard to follow, though," he said. "If you can't see it."

Noah shrugged. "Follow the compass straight east to Breven."

"Well, the road's going to curve now and then. Obstructions in the way. Natural human error. How will we know which way it's bending? We run off the road into the muck, we'll never tow the Beast out."

Noah grinned. "Drive carefully," he suggested. "Pay attention. You'll feel the front wheels drop off."

"Going to slow us up some."

"That's all right. We've made good time so far."

So they swung the Beast back toward the road, since they'd overshot it by about ten yards, and continued their journey on the Jansai caravan route. The Beast's metal tires bit happily into the shattered stone of the roadway; this was, as Noah had guessed, the ideal terrain for the big vehicle. All three passengers could instantly sense the difference in the ride—not necessarily better or worse, Delilah commented later, but more consistent.

"At least you know what you're getting from bounce to bounce," was the way she put it. "It lulls you into a sort of security."

And, as Noah had said, the driver could immediately tell when his wheels had grazed the edge of the track. It was not easy, of course, to wrench the Beast back on course, but by the time they came to a halt for the day, they'd never once completely left the road. Both drivers considered this a promising sign for the remainder of the trip.

There was yet another good omen: They'd arrived on the outskirts of a small town built at the juncture of the road and a minor river. No doubt it had enjoyed greater activity during Breven's more prosperous days, but still, it was a bright oasis of civilization for the three weary travelers.

"Look! I believe it must be Luminaux ahead!" Delilah called out in delight when they came close enough to make out the low stables and silos at the edge of town.

"Ysral itself could not be a more welcome sight," Noah replied.

"They're going to bar the city gates against us if we pull up in this piece of junk," Caleb said more practically. "You want to chance being mobbed, or shall we leave it a few miles away from town?"

"Take it with us," Noah said. "Safer."

Delilah laid her hand on his arm as if she were comforting a lunatic. She and the Edori were riding together in the back while Caleb took his shift as driver. "Noah—trust me—no one is going to steal your precious car. It will be safe no matter where we leave it."

Caleb grinned. "No one could figure out how to run it," he said. "I don't think it will be stolen."

"Well, someone might throw rocks at it or break something," Noah said defiantly. "I'd rather have it near."

"Suits me," Caleb said, and hauled the Beast to the left, leaving the road to head straight for the town.

Predictably, their arrival created quite a stir. Children were the first to come running up, shrieking and pointing, but the men were not far behind. The women mostly watched sensibly from the doorways and windows, calling out to their neighbors across the alleys, "Did you see that?" The travelers did not go very far down the main street that seemed to bisect the town, but pulled over at one of the first stables they saw and motioned an ostler over.

"Is there anywhere we could leave this for the night?" Caleb called over the rumble of the motor. "Not in the stable, of course, but maybe in back where it would be out of the way?"

"We'll pay you," Noah added.

"What in Jovah's name is that damned thing?" the ostler demanded, and variations of his question were repeated by everyone in the crowd that had gathered. "It smells like one of those factories over in the city. You riding in that?"

Obviously, Caleb wanted to reply, but decided to be more diplomatic. "It's a self-propelled traveling vehicle," he said. "We're taking it on a test run from Luminaux to Breven."

"It sure is noisy," the ostler remarked, but his words were drowned out by queries from the other watchers. "How does it run?" "How fast does it go?" "Can I take a ride?" "Dad, Dad, can I go for a ride in the propelled what's-it-called thing?"

Caleb glanced back at Noah, who was having a harder time communicating with the onlookers from the deep well of the passenger compartment. "You have a money-making opportunity here," he said, but Noah merely grinned and climbed nimbly up and out of the car.

"Sure, we'll give rides to anyone who wants," he said. "But kids can't ride unless their parents say so."

"Is it safe?" a man called out.

Noah nodded. "We've been traveling three days now. Nothing's gone wrong. Nothing here to hurt you."

"How fast does it go?"

"Top speed is about twenty miles an hour, but we've been averaging a little less than that."

"How does it run?"

"Fuel and steam and a lot of moving parts." Noah laughed.

"Can I really ride? Can I really ride?" a little boy called.

"Sure. If your mom or dad says so."

"How much does it cost?"

Noah spread his hands. "Free!"

There was a sudden commotion as excited children and boyish men pressed forward at that invitation—and a silence just as sudden that caught Caleb and Noah by surprise. As one, they turned back to look at the Beast, and saw that Delilah had risen to her feet and was now visible to the crowd. With her wings folded behind her and her arms spread for balance, she seemed to be floating above the vehicle like an angel offering benediction. Surely no one had recognized her in those few moments, but there was something—the tilt of her head, the intensity of her gaze—that always had this effect on people, of bringing them, at least briefly, to a state of humility and awe.

"Jovah's bones!" one of the children exclaimed to his friend. "I'd have thought *she'd* be able to *fly* to Breven!"

The ensuing laughter broke the tension and opened up the flurry of questions again, though Noah glanced quickly at Delilah to see how she'd taken that unwitting remark. Unruffled, she held her hand out to Caleb, who helped her from the car.

"I don't believe I would enjoy the amusement rides as much as you and Noah might," she said in the pleasantest voice imaginable. "Why don't I go see if I can find us accommodations for the night? Perhaps an inn that also serves hot meals? Then you can join me when you've quite had your fill of fun."

"Blue Heron sets a nice table, and I know they've two empty rooms right now," the ostler spoke up quickly. No doubt courting the innkeeper's daughter, Caleb thought, but even the worst bed tonight would seem kingly compared to blankets spread thinly over bumpy ground. Besides, they wanted this man's good will if they were to leave the Beast with him.

"Blue Heron," he repeated. "And where would we find that?"

"Up this street to the first cross, then turn to your left, and it's the second building on your right."

Caleb nodded at Delilah and she smiled back. He handed her a bag of coins and watched her make her way gracefully through the crowd. Or, more accurately, watched the crowd part for her as it might part for a mountain cat inexplicably come down from the heights to make its home among humans. Angels were apparently as rare here as self-propelled motorized vehicles, and even more open to suspicion.

Caleb was not crazy about the idea of spending the next few hours piloting the Beast around the outskirts of town while giggling children bounced in the back. But when he saw Noah's joyous expression, his sullenness dissipated. "You drive first," he said to the Edori. "I'll organize the carloads. Let's keep the rides as brief as we can, shall we?"

Noah grinned. "Done in an hour," he promised, and he climbed into the driver's seat and waved his first passengers aboard.

Of course, it was more like two hours before they were able to accommodate all those clamoring for a turn, even crowding four and five people at a time into the passengers' compartment. Caleb was thoroughly exhausted by the time they made their way to the Blue Heron, and famished as well. The innkeeper, a pleasant middle-aged woman who had heard all about the excitement from her son but betrayed no interest in the event herself, gave them their room key and told them dinner would be ready whenever they wished.

"There's a bathing hut out back," she said helpfully, running her eyes over their dusty clothes and soot-streaked faces. "Your friend seemed to think you might want to wash up before you had your dinner."

"When did she say she wanted to eat?" Noah asked.

"Whenever you returned."

"Then we'll bathe," Noah decided. "Dinner in half an hour?" Caleb nodded.

It felt unbelievably good to get completely clean in heated water in a controlled environment, Caleb decided as, a few minutes later, he slid his head all the way under the water in the big metal bathing tub. A quick swim in icy river water or a half-hearted splashing in a shallow stream did little more than wash away the surface dirt, and he felt grimy right down to the bone. It was rare for an inn this small to offer such a luxury; the hot baths must be a service for the whole community. And a damned fine one. He came up for air, soaped his hair, and went under again. In the tub beside his, he heard Noah splashing with equal pleasure. It made him smile underwater.

Soon enough, they were dressed in clean clothes and joining Delilah in the tap room. There were maybe a dozen tables of varying sizes clustered together rather tightly in the low, dark room, and all but two were occupied. Delilah had selected one of the smaller tables in a shadowed corner. The two empty tables were at right angles to hers, as though no one had wanted to get too close to the angel—but everyone in the room glanced over at her repeatedly, in almost helpless fascination, and then quickly looked away.

"Well, don't you two look handsome," was her greeting when Caleb and Noah seated themselves in chairs across from her. "I never dreamed either of you would clean up so nicely."

"I was just thinking the same about you," Caleb replied. "You must be showing off for the townsfolk. You never waste fresh clothes and a new hairstyle on us."

Noah frowned at him, but Delilah laughed. "I've already ordered," she informed them. "They only serve one meal every night, so I ordered three of everything and a pitcher of ale. I assumed that would be fine with everyone."

"Perfect, if this is it," Caleb said, watching a thin young woman approach with a loaded tray. "I could eat the Beast itself, I'm so hungry."

"Give you a stomachache," Noah murmured, and they all laughed.

The meal was one of the best Caleb had ever eaten, though he was sure hunger and three days of road rations were the primary seasonings. Delilah was in the gayest of moods, flirtatious in a way that seemed entirely innocent—merely happy. She drank almost none of the ale, so her lightheartedness could not be put down to alcohol, and Caleb couldn't imagine that just taking a bath and eating a hot meal could lift anyone's spirits so much. But he wasn't complaining. As the candle on their table glowed with flame, Delilah glowed with charm, and the effect was just as cheering.

None of them had the energy to linger long over their wine (which Delilah ordered once the pitcher of ale had been emptied), so as soon as their meal was over they headed upstairs to the chambers the angel had bespoken. "I'm in the room right next to you, so come rescue me if you hear any trouble in the night." She laughed as she unlocked her door. Both men solemnly promised to do so.

"I'm asleep on my feet," Caleb said the instant they were inside their own room with the door closed. It was a small chamber, barely big enough for two narrow beds and a nightstand, but it seemed palatial to him. He stripped off his shirt and trousers and practically fell into bed. It took almost more strength than he had to wriggle his body under the covers. "Don't wake me tomorrow. Let me sleep till Jovah comes looking for me."

"All right," Noah said, blowing out the candle and crawling into his own bed. "But don't blame me if you wake tomorrow at noon and find that the Beast has crawled on to Breven without you."

Caleb remembered laughing, and then he remembered nothing else. Sleep claimed him like a famished lover, and he went willingly into her jealous embrace. He'd been certain he would sleep through till noon, unmoving and oblivious, but something woke him a couple of hours later. He lay there a few moments, trying to recall where he was and then to reconstruct what might have disturbed him. But the streets outside were silent and his companion on the other side of the room slept soundlessly in his own bed.

Except . . .

Caleb rubbed his eyes, then looked again at the formless shape of quilts on the other bed. Moonlight filtered through the shuttered window and threw white bars across the floor, across the crumpled covers on the bed. No one was sleeping in it. Caleb sat up, said "Noah?" very softly, and then came to his feet. It only took three steps to cross the room, and he verified by touch what his eyes had already told him. The bed was empty.

And Noah could only be in the room next door, sleeping in the arms of the fallen Archangel. Bringing some salve to her wounded heart and cruelly wounding his own.

Caleb climbed back onto his mattress and turned his face to the wall, but it was quite a while before he closed his eyes again.

In the morning, when he woke for the second time, Noah was in his own bed, sleeping the noiseless, guarded sleep of the Edori. Caleb lay there a long time, watching his friend's peaceful face, and wondered if he had dreamt the whole.

Chapter Eleven

After spending hours poring over the incomplete genealogy records of the angel Gabriel and his offspring, Alleya reluctantly concluded that she would never be able to track down all of the great Archangel's progeny through such limited resources. Against her better judgment, almost against her will, she decided she must consult an oracle—or rather, work through an oracular interpreter, to ask Jovah himself.

Job would have been the logical choice, since he already knew why she was seeking the sons of Jeremiah, but Mary was closer and somewhat less intimidating. Actually, Sinai was even closer, and Alleya debated the idea of entering the empty caves and attempting to ask Jovah the questions without benefit of an intermediary. She almost thought she could do it. During nights of studying the old histories, glancing at the original text alongside the modern interpretations, she'd become fairly adept at comprehending certain words and phrases in the forgotten tongue. In fact, one night she had rather painstakingly gone through a long chapter of the history before she realized she had read the entire thing in the old language, having somehow turned her eyes to the wrong side of the open pages when she first took up the book. The discovery chilled her (how could she do such a thing *accidentally*?), but elated her at the same time. She had the true scholar's love of knowledge, any knowledge; acquiring a lost language held intrinsic appeal for her.

Lately she had even begun dreaming in those strange, unfamiliar words. At first those dreams were cramped, uncomfortable episodes in which she sat at her desk, hunched over an open volume, laboriously interpreting various passages in books that she had never seen before. In the mornings when she woke, she could remember what she had read, and she remembered it in the old language, and she knew what it meant in her own lexicon. Mostly the phrases were simple, even laughable—"The beautiful tree cries its autumn tears" or "What child laughs in the other chamber?"—but she found it fairly marvelous for all that. She had never heard of anyone learning a language from dreams.

More recently, however, she herself strolled through her dreams talking in this ancient tongue. Sometimes those around her understood what she said and seemed to display no amazement at her new skill; more often, they gaped at her uncomprehendingly, and she was filled with a nightmare's frustration at being unable to communicate. She woke frequently in the middle of the night, tense and angry, with her fists clenched and her face furrowed in a frown.

But Caleb Augustus, when he appeared in her dreams, always understood every word she said; and he appeared in her dreams almost nightly. But there was no use spending every waking moment analyzing *that.*

In any case, because of her growing familiarity with the language the oracles used in communicating with Jovah, Alleya suspected that she could head straight for the interface at Mount Sinai and talk to the god without assistance. Except . . . the interface itself. She was not entirely sure how it was used, what buttons to press and when, how much time she should allow between a question and a reply. And if either of the oracles ever found out what she had done, they would never forgive her.

Although what could they do to her, really? She was the Archangel. It was not as if they could order the priests to shatter her Kiss and tell Jovah she had been removed from the lists of the living. The thought gave her a faint pleasure. She was unused to having any advantages accrue to her from her high position.

But she was also unwilling to risk the experiment—what if it was Jovah she angered by her inept questioning?—and she needed information only an oracle could supply. So she told Samuel she would be gone for a day, perhaps two, and she packed a travel kit for a short visit to Gaza.

Mary worked in a stone retreat quite close to Monteverde—in the same mountain range, in fact, though Mount Sudan was at a much higher, colder altitude than the angel hold, and it was much harder to get to. For anyone who was not an angel, at any rate. Alleya coasted in to the narrow, flat landing place that was instantly swallowed by an overhang of rock, and made her way inside the caverns where Mary did her work.

As was the case at Mount Egypt, Mount Sudan had a small cluster of acolytes and petitioners moving through the outer rooms. A respectful silence muted all voices, even kept footsteps to a cautious, hollow tiptoe. Alleya practically whispered her request to the acolyte who came up to ask her business ("I would like to see the oracle Mary as soon as she has time"), and then waited as quietly as the rest.

Naturally, it was not long before the acolyte scurried back to escort her to Mary's inner sanctum. The oracle was standing by the blue interface, her hand resting on the keyboard, her eyes watching the door.

"Angela," she said, inclining her head slightly. "I'm honored by your visit. What can I do to serve you?"

It was strange to receive such a respectful greeting from someone only five or six years older than she was—especially someone like Mary, a sharp-featured, sharp-tongued, no-nonsense woman.

"First, do you have time to spare for me? This is not an emergency, and I know you have much to do," Alleya said.

Mary smiled faintly. "The work of the Archangel is the preservation of the realm, and the task of the oracles is to support the Archangel," she said didactically. "Even your small questions carry weight for us."

"Actually, it might not be a small question," Alleya said. Mary indicated two rolling chairs arranged close to the glowing screen. Alleya came forward, and they both sat. "Some weeks ago, I was in Mount Egypt and I conferred with Job about troubles in

Samaria. We asked Jovah if he was angry with us, why he sent so much storm, who he—" She hesitated, then plunged on. "Who he had selected as my angelico. To every question we asked, Jovah replied, 'Ask the son of Jeremiah.' "

Mary nodded. "Job mentioned some of this to me. He wanted to know if I was familiar with any Jeremiah who might have caught Jovah's attention. I had to confess I was not."

"Jerusha reminded me that Jeremiah was the name of Gabriel's father. And we thought perhaps, since Jovah was speaking so vaguely, he might mean one of Gabriel's descendants living today."

"But which descendant? There must be a hundred—"

"And not all accounted for," Alleya finished. "I checked records at the Eyrie, but they scarcely list anyone except the angelic offspring, and even those erratically. But if, as I believe, Jovah tracks all the sons and daughters of everyone on Samaria—"

"Everyone who has been dedicated," Mary said automatically.

"Then perhaps he could tell us where all of Gabriel's 'sons' are today. And this man *must* have been dedicated for Jovah to know of his existence."

Mary nodded briefly, not as if she agreed, but as if she was thinking everything over. "But if he has been dedicated," she said slowly, "why will Jovah not call him by name?"

Alleya spread her hands. "I don't know. I don't understand why Jovah does many of the things he does. But since Jovah seemed to think this man held so many keys, I thought it behooved me to try and find him. If, that is, there is a way to phrase the question to Jovah."

"Well, we can certainly ask," Mary said, swiveling around to face the blue interface. "I cannot promise that he will answer. These days—"

"I know," Alleya said. "It is the same with me."

The angel pulled her chair closer to the oracle's and watched intently as Mary played her fingers over the keyboard. Ah—it was so simple—the buttons that Mary pressed were marked with the letters of the foreign alphabet; and after she had framed a polite question (which appeared on the screen before her), she pressed a square green key which, apparently, signaled to Jovah that her message was complete. Alleya could not believe how straightforward it was. All these years of mystery solved by a single textbook!

It was still impressive, she had to admit, when Jovah's reply materialized in glowing blue letters on the pale screen. Mary's inquiry had been a repeat of one of Job's questions: "Who should be the angelico to the Archangel Alleluia?" This time Alleya did not need to guess at the reply; she could read the words for herself. "The son of Jeremiah."

Mary glanced over at her. "Well, at least it's the same answer."

"I thought it would be. Ask him about Gabriel."

Mary typed in: "Is the Archangel Gabriel the son of Jeremiah?"

Jovah replied almost immediately in the affirmative.

"This is where it gets interesting," Mary remarked, and entered her next question: "Can you tell us the names of the children of Gabriel who are living today?"

This time there was a lengthy pause between the query and the response. "Why does he wait so long to answer?" Alleya asked. She found herself speaking in a low voice, almost in a whisper, as if she were afraid of disturbing Jovah while he meditated.

"The more complex the answer, the longer it takes."

But a few minutes later, the requested information filled the screen. There were fewer names than Alleya had expected and most of them were women.

"It looks like this generation didn't breed many sons," Mary said, voicing aloud Alleya's thought. She skimmed the list rapidly, tapping her finger next to a few of the names. "I know this boy—he's a Manadavvi heir who is about eight years old. Not the one you're looking for. And this one—he's in his eighties, at least."

"But—perhaps that does not matter to Jovah. Perhaps the god does not think of age as a relevant factor, as it would be for those of us who are human—"

Mary shook her head, her eyes still fixed on the screen. "He *always* considers the age factor," she said. "We oracles have come to believe that Jovah makes all of his marriage selections based on some kind of genetic desirability that none of us has been able to understand. He never chooses a wife who is not of child-bearing age, never chooses a husband who is not from a virile line. That must be more than mere coincidence."

"Then if we eliminate those two—and I know that one. He's an angel at Cedar Hills, and so is his brother. Clearly they are not eligible. But this man—I don't know him."

"I don't know him either," Mary echoed. She touched her finger to a knob on the side of the screen, then drew her fingertip across the name of the man they had both failed to identify. To Alleya's astonishment, a glowing grid formed around the name, then the entire list blinked away.

"What did you *do*?" she exclaimed.

"Hush. We can retrieve it," Mary said absently. Even as she spoke, new words came to life on the blank screen and Mary read them out loud.

"Paul, son of Abel, born in Castelana five hundred and eighty-seven years after the glorious day of the founding of Samaria . . . Why, he's sixty-three years old!" she exclaimed.

"Not my angelico?" Alleya asked.

"Not even close."

"Who else was on the list?"

Another touch on that peripheral button, and the original catalog of names reappeared. There was only one male name that they had not eliminated and could not identify. But when they checked the screen which carried personal information about his background, Mary made a small *tsking* sound of irritation.

"He's too old, is that it?" Alleya asked, for she was having trouble reading the small text over Mary's shoulder.

"Possibly not. He's only fifty, although in general Jovah would choose a younger man. But it notes here that he had a son by an Edori woman thirty years ago." Mary swung around to stare at Alleya. "Which would make him approximately your age."

"What's this son's name?"

"It doesn't say. Probably he was never dedicated. Edori children most often are not, you know."

"Yes, I know. But then how does Jovah know this man exists? I thought he was only able to track those who have been dedicated."

Mary nodded. "I suspect that an oracle who knew this man or met him one day simply supplied Jovah with the information. See, Jovah does not even list that son as being alive or dead, of even having a name. Jovah knows nothing about him."

"Except that he was born." Alleya felt her voice come from a constricted, hollow place behind her heart. She should no doubt be feeling a certain blushing excitement at the thought that, with a little effort, she would be able to locate the man that her god expected her to marry. Certainly she was curious and she did not feel apprehensive, exactly, but she would have to identify her foremost emotion as reluctance. She was sure she would not like this unfamiliar Edori, this man so far removed from the god that Jovah did not even know his name. Actually, until Job had mentioned it, she had given no thought at all to the notion that she must marry, or at least find a man to stand beside her when she sang the Gloria in a few months. She did not want to marry, that was the truth of it, certainly not a stranger selected for her by another. Jovah could not know, he could not read her heart; how could he choose for her better than she could choose for herself?

But that was sacrilege; that was a degree of doubt she could not allow herself to feel. He was her god, he loved her. He would not lead her astray. If she did not trust him to do right by her, there was nothing she could trust in her world at all.

"What is this man's name?" she asked, still in that small, scraped voice. "This man who mated with an Edori woman."

"Cyrus. And the woman is of the Cholita tribe of the Edori."

"I wonder where they might be found?"

"You could wait till the Gathering and ask among all the Edori then."

Alleya shook her head, attempting to shake away some of her bleakness as well. "That is only weeks before the Gloria. I must surely find him before that. I suppose I could travel to all the sanctuaries, although some Edori never go there, I know—"

"As I understand it, many Edori are meeting in Breven at the end of this week," Mary said. "You could go there and see if he is present or if anyone could guess his whereabouts."

"Breven? Why there?"

Mary shrugged. "Why do the Edori do anything?"

Alleya smiled. "Maybe I should find out. Finding this son of

Jeremiah seems as important as soothing the Manadavvi and outwitting the merchants, don't you think?"

"I think you have waited too long already to seek your angelico," Mary said sternly. "It is clearly a matter of urgency. And, yes, I think Breven would be a good place to start."

Alleya spent the rest of the day with Mary, inquiring as artlessly as possible into the workings of the interface and the communication with Jovah. Mary obliged her by demonstrating a few more interactions with the god, and Alleya was quite sure she understood how the whole system worked. Simple, so simple, once you knew the language.

"And Jovah always responds?" Alleya asked when they were done.

"Always, although not always intelligibly," Mary replied. "And sometimes more slowly than I would like. They say the interface at Sinai is the most direct link to the god and that Jovah communicates more rapidly with the oracle there."

"Why would that be?"

Mary shrugged. "They say Sinai is where the first settlers learned to interact with the god. Some say Jovah actually stood in that room and spoke to the first oracle. Others say, no, the first oracle stood in that room and was swept up by Jovah's hand to meet face to face with the god. But as far as I know, the god has never entered this room or the room in Mount Egypt."

"It concerns me that Sinai is still empty," Alleya said. "Is that one of the tasks that falls to the Archangel—discovering the next oracle? I must confess I have no idea where to look."

Mary frowned slightly. "It should not be your task—it should not be anyone's," she said shortly. "Oracles reveal themselves. Often they are acolytes, and they feel the god's call from the time they are very young. It is an inescapable call—it makes you shiver like plague, and pine like love. Anyone who feels it surely will be made miserable until he or she comes forward and identifies himself."

"What if someone claims to be an oracle but is not?"

Now Mary smiled faintly. "To my knowledge, that has never happened. What would be the point? Who would lie or cheat to achieve this place?" She waved vaguely at the somber gray walls around her.

"It is a place of honor," Alleya said quietly.

Mary nodded. "Indeed. But a place set apart from the rest of the world, dealing in mysterious and holy relics. Most people are afraid of such an odd life. Most people fear more than anything being estranged from their fellow men. No one who sought this life would be unfitted for it. Besides," she added, now smiling almost naturally, "it would be fairly simple to tell if the candidate was an imposter. He or she would be unable to communicate with the god. Jovah would not answer. After a day or two of that, anyone would give up and go home."

"But doesn't someone train the new oracles?"

"After a fashion. There are some rules and procedures no one would be able to guess by intuition. But for the most part—" Mary spread her hands to convey the inadequacies of speech. "If you are the oracle, you know. Already. The knowledge is in your head. I cannot explain it to you. There is no way to counterfeit it."

"And so you knew. When you were—how old?"

"A child. Ten, maybe. I had been one of the children selected to serve as acolyte for two years—a high honor, mind you, and one that rendered me speechless for nearly a day. I had not been here a month when Peter—he was oracle then—called me into this room." Mary looked around, as if seeing the stone chamber for the first time. "He called me over to the interface, and asked me to read the words printed on the screen. I did. The words said, 'Mary will succeed me as oracle at Mount Sudan.' I turned to him and exclaimed, 'I thought so! But how did you know?' And he said, 'I know now. Because you could read the words on the screen.' And only then did I realize they were written in the old tongue, the only language that the god knows."

"And had you been studying this language?"

Mary shook her head. "Not then. Afterward, of course, Peter gave me all the textbooks *he* had learned from, and I studied very systematically. But it is considered the one true test, for only oracles can understand the old tongue."

Alleya would have liked to dispute that, but caution won the day. "Well, then, have you examined any of your acolytes to see if one of them might be suited for the role at Sinai?"

Mary shook her head again. Her expression was one of faint disdain. "They are all Manadavvi lordlings who are here because it adds prestige to their parents' houses," she said. "They behave well enough, but they have no calling. None of them will go on to be priests. And none of them is suited to be oracle."

"Perhaps we should widen the pool, then," Alleya said, smiling a little. "Offer the posts to the farmers' children and a few of the Edori."

Mary did not look amused. "The acolytes must serve the highest and the lowest citizens of Samaria, who come with questions," she said. "They must be versed in all courtesies. I hardly think Edori or serfs' offspring are suited for the roles."

Alleya raised her eyebrows, for she hadn't expected to evoke such a response. She tilted her head to one side, more carefully examining this intense, cloistered woman who had given up the outside world to be a servant of the god's. Yes, there were the telltale high cheekbones, the delicate, long-fingered hands. How could she have overlooked such obvious clues? "So, you were born Manadavvi," she said softly. "Indeed, you have given up much to serve the god."

The slightest blush of color heightened the contours of those perfect cheekbones. "I have given up nothing," Mary said haughtily. "And I have gained all."

It was late by the time Alleya and Mary finished their dinner, so the angel elected to stay the night. She had never slept anyplace so still. Compared to the Eyrie, of course, any venue seemed quiet, but at Mount Sudan, the silence seemed absolute. Alleya loved it. She would have stayed a week if she could.

But she had promised Samuel she would return within a day and, really, there was little to occupy her here. So she left early the following morning and made the lazy, easy flight back to the Velo Mountains and their tireless, bustling heart, the Eyrie.

Where life was anything but still.

She had made it to her private chambers without actually encountering anyone who wished to speak to her, which was good, but within five minutes, someone was urgently sounding her door chime. She opened the door to find Asher outside, ready to pounce.

"Good. You're back. I thought I saw you landing," he said, greeting her with his usual impetuousness. "Angela, it's disaster!"

She held onto her temper; always the best course with Asher. "What is? What's happening?"

"The merchants, the Manadavvi—even the Jansai, I believe—are meeting in Semorrah to decide what to do!"

"About?"

He waved his arms, indicating the world, all it contained. "Everything! What to do about the angels, what to do about the storms, what to do about the Edori—"

"I don't suppose they can do anything about any of them," Alleya said somewhat sharply. "Where do you get this information?"

"You think I was spying, but I wasn't," he replied somewhat hotly. "Gideon Fairwen sent a message here, alerting you to the upcoming conference, and he—"

"And if you weren't spying, how do you come to know the contents of mail addressed to me?"

Asher flushed, but Samuel's voice answered her. "It became common knowledge almost instantly, the way such things do," the older angel said. He pulled back his wings and brushed past Asher to enter Alleya's room, so Asher immediately followed suit. "Gideon sent his message with a courier who was none too discreet. We knew what the package contained before we had broken the seal." He handed a sheaf of folded pages to Alleya. "It seemed pointless to wait for your return, since everyone was already speculating wildly. It seemed better to know the worst."

Alleya nodded; she was already reading the text. It was couched in language that was both formal and hysterical ("And since this is a crisis of monumental proportions, affecting every citizen of Samaria from the smallest babe to the wealthiest landowner, we deem it extremely urgent to act with all haste and gravity . . .") The meeting was scheduled to take place in three weeks. Alleya felt sick and fearful as she finished the letter and looked up at Samuel.

"But what exactly do they think they can *do*?" she asked.

"Divorce themselves from the protection of the angels? Is that really what they intend? How will that improve anything?"

"It gives them more power, for good or ill," Samuel said.

"What power? The power to disperse the storms? If that is truly what they intend to try, I wish them luck, but I cannot think that mortals will succeed where angels have repeatedly failed."

"I don't think they expect to control the weather," Samuel said softly. "I think they are merely looking to slip the angelic yoke. If you cannot get Jovah to respond as you bid, why should they honor *you*? They do not like some of the divine decrees. This gives them an excuse to ignore them."

Alleya nodded, then shook her head. "And I have only three weeks to come up with an argument so strong they must listen to me."

"You will go, then?" Samuel asked.

"Let me come with you," Asher said quickly.

In spite of her turmoil, Alleya could not help smiling at the eager young angel. "If you like," she said. "I shall need support." She looked back at Samuel. "Of course I shall go. I shall inform Jerusha and Micah of the conference as well, in case their words are stronger than mine."

"Not Micah," Asher said scornfully. "He'd just nod and hand Samaria over to the merchants on an engraved platter."

Samuel gave him a reproving look, then transferred his attention to Alleya. "I will help any way I can. I will go with you, if you like. Or stay here to control things in your absence."

"I don't know—but thank you—I can't think clearly right now. I don't know what would be best." She hesitated, still trying to find some order in her whirling brain, and then she cried the words that had leapt to her mind the instant she read Gideon's note. "I wish Delilah was here!"

Samuel nodded. "So do we all. But this is your task, and you must be equal to it."

Alleya would never forget the surprise she felt when Asher turned on Samuel with a sort of proud fury. "Alleya is as clever as Delilah! She is! She will know just what to do when the time comes!"

Samuel looked just as astonished as Alleya felt, and then, though he hid it well, amused. "I'm sorry. You are absolutely right," he said gravely. "I apologize to the Archangel. I believe she will handle this crisis with her usual brave aplomb."

Asher nodded sharply, then turned to Alleya. "You will let me come with you, then? Just tell me when you need me."

"I will certainly do that," Alleya said, and watched him dash out the door. Then she turned laughing eyes to Samuel. "Well! I see I have partisans! I would not have thought it."

"There is something of a cult surrounding you, actually. You were not aware of it?"

"*No!* Around *me*? But why?"

"Because you can stop the rain and no one else can, and because your quiet self-control appeals to some people who were not exactly fans of the exuberant Delilah."

Alleya couldn't keep herself from laughing, but the laugh had a despairing edge. "I keep a sober look on my face most of the time to cover the fact that I am racked with terror," she said. "But some people are actually impressed! This is even more unsettling than the news from Semorrah."

"But the news from Semorrah is grave, indeed," Samuel said. "I think you're right—you must inform Micah and Jerusha."

"And Asher was right about Micah," Alleya murmured, "though I don't like to say so."

Samuel nodded. "So I fear you will be the one who must win the argument, if the argument is to be won."

Alleya shook her head. "The god defend me, I *do* wish Delilah were here. Sometimes I even wish—" She stopped, shrugged. "I wish I could go to her in Luminaux and ask for advice."

"She might be pleased if you did."

"No. She was not pleased last time I wanted her opinion. Even if the world falls down around our heads, I don't think she will help me calm the dissidents. But she could do it. I have no doubt of that."

Alleya sighed fretfully. When Samuel laid a hand on her arm she thought it was meant to be no more than a comforting gesture. But when she glanced up at him, there was a rueful look on his face.

"Asher was right to chide me," he said. "I did not mean to express doubt of you by wishing Delilah back."

She smiled at him. "You never make me feel as if you doubt

me," she said. "If anything, you make me believe in myself. I have always meant to thank you for that."

"I am like Asher," he said. "I too believe you have a special place in the god's heart. These days it is the only thing that gives me hope."

Two days later, Alleya left for Breven. She had composed careful letters to Gideon Fairwen, to Jerusha, to Micah, and sent them by angel courier to the relevant locations. She invited the angels to meet her in Semorrah a day before the conference was scheduled to begin, so that they could discuss any strategies that occurred to them. She was afraid that Samuel was right, however; most of the arguing would probably be left up to her. And she could not think of a thing to say.

That looming before her, the trip to Breven seemed to come at an inopportune time; still, she had three weeks' grace, and it would not take her that long to fly to and from the Jansai city. Though it might take some time to canvass the gathered Edori and find the man she was looking for.

The man Jovah had chosen for her. She shook her head, tossed the thought away.

It was nearly seven hundred miles to Breven, a trip Alleya did not care to attempt in one day. She broke her flight at Castelana, one of the river cities only slightly less important than Semorrah, and kept to her hotel room the whole time she was there. She was not in the mood to advertise her presence to the merchants. Three weeks would be soon enough to confront them all.

She arrived in Breven in the middle of the afternoon on the following day, though she could spot the Jansai city from the air well before she could make out individual buildings and complexes. Breven was a long, dark smudge of smoke, an evil exhalation of noxious fumes, a bruise against the grainy gray of the overcast sky. Long before she could hear or smell anything escaping the city limits, Alleya imagined piteous voices raised up to her, malodorous vapors threading themselves through her tangled hair, clinging with unwelcome tenacity to her beating wings. She hated Breven. It was a city of horrors.

When she got closer to the city, she got caught in a steady, slow drizzle of tainted winter rain. It was not her fancy this time: When she cupped her hands, the droplets she caught were slivered through with black cinders and gray ash. Almost, she sympathized with Jovah in this instance: This was a city that needed to be washed clean, or maybe washed away.

She landed on the dirty outskirts of the sprawling city and made her way by foot toward the central business district. As much as anything, this was an exercise in self-torture, although she told herself it was a learning expedition. The farflung edges of Breven consisted mostly of slovenly shacks piled together in the most promiscuous, helter-skelter manner imaginable. Because Breven had been dug from the desert, and because it now suffered from a never-ending rain, all the huts were half-sunk in a sandy mud in which footprints and other marks seemed to heal over almost as soon as they were made. There were no gardens, no trees, no weeds or greenery of any kind surrounding these miserable neighborhoods. There was nothing but mud, and broken shelters, and rain.

There were a few inhabitants to be seen at this hour of the day, however—mostly women going to and from the markets or the wells, one or two men carrying wood or peddling goods. Not many children, though; this was a working day, and children were in the factories where they could be made use of. Alleya could not repress a shudder.

She earned occasional sidelong, incurious glances as she passed by, but no one stopped her or addressed her. Even though angels were rare (probably nonexistent) in this part of town, the inhabitants did not have enough energy to wonder why she might be there. They barely had the energy to survive the day.

Conditions improved as she moved closer to the center of town, passing gradually from the poorer districts to the richer residential areas. The demarcation line from middle-class merchants and burghers to wealthy Jansai aristocracy was immediate and distinct. Suddenly the homes were palatial, expensive and ringed by tall fences guaranteeing the owners privacy. Even more conspicuous was the arrangement of the windows, all of them grouped on one half of each house, while the other half of the building remained completely closed, shut off from any view of the world.

She always remembered this with the shock of something she had hated so much that her mind had completely forgotten it: The Jansai women were not allowed to mingle with the world, or even look out upon it. Even the traveling Jansai nomads, who took their women with them on the road, kept them covered with scarves and languishing in their tents when they camped outside a city of any size. Here in the Jansai capital, the wealthy traders kept their wives and daughters off the streets and immured in their huge, gold-plated prisons. Unless you were an eligible Jansai man looking to wed within the proper circle, you would never lay eyes on one of these young women.

Once she passed through the most exclusive neighborhoods, Alleya found herself on the edge of the business district. It was nothing like the collection of offices, warehouses, restaurants and schools that could be found in Luminaux or Velora—all these structures looked temporary, uncertain, built for easy demolition. Many of them were little more than heavy canvas roofs tied over a framework of metal poles. Not until the past generation or two had the Jansai invested to any extent in the city itself; all their wealth had been gathered on the road, buying and selling both goods and information. More permanent buildings were, in some places, under construction, but this section of town was still clearly in a state of flux.

The heart of Breven's current wealth came from the factories located practically along the shoreline, and these Alleya came to last. Shoulder to shoulder, belching smoke and radiating heat, the huge windowless buildings were clustered together so tightly they seemed to allow room for nothing even so small as a human to pass between them. This close, the noise level was incredible—a combination of metallic screeches, subterranean grindings, and unidentifiable crashings of what could be rocks or tree trunks or bones. And everywhere the inescapable burning stink. And even more threatening than the omnipresent clouds was the low, grim, shadowed ceiling of smoke.

And this was the heart of progress, this was the modern city. No wonder Jovah had turned his heart from his children, no wonder he was deaf to their appeals. How could he hear them over this wretched clamor, how could he remember to love them at all?

* * *

The Edori camp, by contrast, was a place of gaiety and ease. True, the closely packed tents and the amazing density of people were rather overwhelming for someone who valued privacy as much as Alleya did, but the overall mood of the camp was so friendly, so open-hearted, that she could not help but succumb to the general bonhomie. Even before she had her first extended conversation with anyone, the sidelong smiles and casual waves made her feel welcome and hopeful. Well, perhaps the world was not such a bad place after all, if there were still Edori in it.

She wandered more or less aimlessly through the tightly clustered tents for about half an hour before she actually attempted to find someone to speak with. She had spent very little time among the Edori, but as always she was impressed by the efficiency that lay behind their general air of insouciance. All the tents were solidly pitched and in good repair; every campfire burned busily away; details of children appeared to be responsible for fetching water and disposing of trash, while older boys guarded the horses. The workers moved purposefully from task to task, while the unemployed played laughing games with such fervor that they could hardly be faulted for indolence. The air was braided with delicious aromas. No voices were raised in anger or supplication. It was enough to make one want to become Edori.

Eventually, she spied the old man Thomas whom she had met in the Edori camp outside of Luminaux. He was sitting on an upturned log outside his open tent. A broad, overhanging flap was stretched out in front to provide him shelter from the constant cold drizzle. He was smoking a pipe, his only apparent occupation, but he seemed to be enjoying it thoroughly. When Alleya walked slowly up to him, a look of inquiry on her face, he smiled at her broadly and waved her over.

"Welcome, angela, welcome! It is good to have you among us once more! Are you looking for someone again? Are you hungry? Are you thirsty? I'm afraid I left all my chairs behind near Luminaux, so there's not much to sit on, but make yourself comfortable if you can."

"Hello, Thomas," she said, perching with some delicacy on

another log beside him. "Not hungry. Maybe a little thirsty. Is there water somewhere that I—"

"Martha! We have a guest who would like a drink of something!" he called over his shoulder, and moments later a smiling, dark-skinned woman emerged from the tent. She was carrying a metal cup, which she handed to Alleya.

"There's fruit juice, if you'd rather," she said. "Or wine. Are you hungry? There's plenty to eat."

More of the famed hospitality of the Edori. No questions, no suspicion. No wonder they had been nearly wiped out a century ago by the predatory Jansai. "No—water is all I want, thank you very much," Alleya said. The woman ducked her head and vanished back inside the tent.

"Had a long flight?" Thomas asked with interest.

Alleya nodded. "I left Castelana this morning."

The old man shook his head admiringly. "Castelana! A trip like that would take a man days on horseback, even riding hard." He laughed. "It might take the Edori weeks, but then, we're dawdlers along the way. Imagine! Castelana to Breven in a day."

"Well, I wouldn't choose to do it every day."

"And so what was the weather like? But you wouldn't care about weather, would you? You can fly above it."

"Most of the way. I dropped down in altitude as I got closer to the city, and then it was nothing but rain."

"As it is day in, day out. Rain over Breven. But we are getting used to it."

"I am amazed to see so many Edori camped here," Alleya remarked, edging the conversation around in the direction she wanted. "I know this is not the time of the Gathering. Is there some other special event taking place?"

Thomas smiled. "The grandest event! The exodus is at hand, and all those who are not afraid have come together to make their plans."

"The exodus? To where?"

"To Ysral."

"To—" Alleya's mouth shut with a snap and her eyebrows arched incredulously. "All of you? Everyone here is going to try to sail to Ysral? But how do you— Do you have any maps? Do you have any idea where you might be going? Do you have any *proof* that you will actually find this place? Because, you know, Ysral—"

The old man laughed. "You sound like my allali friends. They think we are fools and madmen—destined to be drowned fools and madmen, no doubt, when our boats becalm somewhere out in the untracked ocean. But I believe Ysral is there. I believe it can be found—that it has been found. Too many Edori have heard the stories from their grandparents, and their great-grandparents. Edori have sailed there in the past and returned with the good news. So Edori must sail there again."

"But—all of you? Perhaps one boatload, or two—"

Now the smiling, wrinkled face grew sober. "And what is left for Edori on this continent?" Thomas asked gravely. "We live on a few scattered plots of cramped and begrudgingly sheltered land—not enough for all of us, not nearly enough, and still there are those who would take that land away from us. And that is no place for Edori—sanctuaries! Edori should live free, in the mountains and the valleys and along the rivers and in the deserts. Edori should not be tied to"—he waved his hand—"well-tended campsites at Breven and Luminaux! We should be wandering the coasts and exploring the foothills.

"And even if we could bear to live as we are living now, we will find this life slipping away from us," he continued. "Even now, the merchants and the Manadavvi and the Jansai encroach on the land set aside for our use. Even now the angels wonder if perhaps the Edori could be moved to someplace less valuable, someplace a little smaller. Even now, our sons and daughters slip away from the camps at night and go into the cities—and they leave the camps by day to go live in Breven and Velora and Luminaux. They learn allali medicine and allali science and take allali wives. If we do not leave Samaria soon, there will be no Edori left to preserve. Thus, not just one boatload, or two, but all of us, as many as are willing. If we all perish out on the traitorous ocean, so be it. At least we will die Edori, among our brothers. Here we will die anyway, among strangers and no longer remembering the names of our tribes."

Alleya had long since stopped attempting to interrupt his speech, and when he finished, she was not sure how to answer him. In her heart, she believed him; still, his venture seemed so fraught with peril that it was hard not to continue to protest. "You have reasoned yourself to a point from which you cannot turn back," she said quietly. "All I can do is pray that Jovah will protect you on your journey."

He smiled again, all his passion flown. "And an angel's prayers are always welcome," he said. He put his hand out in greeting, and she laid hers on his palm. "You had my name last time we met—I am Thomas of the Rahilo clan. But I failed to secure yours."

He might not even recognize her name, but it did not seem the time or place to put on airs. "I am called Alleya," she said.

"Welcome, Alleya. Have you returned to our camp merely to hear an old man rant, or is there something I can do to help you?"

"I'm looking for someone. I had heard there was a great conference of Edori at Breven, and I thought I might find him here—or someone who could tell me of him."

"He is an Edori man?"

"No, but he took an Edori wife."

Thomas smiled quickly. "Edori do not take wives or husbands," he explained. "They may mate for life, but there is no false ceremony that binds them. Rather, they are tied together by the affection they feel in their hearts."

Alleya smiled back. "A good system," she approved. "In any case, he had a son by an Edori woman, that son now being about thirty years old. The son is actually the man I am looking for, but I don't know his name. His father's name was Cyrus, and he had this child by an Edori woman of the Cholita tribe."

Thomas had listened intently but blankly until she spoke her final sentence; then an expression of regret crossed his face. "Ah, Cyrus. He was a fine man. Not Edori-born, of course, but he took to the people's ways as well as any allali has."

"You speak as if he is dead," Alleya said.

Thomas nodded. "Yes, but Mariah of the Cholitas is still alive. She's not here—I believe she stays in the sanctuary near the Heldora Mountains—but her daughters joined us a few days ago."

"Her daughters? What about her son—Cyrus's son?"

Thomas shook his head. "I never heard of any son they had

together. I only know of their daughters. Their eldest, Sheba, is a fine, strong woman with a good heart. She plans to join us on the journey to Ysral."

Alleya could not hide her dismay. "But—are you sure? No son?"

"You could ask Sheba, of course. But my memory is usually accurate." He smiled briefly, as if at a private joke; no doubt he was the recordkeeper for the whole race of Edori. "Who gave you your information?"

Alleya made a small gesture with her hands. "Jovah, I thought," she said ruefully. "Perhaps someone gave the wrong information to him."

If Thomas was curious about her search, he did not ask questions. "Sheba will help you," he said comfortingly. "I will take you to her tent, and then you can come back and join Martha and me for dinner. It's very good—a rabbit stew. We will have other friends joining us, and they'd all be happy to meet you."

There seemed to be no possible way to refuse; besides, the idea of a solitary meal at one of the grim Breven restaurants did not seem remotely appealing at this moment. "Thank you—you're very kind," Alleya said. "I don't want to be any trouble—"

Thomas waved his hand. "You honor us."

He came nimbly enough to his feet and led her on a winding journey through the camp. The bunched clouds seemed to gather more tightly overhead, which Alleya took as a sign that nightfall was nearing. It was hard to tell. The rain, for the moment, had stopped.

Thomas halted outside a large, noisy tent that seemed to bulge outward from the force of uproarious merrymaking within. "Sheba!" he called. "Sheba sia a Cholita! Stop chasing your man around and come out and greet your visitors!"

There was a shout of laughter from perhaps a dozen people inside—men and women, from the sound of the voices, adults and children—and within moments a tall, well-built young woman emerged. She was somewhat ostentatiously smoothing her hands down her skirt and across her hair, as if to cover up traces of lovemaking, but in fact she looked quite neat and trim.

"Why, Thomas, if I had known you wanted some fun with

me, I would have waited till you arrived," she said with mock innocence. "You know that Laban only satisfies me when I can't have you."

Thomas turned to Alleya. "This is how an old man is teased," he complained. "Age is a sad thing, because youth is so cruel."

Alleya was peering through the open tent flap at the jumble of faces and limbs inside. "How many people are in there?" she asked.

"Ten. Well, nine now that I'm outside," Sheba amended. "Laban, and my two sisters and their lovers, and Laban's brother, and three children. And my sister is expecting a child this spring."

"Do they all have tents nearby?"

Sheba and Thomas both laughed. "Oh, no! We all share one tent. We are never there, of course, except to eat and sleep, so we enjoy the times when we are all together."

"But you—isn't it crowded, ten people in that little tent?"

Sheba glanced back at the tent as if she'd forgotten its dimensions. "It's a *big* tent," she said happily. "Laban wove it for me the first summer we shared a blanket. The others gave away their small tents so we could all stay together."

At Alleya's sustained look of astonishment, Thomas added, "We Edori cannot stand to be apart. A solitary Edori is a wretched man. The more of us that are together, the happier we are."

Alleya laughed and shook her head. "And I find the angel holds to be crowded," she remarked. "And I have a room to myself. No doubt you Edori would find that a lonely place."

Thomas shuddered. "Intolerably," he said.

Sheba gestured back toward the tent. "Have you come to join us for dinner?" she asked. "I assure you, angela, there is plenty of room. Come inside. You'll see."

"No, you can't steal her. She is dining with me," Thomas said. "But she did come here looking for you."

Sheba smiled at the angel with complete unselfconsciousness. "For me? I will be glad to help in any way I can."

"Thank you, but now I'm not sure you can," Alleya said. "I was looking for a man who would have been your brother, a man about my age. But Thomas says there is no such man."

"There was a boy born to my parents three years before my birth," Sheba said readily. "But he died when I was two years old. He ate some poisonous flowers that bloomed on the northern slopes of the Verde Divide. I have never seen those flowers anywhere else."

"No, that is the only place they grow," Thomas said thoughtfully. "A sad tale, though I have heard it before." He turned to Alleya and made a little nod of apology. "I'm sorry, Alleya, I was wrong. There was a son. I am embarrassed that I did not know of him."

"My parents missed the Gatherings for many of those first years they were together," Sheba explained. "My father spent that time working for the Manadavvi. He wanted to be a landowner, my mother said, and he thought he might earn enough money to buy a farm in Gaza."

"From the Manadavvi?" Alleya said, and she could not keep the edge from her voice. "They give up land to no one."

Sheba smiled at her. "That's what my father eventually learned, and so my mother finally persuaded him to return to the Edori way. I remember none of this, of course, but my mother told me the stories many times."

"And you have no other brothers?" Alleya asked. "Your father—Cyrus—he had no other sons?"

Sheba shook her head. "None that were ever mentioned to me. I don't think there could have been any. My father was a very loving man who could not stand to be away from his daughters for more than a day. I don't think he could have left any child behind."

"Well, then . . ." Alleya said, and let her voice trail off. She knew she should be deeply disappointed, even anxious, because she had nowhere else to look for the mysterious son of Jeremiah. But instead she felt relieved, almost exuberant, freed from a sentence of drudgery. It was hard to understand. She did not pause to analyze. "Thank you, anyway. I'm sorry to have kept you from your family for nothing."

Now Sheba's smile was radiant. "It was not nothing to meet you!" she exclaimed. "I wish you would stay for dinner. I think you would like Laban and my sisters. And I am an excellent cook."

"Thank you again, but I promised Thomas—"

"Tomorrow night, then," Sheba urged. "We will have venison cooked in wine—"

"I don't plan to stay through tomorrow," Alleya said. "But perhaps some other time—and I do thank you."

It took a few more exchanges along these lines before Sheba finally let them go, and Alleya followed Thomas back through the narrow alleys to his own tent. It was now full dark and the damp air was thoroughly chilly. Alleya was pleased to see that the large communal campfire a few feet from Thomas's tent was strong enough to beat back both the cold and the dark. A few shadowy shapes moved around its edges, setting up logs to be used as seats and arranging food in convenient sites.

"I hope you don't mind," Thomas said. "I misled you when I invited you to dinner, for Martha and I share our fire with the Canbellas and the Malotas and any strays who care to join us, and there are always several of those. I'll have to introduce you to everyone. And this week we have had three more visitors join our campfire, and I'll introduce you to them as well. Although something tells me that you may already know one or two of them."

For Alleya was staring at a graceful, improbable shape outlined by the leaping firelight—the pristine arch of an angel's folded wings, and the unlikeliest of all angels at that. Delilah stood between two men, her hands stretched out to touch each man lightly on the elbow, her head thrown back in a laugh of genuine delight. Alleya was dumbstruck.

A fresh shock was to follow instantly. For, "Noah!" Thomas called, and the angel and both her escorts turned to face him. One was an Edori man Alleya had not met before, and the other was Caleb Augustus.

CHAPTER TWELVE

If someone had told him Jovah would be joining the Edori campfire that night, Caleb could not have been more surprised to see a visitor appear. For a moment, he truly thought he had conjured the angel by sheer force of longing, for he had been thinking of her a great deal the past few days. That, or he was hallucinating on the strong wine someone had pressed on him a few minutes before. It could not possibly be the Archangel come to join them at the Edori campsite in Breven.

But then he heard Delilah's musical, ironic voice say, "Why, Alleya! You do show up in the oddest places," and the dark-haired woman stepped forward to greet the blond one. "Can it be just coincidence, this second time, or have you been searching for me?"

"Coincidence, this time," Alleya said, her voice a little muffled. She, too, appeared to be wrestling with disbelief. "It had not occurred to me that you would have any business here."

"No business—merely pleasure," Delilah said lightly. "I take it you came on some grave mission?"

"I was looking—it's not important," the Archangel replied, and Caleb thought he saw a flutter of embarrassment briefly decorate her face. "I came on an errand and plan to stay only for the meal. What about you? Are you staying long?"

"I don't quite know," Delilah said, and now she affected a languid tone. "My friends came to—do something mechanical, I think—and I have no idea how long they're staying. I, as you might imagine, am purely ornamental. But I'm dependent on their transport."

"Transport?" Alleya repeated neutrally.

"It's the most amazing vehicle! I'm sure they'd give you a ride in it if you asked them, although it's not as much fun as you might think. Noah invented it—by the way, do you know Noah? I believe you've met Caleb."

Alleya's eyes flickered to Caleb, then back to Delilah. "No, I haven't met Noah. But I've heard of him." She stepped forward as Delilah made the introductions, offering her hand. Caleb watched as the Edori reluctantly took it. "You have a friend in Velora who mentioned your name to me," Alleya said, smiling. "His name is Daniel, but his clan escapes me."

Noah managed to return a small smile. "Oh, yes! Daniel and I go way back. We were always inventing wheels and tools and odd gadgets to make camp life a little easier."

Thomas bustled forward, clapping one hand on Noah's shoulder, offering the other to the Archangel. "Time enough to visit when your plate's full," he said, urging them back into the circle of firelight. "Can't you see everyone else is eating? All the food will be gone if you just stand here talking!"

Once more Alleya's eyes found Caleb's, once more she looked away. "Yes, I'm quite hungry now," she said with her usual courtesy. "Everything smells so good."

There was a general jostling at the food tables as the five of them joined the other latecomers and those returning to the big pots and cauldrons to take their second helpings. Unobtrusively, Caleb maneuvered himself behind Alleya at the serving table, and he was hard on her heels as she moved over to the campfire, looking for a place to sit.

"Here," he said, touching her on the arm. She started so violently, she almost dropped her plate. He responded with a crooked grin. "I didn't mean to frighten you," he said.

Now she smiled. "Not frightened," she murmured, "taken unaware. Is this where you think we should sit?"

It was a half-sawn log draped with a ragged quilt, and it looked a little more comfortable than some of the other perches; more than that, it was separated by a few feet from the other makeshift seating, offering what passed in the Edori camp for privacy. Alleya settled herself carefully, balancing her plate in one hand and spreading her wings behind her. Caleb flopped less gracefully beside her.

"*Tell* me," he said, before she had a chance to speak a word, "what can you possibly be doing here?"

She had taken a bite of food. Maybe he imagined the mischief in her eyes as she took her time about chewing and swallowing. "But I was following you, of course," she said at last.

So he had read the mischief right. "As glad as I would be to hear that," he said dryly, "I cannot believe it's true. But if you don't want to tell me—"

"Oh, it's not a secret," she said. "I was looking for a man whom Jovah had identified—had not, as it turns out, identified very *well*—but he isn't here. Apparently he died as a child."

Caleb shook his head. "That is not a lucid explanation. Why did Jovah single him out? And how did he? And if he's dead—well, what was the point?"

"Exactly," she said on a long sigh. "And if this man wasn't the one Jovah wanted, then who am I really looking for?"

His expression must have been pained, for Alleya laughed and launched into a fuller explanation. "I went to the oracles to ask Jovah about all our recent troubles—storm, flood—you know what I mean. I asked if anyone on Samaria could help us solve these problems, and he told us to look for one of the descendants of the Archangel Gabriel. And the oracle Mary and I were able to eliminate most of them for one reason or another, but he did say that this man Cyrus—who was a descendant—had taken an Edori woman as a mate, and that they'd had a son. And I thought this son might be the man we wanted. But he's dead."

Caleb was still confused; he was convinced she was leaving out vital parts of the story, but he didn't want to press her if she preferred not to tell him. "You were talking to Jovah?" he asked instead. "I didn't know that was possible."

"Well, not face-to-face," she said, laughing. "We weren't actually *speaking*. Haven't you ever been to see one of the oracles?" He shook his head. "Well, all of their retreats have these amazing"—her hands described a square—"panels of glass, except it's not just glass. There's a light behind the glass and it's all connected to some strange machine. It's called an interface. And you can form letters on this interface to ask Jovah questions, and then you wait a while, and his answers appear. It's the most incredible thing."

His mind was racing, trying to fit this description into some familiar context; but it literally made no sense to him. "I can't even guess how something like that might work," he said. "I can't even visualize it. And you say you can ask Jovah—anything?—and he answers? Just like that?"

"Well, sometimes he answers in a more direct way than at other times," Alleya said, and he detected a slight note of bitterness in her voice. "Lately his answers have been very—how can I say?—circuitous. Open to interpretation. But he does answer."

"Can anybody go up to him and ask him questions?"

"No, of course not! You must ask through an oracle, because they're the only ones who know how the interface works—and they're the only ones who know the language Jovah speaks." Alleya fell abruptly silent as she said the last words, then tossed her head as if to shake away a worry. "But if you'd like to see this for yourself, I'll take you sometime to visit Job at Mount Egypt."

"I would like to very much," he said, smiling down at her. "I would be interested in witnessing a communication from the god."

"And would that make you a believer?" she asked softly.

"Well, it might. But I won't make any promises, angela."

She touched the gold clasp in her hair. He had noticed immediately that she was wearing it. "Angela?" she repeated. "You called me Alleya when you left me this."

"I'm more of a coward in person," he admitted.

"Aren't we all. But I wanted to thank you for the gift. It was very thoughtful."

"Not brazen?"

She laughed. "From the adventurous outspoken Caleb Augustus? I thought it was restrained."

He was grinning broadly. "Just wait," he promised. "See what I buy you in Breven."

"I won't be here long enough to qualify for presents. I'll be leaving tomorrow at first light."

"Where are you staying?"

"Well, I didn't think I could turn down the meal, but as soon as I'm done here I'll head on back into the city and find a hotel."

"You can't do that!" he exclaimed. "Alone—in Breven!"

She looked amused. "I hardly think anyone will mistreat me. Unlike our gentle friends here, I think most everyone in the city will recognize me and handle me with caution."

He shook his head again. "It's not like Luminaux, or Velora, or even the river cities. Breven is—it's a nasty place. Especially at night. Especially for a woman. Alleya, they don't even let their women out of the house during the *day*."

"Well, but I think I'll—"

"Here's where you've been hiding!" a voice came booming out of the darkness. Caleb glanced up quickly to find that Thomas, Noah and Delilah had strolled the perimeter of the fire, presumably to find them. "I can't believe the nerve of you allali men! I invited the angel to join *my* campfire, and you've monopolized her all night."

"Happily, it would appear," Delilah murmured.

Caleb was on his feet. "Thomas, tell her," he said urgently. "She can't return alone to Breven tonight."

Thomas's bantering tone instantly vanished. "No, angela, it really isn't safe," he said. "We allow even our children to roam free in Luminaux, but in Breven—no one goes about alone, even by daylight. Surely you weren't thinking of leaving tonight?"

Alleya, looking exasperated, rose slowly, fanning her wings behind her. "Thank you for your concern," she said. "But I think I'll be just fine. I'm used to traveling alone."

But Delilah, of all people, was shaking her head. "I wouldn't, Alleya," she said with unwonted seriousness. "Not Breven. The Jansai are not much to be trusted."

"But then—I suppose I could fly back tonight, as far as Castelana, maybe. . . ."

"Angela!" Thomas exclaimed. "Of course you will stay right here! There is always room for one more. In fact, we would be insulted if you left."

Alleya cast a quick, despairing glance around the densely packed campsite. Caleb had never heard her say so, but he would guess she was not a woman who enjoyed a crowd. "I do not like to trade so much on your hospitality . . ." she began, and Delilah laughed aloud.

"Poor Alleya! She's too polite to say that she can't sleep in a tent with more than a dozen people in it. You can stay with me, all right? I've been given a tent all to myself, as a special mark of favor. It's small, but I think the two of us will fit."

Caleb caught Noah's swift look at Delilah, but the angel appeared oblivious. Ah—probably she had just scotched a rendezvous, Caleb decided, and thought better of her for making the sacrifice on Alleya's behalf. Alleya, on the other hand, looked trapped and unhappy, but she made a valiant effort to cover her unease.

"Well, then—what can I say?" she responded, essaying a smile. "You have convinced me. Thank you for your offers—Thomas, Delilah—and I will certainly stay the night. I do appreciate your concern."

Thomas brought his hands together in a single slap of applause. "Good! That's settled. Now it's time for singing."

As Caleb had learned during the past two days in camp, singing was a nightly occurrence and one that the Edori approached with exuberance. Everyone joined in, or at least came together in the center of the camp to listen. Already the other diners, finished with their meals, were gathering around the most central of the campfires, dragging mats or pillows or small logs with them to sit on. Thomas ushered before him Martha, Noah, Caleb and the two angels, making sure they all had prime seats in the inner ring closest to the fire. Caleb found himself between Noah and the Archangel; Delilah sat on the other side of Noah, and Thomas and Martha on the other side of Alleya.

"So what happens next?" Alleya murmured to Caleb.

"It's very informal," he replied in an undertone. "Whoever feels like singing will rise to his feet, look around to make sure no one else is also standing, and then launch into whatever song moves him."

"Do they sing masses?"

"Not that I've ever heard. Or maybe they have their own version of sacred music, but I haven't been able to identify it."

"Do they—" Alleya began, but instantly fell silent as two young women stood and glanced around the fire. When they had verified that they had the stage, one of the girls nodded three times to give her friend the count, and they began singing at exactly the same moment. Caleb listened appreciatively. These two had sung on the night of his arrival, and he remembered distinctly the sweetness of their blended voices and the plaintive thread of the melody. Thomas had told him that the oldest one was the songwriter, and Caleb had been impressed. She did not look more than fourteen years old.

He glanced at Alleya to see how she liked the music. She was leaning slightly forward, hands braced on her knees, listening intently. When the girls hit a particularly beautiful harmonic, he saw Alleya's head arc backward slightly, as if she'd been struck, and then she smiled faintly. Yes, the Archangel was enjoying the concert.

Enthusiastic applause greeted the end of the song, and another singer was on his feet before the last few cheers had died away. This was a man about Caleb's age, perhaps in his midthirties, with a light, polished voice and a penchant for lively tunes. He, too, had entertained them a couple of nights ago. When he finished, a woman rose to stand beside him, and the two of them sang a rollicking duet that had everyone in the audience laughing and clapping along. They also were zealously applauded after the last note.

The next several singers turned to more sober music—love songs, lullabies and ballads. Caleb remembered hearing Noah sing one of these while they were on the road, and he glanced over at his friend to see if he recognized it. Noah, however, did not seem to be paying much attention. He had leaned over and was whispering in Delilah's ear. But the angel stared straight before her and did not appear to be listening. Caleb swung his eyes back around to the performers.

And soon enough, he had his own distraction whispering in his ear. Politely waiting for the brief pause between acts, Alleya touched him on the arm and murmured, "Do they ever sing in Edori?"

"Every once in a while," he replied softly. "Thomas was bemoaning that fact the other day—that so many of the younger Edori had forgotten their old language. So you rarely hear it."

"I don't know that I've ever even heard it spoken. I understand it's a beautiful language."

"Maybe we'll make a special request," he said.

But they didn't have to. Perhaps an hour into the music, when children had begun to fall asleep and even the moon looked weary, when all the selections had become haunting and sad, one of the older Edori women came to her feet and glanced carefully around at the assembled listeners. All faces turned expectantly in her direction; even the tired ones stirred.

"So that we never forget," she said simply, and then began to sing one of the old ballads in the original Edori tongue. She had a high, true voice, silver and thin, and she delivered her notes plainly. Something about the melody, or the foreign words, or the quality of her voice itself, invested the song with an eerie significance. Caleb felt disembodied, hurled backward, re-created at a campfire hundreds of years ago where the words to this song were being delivered for the first time. Among the faces of the Edori he knew were scattered a few of the long-ago Edori, listening gravely to the message of the lyrics, impressing the words forever on their hearts. The singer's voice became stronger, more urgent; she raised her arms slowly in a gesture of entreaty to the god, and held them out, pleading, a long moment after her final note had sounded.

Silence reigned until she dropped her hands, and then the mad applause went on for more than ten minutes. Alleya tugged on Caleb's sleeve. "What was she singing?" she said in his ear.

He shook his head, and leaned across her to address Thomas. "What was the gist of that song?" he asked.

Thomas almost had to shout to be heard. "It is a recitation about the floods that visited Samaria shortly after the first settlers arrived. It is a reminder to Jovah that we are his people and we worship him, and a prayer to him to never forget us that way again."

Caleb saw Alleya's sharp look at the Edori. "Floods?" she repeated. "I don't remember reading about this."

Thomas smiled. "Well, it happened centuries ago. And I don't suppose it really affected anyone except the Edori. It was, oh, fifty or so years after Samaria was colonized, and most of the settlers were still living in Bethel and southern Gaza. The Edori, of course, had been on the move since their arrival. The floods washed across the southeast tip of Jordana, maybe one hundred miles south of where we are now. Drowned about a dozen Edori. There weren't as many Edori then, so it was quite a tragedy."

"So! They had weather problems six hundred years ago, too," Caleb said cheerfully, and was surprised to earn his own quick look of concern from Alleya. He arched his eyebrows at her. "What?" he said.

She shook her head. "I was just thinking . . . That's the same place that's going to flood now if these rains don't let up." She turned back toward Thomas. "What caused the flood then, do you know? Was it rain? Or was it one of the rivers rising—maybe too much snow melting up in the mountains?"

"The song doesn't say," Thomas replied. "Does it matter?"

"I don't—I was just wondering."

"Odd, though, that what's essentially a desert would flood more than once within our memories," Caleb remarked. He was surprised to receive yet another swift, unhappy look from Alleya.

"Not odd," she said, almost too softly to hear, "if Breven had not been a desert to begin with."

"What?" he said again, but she did not have a chance to answer. A tall, handsome Edori man was standing over them and smiling down.

"It would be such an honor," he said to Alleya, "to have the Archangel sing for us."

More of those rapid glances, as the angel looked from Thomas to the new arrival. Caleb guessed that Alleya had believed she was here incognito; Edori were not big on ceremony, and probably no one had betrayed to her that they knew who she was. Thus she was caught completely off-guard.

"Oh—" she faltered, into what was suddenly an intent and expectant silence. "I've enjoyed hearing all of you so much," she said, clearly improvising. "I would not want to intrude my voice on yours."

"Sing for us, please sing, angela," Thomas urged, and from beside him, Martha added her quiet voice. The tall man held his hand out as if he would help her to her feet.

"No intrusion at all!" he said happily, taking her words at face value. "It is rare the Edori have a chance to hear angel voices lifted around their campfires. Our pleasure would be great if you could consent to sing for us now."

Clearly, there was no possible way to refuse. Caleb remembered what Delilah had said (years ago, it seemed): that it was torture for Alleya to perform in public except on holy occasions. He felt a deep sympathy for her—but had to admit to feeling an equally strong current of excitement. He had a sharp desire to hear this particular angel sing.

Alleya was on her feet, perforce, and then she made a quarter turn in the other angel's direction. "Delilah," she said. "We once sang the Benediccio Duet in D minor together. Do you remember? I wish you would perform it with me now."

For a fraction of a second, Delilah sat frozen, stubborn, as unprepared for this public invitation as Alleya had been. Then she laughed aloud and jumped to her feet.

"Yes, of course I remember it," she said. "I would be happy to sing with you. Only—we don't have quite enough room for both of us to stand here."

There were a few moments of fussing and confusion as the angels found a more suitable spot, and a low murmur of anticipation ran through the gathered Edori. Caleb glanced at Noah to see what he thought of this. In the past three nights of singing, Delilah hadn't once showed any inclination to join in, though it had been clear that her voice would be welcome. But the dark angel must have known, even better than Caleb, how much Alleya dreaded a public exhibition.

Noah's expression was one of guarded pleasure. "That was kind of the Archangel," he whispered to Caleb. "To invite Delilah to sing."

Caleb smiled. "It was kind of Delilah," he whispered back, "to agree."

The two angels now stood about three yards away, side by side but turned slightly toward each other. The whole crowd had grown unbelievably still; even the night birds and chirping insects had fallen quiet, it seemed, to listen. Delilah nodded twice, and the two women began simultaneously to sing.

It was as if the moon exploded, as if the stars spun into an iridescent dance. Light showered through Caleb's brain and careened down the veins in his arms, his legs, with a tingling brilliance. His physical reaction was so strong that for a moment or two he could scarcely distinguish sound from sensation. By a great effort of will, he forced himself to concentrate, to focus on the music itself.

It was not a particularly complicated piece for sacred music, though the intricate harmonies and interlaced fugues were more complex than any of the other singers had attempted tonight. Obviously, the angels had been rigorously trained in delivery and technique; every word was flawlessly pronounced, every note precise. It was also clear that Delilah's voice was the stronger of the two, richer and more mellifluous. But Alleya's . . .

Her voice wove around Caleb's head like a strand of witchlight; it ruffled his hair like a hand stroking back from his face. He felt himself wrapped in her voice, clothed in it, made warm against the winds of the world; and at the same time it sent sparks through the interior of his body, lighting the caverns over his lungs, shooting fire through his hollow bones. He was lit from inside; surely his eyes glowed like lamplight and his lifted hand would be translucent from that inner flame. Even his flesh was burning; he could feel the flickering heat wash once across his body, then coalesce into a sharp, painful brand on his upper right arm. He slapped his left hand across the knot of fire, as if to extinguish it, and felt only the cool, buried glass of the shattered Kiss in his arm.

Involuntarily he glanced down—and then he stared. In the black heart of that cold marble danced a flame of scarlet and opal. The sound of Alleya's voice had brought the fire to life, when the Kiss and everything it stood for had been dead to Caleb for years. He had never heard of such a thing happening. He squeezed his fingers tightly together, but even so, the fey, hot light seemed to leap through, turning his fingers crimson and his palm amber.

In the morning, Caleb's first waking thought was that he must speak to Alleya before she left. And she seemed like the kind of woman who would rise early and be productively on her way before anyone else had stirred. Thus, he rolled to his feet almost as soon as he opened his eyes. Carefully, he tiptoed out of the tent he had shared with Noah, Thomas, Martha, and two of their grandchildren.

He was not the first person in the camp to wake; about a dozen of the Edori women were already at their fires, fanning the flames and mixing bread for breakfast. He asked around; no one had seen either of the angels emerge from their tent. Quickly, he ducked into the water tents which were used for communal bathing, and made himself presentable. Then he snagged a chunk of bread from a smiling Edori woman and loitered until Alleya stepped into view.

He gave her time to visit the water tents as well, but he was waiting for her when she returned. She seemed startled but not displeased to see him.

"What are you doing awake so early?" she asked. "I would have pegged you as a late riser."

"Not at all," he said, smiling down at her. Even under camp conditions, she managed to look clean and fresh. Her hair, now damp from a quick washing, had been combed out of its usual knots, though he imagined it would tumble free of its coiffure in a matter of hours. "And certainly I didn't want you to leave before I had a chance to say goodbye."

"That was thoughtful. Though I'll probably stay for an hour or two. I thought maybe—" She hesitated, shook her head. "Maybe Thomas or one of the other Edori could tell me more of the oral histories. Maybe I could learn something."

He guided her gently toward one of the tenanted fires and nodded to the woman stirring a pot of porridge. She brought them steaming bowls and mugs of milk. They sat to eat.

"Learn something about what?" he asked.

"Weather patterns six hundred years ago."

He couldn't keep the amusement from his voice. "But for what reason?"

Again she paused, as if uncertain whether or not she should tell him. "I've been reading," she said slowly, "old history books that were translated from texts written about the time of the settlement. And I learned—well, I learned many odd things but the oddest was that the original settlers had decided they couldn't live on Samaria unless they could change its weather cycle. Essentially, the whole continent was a flood plain. And one of the reasons Jovah created angels"—she paused to consider something, then moved on—"was to control the storms."

"Which now for some reason they can no longer control," Caleb finished thoughtfully. Now her interest became explicable. "And you want to know what might happen if they can never regain control."

"That, and if such a thing happened in the past. The angels' records are not particularly helpful on these points. Mostly they just glorify the deeds of the past Archangels and gloss over any unpleasant events. But the Edori seem a little more—clear-eyed."

"Yes, I think it's an excellent idea," he said approvingly. "Stay all day. Stay a few days. I think there is much to learn."

She smiled faintly. "Well, I think I'll find out what I need to know this morning. I have to leave this afternoon at the latest, because I must be back at the Eyrie in a few days."

"What's happening at the Eyrie?"

"Well—" She sighed. "I have to prepare for a meeting in Semorrah in, oh, not quite three weeks from now. The Manadavvi and the river merchants and even the Jansai are unhappy with the state of the realm. I need to think of how to calm them."

"Maybe Delilah could help you," he suggested.

She smiled again, ruefully. "A good thought. I had it myself. But she—" Alleya spread her hands wide.

"She won't advise you," he guessed.

"Can't, won't, it's hard to tell. I think she feels so betrayed by Jovah that she no longer trusts herself with men. Does that make sense? She was the most extraordinary politician ever. She could make anyone agree with her. But now that the god won't listen to her, she thinks no one else will either. At least, that's what I think I read behind her words last night. But I did ask her."

"Maybe, in time—"

She rose to her feet. "Maybe in time the sun will shine again and all our worries will dry up and float away," she said. "I see your friend Noah looking for you. You must have plans for the day."

Caleb glanced over his shoulder. It was Noah, all right, but he looked to be loitering much as Caleb had done earlier, and outside the same tent. A waste of time, of course; Delilah would not rise till noon. Caleb turned back toward Alleya.

"Much to do," he admitted. "But I didn't want—I hate to see—I wish I knew when I would see you again."

She flushed but she did not seem annoyed. "I'm usually at the Eyrie," she said. "If you're ever up that way again."

"Then you wouldn't mind? If I traveled there just to see you?"

"Of course, I'm busy much of the time," she told him. "And sometimes I'm *not* there. But no, I wouldn't mind. It would be—sometimes I need to—I enjoy your company," she ended, sounding almost as flustered as he had been. "It is hard being the Archangel," she added. "It's nice to talk to someone who's not too impressed by that."

"I'm impressed!" he exclaimed. "I think you're a wonderful Archangel!"

Now she smiled freely. "You know what I mean."

He smiled back. "I know what you mean. I'm happy to think you feel at ease with me. When can I come see you?"

She was flustered again. "When will you be done here? Of course, I'll be in Semorrah in a few weeks, and I'm not sure how long we'll have to stay—I don't know, a month from now?"

"A month! That's too long to wait. Maybe I'll come to you in Semorrah. How would that be?"

"Well, I'll be *very* busy in Semorrah," she said demurely.

"And I just remembered a project I have waiting for me in Luminaux when I get back," he said, scowling. "It might have to be a month after all. But you could come to Luminaux when you're done in Semorrah."

She laughed. "What would I be doing in Luminaux?"

"Visiting me. Is that not reason enough?"

She made a gesture of uncertainty. "If something brings me to Luminaux, I'll let you know."

"It will be good to see you again, angela," he said softly.

"And you, Caleb Augustus."

He wanted to touch her—take her hand, maybe, although the thought of kissing her did for a wild moment cross his mind—but Noah chose just that moment to join them. Caleb had never been so irritated with his best friend; incredibly, Alleya was laughing.

"I don't suppose Delilah's awake yet, is she?" Noah asked.

Caleb snorted. "In your dreams."

"She said she would go with us to the docks this morning, and I told her we'd be leaving early," the Edori answered.

"She was awake when I got up," Alleya said, "but I don't think she was quite ready to join the world. If you know what I mean."

"We've seen Delilah in the morning," Caleb assured her. "We know what you mean."

But the dark angel belied them all. Even as they were discussing her, she stepped languidly from the tent and looked about her with a disapproving eye.

"Once again, the sun conspires to make me wretched," she announced. "Surely it cannot be morning again so soon."

"Morning, and in less than an hour we're on our way into Breven," Caleb said cheerfully. "So you'd best hurry to make yourself beautiful, or at least passable, for our trip."

She gave him a look dripping with revulsion. "I strive to meet the level of my companions," she drawled. "I could go now."

The men laughed, and the three of them exchanged a few more bantering remarks. When Caleb turned back to finish his goodbye to the Archangel, he found that she had slipped away, for he saw her on the other side of camp, deep in conversation with one of Thomas' cronies. He could not help his sharp sense of loss, though it seemed ridiculous. What did it matter that he would not see her again for three weeks or more? She was a delightful woman, but he scarcely knew her. No need to feel like a heartsick lover on the verge of his last farewell.

The short, uncomfortable trek into Breven did little to help Caleb shake off his unaccustomed depression. They had briefly considered driving the Beast into town, but the thought of attempting to negotiate Breven's narrow streets with the unwieldy vehicle instantly dissuaded them. Since angels had notoriously bad luck attempting to ride horses, and Delilah had flatly refused to attempt such a feat, they had borrowed a cart and a couple of geldings to pull it, and jounced down a bad road into the industrial city. Thomas handled the reins and Caleb sat beside him on the front seat; Noah and the angel arranged themselves as best they could in the back. Riding in the unsprung cart was unpleasant enough, but the constant cold drizzle made the trip even more dismal. And Breven itself was enough to make the happiest man feel despondent. None of them talked much till they arrived at the teeming docks.

But here the atmosphere was so much livelier, and the salt breeze made the damp air seem so much cleaner, that they all began to revive. In the warren of identical tumbledown buildings lining the wharf, it took them a little time to locate the shipbuilder they had visited just the day before, but soon enough they were tying the horses up outside his office and following his call to come inside. Here the walls were lined with sketches of ships of every conceivable design, and fabulously detailed miniature models were scattered on every available surface. Caleb looked around admiringly. This was a man as dedicated to the shipbuilding profession as Caleb was to his own.

That was one fact that had made Caleb feel more comfortable about joining this mad enterprise. The second one was even more potent: The shipbuilder and his partners, both women, were Edori; and they all planned to join the exodus to Ysral. Any ship they built would withstand the worst that the ocean had to offer.

"Come in, come in, you're right on time," the shipbuilder greeted them, pulling up chairs and waving to an array of refreshments on a side table. "Anyone hungry? Thirsty?"

"I could stand something to drink, thank you, Marco," Thomas said, and so with a little more shuffling they all fortified themselves and found their seats. Caleb let Noah and Thomas take the chairs closest to Marco's so they could lean over the unrolled blueprints and diagrams. Noah had done most of the work on the engines themselves, though Caleb had spent long hours going over every formula. His main function had been to question how well certain theories would work in practice and to carp at simple design flaws. But he had been impressed; Noah's work was always sound, but this had been virtually flawless.

"And we're estimating three hundred people per boat," Marco was saying, tapping on his drawing to indicate living quarters or hold space. "So you've allowed for their approximate weight, I assume?"

"Setting an average of two hundred pounds per person, which is high," Noah said, "since some of them will be children."

"And allowing for food, water, a certain tonnage in luggage—?"

"All that."

"How much space would be required? For the equipment itself and for its fuel?"

Caleb let Noah give the answers and ask his own questions; all of this they had gone over before late-night campfires back in Luminaux and on the road to Breven. It still seemed incredible to him, but here were rational human beings seriously discussing the machinery they would use to propel themselves into a fantasy: *four ships carrying three hundred people each; food for twelve hundred people for four months, water, fuel, living quarters . . .*

Jovah spare him the horrors of such a trip. How could anyone be sanguine enough, or fool enough, to contemplate such a venture—no map, no destination, no timetable. No proof. Even the thought of drowning in the rising waters of Samaria would not be enough to induce him to strike out for the mythical Ysral.

Delilah brushed her fingers along his arm to get his attention, then leaned over to whisper in his ear. "What do you think their chances are of finding Ysral?"

"About as good as their chances of surviving the trip," Caleb said dryly. "Zero."

"Really? You don't think they'll find it?"

Caleb spread his hands. "How can they find it if it doesn't exist? I think they will sail till they run out of food and water, and they will die a miserable death in the middle of the salty ocean."

"Even if they don't find Ysral, they may find some kind of land," Delilah said. She was about as serious as Caleb had ever seen her. "Some pretty island in the middle of the sea. Don't you think? And once they find it, they can name it whatever they want, and live there happily the rest of their lives."

Caleb shrugged. "Maybe. I certainly hope so. I hate to think twelve hundred people will just—" He shrugged again.

"I can't believe this talk from you!" she said, keeping her voice low. "You, the experimenter, the inventor—"

"I don't risk my life with my experiments," he said, although that wasn't true; the smoky Kiss in his arm could attest to that. Still. "I take my hazards one at a time. One person at a time, at any rate. If I were going to set off to find Ysral, I'd send one ship with maybe twenty men. I'd let them make the exploration and draw the maps—and I'd have them come back safe and whole before I sent out a thousand men on an idiot's mission."

"But don't you see?" she said softly, "they're not concerned with safety. They're concerned with living."

"Well, they'd better be concerned with dying!"

"That doesn't matter to them. They're dying, anyway. Or at least, they don't consider this life they have worth living. Better to die grandly than to waste slowly and unhappily away."

Caleb glanced over at the three men gathered so tightly around their diagrams. Their expressions were alive, intense, passionate. "I've never met an unhappy Edori," he said. "They've always been among the sanest and most cheerful people I knew. That doesn't look like a slow death to me."

Delilah shook her head slowly. "That's because you have no imagination," she said.

He was about to protest that fairly hotly when the three Edori came to their feet. "Let's go take a look," Marco was saying. "You can tell me if the dimensions meet your specifications."

Caleb and Delilah also rose. "Are we going somewhere?" the angel inquired.

"Two of the ships are almost completed," Noah said. "We're going to go take a look."

"Does anyone need to borrow a cloak? It'll be raining," Marco said. He gestured to a rack hung with a mismatched assortment of coats and jackets.

Noah grinned. "We're getting used to it. We'll be fine."

But when they stepped outside, all of them were nearly blinded by the brilliant reflection of white sunshine off the wet surfaces of the docks. Marco covered his eyes with an exclamation of surprise, and both Thomas and Noah automatically turned their faces up to feel the loving hand of sunshine across their cheeks. Caleb was amazed at how good it felt, that sudden slight warmth in the sluggish, humid air. Like the others, he felt a smile stretch his face; he felt his heart perk up and his feet lighten.

He turned to Delilah to make some joking remark and found her, too, with her face lifted toward the sky. Unlike the others, she was not merely reveling in the miracle of sunlight. She was assessing the clouds, judging the angle of the sun, making some calculations unfathomable to Caleb, who watched her a moment in silence. When she sensed his gaze on her, she turned to him and smiled, but her expression remained sad, a little wistful.

"Alleya," she said simply, and nodded her head. Before Caleb could respond, she hurried forward to catch up with the men, and fell in step beside Noah as they started strolling toward the pier.

Chapter Thirteen

For Caleb, the next two days passed in much the same manner: Days spent at the Breven docks, going over questions and problems with Marco and his partners; nights spent around the Edori campfires, listening to songs and stories. It was a good life and he enjoyed himself, but he had his concerns as well. He liked these people, and he had to admire their nerve, though it grieved him to think that Thomas, Martha, Sheba, Laban and all those he had come to care about would in a matter of months be lost. Noah had warned him not to attempt to dissuade anyone from making the trip, so he kept his mouth shut, but he couldn't keep from looking around the camp every night and tallying up the faces. *Alive now, but soon to be drowned at sea.* It was an eerie, unsettling feeling, and contributed to his growing restlessness. He would be glad enough when this trip was over.

The good weather that Alleya had prayed for lasted only a day. Soon enough, the clouds returned, as dreary and pot-bellied as ever. No doubt the constant rain was contributing to Caleb's malaise, though it appeared to have no ill effect on the moods of his Edori hosts. However, he could tell the weather caused Delilah some stress—more, perhaps, because she knew Alleya could change it and she could not. But she did not complain.

The day before they were scheduled to begin their return journey to Luminaux, only Noah, Caleb and Delilah made the trip into Breven. Noah needed one last set of blueprints, which had not been ready before. The weather was particularly nasty: Instead of the usual chilled drizzle, rain was coming down in a steady slantwise downpour, and there was simply no way to stay dry or comfortable in their borrowed cart. But Delilah insisted on accompanying them anyway, and the men rigged a tarpaulin over a hastily assembled framework to protect her as best they could. Poor visibility and a soggy road made the trip even slower than usual, and it was close to evening by the time they began their return trip to camp, full into the angle of the rain.

"Doesn't get much worse than this, I'd suppose," Caleb shouted to Noah as the Edori urged the horses faster once they were free of the city limits.

"Ice!" Noah shouted back cheerfully. "That's worse."

"But you wouldn't travel in it."

"Sure. Do it all the time."

"Edori are crazy."

Noah grinned. "Allali are weaklings."

"Smart, safe, *dry* weaklings."

But within a matter of minutes it became clear that they were contending with more than rain. The wind had picked up dramatically, and the sky, even allowing for the onset of night, was ominously black. Lightning spiked through the clouds, followed by the low growl of thunder. Caleb looked over at Noah.

"What do you think?" he called. "Should we turn back?"

He expected another derisive comment about gutless allali, but in fact Noah looked worried. The Edori glanced over his shoulder at the outlines of the city behind them, then twisted his head a little to get a look inside their improvised tent.

"I don't know! If there was somewhere to find shelter between here and the camp—"

Caleb thought of those flimsy, fluttering tents anchored so impermanently to the earth. No safety there. "Let's go back!" he shouted. "At least we'll have the wind behind us."

Noah nodded, and fought to turn the horses around back toward the city. They were spooked by another flash of lightning; the horse on the left pulled sharply against his harness, tangling the reins and confusing his yokemate, who came to a dead stop.

Noah whistled at them, shaking the reins free, and tried again to turn them.

Delilah poked her head through the slim opening of her makeshift shelter. "What's going on? Are we turning back?"

"Storm," Caleb said briefly. "Don't want to be stuck out here."

Her eyes widened as she took in the angry sky, which now resembled a purple bruise edged with a thin line of yellow. A sudden gust of wind rocked the cart, almost causing the tarpaulin to collapse on her head. The horses had come to a stubborn halt, legs braced against the sodden ground, refusing to move either forward or back. Impossibly, the rain came down harder.

"Let's go back!" she cried, and over the swelling rumble of the storm, Caleb could hear a note of panic in her voice. "It's getting worse! Let's go back while we can!"

Noah nodded and rose to his feet, sawing on the reins and shouting at the horses. With a start, they both leapt forward, causing Noah to pitch forward almost out of the cart. Caleb grabbed his seat; he heard Delilah give a little scream behind him. Now the rain was sluicing down so hard he could scarcely see—not the road in front of him, not the tarpaulin behind him. The horses were galloping helter-skelter into a gray wash of nothingness. Noah called and cursed, pulling on the reins to no avail.

"Help her!" Noah yelled in a hoarse voice. "We've left the road and we may flip over—"

Caleb turned and threw himself across the seat, reaching inside the tarpaulin for Delilah. The sky danced with lightning, illuminating an underwater world of racing silver lines. The cart rocked dangerously from side to side as it careened more and more violently across the uneven ground. A particularly nasty jolt flattened the soaked canvas over the back of the cart. Caleb had just caught Delilah's wrists when the tarp went down, and now he tried to haul her free. Dear Jovah, her wings, lacy and delicate; if he pulled her out too fast he would strip the feathers from her back.

"What are you doing? Get her out of there!" Noah shouted. Caleb held onto one of the angel's wrists, using his free hand to push back the canvas till her head was clear. In the scrim of rain, it was hard to see her face; she appeared to be crying.

"Noah thinks we're going to crash the cart!" he called to her. "We've got to get you out of here—"

He tugged; she wriggled; Noah fought the horses, who were now in a full-out desperate gallop. The wheels hit a shallow ditch, and the cart flew three feet in the air. Caleb wrenched Delilah into his arms, receiving a faceful of wet feathers. The cart slammed back down, knocking them all into each other, then bounced twice, hard. Suddenly, the world turned sideways and they were tumbled roughly into the morass of mud. Horses shrieked; wood cracked apart with a brisk, snapping sound. The heavens responded with their blazing, thundering applause.

It took a minute for the world to stop spinning, but Caleb forced himself to sit up, clear his head. Delilah lay beside him on the wet ground, facedown, sobbing; Noah, who had been thrown some distance from them, was crawling to her, calling out her name. Caleb staggered to his feet.

"I'll see about the horses!" he cried, and pushed through the curtain of rain to where the two panting animals stood, so caught in their harnesses that they could not move another step. Caleb disentangled them, talking in a low, soothing voice, but he could see by their flattened ears and wide eyes that they were ready to bolt again at any moment. He freed them of everything except their bridles. If they ran again, at least they would trample nothing and no one; at least they might have the sense to eventually find their way back to the camp.

He headed back to where Noah was crouched over Delilah, urging her to a sitting position. She was struggling for composure, breathing hard but no longer crying. All of them were soaked through, hair and clothing plastered to their bodies, rain running into their eyes and washing away vision.

Caleb dropped to a squat beside them. "We could turn the cart over, shelter under it till the rain passes," he suggested, shouting his words as he had shouted everything this afternoon.

"What about the horses?" Noah called back.

Caleb shook his head. "I think they're going to run. I set them free. We'll be walking back." He thought Noah might argue, but instead the Edori nodded. "If the rain ever stops," Caleb added.

"I think it will," Noah said. "It seems to be letting up already."

He was right. The sheets of rain seemed to be thinning out, and the lightning and thunder had subsided. Caleb rose to his feet to see if he could get any encouraging glimpse of shredding clouds and felt Noah stand beside him to look in the other direction. The wind, which had lashed at them all day, had fallen oddly still. The sky, at least where Caleb was looking, had turned a sickly green. But the rain was faltering; that seemed to be a good sign.

He turned to say so to Noah and found the Edori staring back at him with a stark look of terror on his face. Caleb whipped his head around to see what Noah had spotted, and the sight made him freeze: a black funnel-shaped cloud boiling down from the heavens, spinning lower and lower in the seconds that they watched.

"What in the god's name—!" Caleb cried, but Noah didn't stop to speak. The Edori grabbed Delilah's arm, yanked her to her feet, and started off at a dead run for the muddy ditch that had capsized their cart. Caleb sprinted beside them, calling out questions. But it was impossible even to hear himself. A rumbling behind them grew into a tremendous roaring, drowning out the noises of the world, filling everything—ears, eyes, bones—with its deafening commotion. Delilah stumbled and Noah jerked her back to her feet, then flung her down into the ditch and dropped beside her. He shoved her face into the mud and buried his own head. Caleb scrambled in next to them and burrowed in as far as he could go.

It was as if a thousand horses stampeded across them; it was as if the Beast and a dozen of its brothers charged over the ditch. It was like being thrown off a cliff. It was like falling backward into the cacophonous waters churning through the Gabriel Dam. It was like nothing Caleb had ever experienced. The swirling, bellowing mountain of black wind passed over them, raked its thousand fingers across their backs, seemed to lift the very ground they lay upon and spin it in one dizzying circle. The world was nothing but sound and motion.

And then the world was nothing but rain.

It took Caleb a good five minutes to realize that the tornado had passed, dragging its train of destruction behind it. He had trouble hearing, but perhaps that was only because the rain muffled everything; there might be nothing to hear. He pushed his heavy body to an upright position, peered around him as far as he could.

The landscape was barely recognizable. What little shrubbery grew in this part of the world had been ripped up and flung aside; rocks and boulders stood upended or plowed at unnatural angles back into the ground. Splinters of wood and metal strewn all about showed where their cart had been smashed to pieces. The bodies of the horses lay, broken and still, fifty yards apart.

Nothing and no one had survived except the three of them.

Caleb dropped down to his knees again to find Noah once more coaxing Delilah to lift her head, stop her tears, sit up, be all right. Caleb's heart went out to her. He had never seen anyone, not even a child, so frightened of anything, and he would not blame her if her tears did not cease for a week. No doubt she was remembering that last fatal storm she had lived through, but barely, when she lost nearly everything she cared about. That must have been even more terrible than this.

But she was trying. She was sobbing, but she was choking down on her sobs; she had her arms wrapped about her body as if to hold in the screams. She allowed Noah to draw her to her knees, to her feet. She swayed but she did not fall, and she kept only one hand on his arm to achieve her balance.

"The horses are dead," Caleb informed Noah in a low voice. The Edori nodded.

"We have to start back on foot," Noah said.

"Now? Can't we wait a little, till the rain stops?"

Noah shook his head. "This kind of rain never stops. If we don't find shelter somewhere, we'll all wash away. And unless we keep moving—" He glanced at the angel, whose eyes were closed in concentration. Caleb wondered if she was trying to cut off the flow of the tears or if she was trying to remember how to walk. "We'll get sick and die if we stay here," he ended abruptly.

Caleb nodded. "How long on foot?"

"In this? Hard to tell. A few hours. I'm trying to think where there might be shelter somewhere along the way."

But neither of them could remember anything suitable from

their previous journeys over this road. Grimly, they searched the remains of the cart, seeking any provisions that had escaped unharmed. They found no food, but the tarpaulin could be salvaged. Wet and bulky, it made an uncomfortable load, but it might be all they had to shield them against the oncoming night.

Eventually they set off blindly into the falling rain, trusting the Edori's sense of direction. The men took turns carrying the canvas and guiding Delilah along the path. She made no attempt to speak. Caleb had never seen anyone who made so perfect a picture of abject misery, and yet she never complained or asked them to stop. It occurred to him, finally, that she thought this was the end of the world; she was dead, or dying, or already in some unimagined hell. Protestations would avail her nothing now.

And he looked about him at the scarred landscape, ripped apart as by the god's own hand, and thought perhaps she was right. Something was ending, had ended, was self-destructing, here on the plains outside of Breven. And if here, why not in Velora and Luminaux? Why not in Bethel and Gaza? What would keep all of Samaria from coming brutally apart, since neither mortals nor angels could trust Jovah to guard them and keep them safe?

And he plodded forward into the relentless rain and understood a measure of Delilah's fear.

The Edori came for them about an hour later. Thomas and Laban were driving one of the big transport wagons, large enough to hold three wounded men, and following the route they had always taken into the city. Never had Caleb felt such overwhelming relief to see anybody. Quick queries established that the three of them were unharmed, though their horses were dead, and the camp had been out of the main trajectory of the tornado.

"But half the tents were blown apart anyway," Laban reported, helping Caleb dump the tarpaulin into the wagon. "Everything's upended and most of the fires are out. All the wood's wet, so you can hardly get anything to burn. It'll be a cold camp tonight if it doesn't stop raining."

"Was anybody missing but us?" Noah asked.

Laban grinned. He was a big, easygoing man who found life

almost universally agreeable. "Everybody else was smart enough to get back when the rains started," he said.

"Well, we were *coming* back," Noah said. "We were too far away."

"Didn't you think about staying in the city?" Thomas asked.

"Thought of it. Too late. The storm came up too quickly."

"You'll have to tell us about it," Laban said. "After dinner tonight. There's not many who feel a tornado dance across their backs and live to describe the sensation."

Noah glanced at Delilah, seated docilely in the back of the wagon. Caleb's eyes followed his. The angel had wrapped a dry blanket over her lap and shoulders, and she was huddled inside it in as small a shape as she could achieve. Even her wings seemed shrunken. Her dark hair was wildly disarranged, and her face was colorless. Her eyes were open, fixed on some point at the bottom of the wagon.

"I don't think this is going to be a story I'll want to tell tonight," Noah said quietly. "Not at this campfire."

"If there is a campfire," Thomas nodded. "I think we're all ready here. Let's go."

But there was a fire back at the Edori camp—just one, and everyone was gathered around it, but it was the most welcome sight in the three provinces, as far as Caleb was concerned. Noah cleared a place for Delilah right at the edge of the flames and covered her with pillows and blankets, but he was not the only one who fussed over the angel. Martha brought her food and Sheba brought her wine, and the children clustered around her, offering her their toys and their treasures if those would make her feel better. Martha tried to shoo them away once, but Delilah freed a hand from her blankets and waved them all back.

"I like to have them near me," she said, and her voice was husky as if she had been sick for a long time. "Maybe some of them would sing for me."

Which they did willingly enough, lifting their sweet untrained voices in a medley of songs cheerful and sad. Gradually Delilah warmed herself before the fire of their affection. She began to smile; she let the blankets slip from her shoulders and reached her arms out to take the smallest girl on her lap. The girl whispered something in Delilah's ear, and the angel actually laughed. Caleb, watching from the other side of the fire while he let his own bones dry out, felt a great compression ease from around his heart. She would be all right, then. Delilah had survived another devastation.

It was a few days later that he realized he was not entirely correct about that. They were on their way back to Luminaux, none of them looking forward to the tedious, uncomfortable journey in the rumbling Beast, and they had stopped for the night at one of the same campsites they had utilized on the way to Breven. This trip, Delilah joined in the fuel-gathering and fire-building; she was as active as either of the men. Caleb regarded this transformation with suspicion, but Noah seemed to view it as one more proof of the angel's overall wonderfulness.

This night, over the fire, they were discussing the Edori's upcoming voyage to Ysral. Caleb was asking Noah pertinent questions: When did the Edori plan to set sail? When did the engines need to be completed? When did Noah have to return to Breven? Delilah listened carefully to each query and reply.

"They plan to leave the week after the Gathering," Noah said. "One last chance to see all their brothers and sisters and friends. Then—off to Breven, off to the new land."

"Not much time," Caleb commented. "The Gathering is only a couple of months away."

"The boats will be ready by then. And the engines."

"You haven't changed your mind, have you?" Caleb said, as if he were joking, but he was seriously interested in the answer. "You don't intend to join them, do you?"

Noah laughed ruefully. "Half of my heart wants to go. What a splendid adventure! What a story to tell your children and your grandchildren! I sailed for Ysral and lived to tell the tale. But I—" He shook his head. "I have so much I want to do here. I have such a stake in the new technologies we are exploring. In Ysral, it will be a fresh new world, yes, but there will be so much work to be done. And none of it scientific. And science owns most of my heart." As he finished, he glanced at Delilah, but he did not say the words aloud: *And you own the rest of it.*

"Glad to hear it," Caleb said. "I'd hate to lose you to this Ysral venture."

"How many people are going?" Delilah asked.

"Twelve hundred. Well, there's room for twelve hundred,"

Noah amended. "I think, at last count, eight hundred had signed up. Which is a lot. Which is almost a fourth of the Edori."

"So few?" Caleb asked. "I thought the Edori numbered in the tens of thousands."

Noah shook his head. "Not even in our more glorious days. There have always been few of us, because the life is so hard. And now . . . We dwindle away by the hundreds every year. Soon there may be no Edori left—at least, no Edori roving Samaria, living together in tribes. We'll be scattered throughout the towns and villages, forgetting our traditions and our clan names."

"You sound like Thomas."

"All Edori sound like Thomas. These things worry us. That is why so many are sailing for Ysral."

"Freedom forever to live the untrammeled life," Caleb said with a little smile. "And goodbye forever to the angels and the allali."

Noah grinned. "And glad to see the last of them."

"Not all of them," Delilah said unexpectedly.

Both men turned to look at her in surprise. "What do you mean?" Noah asked.

"Not goodbye to all the angels," she said. "I asked. Thomas said it would be an honor."

"What would be an honor?" Caleb said, though the sudden clench of his stomach gave him the answer before she did. The look on Noah's face was one of profound horror.

"To have me along. They've agreed to let me sail with them for Ysral."

Chapter Fourteen

Alleya headed toward the rendezvous in Semorrah with no clear idea what she would say to the merchants and Manadavvi who awaited her there. She and Jerusha and Micah had agreed that their best course was to stress the importance of the Gloria, coming up in three short months, and the opportunities for disaster that it offered. *If we do not present a harmonious front to the god, will he not punish us with thunderbolt and destruction? Did it not happen in the time of Gabriel?* Her adversaries did not seem to have looked that far ahead; they appeared to be interested only in the profit potential of the present.

In her free moments, Alleya had continued reading her purloined history books, looking for more clues to catastrophes in the past. She had found very little that was weather-related once she got past the founding of Samaria, but one odd little story held her interest long enough to keep her up late one night, reading. It was the tale of an oracle named David who claimed to have come face to face with the god, having been whisked by Jovah's hand to a floating tower somewhere in the heavens over Samaria. David was generally considered mad, and his stories had been rigorously repressed even at the time. In fact, Alleya read the account in the old language because the translator had omitted it from his version, as if to keep the story from spreading down through the centuries.

But that did not help her solve the mystery of Jovah's inattentiveness now.

With a sigh, Alleya closed her books and went to look out her small window at the night panorama before her. It was late; she had been reading far too long for someone who planned to take off early the next morning. She had hoped for a comforting glimpse of the glittering night sky, but clouds shut out all light overhead, even the moon. Instead she gazed down at Velora, illuminated even at this hour by a multicolored mix of torchlight, gaslight and the new electrical light that burned with such a cool, unwavering fire. The world was changing even as she watched; no way to avert those changes.

She rested an elbow on the sill and pillowed her cheek in her hand. What was she going to say to Gideon Fairwen and Emmanuel Garone and Aaron Lesh? She had come close to begging Delilah for help, but none of her pleading had moved the dark angel. In fact, that night in the Edori tent, as they endlessly shifted and rearranged themselves in an attempt to get comfortable, they had come close to a shouting match that would have roused the whole camp.

"I understand! You feel hurt and angry and abandoned—I understand all that!" Alleya had exclaimed in what must have seemed like the most unsympathetic of voices. "But this is more important than you, and *you* must understand *that*! If the merchants and the Manadavvi choose to desert us, what happens to Samaria? What happens to the cities and the trade patterns and the lives of the farmers? How can we keep our society functioning at all if the most powerful members withdraw their support? It is not merely a problem of flooding across the eastern plains, Delilah—we are looking at the disintegration of the life we know. *Help* me. Tell me how to deal with them, what to say to them—"

"I don't have any idea!" Delilah had cried. "Even if I were whole, even if I were Archangel, what could I say to these people that you cannot? You think I don't see what is happening, what could happen, to all of us? Of course I do! I don't know how to stop it! Only Jovah can stop it, Alleya, only Jovah can hold us all together—and he can do that only if he listens to us, if he holds back the storms, if he proves to the merchants that he trusts the angels so that they should trust us as well. Does Jovah listen to you, Alleluia? Because he has not listened to me for a long time. How can I make the merchants believe in me if the god does not? How can you?"

But that had not helped at all. Alleya sighed again, propped her other elbow on the windowsill and leaned her other cheek on that hand. What would she say to the merchants, the Manadavvi, the Jansai, the angels? *Jovah listens to me, but only sometimes, and you should listen to me now.* That was sure to hold their attention. That was certain to keep them faithful. She closed her eyes once, tightly, then opened them again, and continued to watch the lights below as if they could flash her some kind of secret message.

She took off for Semorrah at first light—or what would have been first light if the early morning rains hadn't turned everything gray. It didn't seem worth the effort to pause and pray for sunshine, so she just endured the wet, feeling her hair, her clothes, the feathers of her wings, grow slick and sodden within the first five minutes of flight.

She had assumed the rain would clear up within ten or fifteen miles, but in fact, the farther she flew from the Eyrie, the more tempestuous the storm became. Once or twice she was caught by an unexpected gust of wind that tossed her above her course the way a playful father might toss his infant over his head, and she found this most unnerving. She was used to riding the currents, taking advantage of their dips and swirls; she was not used to having them treat her like a snowflake or an autumn leaf to be flung about at random.

Still, she had flown in worse, so she kept going. It was hard to gauge her progress, because the rain made every wingbeat heavier and slower; she thought it might take her half again as long to make it to Semorrah as it usually did. Which meant, if Samuel and her other angels followed her at noon as they planned, they might not make the river city till nightfall. She had told Samuel she wished to arrive alone and separately so the merchants did not feel threatened by a sudden eruption of angels into their city; in fact, she had just wanted a few extra hours of solitude, to think about her strategy and clear her head. As the storm worsened, she was beginning to regret her decision. This was not the sort of weather she liked to be caught in alone.

Another blast of wind shoved her sideways, temporarily causing her to lose her rhythm and her altitude. Alleya drove her wings hard, climbing higher, trying to peer through the curtain of rain below her to get a better sense of her bearings. She almost felt as if she could take her two hands and push aside the misty veil before her, it was that thick and substantial. Hard to see anything, really, not the ground below or the horizon ahead; it would be easy to miss her way. Another snarl of wind spun her backwards, made her dizzy. She fought to right herself and was amazed at how much strength it took.

Perhaps it was time for a weather intervention after all. She began to sing, tilting her head back to aid the prayer in its ascent to Jovah. She felt the words leave her mouth and disintegrate about her head in the sullen air. Hard to believe Jovah would heed that. She must go higher.

She increased the sweep of her wings, aiming for higher elevation, but the air around her was so thick that she felt herself tiring even as she started to climb. So thick that she felt her breath clog in her chest. She could not see, she almost could not move; for a moment she was suspended in a great, gluey web of clouds, wings extended and mouth sucking for air.

And then suddenly the wind shifted, roiled over her, shook her like dice in a cup. It lifted her feet over her head, dropped them back toward the earth as she was wheeled in a sickening circle. Now air currents pummeled her from two directions, rushing in on her, then jetting away. Her wings almost tore from her body. Instinctively she folded them forward, wrapped herself in their cocoon, and immediately felt herself plummeting toward the earth. A cry of panic ripped from her throat; she heard it unravel above her as she fell backward toward death.

Desperately, she unfurled her wings, beat them against the treacherous air. Like a skidding mountain climber grasping at a protruding root, she managed to catch herself, safe for the moment. She hovered briefly, panting for breath, trying to get a sense of the currents around her. Everything was wild, helter-skelter, malevolent; she could not read the pattern of the air.

Sudden small flurries caught her from below, from the left,

but she was able to ride them out, coast back to relative calm. What was happening here? This was no ordered movement of winds, no comprehensible mix of cold air and warm air doing a sinuous but predictable dance. She had tracked wind her whole life; she knew how it was supposed to behave. This was utterly random, mindlessly vicious. This was not wind under anyone's control—not hers, not Jovah's.

Even as the thought crossed her mind, she was rammed from behind by a solid wall of racing air; she was pushed before it like debris brushed away by a hand. Again, she cried out in terror; again, she lost the sound as the wind swept her back and forth, scrubbing her across the empty countertop of air. She tumbled over and back, like a child rolling down a hill. Again, she clamped her wings to her body to keep them from tearing from her back; and she felt herself plunging earthward with no way to halt her fall.

She slammed into a rocky soup of mud, and spun three times before she fetched up hard against a broad tree trunk. She couldn't breathe, she couldn't think, she couldn't see. Everything was pain and darkness and terror. Around her, the rain poured down in a fierce, defiant onslaught. It took her a long time to realize that the surface below her was stable ground, and would not betray her with sudden motion.

Shakily, she forced herself to sit up and check her damages. She was alive, that was one thing; and if she tried, she really could breathe. She could even open her eyes and look around her. The first thing she spotted was blood on her feathers, and the sight made her frantic. Dear Jovah, she had broken her wings. She was a cripple like Delilah. But a few seconds of experimentation brought a flood of relief. Her wings were sore, but functional; she was essentially whole.

But the blood had come from somewhere. Touching her face, her hands came away covered with a watery red liquid, so she must have cut her cheek or her lip or her forehead. Since she could see and could purse her lips, she supposed the injury was not profound. Of course, she might have split her head open, or even suffered a concussion; at the moment, she was too woozy to judge. But that could be dealt with later.

Next, she tentatively moved her arms, her legs. She thought

she had probably sprained her left ankle and she might have broken one or two of her left ribs; that half of her body burned with an excruciating fire. But every muscle responded and nothing appeared to be fixed at an awkward angle, so she didn't think she'd snapped a bone.

"Good news," she whispered, trying to cheer herself up. "The god was watching out for you after all."

And that was so patently untrue that it did her in. She started crying, and it seemed like hours before she was able to stop.

The storm cleared up about an hour later. Alleya had stayed that whole time under the shelter she had been flung to: a great, overhanging beech tree whose weeping branches created a makeshift, somewhat leaky chamber. She had managed to compose herself enough to administer rudimentary first aid, binding her ankle and her visible cuts with strips torn from the clothing in her backpack. Night was falling and the air was growing decidedly cooler. As a rule, angels had no fear of cold weather—their bodies were built to withstand the icy temperatures at flying altitudes—but Alleya felt weak enough to dread the thought of spending a night outside in the cold and the wet.

So she forced herself to her feet and limped her way clear of the clinging tree, and cast a long, considering look at the limpid sky overhead. She would have given anything to not have to take flight again, now, this evening. She was afraid her wings would not hold her suddenly tremendous weight; she was afraid the perfidious wind would rise again and wrench her from the sky. She knew that this was a fear that would never leave her, a fear that would grow stronger and blacker the longer it was left unattended. So she spread her great, damp wings, fluffed them twice, and took off on a slow flight as low to the ground as possible.

She had covered maybe fifteen miles when she saw the lights of a house below her. It had been clear to her from the first mile that she did not have the strength to make Semorrah tonight. Either she had lost more blood than she thought or adrenaline had sapped her body of all its reserves, but she was weak and dizzy and incapable of sustained effort. When she saw the lights, she banked immediately, and came down in a somewhat less than graceful landing in the center of a small assortment of buildings.

One of the modern farming conglomerates, no doubt; she'd swear that the exterior lights were electrically powered. Good. That meant whoever ran the place was probably sophisticated enough to hold a rational conversation with an angel—might even know which angel she was.

She staggered to what appeared to be the main entrance, almost sobbing every time her weight came down on her injured ankle, and wondered what she would say to whoever answered her summons. At the door, she pulled the chain that activated the interior chimes, leaning her head against the solid stone of the wall. *I am the Archangel Alleluia, I am in need of shelter for the night.* The words circled in her head, but she had no chance to utter them. As the door opened and light spilled festively out, onto her ragged clothes and her bloodstained wings, she crumpled silently into a dead faint at the feet of total strangers.

So she was a day late making her rendezvous in Semorrah. But all in all, she had to feel lucky. Her hosts did in fact recognize her—they had been petitioners at the Eyrie not more than three months back—and they instantly sent servants and children running for the proper medical supplies. Once Alleya revived and told her story, they insisted that she spend the night, maybe the next two nights, watching her wounds and recovering her strength.

Once she saw herself in a mirror, she had to agree.

She had a gash in the top of her head, half a dozen smaller slices around her cheeks and chin, and a spectacular bruise forming all around her left eye. Her hands and arms were a crisscross of scratches, and her left leg was purple from thigh to heel. She looked like the angel of death, she thought, smiling a little grimly. She would frighten anyone who laid eyes on her.

Although . . .

After she had been fed and tended and left blessedly alone to sleep, she lay back on her borrowed bed to think. Well, it was not the entrance she had planned to make, but it would be effective nonetheless. Who could fail to listen to her, who could doubt her sincerity, when she showed up with these proofs of Jovah's negligence on her face? She had to be careful, though, or she would misplay this. And it was her last trump in a very thin hand.

She slept past noon the next day and felt wretched enough

that she agreed to stay the rest of the day, trying to recuperate. She did insist on taking a practice flight around the outbuildings of the compound, and was vastly relieved to find her wings fully functional, though a little weary. She did not care if she broke every bone in her body as long as her wings were whole.

She went to bed early and rose with the farmers, eating a quick breakfast and thanking them profusely for their help. *Not at all, not at all, delighted to be of service to the Archangel.* She left as soon as she politely could, heading southeast toward Semorrah. The storm had thrown her decidedly off course, knocking her much farther north than she had thought possible. She had more than a hundred miles to go, and a desperately important meeting to be at in a few short hours.

She flew steadily and carefully through an entirely calm sky. After the first hour, her nerves steadied and she lost most of her fear. Though it was a fear that she was sure would never leave her completely. And she might never have the courage to fly through a storm again.

And this world was turning into nothing but storms.

She made it to the Galilee River about thirty minutes before the noon meeting was scheduled to begin. Coming down in a slow spiral from her flying altitude, she paused a moment to hover over the wondrous city of Semorrah. From any angle, but especially from the air, it was a breathtakingly beautiful place. Built of pure white stone on a tiny island in the middle of the Galilee River, it boasted a magical collection of multistoried buildings ornamented with delicate arches, spiraled obelisks and lacy stone grillwork. The rushing river foamed around its edges, no more white or playful than the stones of Semorrah themselves. To the east, the city reached a thin hand to Jordana with a slender and famous bridge that was the only approach to the city by land. Other visitors booked passage in ferries from the Bethel shore. And, of course, angels could always come and go at will.

Alleya dropped closer, still fascinated by the complex, interlaced architecture below her. She almost wished that she had arrived at night, for then the city was doubly exquisite. The advent of electricity—driven by the mighty Galilee River rushing by the city on all sides—had given Semorrah a decided advantage. Every merchant, every burgher, even the lowliest common-market trader, had wired his home and office for power, and at night, Semorrah was a carnival of lights. Even Luminaux could not rival it for visual enchantment.

Alleya sighed and tightened the circle of her descent. All that was true, and yet there were those who despised Semorrah, and rightfully. Here the wealthiest merchants held absolute sway, and here some of the cruelest abuses of the past few centuries had been welcomed. Semorrah had been a sanctuary for slavers, back when that disgrace had flourished in Samaria; and there was no end to the stories you could hear about the deceptions and trickeries practiced by the rival river merchants. Alleya had often thought that Semorrah looked like a place where angels should live. The merchants deserved to live someplace more like Breven.

She tilted her wings, dropped her feet, and made a neat landing on the narrow stone entryway before Gideon Fairwen's house. Well-trained servants were at the door; she did not need to identify herself or her mission to be ushered wordlessly to a conference room in the heart of the mansion. Someone took her backpack from her and someone else silently offered her a tray of refreshments, but she shook her head. She wanted to appear in the doorway empty-handed.

She also shook her head at the footman who guarded the door to Gideon's meeting hall, when he asked in a murmur, "Shall I announce the Archangel?" But she paused a moment outside, to catch her breath from the agonizing climb up three flights of steps on an injured ankle. Past the closed door she could hear angry voices raised in bitter argument. Either they had started early, or the flight had taken longer than she calculated. The strident voice was Aaron's; the calmer but still angry voice was Jerusha's. Obviously nothing had been settled yet.

She nodded to the footman, and he opened the door. She stepped inside, quickly looking about the room to note the placement of her allies and adversaries. Heads snapped her way in irritation at this interruption, and then abruptly all conversation ceased. Maybe fifty pairs of eyes stared at her in various degrees of concern and consternation. She picked out Samuel's face (relieved and frightened), Jerusha's (appalled), Gideon's (shocked), Aaron's (suspicious). Asher, coming impetuously to his feet, was the first to speak.

"Angela, what happened to you? We have been so worried!"

A babble of voices rose in a series of similar questions, but Alleya held up her hand for silence. Everyone subsided.

"I ran afoul of the temper of the god," she said quietly. "And I hope we have all gathered here today to work together to solve the problems that beset us. For none of us will survive if we attempt to deal with this on our own."

There was a moment of silence, then the expected outcry. Samuel had come forward to urge her to the seat at the head of the table, left empty for her. Asher appeared on her right hand with a glass of water and an anxious expression, and he made no move to leave her side even after she had been settled. Everyone else was still firing questions at her or talking across the table, sharing speculations with others in the room. It was Gideon Fairwen who finally called them to order. Fairwen, a stately, intelligent and dangerous man, sat at the foot of the long table, directly facing her.

"So. Angela. Tell us what happened to you," he said, his voice measured, almost neutral. He had recovered his habitual aplomb. "We had wondered where you were."

"When you were not here when we arrived," Asher murmured in her ear, "we had the worst fears."

"Somewhere a little north of Sinai, I got caught by a storm and was thrown to the ground," she said calmly. "I don't think it's an exaggeration to say I might have been killed."

A small gasp circled the table. "Like Delilah!" Micah exclaimed. Alleya nodded.

"Exactly like Delilah. And like Samuel, and Asher, and the others who were with her that night."

"But are you saying you could not control the storm? That you prayed to Jovah and he did not respond?" Aaron demanded.

"I barely had a chance to begin a prayer to Jovah," Alleya said.

"But if he had heard you, he would have answered. He would have diverted the storm," the Manadavvi said.

"Perhaps. I have never felt Jovah's temper before. I don't think, at that moment, he cared whether or not I survived his gale. I don't think he would have listened."

Now the expression on every face was identical: horrified.

"But Alleya," Jerusha began, only to have her voice drowned out by forty other voices. Finally, Emmanuel made himself heard.

"I thought *you* were the only angel the god always listened to," he said on a rising note. "I thought *you* were the one who could always control the god."

"No one controls the god," Alleya said quietly. "We all petition him. Until now, he has always listened to my voice. This time, he did not."

"But Alleya," Jerusha said, "what does that mean? If the god cannot hear *you*—"

"That is what we have come here to discuss," she said, still in that level voice. "I understand that the Manadavvi"—she nodded at Aaron and Emmanuel—"and the merchants"—a look at Gideon Fairwen and his compatriots—"and some of the Jansai"—she glanced at the Breven contingent, bedecked in their gypsy clothes and their gold chains—"all accuse the angels of manipulating the weather in order to force their hands. I would like to hear why they think that. But I would also like to ask them what they plan to do if their theory is wrong. What they plan to try next to save Samaria from flood and destruction."

Emmanuel stabbed an accusatory finger at her. "You cannot deny that angels have always been able to call forth storms and send them away," he said fiercely.

Alleya nodded. "Until this past year—yes, we have always been able to do so."

"And so when our crops were drowned and our riverways flooded, who should we have thought responsible if not the angels?"

"And why would angels have done such a thing? What reason could we have for destroying your fields—the crops that feed us all?"

"You are angry with us!" Aaron burst out. "Because you think we do not honor our treaties or pay the proper taxes—"

"Well, do you?" she asked mildly.

There was a sizzling pause; then Aaron flung at her: "When they are fair!"

"And I think they are fair, and a council of angels and merchants agreed they were fair, but we can address that later. What would make you think angels would resort to such despicable means to compel you? How could that profit us? If the croplands turn to swampland, we starve with everyone else. How can you ascribe such malice to us? What have we done to deserve this?"

"Then if not the angels—" Gideon began, and let the question hang. Everyone in the room had already figured out the answer, though not the reason.

"It was not the angels," Alleya said. "We have done what we can to stop the storms. If they cannot be stopped, what can we do? What can we all do, working together? We have no other hope of survival."

She paused, letting that sink in, then spoke in a voice so quiet that everyone had to lean forward to listen. "And I ask you to consider this as well," she said. "If Jovah cannot hear the angels—and if you raise your voices and he cannot hear you—who will he hear in three months as we gather on the Plain of Sharon to sing his praises? Will all our voices, combined in the Gloria, be loud enough to catch his wandering attention? And if they are not, how will he respond?"

She waited, but no one had a reply. Dread sharpened every face turned in her direction. "It is written that if we do not all in harmony sing the Gloria, the god will send thunderbolts to destroy the world," she said, her voice even lower. "But what if we sing—and he does not hear us? What will the god do then?"

Later, Samuel told her that she had conducted a magnificent meeting. Alleya was not conscious of feeling much triumph, however; she was tired, and her body ached, and the arguments she had put forth had frightened even her. But the mutiny appeared to be over, and that was a victory of sorts. She no longer feared the damage the Manadavvi or the merchants could do.

No one had had much in the way of helpful suggestions except the Archangel, and hers was a forlorn hope. "I have been reading old history books from the Eyrie archives," she said, glancing at Job and Mary and shading the truth. "They mention weather problems that the settlers had in the early days of colonization. The Edori also tell stories of wind and rain in those first hundred years on Samaria. Perhaps this is a cycle that occurs on this planet, maybe every five hundred years, and we must now simply endure it until it corrects itself.

"But I'm not sure," she added, before the relief around the table could become too palpable. "The histories also mention—things it is difficult to understand—devices that men put in place around Samaria to enable Jovah to hear them more clearly. I wonder if these are machines similar to the interfaces the oracles use. If so, I wonder if I can find them and put them to use."

"Put them to use how?" Job demanded.

"I won't know until I see them. Maybe I won't know even then."

"But how will you find them?" one of the Jansai asked.

"The history books say that one of these devices can be found in the Corinni Mountains. My guess is that it's located at Hagar's Tooth. That's where I propose to look."

"But once you find it," Mary began. She paused, rubbed a hand across her face. She looked very tired. "You won't know how to use it. You can't even use the interfaces. Maybe I should go with you, or Job."

"Maybe," Alleya said gently. "But I thought I would first get help from one of the engineers who live in Luminaux. They've built dams and directed electricity and created incredible equipment. One of them was even able to fix a broken music machine at the Eyrie—a machine also left behind by the original colonists."

"*That's* the man you should get," Samuel exclaimed. "*He* would understand how these—hearing devices work."

A general endorsement of this plan rose from the assembled council. Alleya nodded gravely, but her heart was laughing. As if she would consider any other engineer.

"Then it is agreed," she said solemnly. "I will go to Hagar's Tooth to see what I can discover."

There was a murmur of assent, and the meeting was essentially over. People rose hesitantly to their feet, paused to discuss things with their neighbors. Asher dropped to his knees at Alleya's side, while the other angels in the room made their way to the Archangel's seat.

"Angela, what can I do to ease you?" Asher asked, so intensely that Alleya could not help smiling. "There are healers in the city—I can fetch them. I can bring you wine, or food. Tell me."

"I just need time and sleep," she said. "But thank you for your concern, Asher."

Samuel and Jerusha reached her next, demanding details, exclaiming over the ugliness of her bruises. Micah hovered behind them. Alleya answered their questions as best she could, describing the uncontrolled frenzy of the wind, the suddenness of its attack. "I have never experienced anything like it before," she said.

Samuel met her eyes. "I have," he said quietly.

She nodded at him. "And I'm afraid I may never get over my fear that it will happen again," she added.

He shook his head. "No, you never will."

The conference members spent the rest of the day in Semorrah, enjoying a lavish dinner at Gideon Fairwen's house, and settling for the night in some of his dozens of guest chambers. In the morning, as they all prepared to depart in various directions, half of them tried to convince Alleya to stay another day to recuperate more fully. Even Gideon expressed his concern and offered every amenity of his household. But Alleya was restless.

"The storms grow worse, they do not abate," she said. "I am afraid to linger too long. I must get to Hagar's Tooth as soon as I can."

So they bid her farewell and wished her a safe journey. She promised she would stop for the night in one of the smaller river cities, not attempting to make the whole journey in one day. She was impatient to go, and let them think it was an eagerness to discover what lay hidden at Hagar's Tooth.

In fact, she was elated to be going to Luminaux so soon. To be seeing Caleb Augustus again in a matter of days.

Chapter Fifteen

Alleya arrived in the Blue City a little after noon the following day. She did not have much hope of finding Caleb in his rented room at this hour, but she tried anyway, just in case. No, he was not at home, said the baker's daughter, but she would gladly take a message. Alleya thought a moment before composing a short note. "I have come to Luminaux because I must see you as soon as possible," she wrote, and included the name of her hotel. It seemed certain to fetch him. Then again, perhaps he had been idly flirting with her during that public farewell at the Edori camp. That was a cheerful thought. She almost crumpled up the note to replace it with something more colorless. Then she shrugged and handed it over as written. In any case, she needed him. And he seemed unlikely to ignore her summons.

Well, she was in Luminaux; might as well go shopping. The flying clothes she had worn at the outset of her trip had been completely ruined when she tumbled to the earth, so they had to be replaced. In addition, here was a shop that offered lovely, soft, flowing tunics that could be attractively swathed around any figure. The saleswoman deftly wrapped one of them around and between Alleya's wings, showing her how to attach it, how it appeared both belted and loose. It was impossible to resist. Alleya flashed her gold and sapphire wristlets at the woman, who smilingly nodded. Accounts would be tallied up with the Eyrie at the end of the month.

Back at her hotel, Alleya took a hot bath, then spent some time upgrading her appearance. Her yellow hair, naturally, was clipped back with the gold filigree clasp. She experimented with cosmetics to cover up the worst of her cuts and bruises, then to enhance her cheekbones and her eyes. Not something she was adept at. She surveyed her reflection critically and was not ill-pleased.

"At any rate, you look better than you did when you woke up in the farmers' compound," she told the mirror, and laughed aloud. She liked the way that made her look, so she laughed again.

She glanced out the window; nearly sunset. How long would Caleb Augustus work at his present job? Maybe it would take him past midnight. Maybe he would not go back to his rooms tonight. Maybe he would head directly to Seraph; maybe he would go out to the Edori camp to visit his friends, never seeing her note till the morrow. Maybe he would receive her message, and laugh, and toss the note aside. She was a fool for buying new dresses and spreading rouge across her cheeks to entertain a man who would never arrive.

She had lifted her hand to her head to yank out the barrette when there was a sudden, excited pounding at her door. "Alleya? Are you in there? Alleya?"

Caleb Augustus. She'd known he would come.

She opened the door and he bounded inside, beaming. He carried an armful of cut flowers that instantly perfumed the room. "I couldn't believe it when I got your note," he said, talking so rapidly he might be nervous. "I rushed right out again and only stopped running to buy you these. I hope you like flowers."

"Yes, of course I do," she said, taking the bouquet from him and holding the blossoms to her nose. It was a ploy; she merely wanted to hide her flushed face. "They smell wonderful."

But he was tugging on her wrist, pulling her hands down. "Angela, what happened to you?" he demanded in a completely altered voice. "Your face—you've been hurt. . . ."

She turned away. "Let me find a glass or something to put these in—some water—"

He forcibly turned her back. "Tell me."

She sighed, met his eyes. "A few days ago. Flying to the conference in Semorrah. I ran into a rainstorm and I was flung to the ground."

His breath caught sharply. "Alleya! Were you hurt? Was anyone with you?"

"My hurts are essentially what you see, except for a twisted ankle, which is *much* more painful than I expected," she said, attempting to speak lightly. "And no, no one was with me. It was a very frightening experience."

"What did you do?"

"Took shelter with some farmers, and continued on to Semorrah a day or two later. I told everyone that Jovah had turned his back on me, but—I don't know. My appearance at least convinced everyone to listen to me—convinced Gideon Fairwen and the others that I was not working with Jovah to flood the world. So this was a good thing. So maybe Jovah purposefully cast me down. As I say, I don't know."

He shook his head. "How you can trust such a god—"

"I think our god needs something from us, and does not know how to tell us what that is," she interrupted gently. "I still trust him. But I admit I am worried. And that is why I'm here."

He smiled, though it was clearly a strained attempt. He still looked shocked beyond measure at the thought of the danger she had survived. "What? Not to see me?"

She smiled back. "Yes, as a matter of fact. You see, I think you may be able to help me. And you will be delighted to learn that the council that just met in Semorrah specifically named you as the man I should go to for help."

At that, he smiled more naturally. "I'd be interested in hearing how that came about."

"Well, I sang your praises, of course—"

"Of course."

"And they said I should by all means employ your skill."

"For what daunting but glorious task?"

She moved over to a pair of chairs set before a small table, and they both sat down. "I believe the original settlers left behind a few pieces of equipment that make it easier to communicate with the god."

"You mean the interfaces?"

"No, I think these are different. I think they're listening devices of some kind. The old history books call them 'ears,' which confused me at first—but I think they're some kind of electronic sound enhancers that help Jovah hear. Maybe something has happened to these 'ears,' preventing Jovah from hearing us as clearly. And I thought, since you have repaired complex, foreign machinery before—"

"Oh, I'd be happy to try my hand!" he exclaimed. "But I've never heard of such a thing before. The angels—and the Edori—have always claimed that Jovah could hear them from anywhere. Why would he need special listening devices?"

"I don't know. I'm not even sure that's what they are. But it seemed like it might be something worth trying."

"I agree absolutely. When do we go? *Where* do we go?"

"The history books name the Plain of Sharon and the Corinni Mountains as two possible sites. There's a third one, but I haven't figured out where it is yet. But the Corinnis aren't far."

"Yes, but—that's some pretty broad ground to cover, looking for something we can't even identify."

She nodded. "I can't help thinking the device must be near Hagar's Tooth."

"Near *what*?"

Now she laughed. "Hagar's Tooth. You aren't familiar with it?"

"Obviously not."

"It's a retreat that Uriel built for Hagar shortly after Samaria was settled. It was a place she could go and not be bothered by angels—because the grounds are entirely covered by tall, sharp spikes that would pierce angel wings if they tried to land there. She was the first angelica to use the place, but it was supposed to be available to any angelica after her who needed a place to get away."

"And why are you so sure that's where this ear is?"

"Legend has it that Jovah could always hear the angelica if she went to Hagar's Tooth and prayed. Which makes me think—if there *is* some listening device in the mountains—"

"That it's there," Caleb finished up. "I would guess that

you're right. Well, at least that narrows down the mileage a little. What's this place like?"

"I've never been there—angels are discouraged from going—but I believe it consists of a house and some grounds. Probably in utter disrepair by now, because I don't think anyone's been there for twenty-five years or more. Well, I could be wrong. I remember Levi once saying he was going to make a pilgrimage there, but I don't know that he ever actually went."

"Levi?"

"The last angelico. Delilah's husband," she said. "He died in the accident in which Delilah broke her wing."

"And what was he like?"

Alleya was silent for a moment. It had been months since she'd thought of Levi, that reckless, handsome, mercurial man. It had been so inevitable that Delilah would love him; and it had been so obvious that he was the wrong man for her. What had Jovah been thinking? "Like Delilah," she said. "Charming and impossible. They were like children together, always challenging each other to more outrageous escapades. There were those who were not sorry when he died, thinking Delilah would become more sedate. But that was before—" Alleya spread her hands and did not complete the thought aloud. Before they realized Delilah herself was damaged beyond repair.

"She's never mentioned him to me."

"That doesn't surprise me. Have you seen her lately? How is she?"

He laughed shortly. "She's put us all in shock. She claims she's going to sail with the Edori to Ysral."

Alleya felt her cheeks pale. She sat bolt upright in her chair. "No! That's ridiculous!"

"Try to tell her that. I thought at first she was just toying with the idea, but she seems to be serious. I cannot tell you how frenzied this announcement has made my friend Noah."

"But she can't—I don't mean to mock their enterprise, but Caleb, it is doomed to failure. She *can't* go. She will drown with the rest of them somewhere in the middle of the ocean."

"I know, I know. And maybe that's what she wants. She hates the life she is living now, Alleya. It is so bitter to her that she almost cannot continue from day to day. Since she made this decision, she has been like an excited little girl planning her first trip to the city. I have never seen her so hopeful and so happy. I for one cannot take that away from her."

Alleya was shaking her head, patting her hands against her cheeks. "I must talk to her—I must tell her—"

"Talk to her, by all means," Caleb said gently. "But I don't think you have a hope of changing her mind. I don't mean to be cruel, but she hasn't paid much attention the last few times you've tried to reason with her."

She smiled wanly. "Like Jovah," she said. "Deaf to all appeals."

"But we can go see her tonight," he said. "Or tomorrow or the next day."

"I had hoped to leave for Hagar's Tooth in the morning."

He grimaced. "I can't leave for another two days. I have to finish this job I'm working on or it will completely fall apart. Can you wait that long?"

She was thinking rapidly. The Corinni Mountains were so close to another place that she should visit. She had not been back for months, a shameful omission. "I can meet you there," she said slowly. "In—what? Five days? Six? How long will it take you to travel that far?"

"No more than four days, I imagine, and maybe only three. I'll borrow a horse." He gave her a speculative look. "Though if you waited for me, we could travel together. You could carry me to Hagar's Tooth. If you could manage it."

His doubtful tone caught her attention. "What?" she demanded. "You don't think I could?"

"Well, look at us," he said. "I'm taller by four or five inches, and I must outweigh you by sixty pounds."

"In case you don't know," she said, though she was sure he did, "angels have been blessed with gifts other than their wings."

"Body heat," he murmured. "I've heard that."

"And disproportionate strength," she added. "I could carry a man three times my own weight—though not far, I must admit. But you—I could carry you three hundred miles. Although it might take a full day."

He gave a soft, almost breathless laugh. "I have to admit," he said, "one of my lifelong goals has been to meet an angel I trusted enough to take me on a flight. I am dying to fly—you know that. And you're the first angel I'd want to ask to take me in her arms." She felt herself reddening again; surely he had said that on purpose. "So you can imagine how chagrined I am that I can't leave with you tomorrow for the Corinnis."

"Some other day," she said lightly. "Perhaps I'll fly you back to Luminaux."

"I'll have the horse," he reminded her.

"Another time, then," she said.

"Is it a promise?"

"I promise to do what I can," she said, making no promises at all. "I would like to help you achieve your lifelong ambition. I'd like to take you on a flight. Maybe we'll have time while we're at Hagar's Tooth. Maybe it will be sometime in the future. Does that satisfy you?"

Now he was the one to draw a long breath, reconsider, and answer in a lighter tone than he might have used. "Yes, thank you, angela. I will look forward to the day."

"Good. Then *that's* settled," Alleya said briskly. "Are you hungry? Do you want to go for dinner?"

"Of course I do. What would you like? Someplace simple or someplace elegant? Do you want to eat at Seraph—or go there later?"

Alleya thought about it, then shook her head. "I don't think I can see Delilah right now," she said. "I don't know what I'd say to her about this Ysral trip. When you see her again, tell her I asked about her and wished her well. Tell her I persuaded the merchants to give me more time. Don't tell her—" She touched her finger to the bruises on her face. "Don't tell her about my fall. I don't want her to compare it to hers."

Caleb rose to his feet and held his hand out. Surprised, Alleya gave him her hand and let him pull her out of her chair. "Very well," he said. "We will have the night just to ourselves. Don't bother telling me where you want to go. I think I know just the place."

Late the next morning (later than she had planned), Alleya took off from Luminaux and headed almost straight west. The weather was cold but clear. Her course took her parallel to the coastline, so she flew low enough to enjoy the panorama of the ocean. Along the shore, the water was multicolored, layered patches of teal, indigo and violet edged with white where the breakers foamed and split. Farther out, the sea became darker, more monotonous, more mysterious. She could not imagine setting sail in that unmapped element, striking out for a place that might only exist in legend.

But then, like most creatures of the air, she was afraid of the water—always had been, despite the fact that the first ten years of her life had been spent near the sea. Her wings had made it impossible for her to learn to swim, and she had not even cared much for wading in the cold, salty shallows along the beach. Something about the eternal rise and fall of the tide, the endless pursuit and retreat of the waves along the sand, made her feel frail and at risk. She did not trust the shifting, hungry water; she was not seduced by the hiss and murmur of the waves. She never wanted to get close enough to allow the ocean to spirit her away.

How could Delilah have overcome that fear? Or was she merely running to it headlong, arms outstretched, as she had run to unlikely lovers in the past? Surely she must expect this to be the last embrace. Surely she must expect this one to betray her in the end.

Alleya stopped once to eat lunch and take a brief nap, though it annoyed her to need rest during what should be a fairly easy flight. She stretched out in the soft sand twenty yards from the waterline, wrapping herself in her wings and pillowing her head on her backpack. Not the height of luxury, but it would do. She closed her eyes.

And instantly began dreaming of Caleb Augustus.

He had kissed her last night on the cool streets of Luminaux, under one of those blue lamplights that gave the night there such a haunting quality. She had been as shaken as a schoolgirl taken unaware by the cutest boy in class. Although she had not been surprised. At some point during the meal (which he had seemed to relish, though she could not remember a bite of what she ate), she had looked across the table at him and felt his momentarily unguarded rush of desire.

It had given her a dizzy sense of elation, an almost triumphant sensation; she had felt her laugh grow more languorous and her gestures more deliberate. He watched everything she did with a starved intentness, but at the same time, everything she did pleased him. She could sense his utter delight in her smallest *moue*, her most artless remark. It was as if she were the most alluring woman in the world, the most intelligent, the most insightful. He watched her, and she felt herself grow beautiful.

"Have you ever been in love?" he asked her once, abruptly, apropos of absolutely nothing. They had been talking, if she recalled correctly, of their regret that neither of them had ever learned to play a musical instrument.

"In love?" she repeated, wondering just what to say. In the angel holds, physical gratification was fairly easy to attain. Although angels were forbidden to marry each other (except by special dispensation), there were always plenty of mortals available to satisfy the hungriest desires. Alleya had had desperate crushes on a few of the human boys reared alongside the angels at the Eyrie; she'd had a short, unhappy affair with one of her instructors, and one or two brief and less agonizing relationships with mortals at the Eyrie and elsewhere. But in love? "Not the kind of love that really means anything," she answered.

"You can't call it love at all if it's insignificant."

She laughed. "I've had *affections*, if that pleases you better. How about you?"

He grinned. " 'Affections' covers it well enough. Nothing that changed my life. Nothing that changed me."

"I suppose my handful of romances all changed me to some extent," she said thoughtfully. "If love makes you sad, you acquire a little depth, a little compassion. If it makes you happy—you learn how to be joyous. Every relationship should color your soul to a certain degree, don't you think? Every friendship, every love affair—each one should build up the chambers of your heart the way a sea creature builds the chambers of his shell."

"Until you build the largest one of all, and there you live the rest of your life," he said.

She held up a cautionary finger. "Be sure to make it large enough to last you that long."

"Oh," he said, "there's no doubt about that."

And they had turned from the subject, and talked of other things. After dinner, they wandered the streets of Luminaux for hours, watching the jugglers, listening to the storytellers, standing alongside other strollers to judge impromptu singing contests held on the street corners. The night was very clear, tinged with enough chill to keep them moving. They were no longer hungry, but they had to sample the vendors' treats—flavored ices, chocolate-dipped fruits, fizzing wines. Total strangers stopped to recommend taverns and discuss the merits of various performers. The world seemed young and happy.

On one corner, under a turquoise street lamp, Caleb took her arm and pulled her to a halt. When she turned to face him, a questioning look in her eyes, he pointed at the sky. "See?" he said softly. "In Luminaux, even the moon is blue."

She was sure it was not true—it must have something to do with the sapphire haze generated by the city lights—but indeed the creamy white cup of the quarter moon seemed to be spilling over with drops of azure liquid. "I think it's an illusion," she said, turning back to him with a smile. But before she could say another word, he pulled her into his arms and kissed her.

She felt heat flash from her scalp to her spine; she felt her blood clamor its amazement. His hands had slid so easily under the feathered webs at her back, finding the smooth expanse of muscle below the tough ridges of her wing joints. He drew her closer, kissed her harder, covered her mouth and cheeks with kisses. Even in the blue light, her face must have been scarlet. She gave a single nervous laugh and pulled away.

He put a finger across her mouth before she could think of a word to say. "Don't," he said, an injunction that seemed to cover everything. Then, taking her hand and looping her arm through his, he led her in silence back to her hotel. At the entrance, he paused, looked down at her and smiled.

"In five days, or maybe six," he said. She had already drawn him a map so he would know exactly where to meet her. "I'll see you at the Corinni Mountains."

"All right," she had replied, her voice almost a whisper. They were the first words she'd spoken since he kissed her.

He released her hand and took a step backward. "Dream of me," he said, and turned to walk rapidly away. Stunned and a little unsteady on her feet, she had negotiated the marble lobby and the wide stairway, for the first time realizing that her ankle was throbbing painfully. Once she made it to her room, she could think of nothing useful to do, so she went to bed. It was only when one of the nearby clocks struck the hour that she realized it was three in the morning.

Alleya slept on the beach for an hour and woke feeling much refreshed. Two more hours of easy flying took her to her destination: a small community on the very southwestern corner of Bethel. Maybe a hundred and fifty people lived there in a haphazard collection of houses and dormitories. But there were two roads: the fairly well-traveled coastal highway, and the smaller track that led to the nearest farms and villages a few miles to the northwest. The roads were important, because the place lived on trade. Most of the residents were master craftspeople who wove the finest lace outside of Luminaux. Even the children learned the art at a very early age.

The community had grown since Alleya had been there last. There were two new houses and what looked like a small store. Life appeared to be thriving here in Chahiela, an Edori word meaning "silence." Never had a place been so appropriately named.

Alleya landed a few yards away from the farthest outbuilding and walked slowly toward the center of the tiny town. It was late afternoon and the inhabitants were milling about, this being their liveliest time of day, as they left their classrooms and workrooms and returned to their dormitories or dwellings. Most of them lived in the four communal houses, divided by age and sex (girls, boys, men, women). A few of the instructors had private quarters which they shared with their families. And of course, Hope Wellin lived in a small house all by herself.

Alleya had not advanced very far before someone spotted her, and soon she was at the center of a small, animated group of men and women all trying to communicate with her at once. She laughed and attempted to keep track of every question, every exclamation, but it was a hard group to converse with. Maybe three-quarters of the inhabitants were deaf; most of the others were blind; some were both. All of them had learned an intricate hand language of Hope Wellin's devising, although some were more fluent than others. Most of the blind children could verbalize as well, although—living here in this isolated, mostly silent community—their speech was halting and oddly accented, hard to understand. The flailing arms and high-pitched cries of astonishment were difficult to follow.

"Yes, it is true, I am Archangel . . . Oh, no, they treat me just as they did before . . . A crown? No. A tiara? No, I just wear my regular clothes and my bracelets . . . Yes, it has been storming all over Bethel. In the other provinces, too. Well, I am doing what I can . . . The crop prices? I don't know anything about the crop prices. How about the price of lace? Are you selling what you make? . . . And traffic has been busy? That's good, I'm glad to hear that . . ."

Someone tapped her boldly on the back, and she turned. These people had known her since she was a child, they thought nothing of tugging on her wing feathers or spinning her around to face them when they wanted her attention. Thus she did not have the angel's customary sensitivity about her wings; it did not enrage or upset her to have her feathers stroked. Here, she had always been public property.

"Yes, Mara? You're looking well," she said to the older woman who had addressed her. Mara was one of the first inhabitants of Chahiela, a lacemaker without peer, and born stone deaf. She was one of the few residents who had never been able to hear Alleya's voice.

"Your mother?" Mara asked, weaving her fingers quickly into the question. None of her impatient sentences were complete; Alleya always had to interpret what she meant to say.

"Does my mother know I'm coming? No. I just happened to be flying this way. Is she here?"

"Yes."

"In the house? I'll go to her."

"House."

"Thank you." She waved generally at the small crowd and began to edge gently through their ranks. Some of them followed, still bombarding her with questions. "We'll talk tomorrow. I'll be here a day or two. Yes, lovely to see you, too!"

Finally, she made it to the stone walkway that led to the small gray house where her mother lived. Where she herself had been born. Even though her mother, neither blind nor deaf, could speak as well as any woman, this was the quietest house Alleya had ever been in. As quiet as the oracles' retreats—quieter, when her mother was angry and using silence as her weapon. Alleya remembered entire weeks in which they did not exchange a word.

Before she had gone two steps up the walkway, the front door opened and a small bundle of red hair and wide smile came scrambling down the path. "Alloo! Alloo!" the little girl cried out before flinging herself into Alleya's arms. "Alloo! Here!"

"Deb-o-rah," Alleya chanted into her ear, hugging the small, squirming body to her heart. "How's my silly girl?"

Deborah pulled back to watch Alleya's face as she spoke, but she kept her small hands wrapped tightly around the angel's. "Come to stay?" she asked wistfully. Like many of the other children, Deborah was only partially deaf; she could speak clearly enough to be understood, though her sentences were often incomplete and idiosyncratic. It didn't stop her from chattering continuously and unselfconsciously.

"Oh, sweetie, you know I can't," Alleya replied. "I'm a big important person now! I can only come home for visits."

"Archangel," Deborah said. "Smartest angel in Samaria."

Alleya laughed. "Well, I wish," she said ruefully. "Angel with the most troubles in Samaria."

"Too much rain," Deborah said, nodding sagaciously.

Alleya laughed again. "Among other things. So how's your schooling going? Are you learning your letters? Are you learning your numbers?"

"Can *read*!" Deborah said proudly. "Hear me? Read you story?"

"Yes, I'd love to. I'll come by the dorm tomorrow or the next day, all right? Which story are you going to read me?"

"Pick one. Be good one."

"I'll look forward to it."

Deborah answered, but Alleya didn't catch the words. A movement at the front of the house had caught her attention, and she looked up to find her mother framed in the doorway. Hope Wellin nodded when she saw she had her daughter's attention. Alleya kissed Deborah on the top of her flaming head, then shooed her away toward the girls' dorm. Not hurrying about it, she made her way up the walk.

"Hello, Mother," she said when she got close enough to come to a halt. "I hope my timing isn't inconvenient. I need to make a trip to the Corinni Mountains, and since I was so close—"

"It's good to see you, Alleluia," Hope said without much expression. "How long are you staying?"

"A day or two. Unless that's a problem."

"Certainly not. It will be delightful," Hope replied coolly. "I see you've already had a chance to visit with Deborah."

"She looks like she is doing well. How is she doing in her classes?"

"It's hard to make her settle down and concentrate, but she's intelligent, so she learns quickly. She doesn't have much patience for lacemaking but she doesn't mind menial chores, so we can always put her to work. I think she could do quite well outside of Chahiela, if she decides to leave us when she's older. I have hopes for her."

Alleya smiled. "Maybe she'll go to work in Velora some day. I'd like to have her near me."

"She misses you. She asks about you."

"I would like to come more often, but these days—"

Hope abruptly turned and led the way into the house. "You have had your troubles, I know. Come inside. Tell me what's happening at the Eyrie. And all the gossip of Samaria."

So they spent a pleasant enough hour, mother and daughter, discussing the state of the realm, the worries over the weather, the effect of Breven factories on Chahiela lace, and the latest events in the lives of people they both knew. It was too much to say that Hope was cordial, but she was a little warmer than civil. It was the best her mother was capable of. Alleya let herself fall back into her old familiar patterns, answering what was asked, asking what seemed appropriate, and letting everything else slip away from her.

During pauses in the conversation, she glanced around the house. It had not changed much in the twenty years that had passed since she had lived here. The furniture looked new, and the wall tapestries had been changed, but the colors were very close to the old ones. In one corner of the room, propped on a brass easel, was a faded painting of Hope's parents and brother—

all deaf, all dead. The brother had died quite young, trampled by a runaway horse he could not hear approaching. As far as Alleya could tell, he was the only person Hope had ever truly loved. She talked about him very little, but she had told Alleya once, "My brother could hear me, as these children can hear you. He never heard any voice but mine in his entire life." It was one of the few times Alleya had been able to identify any emotion in her mother's voice: grief.

"While you're here," Hope was saying, "it would be appreciated if you were willing to sing."

"Of course I will, " Alleya said quickly. "I'd be glad to."

"There are two new women here—I don't believe you've met them—and I think you might be able to reach them. One of them lost her hearing when she was a little girl. The other has always been deaf. But I thought they might hear your voice. So many do. It would mean a lot to them."

"I would be glad to try. Tonight?"

"Oh, no. Tonight I will keep you for myself, and Mara and Seth and Evan, who usually take dinner with me. But tomorrow, if you would care to attend some of the classes—"

"Certainly. And I'll sing in the evening."

They talked a little longer, then parted so Alleya could freshen up before the meal. She would stay in her old room, of course, the bare gray chamber with the narrow bed and the single window which never seemed to admit much light. Standing now in the middle of that room, Alleya turned slowly, taking in its hard angles and cold features. It was difficult to remember if she had been happy or unhappy in this room; she'd had nothing to compare it to, no outside life, no privileged or destitute friends. It was just her life. She had not known that she was strange, or shy, or special, because every other child here was scarred or gifted or maimed. They were all odd. She had fit right in.

At the age of ten, given her choice, she never would have left. At the age of thirty, knowing what she knew now, would she have chosen to stay?

The next few days were an oasis of calm sunshine in what Alleya was beginning to consider her stormy life. She distributed her hours among the various classrooms of the deaf students, drawing the children about her in a circle. The older ones knew her from her past visits; some of the younger ones were awed at her presence and her great, gleaming wings, but her smile won them over.

"I want all of you to pay close attention," she said in her first session, saying the words aloud and also making the appropriate motions with her hands. She had learned the language of silence long before she had learned the music of the angels. "I want all of you to cover your eyes with your hands."

Everyone did so; she continued talking. "I know all of you have problems with your ears, but some of you can hear my voice. Raise your hands if you can hear me speaking."

There was an incoherent murmur of amazement from the students who were unused to hearing any voice; more than half the hands went up. Behind her, Alleya heard the teacher's gasp of surprise. It gave her confidence.

"You can put your hands down now," she said. "Now I'm going to sing a little song. If you can hear me, I want you to raise your other hand."

She chose a simple nursery tune, pitched in the high, sweet key that had always reached so many of the children in Chahiela. The ones who had heard her speaking waved their hands in the air. The other children, every one of them, dropped their palms from their eyes and leapt to their feet, staring at her in disbelief. She continued singing, beckoning them closer.

"*Can you hear me, can you hear me?*" she crooned as they crowded around her, reaching out with their small, wondering fingers to touch her lips, her throat. "*Yes, you can. Yes, you can! Hear Alleya singing, hear Alleya singing! Clap your hands. Clap your hands.*"

They applauded crazily, happily, calling out indistinct words of question and excitement. She hushed them with her gestures, and sang the rest of her words, setting them to different, always lilting tunes.

"*Let's count our numbers from one to ten,*" Alleya sang, holding up the fingers of her left hand. "*One . . . two . . . three . . . four . . .* " They listened intently, for most of them had never heard these syllables before, and held up their own fingers along with her. When she finished with numbers, she went through the alphabet, and then she randomly began naming objects in the room: *dress, boat, book, flower.* Some of the children began pointing to themselves, which at first Alleya did not understand.

"They want you to name them," the teacher murmured in her ear.

"Tell me their names." And as the woman introduced each child, Alleya sang the names back. The looks that crossed the small, engrossed faces were indescribable. Alleya felt her heart contract with a strange combination of sorrow and elation.

It was the same in the other classrooms, though she was not successful in reaching everyone. Three of the youngest children, who were both blind and deaf, did not even know that Alleya was singing. Two of the older, teenage boys (who looked as if they resented learning anything and didn't care about hearing their names sung by a stranger) either did not hear her or refused to acknowledge that they did. Mara, who had never responded to Alleya's voice, shook her head regretfully when the angel sang to her again.

But the others heard her—heard her and were moved, delighted, thrilled, thunderstruck. It gave Alleya a fierce pleasure—a gratification so intense that she knew it must be vanity, and should be repressed—to touch so many people with such a simple skill.

"Not my gift, Jovah, but thine," she whispered once, and she knew it was true. But it was the gift of Jovah's that she most cherished.

In the evening, she was the centerpiece of a gala entertainment that started with a feast, was followed by charades and ended with her performance. As she stepped up to the makeshift dais, facing the disordered chairs clustered in a few tight rows, she was gripped with a moment's stage fright. Even in Chahiela, where she had sung her whole life, it panicked her to be the center of attention. But the sight of her mother, cool and waiting at the back of the room, calmed her down; and her glimpse of Deborah, wriggling impatiently in her chair, made her laugh. She took a deep breath and began to sing.

In such a mixed group, it was hard to know what would please most, so she sang a little of everything—the solos from two of the sacred masses, a handful of lullabies, two of the Edori ballads that had stuck in her head well enough for her to remember them now, even a couple of the popular tunes that she had overheard in Velora and Luminaux. Every selection was greeted with extravagant applause, but, even more telling, no one rustled or whispered or even moved while she was actually singing. It was such a rare gift, such an exotic pleasure that she offered them; clearly, they did not want to miss a note.

She sang till the children began to look tired, and then she presented a final number. When she made a little bow to signify that she was done, the protest was so clamorous that she offered a quick, upbeat encore. Even this did not quiet some of the more vehement protests, but Hope Wellin had already come to her feet, and now she made her way to the stage beside her daughter.

"Tomorrow," she spelled out with her fingers. "Alleya will sing for us again in the evening." And with this, everyone was forced to be content. At any rate, no one had the nerve to dispute her; no one ever did.

Alleya stayed behind with her mother and some of the staff to straighten up the room after the crowd had emptied out. One of the women (Alleya thought she was a cook) approached her somewhat shyly as Alleya arranged chairs against the wall.

"I just wanted you to know—I've been able to hear every day of my life, and I've never heard anything so beautiful as your voice," the woman said. "I can't imagine what it must have been like to these people, never hearing a single sound and then suddenly—you singing. I know I saw two women crying."

"Oh, thank you—you're so kind," Alleya said, stammering. She was both pleased and embarrassed by the compliment. "But some of them have heard me sing before, though I haven't been back for months. So it wasn't their first time."

"It may as well have been," the woman said. "I felt like I had been deaf all my life when I first heard you sing. That until I heard your voice, I had only known silence."

It's because you live in Chahiela, where the world is mostly silent, Alleya wanted to say, but it seemed undiplomatic, especially with her mother standing so close. "I'm glad you enjoyed my singing," she said instead. "And I'll sing again tomorrow."

"I'll be right here."

The next two days passed in essentially the same manner, with Alleya moving from classroom to classroom during the day, and giving a cappella concerts at night. The teachers had quickly thought of ways to take advantage of her gift, and devised lesson plans with which she could serenade the students. It felt a little silly to be singing of multiplication and plant biology, but then, some of the prayers she sang to Jovah were laced with technical language that was far from poetic, and those never felt foreign in her mouth. She willingly obliged the teachers.

It was late in the third day of her visit before she finally made good her promise to come to Deborah's dormitory room for a story. All the other little girls came running up happily when Alleya entered the room, though they were not so eager to hear Deborah reading. So Alleya promised to sing them all a lullaby before she left, and they scattered back to their toys while she visited with Deborah.

"This is a story . . . about a tall man," Deborah began somewhat haltingly, painstakingly reading every word, every pronoun, every article. She had waited for Alleya to get comfortable, then perched on the angel's lap like a cat who knew it had every right to be there. Alleya closed her wings around both of them, sheltering them in a white cocoon, and bowed her head over Deborah's.

"He was so tall . . . his head . . . barely fit on the page," the little girl continued. She pointed at the illustration of a thin man whose dark hair grazed the top margin of the printed book, then glanced back to make sure Alleya was smiling. "He was . . . so very tall . . . no one could see . . . the color of his eyes."

It was a childish story, actually a little tedious, but Alleya listened with great patience all the way through. "Very good! You're reading so well!" she exclaimed when Deborah was finally done. "You must be studying hard and practicing every night."

"Most nights," Deborah amended. She wrinkled her nose. "Hard to be good."

"Quite true. Although if you practice being good, it becomes easier."

"That why Alloo Archangel? Good?"

Alleya wrinkled her own nose in response, making Deborah laugh. "I think I'm Archangel because Jovah can hear my voice," she said. "Just like you and all the other little girls can hear me when they can't hear anybody else. Jovah picked me because he can hear me." She sighed, adding under her breath, "*Or because he used to be able to hear me.*"

Deborah, unexpectedly, caught that final comment. "Jovah not hear Alloo?"

"Sometimes he does. I think—sometimes he doesn't."

"Jovah blind too?"

Alleya laughed. "What? I don't know. I don't think so."

Deborah put her fingers up to Alleya's face and began tapping out the slow, complicated language Hope Wellin had invented to communicate with children who could neither hear nor see. Alleya had to concentrate to remember what each separate symbol meant, but Deborah's message was simple: "Hi, Jovah." Alleya laughed.

"Silly girl," she said, whuffling her breath into the flyaway red hair. "Is that what you think I should say to the god?"

Deborah nodded. "Maybe *how* talk to Jovah," she said. "Can't hear, can't see. Touch face."

Alleya rested her chin on the bright head, thinking a minute. "I don't know where Jovah's face is," she said finally, sighing. "Or I might give it a try."

Two days later, Alleya left Chahiela. Everyone turned out to see her off, which was a little unnerving but spared her the ordeal of a private farewell with her mother. They had said formal goodbyes over breakfast, of course, Hope wishing her well in her future endeavors.

"Do you plan to come to the Gloria?" Alleya asked.

Hope looked surprised. "I don't believe I've ever been to one. Why?"

Alleya spread her hands. "Well, as Archangel, I'll be leading the singing—"

"Oh. Of course. I hadn't realized that. Let me think about it. If everything is going well here, I just might. When is it, now?"

"When it always is," Alleya said gently. "At the spring equinox."

"That's just a few months away. Well, I'll try."

And that had been the high point of their conversation. So

Alleya was just as glad to have Deborah crying and clinging to her, and Mara hugging her carefully, and the others—children and adults—crowding close to wave goodbye and hope that she came back soon.

But she still was not sorry to leave.

And she still was more excited than she could believe to be heading for her assignation in the Corinni Mountains.

It took her half a day to fly there, a straight, untroubled journey. The good weather was still holding; maybe Jovah had a special fondness for this corner of the world. Maybe he read her own mood and, for once, was responding to her desires before she had even voiced them. Or maybe the skies could hold no more rain, not a drop, not in any clouds over the whole of Samaria. In any case, she flew in sunshine and felt joyous.

And late in the afternoon, when the sun was its most golden and most supine, she landed at the foot of the Corinni Mountains, at the base of the peak that sheltered Hagar's Tooth. And there, camped like a gypsy before a small fire, sat Caleb Augustus, waiting. He had his hands to his forehead as if to shield his eyes from glare, and she thought he had been protecting himself from the sun, but he did not drop his hands as she came closer; and she realized that she was the bright source, the shining light he was afraid to look at too long. And then he dropped his hands and smiled at her, generating his own incandescence, and she knew a craven impulse to hide her eyes as well, for he was too luminous to gaze upon, and she was afraid of what she might see.

Chapter Sixteen

Caleb had passed a singularly unpleasant two weeks and had almost forgotten what it was like to have something to look forward to or something to fondly remember. First, the trip back from Breven had consisted of hours of wretched tedium relieved only by moments of emotional stress. And the first few days back in Luminaux had been spent struggling to untangle a mess another engineer had created in the home of one of the wealthiest bankers of the city. Normally the challenge of the project would have compensated for its high irritation factor, but for whatever reason, even his work held little appeal for Caleb these days. He was hard put to say why; or rather, he knew well enough why his mind wandered and his soul was discontented, but he chose not to think about it any more often than he had to.

Daily, hourly, minute by minute.

In fact, he had spent most of his time on the uncomfortable drive back from Breven daydreaming about the Archangel. Well, she had promised to see him again; she had seemed to mean it; they would go to some small cabaret and talk late into the night, till the other patrons disappeared and the musicians laid aside their scores and the waiters refused to serve them more wine. Then they would walk through the deserted city streets (sometimes he pictured blue Luminaux, sometimes sparkling Velora), talking endlessly. It was astonishing the number of things he had to tell her. He practiced them all.

He wondered if he would dare to kiss her. He wondered if she would allow it. He wondered if he would survive the experience.

Enjoyable as these musings were, they could not completely counteract the physical wretchedness of the trip itself. First, it rained every day, all day, on the cold journey back. Half-a-dozen times, he or Noah accidentally steered the Beast off the hidden road, and then there was much cursing and exasperation as they strained to find their way again. The first time, there was no budging the hulking vehicle out of the mud until they created a makeshift ramp out of split logs and forced the rear wheels to back along these until they were once more in contact with the road. After that, they made sure to carry the logs with them and employ them in every emergency. Still, each halt was time-consuming and frustrating, and no one's temper was easy.

Conditions did not improve much once they left the Jansai road behind, although, after they'd cleared the sodden desert, the terrain was rockier and a little easier for the spiked wheels to grip. But they made horrible time. More often than not, if late afternoon brought them anywhere near a small town, Delilah would insist that they stop for the night, and neither of the men could think of a reasonable objection. They were no longer on a schedule, and they were no longer being followed by a rescue team of Edori. It could take them the rest of the year to get home, and it would matter to no one. But the stops caused them to lose more time.

The physical discomfort of the trip was compounded by the emotional misery of the passengers—or at least of Noah. It was not hard to tell that the Edori and the angel had had a disagreement shortly after they left Breven, and that Delilah was determined not to allow Noah to patch things up. During Caleb's stints at the wheel, though he tried not to listen, he could hear the low sounds of urgent argument going on in the compartment behind him. Noah's voice ranged from angry to pleading; Delilah's was sometimes sharp, sometimes derisive, but most often implacable. Not wishing to get involved in these quarrels, Caleb drove as long as he could stand it, till his arms ached and his legs were too heavy to move from throttle to brake.

When they stopped, Noah would silently take his place on the front seat, sometimes looking so grim and haggard that it was all Caleb could do to keep from asking him if he were ill. Once, when Noah's face appeared particularly pale, Caleb felt his own anger rising as he climbed in beside the angel.

"What are you doing to him?" he demanded without preamble.

"Torturing him," was the instant response. She looked at him with her dark, fathomless eyes, and appeared lazy and unremorseful. "Would you like a little pain, too? I'm sure I could make you suffer."

"You could make anybody suffer," he said more quietly. "What's the point?"

"Everybody suffers," she replied. "It's a way of equalizing."

"What are you fighting about?" Caleb asked.

She laughed incredulously, as if she could not believe he would expect an answer. "Why do any lovers fight?" she mocked him.

Her use of the word embarrassed him, canceled the sentence on his tongue. "You could be kinder to him," Caleb said at last. "He is a good man and he deserves gentleness."

"I am being kind to him," she said dryly. "If you only knew."

More than that she would not say, and he gave up the effort. It was too exhausting to shout over the roar of the motor, trading barbed comments and elliptical replies. He waited for Noah to draw him aside at some campsite, pour out his heart and beg for advice, but the Edori kept his own counsel. And Caleb could not bring himself to ask.

He had his own guesses, of course; and one night, much against his will, he learned that he was right. It was the first day on which the rain had seemed less onerous, perhaps even intermittent, and they had pushed on as late as possible while travel conditions were passable. They camped that night close to the Heldoras, close enough to find rocky cave formations to serve as shelter for the night. They were able to build a fire and spread their blankets on a dry surface; and this passed for high luxury on this part of the trip. Despite the silence of his companions,

Caleb felt his spirits rise during dinner. He was almost warm, he was almost dry, and he was almost asleep. Life seemed almost good.

He unrolled his blanket close to the fire and fell asleep within minutes of stretching out. It was an hour or two later that he was awakened by the sound of low voices locked in intense battle. By the time he realized he was witnessing another argument, he had heard enough to convince him he should pretend to still be sleeping. Although he thought both of them were too angry to care if he heard every word they said.

"It's crazy, and you know it's crazy," Noah was saying as Caleb swam to consciousness. "It's a death wish, pure and simple."

"Dear Noah, surely you can't have so little faith in your friends' abilities to sail the seas," she said in a light, almost teasing voice. "Why have you helped them if you doubt them so much?"

"Because I love them, and this is what they want to do," he said. "But even they know their chances of survival are very slim."

"They seemed quite confident when I was there."

"Not confident! Fatalistic! They don't care if they die! Is that the death you want, crashing apart in some stormy ocean, all that cold water closing over your head? Is that what you want? Or worse, starving to death, when your food runs out, or dying of thirst? How can you choose that death? How can you choose *death*?"

"It's romantic and strange, and I have had nothing but weariness and monotony for too long," she said, still lightly, still as if she cared about nothing she said, nothing he felt. "And there's always the possibility of finding the miracle at the end of the voyage. I would hazard a lot for the chance to see Ysral."

"You don't give a damn about Ysral. All you care about—the god alone knows what you care about. You don't care about yourself, that's for certain. You don't care about me."

"How do we come to be talking about you again?" she mocked him. "Is that what this conversation has been about all along?"

"You know I love you," Noah said desperately. "You know I would give my life for you. Why isn't that enough for you? To know that someone loves you? Why can't that make you happy? Tell me what you want and I will give it to you."

"Give me my wings back," she said instantly. "Make me fly."

"I can try that," he said steadily. "Caleb and I—"

She laughed aloud, making no attempt to muffle the sound. "You and Caleb! You're boys playing with tools you don't even understand. The god alone could restore me, and he has chosen not to. Don't offer me any promises to make me happy. It can't be done."

"But why this trip?" Noah demanded, his voice anguished. "Why Ysral? Why should I let you die that way?"

"Because you love me and this is what I want to do," she said, her tones slightly more gentle. "You have nothing to say about it, you know. You cannot stop me."

"If I cannot stop you," he said, "then I will come with you."

"No," she said sharply. "I won't have you on that ship."

"Why not?" he asked with renewed energy. "Why should you be allowed to die if I cannot choose to die by your side?"

"Because I don't want you with me," she said flippantly. "Not on the ship to Ysral—not when we return to Luminaux."

There was a long, crackling silence. "You can prevent me from seeing you again in Luminaux," Noah said calmly. "But you cannot keep me from boarding one of those ships."

"You can't go," she said imperiously. "I won't have it."

"Why? Why shouldn't I make the journey? I too would like to see Ysral. I will make this pilgrimage with my friends."

"You," she said scornfully. "You have too much to live for. Too many unrealized dreams. There is no reason for you to court death like that. You won't go."

"I will."

"You won't," she repeated, but now her voice was edged with panic.

Noah must have shrugged. "I don't see how you can stop me."

She took a deep breath, seeming to draw up any reserves of honesty she had. It was as if she played the only winning card in her hand, as if she stopped, for a moment, toying with his heart. "I can tell you—that the only thing of beauty I leave behind in this world is you. I can tell you that you are all that has kept me alive this long. I can tell you that it's the only thing that matters to me at all, knowing that you are still alive, and well, and happy. And surely, for my sake, you will not risk yourself on this terrible journey."

"If you die, I will die," he said simply. "If you board that ship, I will stand beside you."

"If you board that ship," she said, "I will not go."

"Fair enough," he said, and his voice was relaxed, almost amiable. "I will go in your stead, if that means you will stay behind and live."

"No!" she cried. "I will not accept that!"

"Your choice," he said. "I sail with you, or without you if it keeps you safe. You will not leave for Ysral without me."

"And I will not leave for Ysral with you," she said grimly. "If you sail without me, know that I will find some other way to destroy myself. I can do it, you know—I can travel out to the Heldoras or the Corinnis and fling myself off some mountain peak. But I needn't go that far! There are medicines, you can find them in Luminaux, that turn a long sleep into the longest sleep, that ease you painlessly across the threshold of death—"

There was a sudden sharp report; Caleb realized with a shock that Noah had slapped the angel. "Not another word," he said ominously. "Don't say that again, do you hear me? Don't think it. Don't say it. Death is your enemy, you ridiculous child. Don't try to make him your friend."

"He is my best friend," she whispered, her voice muffled. Caleb imagined that she held her hand to her mouth while her wide eyes stared at the Edori. "And you cannot change that by wishing."

After that, there was total silence, but Caleb was fairly sure that no one in the cave slept that night. Certainly he was unable to fall back asleep, and his companions stirred restlessly for the hours of darkness that remained. In the morning, they rose to a renewed onslaught of rain and skies colored an unrelenting gray. No one spoke as they broke camp and wearily clambered back into the Beast. There was nothing left to say.

So that had been the trip; and in the following week, Caleb had seen very little of either Noah or Delilah. Whether they saw each other at all, he did not ask. He did not know how to counsel either one, so he did not lay himself open to requests for advice.

The few times he went to Seraph, Noah was not present. Delilah's repertoire had changed radically; the songs she performed now were upbeat, optimistic, adventurous, ballads about great deeds accomplished and victories won. She seemed, for the first time since he had known her, to be genuinely happy. It was hard to believe that this was the woman who had so forthrightly embraced the promise of death. But perhaps she was happy because she felt finally free—free of pain, of self-loathing, of despair. He could not quarrel with her means of achieving that freedom.

To find Noah, Caleb had to stroll out to the Edori camp and induce Thomas or Sheba or one of his other friends to invite him to dinner. Noah was usually there, invariably glad to see him, always interested in hearing about his engineering projects; but it was not the outgoing, cheerful Noah he had always known. This man was reserved, thoughtful, determined.

"You're really going to go, aren't you?" Caleb finally asked him one night when the two of them were the only ones left around the dying campfire. "You're going to make the journey to sea."

"To Ysral. Yes. I'm finishing up my jobs here and taking on no new commissions. I'll be ready within three weeks."

Caleb shrugged. "You know all my arguments."

Noah looked at him and smiled. "And you know my reasons."

"And if she won't let you go—?"

"Nothing will keep her from boarding that ship. You know that. So I'm going, too. Who knows? Perhaps we'll find the promised land."

"If I could only know for sure—if you were alive or dead . . ."

"Who knows anything for sure? Sooner or later, Yovah brings all of us home. You, me, all of us. I'll watch for you from the circle of Yovah's arms."

It was an Edori farewell; Caleb knew the proper response. "And till I arrive, whisper kindly of me in his ear."

* * *

So he had had nothing to brighten his days until he came back to his apartment one evening to find a brief note from the Archangel. His heart made a clumsy pirouette under his ribs, knocking awkwardly into his bones; he truly forgot the simple requirements for breathing. Surely she must have come for some reason other than to see him. Not that it mattered. She was here.

And, as he learned later that night, she needed him. She could hardly have framed a request he would have refused, but this one intrigued him, and he was glad to agree to help her. However, the intervening six days were interminable, two in Luminaux and four on the road; he had not thought the hours could creak by at such an excruciating pace.

Of course, he had one brilliant memory to sustain him, and he relived it on a pretty much continuous basis for each of those six days. In fact, sometimes he thought he might have dreamed the kiss, hallucinated about it, invented it in his disordered brain.

But when he saw her next, would she allow a second kiss?

He and his borrowed horse arrived at the rendezvous a few hours before Alleluia. Caleb unloaded his mount and prepared a meal. The horse was an Edori mare and should not stray far from this point if Caleb wasn't gone more than two days. So he had been told, anyway. He didn't trust animals; they had minds of their own. A machine would be much more likely to stay where he left it.

Then again, a malfunctioning machine was what had brought him to this meeting place, so perhaps he should be a little less blithe.

He had just finished his meal when he caught a glimpse of movement on the western horizon. His traitorous heart started up again, performing its breathless gyrations. Yes, it was an angel; it was Alleya. She seemed to carry the sun on her back. Her blond head was haloed with light, and her wings seemed to brush color and glitter into the sky with every one of their downward strokes. It hurt to look at her, but there was nowhere else he could possibly turn his eyes. He practiced smiling, he reviewed all the dialogue he had laboriously constructed over the past few days. In the end, he just stood there stupidly as she touched her feet gracefully to the ground and walked toward him.

"You must have traveled fast," she said, an ordinary greeting, smiling at him but not as if it was causing her any great effort. "I thought I would certainly be here before you."

He smiled back, and most of his dizziness left him. "Edori horse," he said, and his voice sounded calm, quite reasonable. "Bred for travel."

"Can we just leave it here while we go up in the mountains?"

"That's the theory. I've been told she'll be here when I get back. Are you hungry? I've got food left over."

"Oh—not now. But once we've made the climb, I might be."

It was easier and easier to talk to her; then again, it was what he had been born to do. "How high do we have to go, anyway?"

"Up the mountain. I think it takes several hours."

"We'd better get started then. Can I carry anything for you?"

"Oh, no. I can manage. But thanks."

So they turned their attention to the rocky slopes that formed the base of the mountain and, after a little study, determined where the trail must lie. Alleya led the way at a brisk but reasonable pace, and the exercise helped counteract the winter chill. The higher they climbed, the more defined the trail became, and within a few miles, it narrowed to a track no more than a couple of yards wide. Both sides were lined with rusting iron stakes, higher than a man's head and ground to a point at the top.

"What are these?" Caleb finally asked, pointing.

She glanced behind her with a grin. "Didn't I tell you about those? When Hagar had this place built, she made it as inaccessible to angels as possible. You can see that no angels could land anywhere along the path, because their wingspan is too great—their feathers would be pierced. Look," she added, and came to a halt. She shook out her wings, which she had folded behind her for the hike, and let them lie on the path behind her. Sure enough, the trailing edge of each landed a few inches behind the perimeter of the slim rods.

"As I understand it, all the grounds around the house are studded with stakes just like these. It would be folly for an angel to try to land there. Which was the point. Hagar didn't want her husband or anyone else dropping in on her without an invitation. She liked the idea that Uriel had to come climbing up the mountain like any lowly petitioner if he wanted to see her here."

"And did he ever make the effort?"

Alleya laughed and resumed walking. "According to the stories, he did. They were always arguing, and she was always leaving him, so he continually had to come here to fetch her."

"I'm surprised he went to the trouble," Caleb observed. "She sounds like a difficult woman."

"Oh, by all accounts she was, but from everything I've read, my sympathies are with Hagar. Uriel comes across as hotheaded and selfish and domineering. Not an easy man to live with."

"Why was he made Archangel, then, if he was so hateful?"

"Uncommon leadership skills. The ability to inspire men. You have to remember, they were the first people on Samaria. Trying to establish—everything. Do everything. Build cities. Build angel holds. Learn how to farm the land. It must have been very rough. You'd need someone a little autocratic to hold everything together."

They didn't talk much after that exchange; they needed their breath and their strength for the climb. The pathway narrowed still more as they ascended, causing Alleya to fold her wings back so tightly they trailed on the ground behind her. Walking a few paces behind, Caleb watched the gleaming white edgefeathers as they played through the dirt, skipped over exposed roots and dislodged tiny rocks. No mud and no debris clung to them; nothing dimmed their radiance.

They halted twice for short breaks, to take sips of water and catch their breath. The sun was quite low in the sky when they trudged up the final rise and broke through to a sort of clearing. Well, there was a house still standing and what looked like the ruins of two or three gardens, but the general undergrowth of the surrounding hillside had certainly encroached on what once was civilized ground. Scattered around the edges of the clearing, and dotting the gardens and the pathways, were more of the metal spikes. Angels not welcome here, indeed.

"Hagar's Tooth," Alleya said, stepping forward again after a long pause. "Let's take a look."

In the immediate grounds, there was not much to see, except cultivated flowers run wild, a cheerful little stream that wound its way tightly around the house and then bubbled away down the mountain, and one or two small outbuildings that may have served for storage. The door to the house was unlocked, and they entered cautiously.

"Spiders inside, I would guess," Alleya said.

"Mice. Maybe rats. Snakes."

"Mountain cats. Bears."

"Too well-built. But I'll bet there's little creatures."

There were no immediate signs of animals or rodents, though there were plenty of cobwebs clinging to the walls in the first room they entered. They moved from room to room to find each one covered with dust but seeming somehow pristine and uncluttered. Each room was sparsely furnished with a few tables or chairs, or a bed and an armoire; but everything looked lovingly chosen and precisely placed.

Alleya stood in the middle of one of the bedrooms and did a slow turn to take in the plain mirror, the single decorative hanging on the wall. "It's strange," she said softly, as if thinking aloud. "Obviously, this place has been neglected for years but it still seems—clean, and serene, and cared for. There's something soothing about it. It's almost like Mount Sinai—a place of calm and quiet, away from the rest of the world."

"I wouldn't have put it that way," Caleb answered, "but I know exactly what you mean. I like it here."

"So do I."

Exploring farther, they stumbled across a cedar closet which seemed to have been effectively closed against insects and small marauders. Inside were blankets and pillows and women's clothes, all apparently unmolested.

"Someone was a good housekeeper," Alleya observed.

"Something to sleep on tonight," Caleb said.

They squandered their daylight hours investigating; it was full dark before they had finished looking over the house. "Which was stupid of us, since now we can't start looking around for the thing we came here to find," Alleya remarked.

"There's always tomorrow morning," Caleb said. "Anyway, it might take us days to find. We don't even know what we're looking for."

"No," she sighed. "Or what to do with it if we find it."

The long day and the physical exercise had made both of them hungry, so they went to the kitchen and took stock of their rations. Each of them had brought enough food to last a couple of days, and they instantly agreed to share items so that there was more variety for both.

They worked together to clean enough of the kitchen to make it usable, building a fire in the large fireplace to heat their food. Alleya found candles in a range of sizes and, lighting them, placed them all around the small room. Their flickering opal light gave the room a festive air.

"You forget how nice candlelight can be," she said. "At the Eyrie, of course, everything is gaslight."

"And in the cities, it's all becoming electricity," Caleb said. "But I like a little candlelight now and then. More romantic."

It had been a calculated remark. She threw him a warning look, but then her face softened to a smile.

"Now if we only had wine and soft music," she said.

"I've got the wine," he said. "And you could sing."

"I'm not singing," she said automatically. "You brought *wine*? All the way from Luminaux?"

"I thought we might need it."

Another one of those looks, followed by a laugh. "Well, we might *enjoy* it," she said primly. "But we won't need it."

It was, all in all, one of the pleasantest evenings Caleb had ever spent. They sat at the small table in the gaily lit kitchen, eating off dishes supplied by some long-ago angelica, sipping their wine without noticing it, eating their food without tasting it. They talked. Caleb recounted in more detail the tale of his trip to Breven and back. Alleya told him about her visit with her mother and then, naturally segueing to the topic, about growing up in Chahiela. That prompted Caleb to reminisce about his own childhood, learning scientific theory at his father's side, learning simple human courtesies from his frail but determined mother. Their conversation was thoughtful, unhurried, built half of memories and half of observations, and Caleb had never felt so completely in tune with himself or another human being.

It was obvious that Alleya felt it, too, that she gave herself up to the pleasure of that conversation, but only for a couple of hours. He could tell when she realized that she must halt this intimacy or lose herself in it completely, for she gave him a bright smile and seemed to draw a polite veil across her face.

"Well! This has been delightful, I know, but after all we didn't come here just to talk about our parents," she said, rising to her feet and beginning to gather up the dishes. "I don't know about you, but I'm exhausted. Why don't I clean up in here, and you see if you can pick out some clean blankets to make up the beds?"

He wanted to protest, but he didn't want to alarm her. They would be here much of tomorrow, most likely; he might even have another evening like this in store for him. A plea now would only put her more on guard for the duration of the visit.

"Very well," he said instead. "Which bedroom do you want?"

"Oh, the one with the blue wall hanging, I think."

"I'll take the one with the big wooden bedstead. I'll see what I can find for us to sleep on."

In another thirty minutes or so, they were settling themselves in for the night and promising to wake early in the morning. Caleb waited for the sound of her door closing, then stretched himself out on his bed, wondering what odd sequence of events had led him to this place, this evening, this company. Not that he was complaining. At the moment he could not think of a place he'd rather be, a person he'd rather be with. He turned on his side, prepared to spend a wakeful night wishing he was closer to that same person, and fell instantly asleep.

Alleya was awake before he was in the morning, and he scrambled to catch up, eating and dressing as quickly as he could. When he joined her outside a few minutes later, he found her prowling through the ruined gardens. She straightened as he approached her and wrinkled her nose in a fatalistic smile.

"No listening device here," she said. "I didn't think there would be."

"Where do you think we should begin looking?" Caleb asked.

She hesitated, and did one slow pivot, inspecting the grounds. It was a rare, glorious day; the sun, looking big and lazy, made just enough effort to spin a silken cocoon of warmth around them. Every rocky outcrop, every mossy log, looked rich with possibility.

"Well, we didn't find anything in the house," she said. "I'd say we start in the near gardens and work our way outward. See how far we get."

"Has it occurred to you," he asked, "that this listening device might be hidden or buried? Or someplace completely inaccessible?"

"Oh, it's occurred to me," she said wryly. "But all we can do is look."

Look they did for the rest of the morning, moving in ever-widening circles around the perimeter of the grounds. Caleb had given some thought to what they were seeking, and he considered it unlikely that it had, in fact, been buried (because why stop up your artificial ears with rock and dirt?), though he assumed it must be in some protected place. And if it had been here since the founding of Samaria, some 650 years ago, it was unlikely to have been snugged under the protruding roots of even the most ancient tree (where Alleya persisted in looking). No, it was hidden in a small cave or installed in some stone housing, if it was here at all, and so Caleb turned his attention to rocky outcrops and tumbles of boulders.

They stopped once for a quick lunch, then resumed their search. They were now about a mile from the house and could choose either to go up toward the stony peak or down the overgrown mountain.

"What do you think?" Alleya asked.

"Up," Caleb replied without hesitation.

She seemed willing to trust him, but asked, "Why?"

He smiled. "Closer to Jovah," he said.

She smiled back. "As good a reason as any."

So they made their way slowly up the mountain, where the greenery grew more and more sparse and the little stone caverns grew more and more numerous. Twenty men diligently searching for a week could not have looked inside all the possible hiding sites, Caleb thought in some disgruntlement. If they were to find anything, it would be through sheer luck.

He heard Alleya, a few yards away from him, give a tired laugh. "She even thought angels might try to land here," Alleya said.

Caleb glanced over at her with a frown. "What? Who?"

Alleya pointed to a slim metal spike protruding from a cluster of rocks about twenty yards above them. "See? Another one of the pointed rods. All the way out here."

Caleb glanced behind them, trying to remember where he had last seen one of Hagar's lethal angel deterrents. Yards away, maybe half a mile. "I don't think she's the one who placed that," he said slowly. "It doesn't look like the others."

Alleya shaded her eyes. "You're right. It's thinner. Shorter. Not so sharp-looking." She looked back at Caleb. "What do you think it is, then?"

He moved toward it cautiously, since the rocky slope did not offer easy footing. "Flag, maybe. Tell people where something was buried. Or maybe—"

"What?"

He sought a better handhold and shook his head. "We don't know much about noise and how it travels," he said. "Maybe it's something that facilitates the transmission of sound."

She caught her breath. "The listening device."

"Well, let's see."

Once they arrived at their destination, they had more work ahead of them, for the root of the thin metal rod was buried deep under a pile of heavy stone. Working together, the man and the angel lifted and laid aside twelve or fifteen boulders which had obviously been carefully selected and arranged to create a small, well-protected cairn. Caleb considered himself a fit man, but the angel's strength was greater than his own; she could carry heavy rocks that his own muscles could not have supported. She worked beside him tirelessly for the full hour it took to open the crypt.

"I see something," she said once, breathlessly, when about half the rocks had been removed.

"You have been gifted with special vision as well?" he panted.

"What? No, look, can't you see it? It looks like something silver. And it's—I can see a blue light glowing on top of it—"

So could Caleb, now that he peered more determinedly into the little cave. They redoubled their efforts to move the rocks and free the object inside.

At last, it was clear of all rubble and they both came to their knees to examine it as closely as they could. As Alleya had said, they had discovered a silver metal box encrusted with black knobs and a single glowing sapphire light. It was no bigger than the basket a woman would carry to market, but more square, and the thin rod they had spotted was embedded firmly into its back.

Cautiously, in case it gave off a violent heat, Caleb reached a hand out and placed his fingertips along the unmarked surface. Cool as water, and just as smooth. He touched each knob without adjusting it, ran his fingers down the back of the rod to see how it connected with the box. Then, frowning, he flattened his palm along the top plane of the device.

"What?" Alleya asked quickly.

"It feels like—there's the slightest tremor inside."

"Like it's alive?" she demanded.

"No—like it has a motor running. A more finely tuned motor than I've ever encountered, but—there's that electric vibration."

"Let me feel."

She laid her own hand along the top of the box, then moved it experimentally to the sides and the front. She nodded. "I can feel it, but barely. What does that mean?"

Caleb took a deep breath. "Well. That, and the blue light, would seem to indicate that it's switched on. That it's working."

At first, she seemed excited. "It's working? You mean, it's listening to our words and sending them to Jovah?"

He nodded. "If that's what it's intended for."

"Of course it is! And that means—" Suddenly the excitement faded from her face; now she appeared anxious. "But if it's been working all along—if it's been relaying our prayers to Jovah—"

"Well, I don't know how great its range is, but I would assume pretty far—"

"Then he has been hearing our prayers and choosing to ignore them," she finished quietly.

Caleb turned a hand palm-up in a gesture empty of comfort. "It's only a guess," he said. "Perhaps this thing isn't working after all. Or perhaps—something else is blocking the songs of the angels."

She shook her head. "Perhaps," she said, but she did not sound convinced. "But I think he just has chosen not to listen."

Caleb was fingering the foreign silver box again. He was dying to take it apart and examine every minute detail, but he knew there was no justification for such an action if it really was still functioning. "Sing for me," he said suddenly. "Let's see if that has any effect on the box. Maybe we'll be able to tell if it's really transmitting."

She sat back on her heels, too discouraged to make her usual protest against performing. "What should I sing?" she asked helplessly.

"Anything. A prayer for sunshine."

She did smile at that. "We already have sunshine."

"Well, you must know more prayers than I do."

She nodded abstractedly and thought for a moment. Then she folded her hands together and began a soft, musical incantation—so soft that neither Caleb nor the machine registered the beginning of her song. But her voice grew stronger, sweeter, rich with its own peculiar cadences, and for a moment Caleb suspended his breath to listen. Almost on the instant, a ripple of green lights played down the left edge of the silver box, and a blinking light, also green, set up a fluttering pattern next to the steady blue one. Alleya faltered briefly, then recovered, her voice soaring in a high, pure loop that seemed to brighten each individual bulb to a point of ecstatic radiance.

Caleb understood their frenzy. As soon as Alleya hit her first gorgeous trill, he felt a pulse of fever in the black Kiss on his arm. As the intensity of her song built, so did the heat in his Kiss, till he felt as if a brand were being pressed against his skin. He made no protest, though he glanced down once to see the scarlet light filtering through the charred nodule on his arm. He merely clenched one fist and listened intently to the heavenly sweep and circle of the angel's song.

He had kept his eyes mostly on the antics of the machine; he did not feel capable of looking at Alleya while she sang so close beside him. So when she abruptly fell silent, he swung his eyes over in surprise, to find her staring at him with something like panic. Her eyes flicked from his burning Kiss to his face and back to his Kiss, and she put a hand across her mouth as if to hold back unspeakable words.

"What is it? What's wrong?" he demanded, relieved to feel the heat beginning to fade from his arm.

She shook her head. "I think the machine is working," she said in a whisper.

"No question," he answered. "At least on this end. So what do we do now, angela?"

She was still shaken by some unexpected anxiety, but she was recovering fast, and she clearly was not going to offer him an explanation. "We bury the device again, and we leave it alone," she said. "And we find some other way to reach Jovah."

A few hours later, they were back at the cottage, making unenthusiastic plans for leaving in the morning. They had said very little on the way back down the mountain, leaving Caleb to wonder what exactly had caused Alleya's perturbation. Soon enough, he thought it might be physical pain, for he caught her favoring her injured ankle more and more.

"Would it be easier if I carried you?" he asked once, stopping her with a hand on her shoulder.

She shook her head. "Hard to carry an angel," she said with an attempt at humor. "The wings get in the way."

"Then fly back down," he said.

"Nowhere to land safely," she answered briefly. "I'll be fine."

But she looked haggard and worn when they finally made it to the door of Hagar's cabin, and Caleb ordered her to rest while he prepared a meal. She slept longer than he expected, for it was well past nightfall by the time she reappeared. The food had been ready for an hour; he had kept it warming by the fire.

"How do you feel?" he asked.

"Better. I don't think I'll enjoy the climb down the mountain tomorrow, but after that I shouldn't have to walk much till my foot is healed."

"Couldn't you take off from here? Isn't that easier than landing?"

"If I climbed to the roof, maybe." She was joking.

He took her seriously. "We should try that. Figure out a way to get you up there."

"Caleb, I'll be fine."

"Well, we'll think about it in the morning."

Dinner this night was much more subdued than the meal the night before, though Alleya made no demur about finishing up the wine Caleb had brought. Neither did she protest when he suggested moving to a more comfortable place in the main room, where he had also built a fire. He settled her on a pile of clean blankets before the hearth, placing a large cushion at her back and a small pillow under her foot. He sat cross-legged a few feet away from her, turned toward her, watching her face. She looked into the fire.

"Tell me something," he said softly, after neither of them had spoken for a couple of minutes. "What alarmed you so much up there on the mountain? You stared at me as if I were a ghost."

The wine had mellowed her a little; she gave a faint smile. "Did I? I was surprised. I thought you had said the Kiss in your arm was dead."

"I thought it was. But it hurt like fire today."

"Do you know what caused it to burn like that?" she asked.

The question sounded idle, but he had seen her tense; this, then, was the cause of her uneasiness. "No," he said. "But it burned like that once before, too."

"Did it? When?"

"When you sang before the Edori fire outside of Breven."

She nodded once and did not reply. When he was sure she would volunteer no more, Caleb asked, "Do you know why? I've never heard of such a thing before."

She made an indecisive gesture. "There are legends . . . I suppose you don't know them? I suppose your mother never told you about how each Kiss is supposed to light when true lovers meet for the first time?"

"Stories," he said, and now his own voice was a whisper. "But I never believed them . . . And I had met you several times before that."

She nodded again. She still had all her attention on the balletic antics of the leaping flames. "They say," she murmured, "that the Archangel Gabriel and his angelica, Rachel, felt their Kisses light with fire when they heard the other sing. All through their lives, when one sang, the other burned. So go the legends. I don't know if there's any truth to them."

"The Kiss on my arm was dead," Caleb said, "until I heard you sing. And what do you think that means?"

She was silent a long time, then sighed and shifted position. "I don't know," she said. "Perhaps that, when you hear me sing, you believe again in the god."

Caleb shook his head. "That's not true," he said. "When I hear you sing, you are all I can think about. I can't even clear my head long enough to remember to breathe. No god could make me feel like that."

"But it is Jovah who controls each Kiss, Jovah who chooses lovers," she reminded him. "It is Jovah who makes you react as you do."

"I could dig this Kiss from my arm—I could crush it underfoot," he said deliberately. "I could destroy it completely, and still I would turn into a fool every time I heard your voice. Don't you understand, Alleya? You have struck me to the soul. My heart lights with its own bright fire when I hear your name. If I could show you that, then you might believe how much I love you."

Now, finally, she turned her eyes his way. Her own were wide and wondering, almost childlike in their directness. "How can you love someone you know so little?" she asked. "How can you think of him by day and dream of him by night—and yet have only a few dozen words to remember that he has ever spoken to you? I have schemed to find ways to see you again. I have imagined so many things you might say to me. And yet I have met you—what?—three or four times in my life. Love cannot grow that quickly. Nothing can, that is to last."

"Love grows as it will," Caleb said. Taking her hand, he moved closer to her, settling by her side. He reached out his free hand to feel the smooth contours of her face. "And I do not believe it can be either altered or turned aside."

He leaned in to kiss her, but she drew back, her eyes wide. "You can't be afraid of me," he protested.

"I am afraid of everything," she whispered. "The world grows perilous around us and the god turns his back on the angels. If I allow myself to love you, I will forget the other things I am supposed to do. I cannot concentrate when you are near. I cannot think."

"Don't think," he said, and kissed her. He felt the world shake loose of its moorings; he felt the air around him dance. No, it was the intimate wind created by the flutter of her wings, lifting, folding around them both. The world spun into a whorl of whiteness; she was the only solid thing to cling to. He felt her hands grip his shoulders, he felt her feathers wrapping around his back. Every inch of his body blazed with fever.

"Are you still afraid?" he asked her once, lifting his head just so he could look down at her. Her face was flushed, her eyes tilted languorously. She laughed up at him.

"No," she whispered. "But I cannot think."

"You don't need to think," he whispered back, and kissed her once more.

They did not speak again for a long time; they had no need for any language as clumsy as words. But their fingers and mouths communicated everything they needed to know. They undressed each other slowly, lingering over buttons, laughing over knots, murmuring delight at each new beauty of the flesh revealed. Alleya cupped her palms over Caleb's cheeks then brought her fingertips to his lips, then placed her hands flat on the muscles of his chest. A second time, the same motions, repeated with a luxurious slowness.

"What was that?" he asked in her ear. "With your hands?"

"Thc languagc of thc dcaf and blind, who cannot hear or see," she replied in a voice so low he could barely catch her words. "We touch their faces and their bodies to speak to them."

"What did you just say to me?"

For a reply, she lifted his hand and placed it first along her cheekbone, then across her mouth, then against her breast. "See? You have just replied."

"And what have we said?"

"I told you I loved you. And you replied in kind."

"That was not a secret," he said.

"But it is always good to be told."

"I love you," he whispered. "And I will tell you often."

She placed her hands against his face again, spelling out some complicated reply, but this time he did not bother to ask for a translation. What she wanted was clear enough, and it was what he wanted; and it was a long time before they spoke aloud again.

But in the morning, everything was changed. Sometime in the night, they had moved together to the bedroom Alleya had taken as hers, and there they had lain together under the cedar-scented blanket and the angel's palely glowing wings. Caleb had run the flat of his hand slowly, sensuously, over the plaited mesh of feathers, feeling them flex and give and spring back under his fingers, until Alleya had turned to him with a muffled protest.

"What? I'm sorry. Does that bother you?" he asked, instantly contrite.

Her laugh was breathless. "No, I like it. But it makes it very hard to fall asleep."

He smiled in the dark. "Ah. It is not soothing, in other words."

By reply, she lifted her hands and drew them in a light, tickling motion up the side of his ribcage. "Is that soothing?" she asked.

"Not exactly. But I like it."

And that led to another wordless discussion of what calmed their bodies and what roused them, and that, finally, led to exhaustion and sleep. Caleb woke late, a smile already on his lips and his hands reaching for the woman beside him; but she was gone, and only the morning sunshine laid its golden head on the pillow next to his.

So that was a bad sign, but there was worse to come. Dressing quickly, he hurried through the small house till he came across the angel in the kitchen, sorting through their provisions and making herself a small packet. Her hair was still damp from washing, and everything about her looked clean, newly made; she was as fresh as the morning itself. But the set of her shoulders bespoke strain, and her movements were rushed and purposeful.

"I have farther to go, but it will take you longer to get where you're going," she said, glancing up briefly, then returning her attention to her task. "So I'm leaving you most of the food."

"Not the greeting I had hoped for," he said, moving forward very slowly. "Something more romantic, perhaps. Even a simple 'I hope you slept well, my love' would have pleased me."

Her hands stilled and she was motionless for a moment, before looking over at him with a rueful smile. "I enjoyed sleeping beside you, Caleb," she said, "but I have to leave within the hour."

"Can you tell me why?"

"It's complicated."

"Can you at least kiss me farewell?"

She made a helpless gesture with her hands, but now he was beside her, and it was simpler to say silently. He took her into a gentle embrace, and she wrapped her arms around his back, resting her head on his shoulder. For a moment, he bore her full weight as she pressed herself against him, hugging him like a child fearful of the word goodbye, and then she freed herself and stepped back.

"I can't stay," she said. "You confuse me."

He took her shoulders in a light grip and held her so that she faced him. She let him hold her but looked unhappy about it.

"I don't mean to confuse you," he said. "What I want is simple enough. I love you. I want to be with you. How does that distress you or complicate your life?"

"I'm the Archangel," she said, her voice barely above a whisper. "It is my duty to find—and marry—the man Jovah has chosen for me. So far I have not had the time or inclination to look for my angelico too hard. But I must seek him out—soon, now, because he must sing beside me at the Gloria. And that is scarcely more than two months away. I have been terribly lax in my duty. But I cannot disregard it any longer."

It was a blow; he knew very little of the conventions governing Archangels and their mates, but the word "marry" gave him a fair estimate. "How do you identify this angelico? What does he do? Is he a mortal man?"

She shook her head to signify she was not entirely sure of the answers. "Jovah selects him. I don't know the god's criteria. What the angelico does is—sing, and hear petitions that are not brought to the Archangel directly, and—and be spouse to the Archangel. Yes, he is a mortal man. Angels do not marry angels."

"I am a mortal man," Caleb said. "Why could I not be angelico?"

At that she wrenched herself away, and began pacing the room in some distress. "Jovah names him! Jovah chooses him! I cannot just petition the god for the man I would select on my own!"

"Why not?"

"Because—because Jovah has his reasons. Because that is not the way it is done. Because Jovah has already made his selection."

Another blow; he was beginning to feel physically bruised.

But he kept up his dogged questions. "Who is he, then? Why have you not gone to him?"

She tossed him a look over her shoulder and continued her fretful pacing. "Because Jovah is sometimes obscure. He told me to seek out the son of Jeremiah, which I have learned means one of the descendants of the Archangel Gabriel. That's who I was looking for when I came to the Edori camp in Breven, because I thought the man might be an Edori. . . . But it turned out to be a false lead. I need to keep looking." She sighed, stopped in her tracks, threw her hands into the air. "I need to do so many things."

Caleb came closer. "What if I told you my father's name was Jeremiah?"

She actually laughed. "You would be lying. And anyway, I am fairly certain that the Jeremiah referred to is a man dead these hundred and fifty years."

"And if you cannot find this man?"

She sighed. "I don't know. I don't know. I don't know if Jovah would allow an imposter to sing at my side. According to the legends, an Archangel may only replace the angelico—or the angelica—if the one chosen by Jovah is dead. And Jovah seems certain this man is alive, though he is, for whatever reason, unable to name him."

"And if you find him, then what?" Caleb finally asked, the only question with an answer he cared about. "You will love him? You will cleave to him? You will not willingly see me again?"

Alleya spoke to the floor. "He will be my husband," she said. "There are angels who care little about the implications of such a bond, but they would be difficult for me to cast aside lightly. It is hard to imagine that I will love him." She looked up at him now, her face both defiant and oddly pure. "It is hard to imagine that I will love anyone but you. But they say the god is wise and chooses well. I must believe him."

"The god," Caleb said deliberately, "cannot even hear you when you pray to him. How can you think he has your best interests at the core of his heart?"

She nodded. "Perhaps he does not. But as far as I am able, I must do his will. That is why I am Archangel, to carry out the laws and commandments of my god. I cannot choose which of those laws I am to obey and which I can with impunity break. It is everything or nothing."

"Then nothing," he said.

She shook her head. "And I am also Archangel because, of all the voices raised to him, mine is the only one Jovah heeds," she said gently. "If I cannot reach Jovah, we are all lost. I cannot walk away now from the task I have been given. If we were all safe, if the storms had all abated, if someone else could make the god listen, I would go with you this morning. But you cannot ask me to abandon a whole world. There must be something I can do to save us."

"Then abandon no one," he said. "Do not abandon me."

"I must," she said, and turned away. "No other course is open."

And she would not say another word to him, though he followed her from room to room, cajoling, pleading, trying to interfere with the knots she made on her packet of food, on her backpack of clothing. It was as if he were invisible, bodiless, a man she had dreamed, perhaps, not a mortal man with whom she must actually contend. Feeling less and less corporeal as the hour wore on, he trailed helplessly behind her as she finally left the house, carrying a kitchen chair in her hands.

"I've thought about what you said," she remarked, as if they had been engaged all this while in easy conversation. "I think perhaps I can take off from the roof. If I can get up there. Could you hold the chair steady for me?"

So they found the point at which the roof made its lowest slope, and he grasped the chair firmly, giving her a hand while she clambered up the slanted grade. The green tile made a slippery climb, but there was a flat section in the middle near the back. Alleya picked her way there surefootedly, spreading her wings to help her balance. As soon as she found her footing, Caleb scrambled up after her, catching up with her just as she made it to the level place. A touch of his hands turned her to face him.

"This cannot be the last time we see each other," he said.

"Maybe so, maybe not," she said, kindly enough. "It is hard to guess what will happen."

"Promise," he said.

She gave a soft laugh. "I can't."

"Promise," he repeated. "Please."

She lifted her fingers to his face, stroked the rough stubble of his morning beard as if it pleased her. "So often we don't get any of the things we want," she said. "Be content with what you've been given."

"My desire is too great to feed on so little."

"It is not a little thing," she whispered. "My heart—and it is yours, although you cannot keep it."

"Don't leave," he said. "Stay another day."

Now she lifted her other hand, so that one of her palms lay against each side of his face. "Stay well, be happy," she whispered. "I shall think of you every day of my life."

"Alleya," he said desperately, and she stopped his mouth with a brief, impassioned kiss. When she drew back, he saw tears standing in her eyes, but she smiled up at him nonetheless.

"Till we can see each other again," she said. "If we can."

"I love you," he said.

She did not repeat it. Instead she moved her fingers from his cheeks, to his mouth, to his chest. He raised his hands to cover hers but she slipped away from him, took a step backward. Her wings spread, catching the white morning light, filling his sight, blocking the whole world. She was encased in brilliance; he could not go near enough to touch her. Then the great wings swept downward and up, and the air around him whirled with a speckled light. He fell backward a pace as she continued to ascend, and within three wingbeats, three heartbeats, she was a small, bird-sized shape above him in the cloudless sky. He watched until she disappeared, and then he stood there another ten minutes, another thirty, looking toward the horizon where she had disappeared.

Finally, he shook himself free of his stupor and descended cautiously to the ground. Moving methodically around Hagar's cabin, he went from room to room, erasing traces of their presence and making sure every window was tightly secured.

It was a little before noon when he began the long, wearisome hike down to the base of the mountain. The descent was easier than the climb had been, though on the way up he had had company; now his only companion was his brooding memory. But it kept him completely engrossed until he reached the foot of the mountain, and looked around for his horse.

She was there, quietly grazing, and she made no demur when he came over and instantly threw on the bridle. Caleb glanced up once at the westering sun, gauging how many hours of daylight travel he had left; not many. But he was not in a mood to wait for the morrow. He had a long ride ahead and wanted to reach his destination as soon as possible.

In minutes the mare was saddled and his gear was stowed on her back. Caleb swung himself up and lightly pulled on the reins, and the mare obligingly turned her head toward the northwest.

He expected to take three or four days to reach Velora. And even that would be too long.

Chapter Seventeen

Having declared her primary mission to be finding the son of Jeremiah, Alleya returned to the Eyrie with no clear idea of how to accomplish the task. And feeling so weighted down with depression that she wasn't sure she had the strength to undertake it. It didn't help much that she had spoken nothing but the absolute truth to Caleb Augustus; she couldn't imagine spending the rest of her life without him. Knowing he was alive, eager, in love with her, and failing to go to him—this was a dreadful prospect to face for the rest of her days. Surely even stern Jovah could not ask so much of her.

Although he was asking a great deal in other ways. Alleya had not flown an hour from the Corinnis when she plunged headlong into a storm that could have passed for a standing pool of water, so thickly did the raindrops fall. She felt her wingbeats slow as her heartbeat speeded up; the first strong buffet of wind made her want to cry out in fear. But she could not give in, she could not succumb to terror. She gulped down deep breaths and forced her wings to gather power.

Once above the worst of the clouds, she made her ritual prayer for clear weather. She was surprised and more than a little pleased when, less than thirty minutes later, the clouds began to part and the rain thinned away to nothing. So he still loved her a little bit, Jovah did; she could take comfort from that.

Though love, she was beginning to think, was more often a heartache than a comfort.

But she would not think about love.

When she made it to the Eyrie later that day—damp, bedraggled and tired—she found she had almost certainly been away too long. Everyone in the confines of the hold had some specific, personal reason to see her in private; every single citizen of Velora had apparently walked up the grand stairway to approach her with his own petition; and half the angels of the other two provinces had dropped by to inquire about her health and well-being. She did not know where to begin or who to see.

She managed to avoid them all for that first evening and take a solitary dinner, but the next morning, all of her visitors and all of her problems still remained. She closeted herself with Samuel for the first hour of the day, reviewing the priorities as he saw them and delegating to him any tasks he was willing to take on.

"I don't know where I'd be without you," she said with a sigh as he rose to his feet and prepared to tackle his own assignments. "You're so much more efficient than I am."

"You'd be back in the archives, reading till midnight, like you used to be before you were chosen," he said with a sad smile. "And I'd lay money that there's not a day you wouldn't still rather be back there than out here."

"And you'd win your bet," she said with a little laugh. "But *Jovah's cause, and not our laws*. We do as the god directs us."

"How's your foot?" he asked abruptly. "I notice you've been favoring it."

"Oh, it's much better! And my face hardly shows any bruises at all. I'm quite healed, I think."

"Do you know what you plan to do next?" he asked, lingering at the door. She had already given him the outlines of her search at Hagar's Tooth—the discovery of the listening device, the proof that it was working. He had interpreted it just as she had.

"No," she said, which was a lie. "Do you have any suggestions?"

"No, but Mary might."

She felt an instant tickle of alarm. "Mary! Is she here, too?"

He nodded. "Arrived last night after you'd gone to your

bed." His face lit with a grim smile of satisfaction. "Asher would not let her come to your room, though she insisted she just wanted to make a short visit. I've never liked the boy so well."

"I wonder if she's learned anything," Alleya said, half to herself. "Well! Certainly she should be the person I meet with next."

But Mary, when she was ushered into Alleya's formal receiving room, had nothing but questions. "I cannot believe I forgot to ask you this when we met in Semorrah! Did you find the Edori man you were looking for? Is he the one we wanted?"

That seemed so long ago; so much else had happened since then. Alleya repressed a sigh. "He died when he was still a child," the angel answered. "No help there."

The oracle looked stern. "Then you must turn your attention back to the search for your angelico. Alleluia, the Gloria is only two months away. How can you expect to find and groom this man with such a limited amount of time? What if he is an untrained singer? What if he does not know a single mass? He must lead the Gloria, you know. There is so much he has to learn."

"I know—I know. I'm sorry," Alleya murmured.

"I blame myself. I should have paid more attention, made sure you were devoting your time to the search. But there have been so many problems needing our attention—"

"And we still do not know," Alleya interrupted, "if—whether or not the angelico is at my side—the god will hear any of us sing the Gloria."

Anxiety briefly etched deep lines in Mary's face; she looked almost hunted. "I know," the oracle said. "I think of that night and day. What if the god does not hear us, no matter who sings?"

"What, indeed?" Alleya responded. "I too think of it, day and night, night and day. When I am not worrying about the storms, and the floods, and the Jansai, and the Manadavvi, and my angelico—"

"Whom you *must* find."

"I will leave in a few days to seek him."

"Seek him where?" the oracle asked sharply.

"I have an idea where I might find him. I prefer to look first and tell you about it afterward. In case I am wrong."

"But Alleya—"

"And you," the Archangel added, almost playfully, "bend

your mind to the answer of this riddle: What happens if we do not find him? Who sings beside me on the Plain of Sharon?"

"I don't know . . ." Mary said very slowly, staring at her with painful intensity. "It has never happened before, that the Archangel has failed to find the one selected for him—or her—by Jovah."

"One more question, and then you can go," Alleya said, pleased with herself for that felicitous way of asking the oracle to leave. "When Delilah came to you asking Jovah to identify her angelico, did the god speak plainly? Or did he speak in cryptic words, as he did when we asked for my sake?"

"Delilah did not come to me for that information," Mary answered. "Job was the one who questioned the god on her behalf."

Alleya nodded wisely. "Ah. Well, then, I'll ask him next time I see him."

"Why? Is that important?"

"I'm not sure," Alleya said mysteriously. "Perhaps not."

Mary left the room reluctantly enough, and Alleya waited a moment before she summoned the next petitioner through the door. She would have to confirm it, of course, but she remembered Job once telling her that he thought Mary had misread the god; surely Jovah was too wise to choose Levi to be Delilah's angelico. In any case, Alleya had always thought Delilah had asked Mary to petition the god for her husband's name, but Mary had just denied it.

Certainly it would not be beyond Delilah's ability to pretend to each oracle that she had consulted the other on this most delicate, most momentous of matters. Delilah had been in love with Levi all her life; she had been determined to have him. No one had been surprised when the god granted her this dearest wish, because the god had always loved Delilah.

But Alleya suspected that Delilah had not even asked the god.

And that was a precedent that, once set, could be followed.

Unless the god had already named the angelico. And could he then be ignored or countermanded?

And if he was?

* * *

The day was filled with similar conferences: Samuel and the other angels could generally handle the problems of most of the petitioners, but Alleya tried to make it a point to personally meet with the river merchants, the wealthy landowners—and the ordinary farmers and shopkeepers who absolutely insisted on seeing the Archangel and no one else. Timothy, who had been monitoring for her the trade routes along the upper Galilee River, reported harmony for the moment between the Edori and the burghers who wanted to use that road.

"But there could be trouble," he added as he finished his story. "There were a couple of dry weeks, and then the rains started again. Jerusha said the Manadavvi came to her humbly enough, asking that she invite you to pray the showers away. She said you would, of course, and there was no hint—this time—that they blamed you for the rain. But we did not know when you would be available."

Alleya sighed. And how could she search for her angelico if she was constantly flying off to control urgent problems? "I can leave tomorrow—or, more likely, the day after," she said. "If you would like to send that message—"

"One of Jerusha's angels is here, to carry the news back."

"Very well. Tell them I will come as quickly as I can."

At the end of a long day of meetings, she was touched when a gentle knock at the conference door was followed by Asher, entering with a tray of food in his hands.

"I don't believe you've paused all day to take a bite of food, angela," he said somewhat reproachfully. "Now would be a good time for you to eat something."

She could not help smiling at him; his sweet fierceness appealed to her irresistibly. "How many people are still waiting to see me?"

"Three, but they have a great deal of patience," he assured her. "You have time for a quick meal."

"And will you share it with me?"

"I have dined, thank you. But I will sit with you, if you like."

So he sat across from her and entertained her with recent gossip about the Eyrie residents. He did not consider it gossip, of course. His eyes would darken with scorn as he recounted one mortal's actions, and his voice would lighten to admiration as he described a new song that Dinah had written.

"And that new mortal girl that I saw this morning in the kitchen—what was her name?" Alleya asked. "Attarah? How long has she been here and where did she come from?"

Unexpectedly, Asher blushed, but he answered readily enough. "She is from one of the conglomerate farms in the heart of Bethel," he said. "Her father is Omar Avinmass."

"Oh, I know him. And she came here because—?"

"Timothy says she is here for the same reason any mortal girl comes to an angel hold, but I'm sure she has a deeper commitment," Asher said in a rush. "Her father brought her here three weeks ago so she could apprentice and learn the way of the holds—it is not like she is some angel-seeker from the streets of Velora."

No, but many an ambitious father before Omar Avinmass had introduced comely daughters to the angels and then waited hopefully for the likely result. Alleya hid a smile. "Well, and it would not be such an awful thing if Timothy or you or one of the other angels came to enjoy her company," Alleya said. "After all, there are very few of us, and we must mate with mortals to bear more angel children. In some respects, it is your duty, you know, to find an attractive woman—"

Now she had offended him. He replied stiffly. "I realize that angels mate where they will and call it duty, but I think there should be more involved than lust and—and procreation. To mate without love is shallow and—barbaric. It makes angels no better than animals."

"I did not suggest you should proceed without love," Alleya said gently. "All I meant to say is that you should not be suspicious of her motives, or her father's motives. She looked like a pretty and thoughtful girl to me. She might be saving herself for love as well."

"Yes, that's what I thought, but Timothy said—" Asher began, and then launched into a comprehensive catalog of Timothy's jocular comments. The last thing Alleya had expected at this juncture, on this day, was to be counseling lovesick young angels first navigating the tricky seas of romance, but it wasn't in her to be abrupt with him. She knew well enough the torments passion could inflict.

"My advice?" she said at last. "Take Attarah to one of the nice music bars in Velora. Buy a couple of bottles of wine. Get to know her. You'll be able to resolve all of this much more easily than you thought."

"Yes, that's what Samuel said," Asher replied. "But I wasn't sure—but if you think it's all right . . ."

"It's perfect. Do it tomorrow. Tell me how it goes."

At last she was rid of him and could speak to her last three petitioners, and finally they, too, were gone. Weary past telling, she returned to her room, fell instantly into bed, and dreamed the short night away. When she woke, her thoughts went instantly to Caleb Augustus (*Where is he right now? What is he doing, what is he thinking? Are his eyes turned in the direction of Velora?*), as they always did. She assumed that thoughts of him would accompany her the rest of her life.

She'd had worse company. She pulled herself almost painfully to her feet, and forced herself to face the morning.

This day was identical to the one before, but the next day she varied her routine: In the morning, she prepared to set out for northeastern Gaza. Manadavvi country.

"And from there you'll be returning here?" Samuel asked her.

Alleya hesitated and then, unaccountably, told the truth. "No," she said slowly, "I'm going to Sinai for a day or two."

He looked at her sharply; something in her manner must have given away her reluctance to name her destination. "And why?" he asked.

"When I was at Chahiela, I was talking with one of the little girls there. Deborah. She treats me like her big sister, and I always try to spend time with her when I visit. Anyway, she said something about Jovah no longer being able to hear us. She told me I should touch his face instead."

"Touch his face?"

"At Chahiela, they have developed a method of communicating with those who are both blind and deaf. Touching your hand to a person's face, you can spell out letters and words with your fingers. And that was how Deborah suggested I talk to the god."

"But—I don't understand."

"There is an interface at Sinai. Maybe I can use it to communicate with the god."

Samuel looked thunderstruck. "Those are for the use of the oracles!"

"Perhaps the oracles have not used them correctly."

"And you think *you* can?"

"Maybe not. But I want to try."

"You don't even know the language the oracles use to speak to Jovah."

"I know enough of it."

Now he gave her another quick, worried look, but she chose to ignore it. "This is not something I would want to be generally known," she said. "But if there is an emergency, I want you to be able to find me."

"I will have no trouble keeping this secret," he said somewhat grimly. "If anyone asks after you, I'll tell them you're still in Gaza."

"Good enough. And I should be back in three or four days."

She turned to go, but he stopped her with a word. "Alleya."

She looked back at him. "Yes?"

"What do you plan to ask the god, when you touch his face?"

Who I should marry, and if I can select the man that I love. "Why he has abandoned us," she said aloud, "and how we can make him love us again."

"I hope he hears you."

"I hope he answers."

It was half a day's flight to Monteverde, and then another hour or two to the Manadavvi holdings that so richly bordered the northeastern seacoast of Gaza. Jerusha accompanied Alleya to the home of Aaron Lesh, a courtesy that Alleya appreciated. Much as she hated to admit it, she was intimidated by the vast holdings and palatial mansions of the Manadavvi gentry. Theirs was a luxury beyond anything she could comprehend. She was never so aware of her roots in tiny Chahiela as she was when she touched down on one of those sloping emerald Manadavvi lawns.

They flew through a light but ceaseless rain the whole way from Monteverde to the Lesh estate. Well, "estate" was not a grand enough word. Aaron Lesh owned miles and miles of the finest cropland in Gaza; a man could not walk from end to end of his property in a single day. His home was twice the size of the Eyrie and far more luxurious. He employed more servants than there were angels in Monteverde. And he was not the wealthiest of the Manadavvi.

"Wet and bedraggled—just the way I wish to present myself to Aaron Lesh," Alleya commented to Jerusha as they waited in a plush drawing room while a servant informed his master of their arrival. Jerusha looked surprised.

"We are not here to advise him about beauty or fashion," the other angel replied in apparent seriousness. Alleya sighed, and combed her damp hair with her fingertips.

But Jerusha was right. Aaron, who had them instantly shown into a small, pretty dining room, did not seem to notice their splashed clothes or dripping wings. "I'm glad you could come so quickly," he said, directing them to a round table already set with fine china and silver. "I know how busy you both are. I assume you are hungry from your long flight? We will be serving a formal dinner later, of course, but I thought you would want to refresh yourselves now."

"Yes, thank you," Alleya murmured, seating herself beside Jerusha. The chairs, expressly designed with cutaway backs to accommodate angel wings, were extremely comfortable; and mouth-watering aromas rose from the platters brought in. This was a different Aaron Lesh than Alleya was used to dealing with. Then again, Manadavvi considered themselves the most civilized of hosts. It was a point of honor with them to treat their visitors well.

Jerusha, of course, was not the woman for any circumlocution. She leaned forward across the table and said, "We flew in through rain. How long has it been storming?"

Aaron waited till the servants spooned food onto each of their plates before replying. "It has been raining for nine days now without cessation. Nothing worse than what you saw coming in. But so much rain—with no sun—it is not good for us."

"No, I'm sure it's not," Alleya said. The food was delicious. She took a small bite so she could swallow quickly and keep talking. "I will gladly do a weather intercession, but I must warn you—"

"I know. The god does not always listen to you, either."

"True. And even when he listens, sometimes the weather only lifts for a day or two. If you like, I will return as often as I can, but I cannot stay here long. I'm sorry."

"I understand," he said, and he sounded almost humble. "We will be grateful for whatever help you can offer."

In the end, they agreed that the angels would sing that afternoon, stay the night, and sing again in the morning, hoping that way to reinforce whatever effect their prayers might have. And to allow the Manadavvi to show off his hospitality.

So, shortly after their light meal, Jerusha and Alleya returned to the snarling skies to raise their voices to Jovah. Although she was used to singing in harmony (all angels were; harmony was the foundation of their existence), Alleya found it strange to offer these particular prayers as a duet. Jerusha signaled that Alleya should sing the primary part, and added her low, dark alto only after the Archangel had sung the opening verse. Alleya had always marveled at Jerusha's voice, smoky and textured, not at all the voice she would have expected from someone so cool and rational.

But their voices blended well enough, Alleya's light and restless, Jerusha's burred and throaty. Strange images came to Alleya's head, of opals laid across black velvet, of sparks shooting from a burning branch of ebony; those were the complements their voices evoked. And the god heard both of them, Alleya could sense it. It was as if Jerusha's rough voice hooked into the silken fabric of her own and rode it all the way to Jovah's ear.

The rain had not ended by the time they stopped, but they knew it would. The air changed around them in imperceptible shifts of weight and temperature. Even the color of the skies seemed less leaden. Alleya glanced at Jerusha as they finished their last song, and the other angel nodded, and soon enough they were back on the ground in front of Aaron Lesh's compound.

"I wonder how you do that," were Jerusha's first words.

"Do what?"

"Make the god hear you. Because he did. I could tell. It's the first time I could feel my prayers reach him since—since I don't know when. Since before Delilah fell."

"I don't know what I'm doing that's any different from what everyone else is doing."

"I know. I listened to you. It was a prayer we have all recited. Yet something in your voice reaches him."

"I'm glad it does."

"So are we all."

The rain had completely stopped by dinner time, which was a predictably lavish affair. The angels had anticipated that, of course, and brought with them formal attire, though Alleya found hers somewhat crushed from transport. She had packed a thin silver gown cut high in front, but daringly backless to accommodate her wings. It usually draped well over the curves of her body, but it usually hadn't been carried five hundred miles folded in a backpack.

"I hope I'll do," she said to Jerusha when the other angel stopped by her door on the way to dinner. "This gown is a little wrinkled. And I have no jewels besides my bracelets."

Jerusha wore an embroidered silk shirt over matching pants, and a collar of gold and emeralds, but she was no clotheshorse either. Although clearly she didn't care. "I wouldn't worry about it," she said, giving Alleya a cursory inspection. "My mother always said neither a man nor a woman could wear any greater adornment than a set of well-groomed wings."

Alleya repressed a sigh.

There were maybe fifty people awaiting them in the dining hall, all of them Manadavvi, all of them dressed as for some gala occasion. This was pretty much Alleya's definition of torture, but she endured the evening as best she could. Conversation ranged from trivial observations to barbed political comments to gossip covering every family of any financial status in the three realms. Alleya smiled and joined in where she could.

It was during dinner that she had her only real trial. She sat at the head table, the place of honor between Aaron and his brother; a few seats down from her was Emmanuel Garone. He was the one who broke conventional etiquette to lean over his dinner partners and confound her with a most unexpected question.

"I hear odd rumors from Breven," he said into what seemed to become an instant silence. "The Edori are engaging in shipbuilding for a most unbelievable enterprise."

Alleya carefully laid down her fork. "So I understand," she said.

"Ah, you'd heard of this mad plan? Romantic and desperate, wouldn't you agree?"

"They seem set on carrying it out," she said neutrally.

"What plan? What are the Edori doing now?" Various voices chimed in with questions. Emmanuel glanced quickly around the table.

"They're building ships to take them to Ysral," he said. "And all of them are going."

"No! That's crazy!"

"Ysral! But there's absolutely no proof—"

"All of them?" Aaron's voice cut in decisively.

"Well, hundreds," Emmanuel amended. "I don't know the exact head count."

"That's good news, isn't it?" someone else asked. "I mean, if all the Edori leave Samaria—"

Alleya stiffened. Aaron and Emmanuel shot quick glances in her direction. So it had been more than idle chatter after all. "If all the Edori leave," Emmanuel said slowly, "we might not have much need for the Edori sanctuaries after all."

"No need for them," Aaron agreed instantly. "No one living there."

"Of course, we'd have to put it up to a vote by the council—"

"That's all fairly premature," Alleya said in as level a voice as she could manage. "In the first place, the Edori haven't sailed yet—anything could occur to change their plans. In the second place, as Emmanuel said, we have no idea how many Edori are actually planning to leave. In the third place, who's to say that they won't come back? The sea is tricky, and these are not born sailors. I don't think you can assume there will be no need of the sanctuaries any time soon."

"But maybe not all of them," someone said in an urgent voice. "We'll keep a few, of course, for those who don't sail, but some of the bigger ones—"

Alleya lifted her index finger in an abrupt motion to demand silence. She kept a pleasant smile on her face, but she was seething; and she wanted them to know it. "Not another word," she said, enunciating clearly. "I came here to ask the god for sunshine, not to debate political ethics. And I will not taint a heartfelt prayer with a selfish, opportunistic discussion on how the Manadavvi can increase their holdings at the expense of a few hapless Edori. If they sail, if their numbers drop, if everything changes, we can talk about it later. But for now"—she picked up her fork again—"let's just enjoy the meal."

And she took another bite of food. There was a moment of complete silence and then Aaron's wife pointedly asked the man beside her how his son was faring, and a low murmur of conversation slowly rose around the table. Alleya saw Emmanuel give Aaron a long, steady look; the younger man shrugged and sipped from his wine. But she sensed they were not entirely disappointed. The topic had been broached, and even though it had not gone over well, they had lodged the thought in her mind. They could not have expected a much better reception.

The evening was interminable. The meal itself was a dozen courses (or so it seemed), and it was followed by a musical program. For a moment, as they were all shepherded into the recital hall, Alleya had a fear that she would be asked to perform; but the Manadavvi were too well-bred for that. Instead, the guests were entertained with flute players and a harpsichordist as well as a procession of exquisitely trained singers. Alleya enjoyed music, as a rule, but it had been a long day and she was tired of socializing. When the final notes had been played and the guests were invited into an adjoining room to play card games, she excused herself and went to bed.

The next morning, she woke to sunshine, and could not help a small surge of triumph from quirking her mouth into a grin. Nonetheless, she and Jerusha made good on their promise and returned to the skies above the lush Manadavvi land. They repeated their prayers, adding a few songs of thanksgiving to show their appreciation for Jovah's quick response.

"Good enough, I think!" Jerusha called to Alleya over the fluttering sound of their mingled wingbeats.

"Send a messenger if you need me to return," Alleya called back.

"You'll be at the Eyrie? No more jaunting around?"

Alleya could not help laughing. "I may make one quick detour before I go back but—yes, I should be at the Eyrie."

Jerusha nodded and waved. "Jovah guard you," she said.

"And you," Alleya replied. She dropped downward to catch a southeasterly breeze while Jerusha drove her wings against the thin air to achieve greater altitude. In a few minutes, they were far apart; and soon enough, Alleya had left the Manadavvi lands behind.

Back toward Bethel; on to Sinai.

As before, Alleya felt a certain peace descend upon her the instant she landed on the gray rock of Sinai. She moved with a sort of calm delight through the empty, echoing hallways, sparing a moment to wonder if she would like the place quite so well once it was tenanted again with petitioners and priests and acolytes. But she thought she would; the serenity of Sinai was imprinted on the very rocks and corridors. Voices were lost in that determined stillness; the soul's turbulence was soothed away.

But when would there be an oracle and his or her attendants here again? Alleya sighed. One more problem to worry over, once she had the time.

She made her way finally to the main chamber, where the interface was situated, pausing at the threshold of the room to kneel and empty her backpack. There, in with the silver gown, was an item that might have raised Jerusha's eyebrows: the book of translated phrases that the novice was to learn when he first began to use the interface to communicate with Jovah.

Well, she was a novice, and she was here to communicate. It still made her a little nervous to usurp the oracles' function, but she felt as if she had no choice. She needed, as Deborah had suggested, to touch the face of the god.

Still, it was with a certain awe tinged with apprehension that she approached the glowing blue screen at the far end of the chamber. The last time she had been here, the messages on the interface might as well have been printed in gibberish for all she could make of them. Now, having studied the ancient tongue for so many weeks, would she actually be able to understand what the god was trying to say?

As before, there were hieroglyphics crowding together, dark blue against the sky-colored background. Alleya pulled up the chair and seated herself before the screen, reading even before she sat down. Yes, these were words and phrases she recognized, though the syntax was difficult and there were technical references that did not make sense to her. She throttled her leaping excitement and forced herself to remain cool. So much depended on this; she must think calmly.

"Welcome, user. Station One of the J/S ship/land Internet stands open and ready for commands. Press the Enter key to initiate program. If you are asked for your password, type it in; if you have no password, type in 'new user' followed by the password you wish to use. If in the future you need to change your password, you may do so, but you must activate the 'change directory' program to do so."

She opened her book to the first few pages and skimmed them; yes, this was a standard screen, something the novice must read and respond to before going on. According to the instruction book, she must first press the square green key on the left side of the keyboard and then, when the screen emptied, type in her name. Not until then could she communicate with the god.

Cautiously, fearfully, she put her fingers against the square button, and gasped aloud when everything disappeared from the screen except a single blinking line. *That's what's supposed to happen*, she assured herself, but nonetheless, a momentary feeling of sickness threatened to overwhelm her. What if she did something awful? What if she unthinkingly destroyed this frail link to Jovah's heart?

She would not. She would be careful. She had no choice.

She was now supposed to identify herself to the god. Painstakingly, because not all the symbols on the keyboard corresponded to the ones she knew, she picked out her message ("new user") and then the letters of her name: A-L-L-E-L-U-I-A. Then she sat back in the chair and waited.

Nothing happened.

She glanced back at her textbook, worried again, but the mystery was soon solved. "Every time you wish to clear the screen or transmit a question, you must touch the Enter key," the instructions said. Ah—the square button must be pressed again. Alleya complied.

Instantly, the screen dissolved into blackness and just as rapidly re-formed with a new message across the top of the glass. Alleya leaned forward and puzzled out the words.

"Welcome, Archangel Alleluia, daughter of the woman Hope and the angel Jude," the god said. Alleya bounced in her chair, clapping her hands together like a child. He recognized her name! He knew her! She was right to have sought him out like this!

There was more, as the primer had told her there would be. "What do you wish to ask me?" was the brief question following the formal greeting.

She had more to ask than she could begin to formulate, and she wasn't sure how many questions the god's patience would endure. But she started with one of personal importance—it did, after all, have some bearing on the fate of the world.

"I must find my angelico," she typed in slowly, hunting for each individual letter on the keyboard. "Can you name him?"

The answer was the one she expected. "Seek the son of Jeremiah."

"Is the Archangel Gabriel the son of Jeremiah?" she asked.

"Yes," the god replied.

"So I must seek one of his descendants?"

"No," the answer appeared on the screen.

She had never been so taken aback. She stared for a moment at the single uncompromising syllable, then cleared the screen and restated her question.

"I am not to seek one of Gabriel's descendants to be my angelico?"

"No," the god said again.

"Then who am I to seek?"

"The son of Jeremiah."

It came to her slowly, stupidly, the solution filtering into her brain like water sieving through sand: Jeremiah had had more than one son. To herself, Alleya said, *Gabriel had a brother . . . and that would be* . . . She knew this; every scholar knew this, but just for a moment her brain would not yield the information. "Nathaniel," she whispered at last. "Gabriel's half-brother. Who founded the angel hold at Cedar Hills, and, by divine dispensation, married the angel Magdalena . . ."

Her fingers curled into fists on either side of the keyboard, her eyes squeezed shut in an effort to slow the whirling thoughts in her head. "And they had six daughters, all but one of them angelic, and that mortal daughter was named Tamar . . ."

Her eyes flew open. And Tamar had a great-great-grandson named Caleb Augustus. Could it possibly be—?

Alleya unfurled her fingers above the keyboard, ready to ask this most momentous of questions, but before she could begin typing, the colors on the screen swirled and went blank. She sat motionless, her hands frozen in position, afraid of what she might see next. And indeed, the image that formed on the glowing glass sent a chill from her shoulders to her heels. Two words, each three or four inches high, stacked on top of each other. She remembered the last time she had been here, watching in apprehension as the screen changed to flash her just this message, before she knew how to read it. Even then, the words had filled her with an indefinable dread; now she was washed with a helpless sense of terror.

"SEND HELP," the god was saying.

Chapter Eighteen

Three days of hard travel had brought Caleb to Velora, exhausted but determined. He arrived in the bustling little city in the morning and considered tying his mount up at the bottom of the grand staircase and immediately charging up the steps to look for Alleya. But he was famished, and dirty from three days of riding, and his long-suffering mare deserved a little better treatment than that. So he found an inn, stabled the horse, had a late breakfast and cleaned himself thoroughly. Then he was ready to seek a conference with the Archangel.

It was not such an easy thing as it had been the first time, for there were throngs of people gathered in the open plateau of the Eyrie, having come for exactly the same purpose. Caleb overheard a group of farmers grumbling, and edged closer to listen.

"Wasn't this way when Delilah was Archangel," one of them said. "You could count on her to be here on public days. Not flying off to the river cities and Breven and such. She serves in Bethel, she should stay in Bethel."

"Well, I heard they've got rain in northern Gaza," one of his companions was saying. "She's got to take care of things everywhere. That's why she's Archangel."

"Well, all I can say is, she should be *here* when she's needed."

Caleb drifted away, now frowning deeply. Was Alleya gone, then? Had he traveled all this way for nothing? When would she return? He was suffused with a violent impatience, totally foreign to his nature. He did not think he could wait another week or more to speak with her.

Half-a-dozen angels formed a crescent on the far end of the plateau, apparently taking complaints and offering what assistance they could in the Archangel's absence. Caleb pushed through the crowd till he arrived at the side of a young, handsome angel with a sulky expression on his face.

"I'm looking for the Archangel," Caleb said without preamble. "It's important that I talk to her, but I understand she is not here?"

The angel gave him a haughty, considering look and shook his head. "She left an hour ago for other duties."

An hour ago! Caleb knew his face registered dismay. "And where did she go? Can I find her somewhere else?"

"I am not free to repeat such details," the angel said.

"One of those men over there—I heard them say something about Gaza. Is that where she's gone?"

"The Archangel travels many places. Gaza may be one of the sites she plans to visit."

Caleb wanted to strangle him. "Do you know—can you tell me—when she'll be back at the Eyrie?"

"It is impossible to tell when the Archangel will return. If you are having problems with weather or plague, one of the other angels will be happy to hear your complaint."

"No, I must talk to Alleya."

The angel gave him a sharp look when Caleb used the familiar name. "If you wish to leave a message for the Archangel—" he began stiffly, but he was suddenly interrupted by one of the older angels standing nearby.

"You're Caleb Augustus, aren't you?" the second angel asked.

Caleb turned to him eagerly. "Yes. I'm sorry, do I know you?"

The older man waved his hand. "I'm Samuel. I was the one who directed you to Alleya last time you came. To fix the machines."

"I need to talk to her."

Samuel nodded. The younger angel stood listening, protest

written in every line of his body, but Samuel took Caleb by the arm and drew him aside. "Asher's a little protective of the Archangel, but he means well," Samuel said with a slight smile. "She can do with a few protectors."

"Yes," Caleb agreed instantly. "Can you tell me where she is? I want to go to her."

Samuel gave him a quick, appraising glance, but it was clear he had already made up his mind, or he would not have circumvented Asher. "She's in Gaza at the moment, or on her way there," he said. "But she plans to go to Sinai when she's through with the Manadavvi."

"Sinai! Did she say why?"

"She can be most evasive," was Samuel's dry response. "I believe she's looking for information."

Caleb was frowning. "So—how long do you think she'll be gone?"

"A day there, a day to Sinai—" The angel paused. "Do you have transportation?"

"A horse."

"If you leave now, you could get to Sinai at about the same time she will."

Caleb nodded. "Yes, I think I'll do that. Stop for some more provisions before I leave Velora, and ride straight for the mountains."

"Do you know how to get there? Do you need a map?"

"Thank you, I know the route. I can't tell you how much I appreciate your help—"

Samuel smiled. "A guess only," he replied.

"A guess?"

"I think she'll be glad to see you."

Caleb held out his hand and was pleased when Samuel shook it firmly. "Thank you again. If she's happy to see me, I'll tell her you sent me. If not"—he laughed—"I won't mention your name."

"Jovah guard you," Samuel said. "Travel safely."

A few short hours later, having taken a brief nap and restocked his supplies, Caleb and his sturdy mare were back on the road. He was chasing across the entire province after this particular woman. Not that he minded. He would cross the world for her.

The journey took him that whole day and most of the next one; and then there was the problem of the mountain. Well, the oracles expected company, so there was a path, but it was steeper than the one to Hagar's Tooth and even rockier. Caleb stood at the base of the mountain and looked up as far as he could see, sighing a little. Oh, to be an angel and merely glide to the top of the peak on the most convenient spiral of wind. And this was clearly not a road he could expect his horse to climb, so he was back to his own two feet again.

"You did so well last time, let's hope you can take care of yourself again," he murmured to his mare as he unpacked his bags and set her free. Ground cover was sparse in this part of the world, but adequate, he thought; she should stay content enough for a day or two. If she was gone when he returned, well, he would walk back to Velora, or wherever Alleya had flown to next.

He settled his saddlebags over his shoulders, took one more measuring glance at the trail in front of him, then resolutely took his first step forward and started the wearisome climb.

For a long moment, Alleya stared at the screen, incapable of responding, unable to believe she was correctly interpreting the words that the god had spelled out. That was it, of course; she had misunderstood. Her book would explain what Jovah was really trying to say.

But she paged through the entire slim textbook, and nowhere did it offer an alternative definition of the words "SEND HELP."

She pursed her lips, took a deep breath, and spread her hands once more over the keyboard. "You need assistance?" she asked the god.

The reply came back with unnerving swiftness. "Yes. Send technician immediately."

Technician? "How can a technician help you?" she queried.

The reply made no sense to her at all, though she could pick out certain words: "repair," "circuit board," "malfunction." None of these words appeared in her guidebook, either.

"How can I help you?" she asked when Jovah's words came to a halt.

A one-word reply. "Teleport."

As before, incomprehensible. She continued to ask questions

as if they were reasonable, as if she were carrying on a logical conversation that she understood. "How can I teleport?"

This reply, at least, sounded sane. "Type in the word 'teleport' at the prompt, hit Enter, and within twenty seconds move to the inscribed pentagram on the floor in the center of the room."

She glanced over to the middle of the chamber, but from this angle she could make out no sigils on the stone floor. She pushed the chair back, crossed the room and, bending low, inspected the floor. At first she could detect nothing through centuries of wear, but then, faintly, she was able to trace a star-shaped pattern that had been cut into the rock itself. She took a few moments to mark its five points with books snatched at random from the nearby archives. Twenty seconds was not long; she did not want to waste them seeking the pentagram again.

Although what would happen at the end of the twenty seconds, she could not even begin to guess.

Returning to the interface, she stood over the keyboard and typed in a message to Jovah. "I am ready," she said. "Is there anything else I must do?"

"Only what I told you," he replied. "Come quickly."

She nodded, as if he could see her, and carefully keyed in the letters one at a time. "Teleport," she wrote, then hesitated a moment, and touched the Enter key.

She ran to the pentagram, being careful not to disturb her books, and then stood there for the longest time, waiting for something indescribable to happen. Would a door open, would a voice speak, would the world around her magically change? But nothing moved or reacted. How long had she stood here—five seconds, fifteen seconds, forty-five? She should have begun a countdown when she first touched the keyboard. Perhaps nothing would happen. Perhaps the interface was broken, perhaps even that method of communicating with Jovah had failed. She would stand here a moment longer, she would begin counting now. Once she reached one *hundred* and twenty, she would know something had gone wrong, and she would return to the interface.

She had reached the number five when two things happened at once. The air around her began to haze over with a glittering golden aura, and she heard someone shout her name. "The god is calling me!" she thought, a certain happiness cutting through the apprehension that had wrapped around her heart, and then the metallic, iridescent curtain drew taut around her.

She felt her body explode into a million tiny fragments, felt her hair and her fingertips and her toenails separately and distinctly detach from her body. She wanted to scream, but her throat had been ripped out; her heart clamped down and vanished. Something colder than ice, hotter than flame, washed over every inch of her body, and then her skin dissolved. In that instant, she once again heard a voice call out her name.

She could not tell how much time passed before she attempted to open her eyes again. She spent a good long time marveling over the fact that she was not dead, though she could not with certainty say she was alive. She seemed to be lying on some kind of cool, level surface, perhaps marble, perhaps not. She felt—odd—disembodied, as if she did not weigh as much as she should, as if she had been hollowed out and laid aside. As if her thoughts were no longer in her head. As if she had been disconnected from her body.

But she could flex her fingers and curl her toes; and her hands, when she put them to her face, found only the smooth contours of her spare cheeks and her closed eyelids. And she was breathing, and she could feel the galloping pace of her heart. And odd little hissing and gurgling noises were skirling past her ears, so she could still hear. So if she could still see, then presumably she was more or less whole.

But when she opened her eyes, she had no idea what she was looking at. The world seemed a mishmash of white and chrome and blinking lights. She shut her eyes again quickly.

She lay there another moment or two, but she would learn nothing this way—not where she was, not what Jovah wanted from her. He was her god; surely he had not brought her here to harm her. She opened her eyes again and pushed herself to a sitting position.

She seemed to be in some kind of round room walled in white, though it was not constructed of stone or wood or even any metal that she could recognize. She was indeed on the floor, which seemed to be made of the same material used for the walls. In a near-perfect circle lining the interior of the room was a bank of screens much like the interface at Sinai, though the keyboards beneath the screens varied radically. Some were not keyboards at all, but consisted of a series of flashing lights arranged in colorful rows. Indeed, now that she examined the screens, most of them looked very little like the interface she knew: They displayed images of lines and dots in mysterious configurations, and as she watched, they altered.

She did not know where she was or how she had arrived here, but surely Jovah had sent her here for a purpose. Surely there would be a way for him to tell her what that purpose was. She made herself stand up and examine the screens more closely. And there was, as she had been sure there must be, an interface like the one she knew.

She approached it cautiously and examined the keyboard. Yes, laid out just like the one at Sinai. She breathed a soundless sigh of relief. Then Jovah was still available to her somehow. She positioned her fingers over the keyboard and typed, "Jovah, are you here?"

But the reply was not what she had expected. Sonorous, mighty, echoing from the round walls around her, a man's deep voice replied, "Yes, Alleluia, I am."

She shrieked and fell to her knees, weak with a primeval terror. She had wanted to touch the face of the god but she had not thought she could do it; and she had not thought his face would look like this. "Jovah!" she cried out, her hands cradling her head as if to shield herself from his sight. "Jovah, I am afraid!"

But the voice did not immediately speak again. Instead, even more terrifying, the texture of the air changed. A golden glow began to build up beside her in the chamber, a whirling luminescent cloud of ensorcelled dust. Crying out Jovah's name again, Alleya flattened herself on the floor in supplication, and waited for the god to strike.

Caleb had never been to Sinai, or, indeed, any of the retreats of the oracles, so it had taken him a little time to navigate the echoing gray halls. "Alleya?" he had called out once or twice, but he could not bring himself to raise his voice to the level of a shout;

there was something about this place that discouraged violence, even violent sound.

So he made a few fruitless investigations of small waiting rooms and obviously disused passageways before the hallway abruptly widened and he sensed that he was approaching the main living quarters. He quickened his pace and forbore to call out the Archangel's name again.

When he moved into the great chamber that was clearly the heart of the maze, it took him only a few seconds to glance around and realize he had found his quarry. She was standing unnaturally still in the middle of the room, her head tilted as if she was listening to some voice inaudible to him. He took a deep breath and another step forward—and then stood frozen to the spot in horror. Alleya was enveloped in a mist of gold and topaz, and the look on her face was one of stark terror. "*Alleya!*" he screamed, bounding forward, but he did not reach her in time. "*Alleya!*"

She was gone. Where she had stood was nothing but gray, unimaginative stone, and not even a sparkle of the traitorous haze remained.

Frantic, he ran back and forth across the confines of the room, touching each wall, as if she could be lurking behind those solid stones, as if only the effect of mirrors or illusion had caused her to disappear. He hurriedly inspected a book room off to one side, peering around each shelf, as if she had taken shelter behind one, as if she was merely hiding. But she was gone. He had seen her vanish.

Well, this was the god's waiting room, after all. Although Caleb could not even guess how she had been removed, surely Jovah's had been the hand that had taken her. And he knew of only one instrument on Samaria that anyone could use to directly question the god.

Slowly, battling a mind-numbing fear, Caleb approached the glowing blue screen set into the far wall. The interface, that was what Alleya had called it. He forced himself to concentrate, to remember what little Alleya had told him about the machine. The oracle wrote a question on the screen and the god replied through the same medium. Fabulous technology, if indeed it worked, if indeed the god replied and the oracle did not just fabricate his own replies to awe and delight credulous visitors.

But now Caleb was almost willing to concede the existence of the god, if the god could help him retrieve Alleya.

He stood for a long time before the alien equipment, studying it, trying to analyze it. It did not much resemble either the music machine at the Eyrie or the listening device at Hagar's Tooth, except it could easily have been constructed of the same materials and featured some kind of lighted display. The buttons on the panel below the screen were lettered with an unfamiliar alphabet; apparently, these were used to form the words and sentences that were then somehow relayed to the god.

Caleb surveyed the screen itself, even now offering him an unreadable message. It was clearly a question, however; the sentence ended with the same interrogative symbol Samarians still used in their written language. So the god was asking him—something. Asking him what had happened to Alleya. No, the god knew that. Asking him what he wanted to do next.

Asking him if he wanted to go where Alleya had gone.

How did he tell Jovah yes?

He dropped his eyes again to the arrangement of buttons on the lower panel. All but one were marked with a letter or a symbol that would seem to pass for a part of speech. On the left hand side of the panel was a large, square green key with an entire word printed on it. Not a word that Caleb recognized.

But green—that was the color that meant "proceed" or "in use" in the other pieces of early technology that Caleb had encountered. Green meant "go forward." Green meant "yes."

He glanced back over his shoulder to try to identify exactly where Alleya had been standing when he saw her melt away. Ah—she had marked the very location with a collection of textbooks. Certainly he must stand in the same place if he hoped to follow her. If indeed he could follow her. If he had guessed correctly.

He took a deep breath and pressed the green key. Then he sprinted for the marked spot in the center of the room. He fought down his dismay when nothing immediately happened; there must be a delay of some sort, because he had clearly seen Alleya's face for a few moments before she was enveloped in the coruscating fire. But not a long delay. There would be no point.

He was afraid, but when the glittering veil fell around him and tickled his skin with needles, his predominant emotion was one of fierce elation. He would follow the Archangel to the lair of the god himself.

Nothing, not even her arrival in this fantastic place, had shocked Alleya as much as the sudden appearance of Caleb Augustus by her side. For a moment, while he overcame his dizzy disorientation, she could not even speak. She merely stared at him, marveling.

He recovered more quickly than she. "Thank the god I found you," he exclaimed, scrambling to his feet and pulling her up into a fervent embrace. "When I saw you—disintegrate like that—before my very eyes—"

"What are you *doing* here?" she whispered. "How did you come to be here?"

"I followed you," he said. "At the Eyrie, they told me you were coming here. And I arrived at Sinai just in time to see you—do whatever it is we have just done."

She pulled back from him to stare at his face. She was still frightened, but less so; just his presence, no matter how helpless he might be, comforted her to an amazing degree. "We have achieved teleport," she said. "But I don't know what that means."

"Teleport," he repeated, and, still holding her in the circle of his arms, looked slowly around him. Alleya watched him, wondering what his scientific mind might make of the screens and equipment arrayed before them. *The son of Jeremiah.* Well, the god had asked for him. The god must have expected him to feel an affinity for this foreign machinery.

"Where *are* we?" Caleb asked at last, his face a study in puzzlement tempered by eagerness.

"I can't even guess."

He released her and walked idly from station to station, examining each with a minute, fascinated attention. Evidently the symbols meant more to him than to her, for now and then he released a small, surprised grunt of recognition, and then moved on. Alleya pivoted slowly to watch him.

"So where are we?" she asked at last.

He was still gazing down at one of the keyboards. He had lifted his hand as if he wanted to stroke the keys, but his fingers were suspended inches above the panel, as if he didn't quite dare. "At a guess, I would say we were in some technological nerve center directing the operations of a million engineering tasks at once," he said. "This is monitoring equipment—this is navigational equipment—this looks like it's simply a communications console . . ."

"Navigational equipment?" she queried.

He nodded. "Star charts, but more complicated than any I've ever seen, and not—" He hesitated. "They're the Samarian constellations, but not taken from the horizons we know."

She felt herself gasp. "From—from Ysral? The other continent?"

He looked over at her. His face was sober, but his eyes blazed with excitement. "I don't think so. I'd almost say—taken from a vantage point far above the ground."

She shook her head. "The stars look the same to me even when I'm flying."

He nodded. "Higher than that. Hundreds of miles higher or farther away. Maybe as far away as the next star. You could never fly so far."

She was bewildered. "But nothing could."

"A machine could."

"Don't be ridiculous!"

"Of course it could. I showed you Noah's traveling vehicle when we were in Breven. I've told you how I've tried to build wings for myself. There's a way to do it—I haven't figured it out yet—but there's a way to build machines that fly. Fly from one city on Samaria to the next. And if they can fly across land, why can't they fly through the atmosphere and to the stars?"

"Because they can't! Because no one can build machines like that! Because—because it doesn't make sense!"

"It makes sense," he said. "I think we're on just such a machine."

Alleya stared at him and felt all the blood drain away from her face, squeeze from her heart, and puddle in tingling pools at her knees and elbows. "You're saying we're in some machine miles above Samaria?" she whispered.

He nodded. "That would be my guess. We could confirm it, I think, if we could find an outside window. Although there may be no such thing as a window on a vessel like this. Probably has to have an outside surface that can withstand—well, anything—pressure, storms, meteorites—"

"Wait—don't—I don't understand what you're talking about," she interrupted, shaking her head. Now she was beginning to feel nauseous and ill, and fearful all over again. "And none of that matters, really. We're here to find out how Jovah wants us to help him."

Now Caleb was the one to stare. "Jovah wants us to help him? Why do you—"

"The message on the screen at Sinai. It said, 'Send help.' And when I asked how, it said, 'Teleport.' And that's how we got here. And now we need to find out how we can render assistance to Jovah."

He glanced around again. "Is there anything here that looks familiar to you—looks like one of the interfaces?"

She nodded and pointed. "Yes, but when I used it before—"

His head whipped back. "Yes?"

"He spoke to me," she whispered.

"Spoke? Aloud?"

She nodded.

"What did he say?"

"I had written, 'Jovah, are you here?' and the voice said, 'Yes, Alleluia, I am.' "

"Has the god ever spoken to you before? Has he ever spoken to any of the oracles?"

She shook her head. "Not that I have ever heard."

"Then—"

"I don't know."

"Are you sure it was Jovah?"

Now she felt a surge of impatience. "Who else would it be?"

"Who else, indeed . . ." He frowned down at the keyboard under the interface and then, without warning, lifted his head and addressed the empty air. "Jovah, can you hear me?"

Alleya did not even have time to catch her breath before the resonant voice replied, "Yes, I can."

She was stricken, paralyzed in place, but Caleb seemed unfazed. "Do you know me?" he asked next.

"Your name is hidden from me," the reply came. "Because the Kiss in your arm has been destroyed. If you told me your name, I could identify you."

"I am called Caleb Augustus. My father was Jacob Augustus."

"Ah," said the rich, deep voice. "Caleb, son of Jacob, son of Zakary, son of Ruth, daughter of Tamar, daughter of Nathaniel, who was son of Jeremiah."

The son of Jeremiah. Hearing the words aloud, Alleya could not repress a slight shiver. All the weeks of searching, and all this time, he was as close as her own hand.

"Can you tell us where we are?" Caleb asked next.

"You are aboard the spaceship *Jehovah*."

"Spaceship?" Caleb asked sharply. "What is that?"

"It is a vehicle designed for transport across interplanetary distances. It is self-sustaining, self-renewing, powered by crystals which release their radioactive energy over a period of centuries, giving the ship an effective lifespan of several thousand years."

"And how old is this ship?"

"It is entering its nine hundredth year of service."

"And how did it come to be flying above Samaria?"

"When the members of the Harmonic Christers sect elected to leave their home planet, they chose this spaceship to carry them from Eleison to whatever world they might find and deem to be suitable. This planet, which they named Samaria, was the one selected."

Caleb, whom Alleya was watching with an almost painful intensity, seemed to be half listening—and half remembering other stories. "Carried in Jovah's hands to their new home," he murmured. "Carried in Jovah's hands—in Jehovah's hands—in the spaceship *Jehovah*."

Alleya stirred and put a hand on his arm. "No," she said. "That is not how it happened. The god took us in his palm—"

"The settlers were carried in the spaceship," the voice interrupted. "As Caleb Augustus says."

Caleb covered Alleya's hand with his to reassure her, but his mind was clearly locked into this particular investigative groove. "So they came here in the ship—and then what happened to the ship? It just stayed floating above Samaria for the next six and a half centuries? What a waste! What we could have learned from it!"

"Orbiting," the voice said.

"What?"

"The ship was not floating, it was orbiting around the planet on a regular and calculated basis."

"On some kind of schedule that had been programmed into its machinery before the settlers landed?"

"That is correct."

"But why didn't they—" Caleb gave a laugh of sheer frustration. "I mean, to have this incredible piece of technology so close, and then to cut themselves off from it completely— It makes no sense to me."

"They did not cut themselves off completely. They installed computer interfaces at three stations on the planet which allowed them to communicate directly with the ship."

"Interfaces," Alleya whispered. "No—"

"To communicate—what?" Caleb asked.

"Information, mostly. Genealogical information about the population shifts on Samaria. Information about weather patterns and crop rotations. Information about technological advances and where they were centered."

"Tracking us," Caleb said below his breath. "Learning how quickly we were evolving." He slapped his hand across the black Kiss in his arm. "Guessing—and pretty damn accurately, too—what bloodlines could be profitably mixed with others—" He refocused his attention on the point above his head, to the right, which seemed to be the source of the voice. "But how were the *settlers* benefiting from the ship's continued orbit over the planet?"

"In many ways," the voice replied. "For example, the weather on Samaria was a concern from the very beginning."

Alleya felt her fingers bite into Caleb's arm. "This is *not* true," she said fiercely. Caleb hushed her, but the voice seemed not to notice.

"The ship is able, through a combination of chemicals and heat rays and solar mirror panels, to cause sudden and dramatic shifts in the wind and temperature patterns—"

"This is *not* true," Alleya repeated, more loudly. "Jovah causes the weather to change, when the angels request it of him—"

"My dear child, who do you think is speaking to us?" Caleb whispered in her ear.

She snatched her hand back, took a pace away from Caleb when he reached for her again. "I don't—it is a voice Jovah is using to speak to us—"

Still watching her sympathetically, Caleb lifted his own voice. "Who is addressing us in this conversation?"

"I am the voice of the computer that operates the starship *Jehovah*."

"*No*," Alleya said instantly just as Caleb asked his next question. "Computer? What is that?"

"A computer is an artificial, electronic brain. It is capable of performing myriads of complicated logical, logistical, mathematical and theoretical calculations that simulate the thought processes of human brains. Although it is more sophisticated than a human brain, boasts more memory than a human brain and can handle functions a human brain cannot."

"It can—think—and make decisions—and learn?"

"No. It must be given instructions and directions in a manner that conform to its programming. Some rote, unchanging tasks it can perform on its own, according to existing programming, but it cannot, on its own, decide to interfere in weather patterns or release antibiotic doses or dispense grain seed."

"Or send down thunderbolts to smite mountains—unless it is directed to do so," Caleb suggested.

"Precisely."

Alleya took hold of Caleb by his forearms and shook him; but her grip was weak and her hands were trembling. "What you are saying—what you are suggesting—is that this, this spaceship is performing all the functions of the god. . . ."

His expression was compassionate. He pulled his arms free and took her in a gentle embrace. "That's what I'm saying. That's what I believe to be true. The settlers traveled to Samaria on this very ship, and left it in orbit above us, and gave angels and oracles the ability to communicate with it, and gave it the ability to respond. And over the years, we, forgetting our technological roots—"

She jerked back from him and stamped her foot. "*No!* That cannot be true! The god is not some—some *machine* left behind by Hagar and Uriel and the others. Not some mindless, soulless piece of equipment that floats in space and waits for some kind of—signal—to begin working. The god is—the god is the god. He is all-powerful. He knows everything. He loves everyone. He is *real*."

"This spaceship is real, Alleya," Caleb said soberly. "You will never find anything more real. Look around you! This is science beyond anything we could have dreamed of, but you will admit it reminds you of technology you have seen before. It is technology our race had once, and deliberately lost, and now stands in need of again. This ship is skilled enough to travel more miles than we can count—powerful enough to scatter storms and strike down mountains. You want a god? The machine is the god, and more believable and less capricious than any deity I could imagine. You have always wanted to be close to your god. Well, you are looking straight into his lighted, unwavering eyes."

"No," she said, and her voice was almost too soft to be heard. "No. I cannot believe in a god who was created by men—built by men to serve them, not to oversee them. Where is the challenge to the spirit in that? Who is to ensure that we live wisely, that we treat others fairly, that we perform our obligations and avoid temptations? If there is no one to punish us for wrongdoing, what is to prevent us from doing evil? What is to keep us honest and good? Who is to guard our souls, and gather us into his arms when we die? A machine? A machine built by men? How can this be the thing we have called a god for so many centuries?"

"It does not matter what we have believed," Caleb said. "What matters is the truth. And the truth is, we have been watched and defended and punished by a machine called *Jehovah*. And the further truth is that this machine has somehow broken. And the final truth is that we were brought to this machine to fix it. And may *Jehovah* correct me if I am wrong."

"No," said *Jehovah*. "You are not wrong. I am in need of

repair to my ancillary audio-coordinator. It is what enables me to pick up transmissions from the external satellites, but the circuitry became overburdened and has almost completely shut down."

"You haven't been able to hear us," Caleb clarified.

"That is correct."

"I am not proficient in settler technology," Caleb added. "Is this something I will be able to repair?"

"Easily enough, if you follow my instructions. But the operation requires fingers, hands and a new circuit board, which I cannot insert on my own."

"But there is a new circuit board?"

"There are dozens."

"Then direct me there." He stepped forward, and turned back to the Archangel. "Alleya? Would you like to come with me and watch?"

She shook her head. She had never felt so miserable and abandoned in her life, not when the storm flung her carelessly to the ground, not when her mother left her at Mount Sinai to learn the ways of the angels. She could not stand by and watch the guts of the god undergo profane surgery.

"No," she said. "I will wait for you here."

Caleb was gone for more than two hours. Alleya spent that whole time sitting motionlessly in one of the cushioned chairs set up in front of each of the lighted panels. Although the room was nearly silent, she could sometimes faintly catch the echoes of Caleb's conversation with the ship's computer, two or three rooms away. And the occasional beep and gurgle of machinery in this room now and then caught her random attention. But mostly she sat there, still and patient, deafened by the tumultuous storm raging inside her head.

Jovah was a machine. Jovah was an electronic brain. Jovah was a starship named *Jehovah* that had traveled incalculable miles, carrying the original settlers in its chambers. She had not strayed from this small space, but she realized the ship must be unbelievably vast, the size of the Eyrie, perhaps, or one of the Manadavvi mansions, to shelter so many people for what must have been a journey of dozens of years. The existence of the spaceship, the mechanics of the trip—that she could understand, that she could accept. Jovah had carried them from another planet to this one, and he must have had some vessel with which to do so, and she was willing to accept this spaceship for the metaphor of his hands.

But she was not willing to accept a computer for her god. Who had listened to her all those years, as she sang prayers of supplication and thanksgiving? Who had heard her voice above all other voices, given her faith in herself, faith in her god? There had been—something—some sentient presence receiving her words and responding to them. She believed that. She had felt that presence at the core of her heart as she had felt Caleb's pulse beating against her own when he held her in his arms.

She might have touched the face of Jovah, but she had not yet touched the face of her god.

When Caleb returned, he was as excited as a boy.

"You should see this place!" he exclaimed. "It's huge! Like a small city, but laid out with such efficiency—the air ducts, the power outlets, the plumbing—And it all recycles. Nothing is wasted. You'd never run out of water or air or food—"

She managed to smile up at him, though it took an effort. "You've been on a tour of the ship, then, I take it?"

"Yes, the whole thing, or at least the living quarters. And, Alleya, you wouldn't believe it! There are these entire farms of grain—wheat and soy and corn and a few I didn't recognize—and there are these automatic harvesting arms, and bins for drying the grain, and silos for storing them, and hatches for ejecting them onto Samaria when we ask for them! I didn't get a chance to inspect the—he called them heat guns, I wasn't quite sure how they operated—anyway, they're on the outside of the ship, so I couldn't get to them. I'm sure they're awesome."

"And what else did you learn?"

"Well, he offered me a—text of some sort, a printout, he called it—of some of his engineering specifications, but then he said it was in the old language, which I don't know, so I didn't think it would benefit me much. And then I asked him how he was able to talk to us in our language if he was only programmed with the settlers' original language, and he tried to explain it—

something about predictable phonetic shift and the universal evolution of language, but I didn't understand it."

"Well, he has been communicating with the oracles for all these years. Maybe he's followed the language shifts through them."

"Maybe. And then I asked him about some of the old technology that I've seen on Samaria, and I told him about your failed music machines, and he directed me to some kind of storeroom where I found—these." Caleb held out a small box holding maybe seventy little metal cylinders which he was regarding as if they were made of stamped gold. Alleya glanced from his hand to his face. She was so tired; it was an effort to think, an effort to group her thoughts into coherent speech.

"And what are those?" she asked at last.

"He called them batteries. Well, he called them something else first, then said I may as well just refer to them as batteries, although they were far more complex."

"And what's a battery?"

"As far as I can tell, stored energy which can be used to power something that doesn't have an outside electrical or steam-driven source."

"Ah."

"Something like this is what ran your music equipment, till the energy was all drained. I got enough to replace the batteries in all of the machines, at the Eyrie and Monteverde. And I picked up a few extras."

"Why? What else can they be used for?"

He was again studying his booty as if he'd discovered the last key to the mysteries of the universe. "I can think of lots of things," he said to himself. "Lots of potential things. We'll have to go back and try them out."

Alleya came to her feet. "I'm ready."

"Don't you want to look around a little?"

She shook her head. "I have had enough of miracles for one day. I don't think I can absorb any more."

He laughed ruefully. "I don't think I could ever be here long enough. But maybe if I come back—"

"No!" she said fiercely. He narrowed his eyes at her, for the first time since his return seeming to focus on her completely.

"You don't want me to return here?"

"Take what you need now," she said. "If you need more time, then we'll wait. But we are not coming back here."

"Why not?"

"Because we are not meant to be here. Because the settlers deliberately hid from their children and their children's children the knowledge of this ship's existence. Because we were placed on Samaria to found a society untainted by the corruption of technology, to see if men could live in harmony with men. You know the stories as well as I do, Caleb. The Christers came here from a planet that exploded from internal war shortly after they were able to escape it. They believed that science leads to self-destruction and they wanted Samaria free of that fear. They wanted us to evolve differently than their ancestors had."

"But that's ridiculous! Technology in and of itself is not evil! Technology leads to music machines and electrical light and vehicles that can travel faster than a horse—"

"And to factories which rearrange the whole manufacturing structure of the country and affect the entire population alignment—"

"All right, progress breeds change, but change is so often for the better. Are you telling me that, right now, you would go to Breven and tear down the factories—you would go to Semorrah and Luminaux, and disconnect the power cords that give the cities their lights? You would halt technological advances—you would refuse to grow?"

"No. I am saying that if we must have technology, we will discover our own. Perhaps the discoveries we make will be different than the discoveries made on Eleison. Perhaps we will not invent the same weapons of destruction, and so we will not be at risk. Perhaps everything we create will be like electricity and your friend Noah's machine. But to ensure that, we cannot go back to the technology of our ancestors. We cannot, you and I, come to this ship for secrets. We must discover our own way. Write our own future, not steal from an unsavory past. Don't you agree with me? Don't you understand?"

"I understand," he said slowly. "But I don't know that I agree. There is so much we don't know—so much that this ship could tell us. We could circumvent decades of experimentation and failure with five minutes of examining the spaceship's circuitry—"

"You've had your five minutes," she said calmly. "You are decades ahead of Noah and the other engineers on Samaria. You know what is possible. It is up to you to discover how to make it work."

"You're serious," he said. "You will never let me return to this ship."

"Not only that," she said, "I want you to promise me—swear to me—that you will never mention to another living soul what you have seen here and what you have done."

"Why? If others know what I know—"

"You may not believe in Jovah, in the existence of a god, but how many others do you know on Samaria who are doubters? Can you name me five? Can you name me one?"

He appeared to think about it. She imagined he must be reviewing his Edori friends, his family members, maybe his fellow engineers. "I can name you one besides myself," he said finally, "and even he believes there is a god. He is just not sure how much power the god can wield."

Alleya stepped toward him, as if she could, from a closer range, make her words more surely penetrate his brain. "What would happen to them, do you think, if you told them that their god was really a machine? Would they believe you? Would they stone you for a heretic? Would they curse themselves and their ignorance and the priests and the oracles who had lied to them? Would they still trust the angels to pray for rain and seed and medicine? If they turned against the angels, who would intercede for them with Jovah—for, god or machine, *Jehovah* the spaceship still hears the songs of the angels, does he not, or will now that you have repaired him? If people are told their god is a machine, how will they go on with their lives? The myth of Jovah is too strong in our society. He binds us all together.

"If we do not come together for the annual Gloria, all peoples singing in harmony, will harmony cease to exist on Samaria? Will Jansai turn against Manadavvi, will farmers turn against the merchantmen? If we do not have a god, no matter how false, to keep us all in order, will we then fall into chaos? Caleb Augustus, think very hard about what it would mean to tell this world that there is no god. Are you willing to be the man who destroys Jovah?"

He had bowed his head as she spoke and appeared to be listening intently, half in protest, half in agreement. When she finished, he raised his eyes to her, and his face was very sober. "The time will come," he said, "when others will discover what Jovah really is. Even now, I know men who are experimenting with disks of glass that enable them to see farther distances than the human eye can manage. It is inevitable that they will train these instruments on the sky—that they will begin to see the stars more closely, or catch a glimpse of Jovah as he circles overhead.

"And there are those besides Noah who are building traveling vehicles—and those besides me who are attempting to discover how to fly. Sooner or later, centuries from now, maybe, they will learn how to build spaceships and they will encounter Jovah, or extrapolate from what they've learned that a thing such as this ship must exist. Sooner or later, this great secret will be a secret no more. And then how will your society recover?"

"By then, it will be a different society, and people will be used to marvels. By then, they will not be afraid of flying machines, and they will know how to make their own—batteries. By then, the world will run more on electricity than faith. Science will replace mysticism, but gradually. We would be fools to force it. And we would be wrong."

He was not entirely convinced; she could tell that by the set, stubborn look on his face. On the other hand, he was still listening. "Perhaps you are right," he said slowly. "Perhaps the world is not ready for the bright knowledge we have uncovered. But what would have happened to us, to all of Samaria, if you and I had not stumbled upon the truth of this ship—if we had not teleported here, and repaired the circuits, and made it possible for Jovah to hear the angels again? We would have been lost to flood and disease—we would have been destroyed when the Gloria came round, for even ten thousand voices raised in harmony would not have reached the god's ear. He would have thought we did not sing to him, and he would have released the thunderbolts that would have demolished the world."

"Jovah, is that true?" Alleya asked, for she had feared it long enough.

"It is true," the voice confirmed.

"So you see," Caleb said, his voice gathering energy, "the risks are just as great if no one knows the truth. As long as Jovah guards us, someone must know who Jovah is, and guard him as well."

Alleya nodded. "You're right. And I believe that, until now, one of the oracles has always known who Jovah is and how to reach him. My guess is that the oracle Rebekah was the one with the knowledge in this generation, but she died before it could be passed on."

"So you will now tell one of the other oracles? You will share this incredible information with Job, or Mary, someone who will be shocked to his soul, but you won't allow me to tell Noah or another engineer?"

"One of the oracles must know," Alleya said. "I will decide who."

"That's a grave decision for one person to make."

"That is why Jovah chose me as Archangel," she replied calmly. "To make such decisions."

Caleb spread his hands and turned away, defeated. "I cannot spread this news without your consent," he said at last. "At the very least, I need your corroboration, because no one would believe me. Once I leave this ship, I may start to doubt it myself."

"Then are we ready to go?"

Caleb looked around one last time, as if memorizing the placement of equipment and the pattern of lights. He sighed. "No," he said. "I will never be ready to leave. But let us go now, anyway."

"Jovah, how do we return to Sinai?" Alleya asked.

"Stand where you are, in the center of the room. When you are ready, merely say, 'Teleport now.' "

Alleya raised her eyebrows at Caleb; a question. He sighed again, nodded, and took her hand. "Teleport now," she said.

It was less frightening the second time but no less strange. She felt again that instantaneous, complete dissolution of her muscles and bones, the disconnection of skin to tissue, the unhooking of cell from cell. She felt her skull melt and her bones disintegrate and every part of her body vaporize, but still her fingers were caught fast in Caleb's hand. And when, seconds later, her body re-formed in the pentagram carved in the stone floor of Mount Sinai, her hand was still locked in Caleb's, and she believed he had never once relaxed his grip.

He was bending over her solicitously, making sure she had survived the transportation intact, both body and spirit reviving. She managed a shaky smile at him.

"What exactly is it that we have just done?" she asked.

"I have no idea. I feel like I have been completely pulled apart and reassembled. Incompletely. Are you all right?"

"Oh, yes. It's less terrifying when you know what to expect."

He glanced around the inner chamber as if seeking points of reference. "I wonder what time it is. Do you have any idea?"

"When did you arrive here?"

"Days ago. Years ago."

"I think it must be late at night. In any case, I'm starving."

"Me, too," he said. "I have some food—"

"Me, too. And I'm tired. I have to sleep, and soon."

He smiled. "Me, too. Shall we throw together a meal, then spend the night here together?"

She nodded. "And then think about what we must do next."

It was a quiet, almost luxurious meal, despite the fact that their dried provisions were neither plentiful nor exotic. They had found the oracle's living quarters and made themselves comfortable on more opulent furniture than they would have expected from a supposed ascetic. When they had finished their meal, they sat quietly together on the sofa, loosely embraced, talking in a relaxed and idle way. It was as if—between terror, betrayal, wonder and argument—all their passion had been spent earlier in the day, and now there was nothing left but to rest in each other's arms.

"There was a great deal else to think about," Caleb said at last, speaking the words into her hair. "But while we were aboard the spaceship, Jovah called me by name. You must have noticed."

She gave a small laugh. "The son of Jeremiah. I noticed."

He kissed the back of her head. "And, as I recall, when you left me at Hagar's Tooth, it was to go off in search of just such a man. The son of Jeremiah. When it appears I am the man you have been seeking all along."

"Strange but true," Alleya said. "I have not had time yet to assimilate the glad news."

"And does this mean you must marry me? And name me as your angelico? In fact, I believe it means you have no choice. Your god has spoken, and you must obey."

"My god is not who I believed he was," Alleya retorted. "I may no longer be subject to his dictates."

"Well, then, what does your heart require?" he asked. "That is where you should look for your true answer."

"My heart is willing, but my head is suspicious," she said. "If a man is to be angelico, he must, first of all, be prepared to carry on his religious and civic duties. In short, he must be ready to lead the masses at the Gloria and sing before a crowd of thousands."

"Ah," Caleb said. "Maybe I am not so eager for the role after all."

"And he must be a patient man, willing to give his time to the petitioners who will come to him, seeking to curry favor with his wife, the Archangel, but afraid to approach her directly—"

"Well, I am sociable enough, though I do not gladly endure fools."

"And he must, of course, put aside his own pursuits so that he can devote his time fully and completely to the life of the Archangel and the business of the hold."

With a palm on her cheek, Caleb turned her face toward his. "Must he really?" he asked seriously. "I admit, that would be difficult."

"Actually, I wouldn't think you'd have to give up anything," she said. "If Hagar could disappear for months at a time to the Corinni Mountains, I don't see why you couldn't be down in Luminaux, inventing things."

"Or Velora," he said. "I could set up a workshop there."

"Well, then. One problem solved. How's your voice?"

"My voice is—adequate. Not something people would pay to listen to."

"Do you know any of the sacred masses?"

"I'm not sure what a sacred mass is."

"How quickly do you learn?"

"How hard is it?"

"Hard enough. But if you only have to learn one mass—"

"Can someone teach me?"

"There are the music rooms at the hold," she reminded them. "You can go there and listen for hours. If you left tomorrow morning—"

"I can't go directly to the Eyrie," he interrupted. "In two or three weeks, I could be there."

She shifted her body so she could face him more comfortably. "Where do you have to go first?"

"To Luminaux. To see Delilah."

"Delilah?"

He nodded. "I think—I may be wrong—I think one of those little batteries might be able to mend her. I have to try. And soon. Before she leaves with the Edori ships for Ysral."

"I agree. Go to Luminaux first, and come to the Eyrie as soon as you can."

"And you'll be there?"

She was silent a moment, thinking, then she settled back into his arms. "I'll be there by the time you arrive," she said.

In the morning, they prepared to go their separate ways. It was the first time that they had parted without the fear that they would never see each other again, and so their farewells were almost lighthearted. Still, as they stood on the landing ledge at the opening to the cavern, they were each touched by a vagrant sadness.

"It is always hard to leave you," Caleb said, "or to watch you leave."

"Travel carefully, and think of me."

"Jovah guard you," he said.

She gave him a quizzical look. "You commend me to a machine?"

"I trust him now more than I ever did."

She kissed him quickly. "You're a strange man, son of Jeremiah."

"Strange but faithful," he said, kissing her in return. "Till I see you again."

"In Velora."

"Till then."

And they kissed again and parted. Alleya watched for a moment as Caleb began his slow descent down the mountain; then she launched herself into the turquoise skies. She flew southwest for half an hour before making a quick landing at a small town situated on one of the main east-west roads.

"I have a message to be taken to the Eyrie," she said after she had introduced herself to the burgher who resided in the largest house. "Can you perform that office for me?"

"With pleasure, angela," he said. So she wrote Samuel a brief note ("I have conferred with the god, and he can once again hear all angels. Spread the news. I will be at the Eyrie in fifteen or twenty days") and sealed it with the proffered wax.

"It is urgent," she said. "I will appreciate your hurrying."

Within minutes, she was on her way again. There was no reason she could not have carried her own message to the holds, of course, for she was on no desperate mission and no one was expecting her in Chahiela. But the truth was, she could not face Samuel's sharp eyes and Asher's eager questions; she needed time to think, time to reorder her numb brain. Time to reassess her role. Time to come to terms with her god.

She stopped only twice more, briefly, and made it to Chahiela by nightfall.

Chapter Nineteen

Delilah was no longer singing at Seraph.

Caleb had arrived in Luminaux early enough in the afternoon to run a few errands before making his way to the club. The crowd was thin, and the reason was soon evident. Two singers, a mandolin player and a flautist all played adequate, even exquisite music, but never once did the angel appear.

Caleb spotted Joseph lounging against the back wall, glumly surveying his clientele, and he made his over way to the Jansai. "You look bereft," he observed. "I take it your star attraction has finally set?"

Joseph nodded. "Came in a week ago and said she was packing to leave. I offered her twice the money and she laughed at me. I couldn't go any higher than three times—a man's got to make a profit, or it makes no sense—but she wouldn't change her mind. She hasn't told me who she's going to, but I'll find out. It's a small city, and she's not the kind of singer you can keep secret."

"I don't think she's planning to continue her career," Caleb said. "So what are you going to do?"

Joseph shrugged. "Something better than them," he said, gesturing toward the stage. "I'll find someone. Don't worry about me."

Caleb turned away. "I wasn't worried."

In the morning, knowing it was pointless to seek Delilah out before noon, he headed to the Edori camp to return the horse he had borrowed so long ago. Thomas was pleased to see him and waved off his apologies for tardiness.

"I knew you would return with the mare, this month or next year, or the year after that," said the old Edori. "You're an honest man."

"If I'd kept her long enough, you'd be on board ship, and I'd never have to return her," Caleb said with a smile.

Thomas laughed. "Well, then, I'd be happy knowing you were caring for her and still meeting your obligation to me."

"But I didn't come just to return the horse," Caleb added. "If you're in a mood to sell her, I'll buy. And I can't imagine you'll have much room for horses on your boats."

Thomas beamed at him. "No, indeed. I was thinking to just set her free, but this pleases me much better. Name your price—I won't haggle."

They came to a quick agreement and Caleb handed over his cash. Then he glanced around the campsite, which was in a frenzy of packing and dismantling. "You look like you're all getting ready to move."

"Yes, the Gathering's in about two weeks now, and the whole clan must be in Breven by then. And most of us won't be coming back, though some will. Had you come even a day later, you would have missed us entirely."

"Is Noah traveling with you? I don't see him."

"No, he's in Breven already. Working on the ships."

Caleb felt a sudden sharp sense of loss, brutal and unexpected. "So he won't be coming back? And is he—is he still set on leaving with you on the voyage to Ysral?"

Thomas nodded happily. "Yes, and we're glad to have him! Skills like his will be sorely needed, both on the journey and after."

There was no way for Caleb to finish his task here, make it quickly to Breven to say farewell, and still get to the Eyrie in three weeks or less. Well, perhaps he could be late. Alleya would no doubt be sympathetic. And yet, he had so much to learn and so little time.

"If I give you a message, will you take it to him? I can't

believe—I didn't realize—I hadn't thought he would set sail before I had a chance to see him again."

Thomas laid a hand on Caleb's shoulder. "Yes, any farewell is difficult, and this one is hard on us all. I wish all the Edori would board those boats, and live or die together. As it is, to leave so many behind— It's tearing many apart. Edori have a close bond, and this trip will sever it. Yet still I am impatient to set sail."

"And if you find Ysral?" Caleb demanded. "Will some of you come back and tell the rest?"

"If we can," Thomas said. "If the boats are still seaworthy, if our navigation has been good enough to allow us to retrace our route. I am not thinking of the return journey as much as the voyage out. Turn your face forward, and don't be afraid of the next horizon."

Scant comfort in that. Caleb stayed only a few more moments before heading back to town. A leaden depression weighed him down as he thought of never seeing Noah again, he with his quick mind and his easy soul. He felt a flare of hatred for Delilah, who had driven Noah to this desperate venture; but he could not long curse the follies caused by love. He was about to pray to a manufactured god before an audience of thousands, and nothing but love could drive him to that.

He was in Luminaux again before noon, making his first stop at the house of a man named Nathan Lowell. Caleb had come by this house the night before to make arrangements, and he found Nathan awaiting him with a small blue suitcase at his feet.

"Ready?" Caleb asked.

"Eager," the man replied.

The housekeeper at Delilah's place informed them that the angel had just risen and might not be interested in company, but Caleb laughed at her and said, "She must see me. Tell her Caleb is here and that I won't leave."

In a few minutes, the housekeeper ushered them into a room Caleb hadn't seen before, pink and plush with fatly padded furniture. "It is my curiosity and not your impudence that brings you to this room," the angel told him. She was lounging in a narrow-backed chaise, her wings spread carelessly around her on the floor like so much drifted milkweed. They had apparently interrupted her at breakfast, for she was sipping on some bubbling juice, and a plate of fruit was set on a table to her right.

"Were you expecting me to feed you?" she inquired next. "I don't know that there's much in the kitchen, but I could ask—"

"We've had breakfast and lunch, thank you very much," Caleb replied. "Delilah, I want you to meet a friend of mine, Nathan Lowell."

"Yes, I noticed you brought company. Do excuse my atrocious manners, Nathan Lowell, but Caleb Augustus brings out the worst in me. You I am truly delighted to meet." She extended her hand but made no effort to get up. Nathan came forward and kissed her fingers, which pleased her and surprised Caleb. Nathan was a staid middle-aged man with a near-fanatical intensity when his professional skills were called upon; Caleb had not expected him to fall so instantly to the angel's charm.

"You I have heard much of, all to your credit," Nathan replied. "The honor of the meeting is mine."

Delilah waved lazy hands toward various chairs. "So, sit down! Tell me what has brought you here so early that you almost found me still sleeping in my bed."

Caleb perched on the edge of a footstool, thinking he might be leaping to his feet any moment. "I've come to ask a favor."

"Don't you always?"

"Which you are going to refuse. But you can't refuse it. It's too important."

Delilah turned toward Nathan Lowell and said conversationally, "I distrust this man most when he sounds so sincere. He is quite manipulative."

"The favor is to me, really," Nathan said seriously. "I've been the one studying the effect of artificial stimulation on damaged nerve tissue—"

Delilah's head whipped back toward Caleb. "No," she said flatly. "Once before I agreed—"

"And I didn't have the tools to help you," he interrupted. "Now I might. Now I think I do. With Dr. Lowell's help—"

"*Doctor* Lowell!" she cried, sitting up so swiftly that her wings made a slurring, sibilant sound. "How *could* you bring a surgeon into my house without asking me—knowing how I hate the very thought of doctors—"

"I knew you would be angry," he said. "I knew I had only one chance. Delilah, I have discovered a device that supplies directed independent energy—it can stimulate the muscles in your wings that have been disconnected from—"

"I will not listen," she broke in, clapping her hands over her ears and shutting her eyes. "I will not listen to you—"

He came to his feet, crossed to her side, and knelt before her. "You must do it," he said quietly, putting his fingers around her wrists and seeking to pull her hands away. She resisted. "You must. Before you fling your life away on a doomed voyage across the sea."

"I will not listen to you. Go away."

"It is your last chance, do you understand me? If you leave for Ysral, no one else, not Noah, not any of the Edori, not Jovah, not you—no one can ever give you another hope of regaining your wings. It is all I have, Delilah, a hope—but it's a good hope. It might make you whole. How can you throw that away? How can you say no? No one will ever ask you again. This is the last time I will importune you. Delilah, you have to try."

Slowly, she allowed the insistence of his fingers to ease her hands from her head. She looked pale, defeated and sad. "You hurt me more than anyone else by making me hope again," she whispered. "Why do you do that? Why can't you leave me in peace?"

"Because I can't give up on you," he said, standing. He held out his hand imperiously, and she laid hers in his, allowed him to pull her to her feet. Nathan Lowell had also risen, clutching his blue bag. "Doctor? Where would you like to perform the operation?"

"Some place that's very clean."

Delilah laughed mirthlessly. "Not here, then."

"I have room at my clinic. Would you like to meet me there in an hour or so?"

"No," Caleb said instantly. "We will come with you now."

The room was white and sterile, though someone had painted a border of violets along the baseboard. Delilah, lying facedown on a narrow cot, seemed absorbed in the repetitive pattern of purple and green. Since they had left her house, she had spoken only to answer direct questions; she seemed disengaged from the whole operation, as if they were not about to touch her body, change her life. On Nathan's instructions, she had unfolded her damaged wing as best she could. Caleb and the doctor spread the chiaroscuro feathers over a long metal table.

There followed a series of exercises similar to the ones Noah and Caleb had performed so many weeks ago, as the doctor determined exactly where the break lay and how the wing was affected. The two men laid the battery over the severed tissue and debated where to insert it, how to connect the working muscles to the alien cylinder, and how to conduct its power through the failed synapses. They had discussed this the night before—and weeks before when Caleb had brought the doctor the existence of the battery as a hypothesis—and they had theoretically determined that such a patch would be effective.

"Well, then. I'm ready if the angela is," Nathan finally said.

"Oh, I'm ready," she said.

"You must take a sleeping drug," Caleb told her.

"I don't want one."

"Well, this would be very painful without one," the doctor told her briskly, measuring out a draught in a silver cup. "So no quarreling now, drink up."

She had propped herself up on one elbow to protest, but the doctor's chiding tone caught her off-guard. She gave Caleb a smoldering look, but accepted the drink meekly enough from Nathan's hands. "What will I feel like when I wake up?" she asked.

"The area of your wing where you still have feeling will hurt," Nathan said.

"And the part beyond that?"

"If you have any sensation, it will be dull and muffled. I expect the battery to give you back gross motor skill but not much refined sensation. I could be wrong."

Delilah pillowed her head on her folded arms and closed her eyes. "I expect nothing," she said, and drifted off to sleep.

Nathan nodded. "Good. Let's begin. This shouldn't take long, but there's no need to dawdle."

It was a strange, fascinating brand of engineering, Caleb decided, this rewiring of the human body with its own circuits and cables. Nathan Lowell worked with painstaking care, knitting the living tissue to the metallic to the dormant; and then he neatly sewed up every cut and fissure.

"It's small enough and light enough that I can't imagine it will disturb her, but there will be a period of adjustment all the same," Nathan commented. He gave a final pat to the small lump that marred the perfect fluid line of the white wings.

"If it works at all," Caleb said.

"If it works at all," the doctor concurred.

"When will we know? How long before she wakes up?"

"She may sleep another hour or so, depending on the condition of her body and the strength of her will. We may as well let her sleep in peace."

But Caleb lingered a moment after the doctor left, looking down at the slumbering angel. "The strength of her will is immeasurable," he murmured. "But I don't know that she has ever slept in peace."

He joined the doctor for a brief snack and to discuss the possible complications from surgery. "You never told me," Nathan said at last, "where you discovered these—batteries."

"At Mount Sinai, in an old library room," Caleb said, lying smoothly. "I wouldn't have recognized them if I hadn't seen a nonfunctioning one in a machine at the Eyrie."

"It's amazing. I wonder how they work—what their components are."

Caleb grinned. "I plan to try and find out."

Long before Nathan expected the angel to awaken, Caleb took an engineering manual with him into the operating room, and sat beside her, reading. He could not bear for her to wake up, alone and in pain and choking down hope. He had brought her here; he would, to the best of his ability, see her through.

It was early evening when she first stirred, murmuring wordlessly, rubbing her forehead against her forearms. Caleb laid his book aside and scooted nearer, wondering if she might just be dreaming. But a few minutes later, she opened her eyes, rolled halfway to her side and looked around her.

"I feel horrible," she said in a slow voice. "What did you make me drink?"

"Some evil medical potion," he said, handing her a glass of water. "Are you in pain or just feeling groggy?"

"Both," she said, accepting the water and swallowing half the contents. "So I take it the operation was a failure."

"Why do you think that?"

"Because you haven't greeted me with ecstatic smiles and cries of good news."

"I don't think we can tell anything until you try to work your wing. But you don't look strong enough even to stand—"

She laughed weakly. "Well, let us see what we can discover." She pushed herself to a sitting position, then closed her eyes briefly, waiting out a dizzy spell. Then she smiled at Caleb and held out her hands. He pulled her to her feet and kept his hold on her.

"You could wait a little," he suggested. "If you're so disoriented, you shouldn't—"

"I think I'm well enough to flap my wings," she said. "My wing. Now watch me."

And she unfurled her wings with a rippling, stretching motion, as a man might extend his arms to loosen his muscles after a long sleep. The feathers made a shushing noise across the floor; the black-tipped edges made a serrated pattern against the stark walls of the office. Right side and left, the wings made mirror images of themselves behind her back.

"You moved it," Caleb said neutrally.

She glanced automatically to her right side, where the damaged wing had never responded to her will, clearly expecting to see it trailing limply on the floor behind her. Her breath caught; her pale face grew chalky white.

"I cannot feel it," she whispered.

"Move it—flutter it—do whatever it is you do," Caleb instructed. "See if it responds."

Slowly, as if her feathers were made of glass, Delilah worked the right wing, extending it, bringing it forward over her shoulder, folding it backward toward the wall. The whole time, she watched in amazement as the wing advanced and retreated, as if it were animated by a power other than her own will.

"I cannot feel it," she said again. "At least—there is a sort of weight there, like a pile of pillows—but I cannot feel it moving."

Caleb stepped forward, ran his hand lightly over the portion of the wing severed from the nerve. "Can you feel my touch?"

She shook her head. "No. I can feel a kind of pressure if you push against the wing, but I cannot feel your fingertips—"

He moved the wing forcibly forward. "You mean, you can feel that?"

"It's like that weight shifts."

"And you can shift that weight yourself."

Again, she shuffled the wing back and forth. "Yes, although I don't have a real sense of control—"

"That would take time, I imagine," he said calmly. He wanted to jump up and down, to shout hallelujahs, but he was not sure of Delilah yet. To learn to operate a mechanically stimulated wing, where she had no sensation and little control, would be a tremendously difficult task; and yet, it *was* responding, she could manipulate it. Would she realize what a gift she had been given, or would she find it even more bitter to have only half of her desire fulfilled?

But this was Delilah; he had forgotten, for a moment, the blazing intensity of her soul. Even now she was frowning as she attempted some invisible contraction of muscles. "I can feel *that*," she was saying, more to herself than to him. "But if I move that way—"

"I think, if you experiment and exercise, you will learn how to control it better and how to tell when it is positioned the way you want—"

She looked at him now as if suddenly remembering he was in the room. "Will I be able to fly?" she asked directly. "Will it bear my weight?"

"I would try to strengthen the muscles before I attempted to fly," he said. "They have been unused for a long time, and I don't know how much power they will regain—"

"Then why give me back any movement at all, if I won't be able to fly?" she snapped.

"I believe you will be able to compensate for the lack of feeling and retrain your muscles," he said quietly. "But I don't know. I have done what I can for you. Dr. Lowell has a therapy program worked out that should gradually improve the muscle tone and your ability to work the wing, but it may take months—"

She brushed past him, so determined that he did not attempt to stop her. "I will fly by the end of the week," she said over her shoulder, heading out the door. "Or I will never fly again."

Although he should have left for the Eyrie the next morning, Caleb postponed his departure for another day—and then another. He was waiting for Delilah, who was nowhere to be found. The housekeeper disavowed any knowledge of her whereabouts, and Joseph, whom he approached when all other avenues proved fruitless, merely shrugged his disinterest.

Well, she had clearly gone somewhere to try out her wings, to retrain them if she could, and if she could not—then what? What if she were to attempt flight too soon, before the shriveled muscle had remembered how to react? What if she were to achieve some grand aerial height, then tire suddenly or misread her strength, and come somersaulting down a stairwell of cruel breezes? Caleb imagined her lying on the ground somewhere, bleeding and broken, miles from Luminaux, hours from help. If anything happened to Delilah, it would be entirely his fault. He watched the skies, and waited out the laggard days.

It was midnight on the second day, and he had, reluctantly and anxiously, sought his bed, when he was roused by a terrific clamor at his door. He had not actually been asleep, nor had he slept the night before, but still he felt dazed and disoriented as he stumbled to the door and opened it.

Delilah strode in like a stormcloud rolling through a valley; she seemed to throw off stray bolts of energy and churn like a whirlwind. Everything about her was alive—her skin, her hair, her eyes, her wings. She glowed like a haloed woman.

"You look tousled. Did I wake you?" was her opening remark.

"Where have you been?" he demanded. "I've been so worried about you—"

She laughed and shook her hair back. It seemed damp with some kind of celestial dew. "Flying," she said. "I love night flying—it's like swimming among the stars. You can actually feel the starlight on your face when you turn your head from side to side. It feels like hot raindrops or—no—I can't describe it. And there are no words to tell you what moonlight feels like across the feathers of your wings."

"So you've done it," he said, just now remembering to shut the door. He motioned her farther inside the room, but it was clear she was too excited to sit. Indeed, already she had begun pacing through the small space, letting her wings brush carelessly over tables, chairs, objects on the floor. "How long did it take you? And don't you think you should have waited a few weeks as I—"

"Oh, I waited a whole day. I did little practice flights down the low foothills just to see if my wings would hold me. It was frightening at first because I couldn't get used to not feeling my right wing. It would be as if you tried to pick up firewood with both hands, but you had no sensation in one of them. You could look at your fingers, and watch them open and close when you wanted them to, but you could not tell by touch if they were responding to your will."

"Yes, I thought that's how it would be. So I think it's risky of you to attempt a long flight—"

"Oh, I've figured it out now. I got caught by a crosscurrent this afternoon, and I had to admit that was a little unnerving, but I just had to *remember* how it was done and I was all right. And it was tiring, I'll grant you that—I used to be able to fly five hundred miles in a day! And today I was worn out after fifty or sixty miles. But I'll get my strength back. Quickly, too. In a few weeks, you won't know that I was ever hurt. *I* won't even remember."

"Take it easy," he advised. "I'm serious, Delilah, listen to me. You've just had a fairly major operation on damaged tissue that is still sensitive, and you could harm yourself—"

She laughed at him again, swept him into a breathless embrace. He could smell the starlight and raindrops in her hair. "I can't slow down," she mocked him when she let him go. "It was always my trouble, Caleb—I wanted too much too fast."

"But now you know what that kind of attitude can cost."

"And I know what months of worrying and hurting and hating can do to the soul," she replied. "I will be a little careful!

Do you think I want to lose my wings again? I could not live through another year like the one I just had. But I have to be happy again. I have to be joyful again. Or I may as well not be alive at all."

He turned his hands palm up, a gesture of resignation. "So what will you do next, oh-so-carefully, as you get used to your wings again?"

She laughed. "I will go to Breven, of course."

"Breven! But surely—"

"No, I no longer plan to make the voyage to Ysral—though I must confess I am consumed with curiosity to see it. Perhaps I will fly there one day, though they say it is too far for an angel to go."

"Then why Breven?"

Her eyes chided him. "Because I believe there is one Edori who will not set sail if I ask him to stay in Samaria with me."

He felt a malicious hand ease its constriction from around his heart. "You're going to fetch Noah," he said, suddenly glad. "You're going to tell him— What are you going to tell him?"

"That I can fly, of course."

"But—he loves you, you know. He may want to sail to Ysral anyway if he thinks you don't love him in return."

Her face softened and she briefly stopped pacing; she was visited by a moment of peace. "How could anyone not love Noah?" she asked. "He deserves better than to love me."

"He would not think so."

She tossed her hair back over her shoulders and resumed both her smiling and her striding. "So I think I will be able to convince him to stay. That will make you happy, yes?"

"Yes. Almost as happy as I am to see you whole again."

"And I still have not thanked you, have I?"

"But you were doing me a favor, remember?" he said with a smile.

She shook her head. "You will never be able to maintain that fiction," she said, and now her voice was serious. "But there is no way I can put into words my gratitude for what you have done. You have given me back my life. You have given me back everything that gives my life meaning. If you had saved me from drowning, you could not have more surely rescued me. There is no way such a debt can be repaid, but if you can think of anything you need, anything I can give you—"

"The debt of friendship is never collected," he interrupted. "And nothing is ever owed."

"Still, I will remember you with awe and affection every day of my life," she said. "And I will speak your name when I ask for blessings from Jovah."

"So now you love the god again," he said.

"How could I not? He has restored me. He has used you as a tool to make me whole again."

Close enough to the truth; perhaps she was even right to worship the god who had done so much for her. "I will be glad to have you pray for me," he said.

She was shaking out her wings as if adjusting a fold of her dress, but she looked up at him now with a rueful smile. "Isn't it strange? Just because he has healed me, I believe he can hear me again. But I have no proof of it. It is just a feeling."

"I would guess you're right," Caleb said solemnly. "Maybe it will rain tomorrow and give you a chance to prove it."

She laughed. "In any case, I have a great deal to do before I leave in the morning. But I couldn't leave without saying goodbye. And—thank you."

"You're welcome," he said.

She took two quick paces forward and kissed him on the mouth. She tasted like wind, night and wildness. No wonder the Edori loved her. "For all the things I don't know how to say," she said, pulling back. Four steps took her to the door, and she was gone.

Caleb lay awake a long time after she left, no longer even attempting to sleep. He had not tested the repairs he had made to *Jehovah*, of course, but he was sure they had worked, and the ship was now once again able to respond to all angels. The storms would cease; the mutinies of the wealthy men would die away to grumbles. The world was back to normal. Time had reversed itself, and they stood now where they had started a year ago.

Only he had changed. An incredible knowledge had illuminated his mind, and a spectacular love had reshaped his heart. The one he must keep secret; the other was to alter every current of his life.

He rolled to his side, content, and finally slept. In the morning, he repacked his bags, saddled his mare, and set out once more on the road to Velora.

Six days of hard traveling took him to the Eyrie, but he needn't have hurried: Alleya was not there. Samuel gave him this news but tempered it with glad tidings.

"I got a note from her a couple of weeks ago, saying Jovah could hear the angels again," the older man confided. "And sure enough, that day when the storms came in, Timothy and Asher went aloft and prayed. And the rains cleared! And the news came in from Cedar Hills and Monteverde—Jovah is listening to the angels again. He has remembered us. And I believe he will not forget us again."

Not in my lifetime, Caleb thought, but of course he did not say so. "Did Alleya say when she would return?" he asked.

"In about two and a half weeks, her note said. I expect her tomorrow or the day after."

"She asked me to do some repairs on the music machines," Caleb said, bending the truth. "Is it all right if I come back tomorrow and start working?"

"You think you'll be able to fix them this time?" Samuel asked skeptically. "I admit I find that noisy motor distracting."

Caleb grinned. "This time, I think I can do it right."

"Then we'll be glad to have you."

So Caleb spent the night in an inexpensive hotel (wondering, *Will I be living at the Eyrie in a few weeks?*) and returned to the angel hold the following morning. Work on the music machines went fairly quickly—there was nothing more complicated than disengaging the spent battery and plugging in the fresh one—though it took him a little longer to dismantle his external motor. He smiled at it with a certain fondness as he took it apart. It had done the job well enough, though it was no match for settler technology; and it had brought him closer to Alleya. It had certainly served its purpose.

Around noon he was finished, and he rolled up his kits and left the labyrinth to emerge on the central plateau. The day was sunny and fine—at last, true spring unmarred by the capricious storms—and he dawdled as he made his way toward the grand stairway through the inevitable throngs of petitioners.

He was wondering when Alleya might appear, and so he was not paying much attention to those around him, but suddenly a low murmur in the crowd erupted into scattered shouts. He glanced around, trying to identify the source of agitation, and he saw a number of people pointing skyward. He looked up. Shading his eyes, he saw nothing more unusual than a single angel making a lazy spiral far overhead, and he turned his eyes back to the people around him. But now everyone was staring at the circling angel, and excited whispers were swelling into cries and cheers and expressions of disbelief.

He gazed upward again, wondering what had excited them so, and just then the angel dropped a few yards closer. Those black-tipped wings, that night-dark hair; suddenly he, too, recognized the vision overhead. "Delilah," he whispered just as someone around him shouted out her name. In minutes, the whole crowd was chanting. *Delilah, Delilah, Delilah . . . !*

There were hundreds of people in the plaza, or so it seemed, but when she finally drifted down for a landing, they parted spontaneously to give her room. Even after her feet touched the rock of the plateau, she seemed to be floating; she sparkled with her own inimitable combination of urgency and delight.

Samuel and Asher were the first to approach her. Everyone else seemed too awestruck to come any nearer. Caleb edged his way through the crowd just to hear what they would say to her; the smile on his face was as wide as the one on her own.

"It is a miracle," Samuel said, his voice quavering. Caleb realized the old man was actually crying. "You were broken, and Jovah has made you whole."

"Yes, the god has been good to me and I thank him daily."

"But when did this happen?" Asher demanded. "Why haven't you come back to us sooner?"

She laughed at him and laid a hand affectionately on his shoulder. "Just days ago," she said. "I have been learning how to fly again, learning everything. I wanted to be sure I was whole before I returned, before I came to you, before I told you all—"

"What?" Samuel said, and the sudden caution in his voice gave Caleb his one brief moment of warning. The angel's next words left both Samuel and Asher dumb, stunned the crowd, turned Caleb sick and dizzy.

"I have returned to the Eyrie to be Archangel again."

Chapter Twenty

Alleya spent more than a week in Chahiela, but there was not enough silence in that place to satisfy her. The children, even the wordless children, managed to be noisy and demanding, and everyone found a way to ask her questions both trivial and unnerving. Even Hope's house, which she remembered as the quietest and most solitary of places, seemed overfull of visitors.

Her mother was not one to ask questions, of course, not even why Alleya had returned to this village so soon after leaving it, looking as though she had seen precipices crumble away beneath her feet. Hope did not ask how long she planned to stay, what she was interested in for dinner, if she would care to sing in the evenings. Certainly, Hope did not ask her daughter to address any of the larger issues that might be thought to concern her.

Have you found the man the god wants you to marry? Have you discovered why the god has turned his face from the angels—and have you learned how to recapture his attention? Indeed, how do you find Jovah these days—warm and loving, or cold, efficient and mechanical?

Hope asked Alleya none of these things. No one did. Still, the questions clamored in her head.

Now and then, during those four days, it nagged at Alleya that she really should be back at the Eyrie. It was now so close to the Gloria that there would be hundreds of petitioners at the holds, bringing special prayers for the angels to present to the god. And she had spent so much time away from the Eyrie lately that these petitioners—indeed, her own angels—could justifiably be annoyed with her for not being present now. And she must learn music, and make arrangements with the vendors who would organize supply tents on the Plain of Sharon, and oversee plans for the pavilion the Eyrie residents would set up for their comfort during the Gloria. And no doubt there were other matters to attend to—storms blowing in over the Galilee River, plague flags raised in the middle plains—the simple day-to-day business which she had neglected so shamefully of late.

But Jovah could hear all the angels again, so there was no special need for her to raise her voice; and until Caleb sojourned to the Eyrie to choose his Gloria mass, there was no need for her to practice any other music. And she needed time to think, to gather her scattered wits, and she could not do that at the Eyrie.

But soon enough it became clear that she could not do that at Chahiela, either.

In fact, she knew of only one place in all of Samaria quiet enough to allow her to think.

So on the evening of her tenth day, Alleya told her mother she would be leaving in the morning. Hope took the news with neither reproach nor surprise.

"I'll see you again, then, when you come back," her mother said.

"Yes. Thanks for letting me stay here so long."

"Of course."

In the morning, she took off at first light, heading northeast through sublimely cloudless skies in the direction of Mount Sinai. The weather was flawless for that entire trip, the wind still, the sun apparently motionless, the color of the heavens an unwavering blue. Alleya felt the first true heat of spring settle across the feathers on her back. The sensation warmed her all the way to her bones.

She was back at Sinai early in the afternoon. Instantly, she felt a beneficent peace gather around her. She had been driven by a sense of urgency to get here as quickly as she could, but now that she had arrived, she became slow-paced, lackadaisical. What did she need to accomplish, after all? She was merely here to relax and sort out her thoughts. There was certainly no timetable for that.

Lazily, she wandered through the corridors of the retreat, glancing into rooms she had not explored before, noting how big the place really was, large enough to accommodate the oracle, the acolytes, visitors, a few servants. All hallways led to the main chamber, of course, but she refused to linger in there more than a moment or two. She had no business in this room, no interest at all in the gleaming blue screen, faintly pulsing, seeming with an almost sentient presence to watch her every time she crossed the floor. She escaped it a few times by ducking into the archives, lingering there to read passages from various books (now that she could read any volume in the library), studying the mystifying maps on the walls. But always when she emerged, there was the living interface, intent, relentless, beckoning.

She had nothing more to say to the god. Nothing to ask him, nothing to relay. Not through this medium, anyway. She would not go near the screen.

The day whittled down to evening. She found the room she had shared with Caleb and went to bed early, falling into a deep exhausted sleep the minute she closed her eyes. When she woke, her senses told her it was the following morning, but she had no great desire to roll immediately out of bed. She lay there an hour or more, feeling relaxed and at ease.

Perhaps she should have gone to Hagar's retreat instead of coming here. That was a still, solitary place with no disquieting instrument of the god overseeing her every move. *Instrument of the spaceship,* she corrected herself, and got out of bed.

She fed herself, continued exploring, continued her investigation into the archives. But every time she walked through the main chamber, she turned involuntarily to glance at the interface; and every time she looked at it, she lingered longer.

And took a few steps closer.

Until finally she was standing before it, close enough for her fingers to touch the keyboard, wondering what Jovah would say to her if she asked him any of the questions revolving ceaselessly in her head.

It didn't matter what he would have to say. He was a man-made machine, nothing but a collection of circuit wires and electrical impulses. He could give her no divine guidance; he was no more brilliant than Caleb, than Noah, than Uriel or any of the first settlers who had colonized Samaria. Men had built him, men had taught him to speak; and men could not give her the answers she so desperately needed.

But very smart men had built him, a voice in her head unexpectedly interjected. *Men who knew more about the world, about the universe, than you will ever know. Men who had traveled who knows how many thousands of miles, through acres of stars, through oceans of unlit space, to come to this one world and declare it home. This machine knows everything they knew. That is the knowledge you want. That is the one thing worth having.*

She had come here planning this, which she only now realized. She had not even moved the marker books from the pentagram on the floor. She typed in a single word, which appeared in bold letters on the bright screen, and pressed the Enter key. This time she did not hurry as she walked to the center of the room. This time she did not gasp or grimace as she was enveloped in that golden haze and split into her smallest invisible components. This time she arrived on her feet as she teleported into the main communication center of the spaceship *Jehovah*.

The quality of silence here was different than anywhere else she had ever been. It was a living silence—not like the silence at the Eyrie, when everyone paused to formulate a private, unvoiced prayer; not like the silence of Sinai, where even the empty hallways echoed with remembered conversations. Here, no one spoke or breathed, but everywhere was the clatter and hum of machinery at work, strange clicks, intermittent muffled chirps. It was an industrious silence, she decided at last, or a thoughtful one; it was like listening to the incessant calculations of a very productive mind.

Which, of course, she was.

"Jovah, can you hear me?" she asked, into that waiting stillness.

"Yes, Alleluia. I can hear you from any point in this ship."

"So you remember me."

"Your Kiss identifies you."

She fingered the marble coolness embedded in her arm. It had meant something so different to her for all of her life. "So it is true, what the priests say," she said. "That you are only aware of those who have been dedicated. That unless a person wears the Kiss, you cannot tell who he is and how he fares."

"Or if he exists at all," Jovah acknowledged. "It is true. But there are other ways to gather information about those living on Samaria. For instance, many oracles have, over the centuries, fed me information about the Edori—clan names, births, deaths, alliances. This has allowed me, although in an imperfect fashion, to track the fortunes of various tribesmen and to understand how they fit into the world."

"So if I were to tell you everything I know about the Edori living today, you would then record their existence and—what? What would that tell you? Why would you need to know?"

"It would help me deduce how far they have traveled along certain predictable evolutionary paths. It would help me gauge their population growth as it relates to the rest of Samaria, and how long they are likely to remain what is essentially a separate race. Even now, for good or ill, they are being absorbed into the mainstream Samarian population."

"Not for long," Alleya said. "They are planning to migrate."

"Ah," said Jovah. "I did not know that. That is the sort of useful information only an oracle can feed me."

She had been making a slow circuit of the consoles as she spoke, trailing her hands experimentally along the curves and surfaces of the keyboards. "What does this do?" she asked suddenly, tapping her fingers against an opaque white screen.

"It monitors the nearest star systems to decode any interesting space activity."

"What does *that* mean?" she asked impatiently.

"Exploding suns, planets that have shifted orbit, space debris that might somehow head this way. As well as any potential human or humanoid space travel or long-distance transmissions, indicating well-developed life on one of these nearby planets."

She digested that a moment in silence. "We came—our ancestors came to Samaria from another planet. From Eleison. On this ship," she said.

"Yes."

"I always thought—well, I never thought about it. It never occurred to me that there were other planets where men lived. But there are?"

"Oh, yes. Maybe a hundred that men had colonized by the time they had settled on Eleison. By now, maybe a hundred more. And men are not the only intelligent beings living in the universe. There were, when the ship left Eleison, sixty-five identified advanced alien species, and hundreds more at a level so unsophisticated that it seemed unlikely they would ever develop to a human level of intelligence."

This was hard to grasp; she felt her mind crunch down in concentration. "Wait. So—so all over the universe there are planets populated by men and women just like us. And *more* planets with people who aren't really people. Who are—well, what are they?"

"The species vary too widely to make a generalization. Some are carbon-based, like you. Some are silicon-based. Some have a basic structure of head, body, limbs. Some have no physical characteristic that you would recognize. Most intelligent species have some kind of functional brain, recognizable as an organ that directs and controls the rest of the operations of the body and that is capable of sustained and logical thought."

She waved her hands to silence him, probably a useless gesture since she had no idea if he could see her. "Stop. It doesn't matter. I don't care about them. But humans. There are humans on hundreds of planets? Did they all come from Eleison?"

"Oh, no. Eleison is a minor planet colonized several centuries after men first discovered space travel. Human life originated on Terra in the Milky Way galaxy. That was several million generations before colonization on Eleison."

"And did they leave Terra too because of war and hatred and self-destruction?"

"Well, war and self-destruction were certainly part of life on Terra, but the original space explorers were motivated more by a desire for knowledge than a need to escape the home planet. Historically, once a race becomes completely at ease with its own environment, it seeks to conquer or at least explore unfamiliar ones—whether those are new continents or new worlds."

She thought of the Edori, setting off any day now on a

chancy, ill-equipped voyage. "That's the only reason they leave? To explore?"

"Oh, no. If a continent, or a world, has become too crowded to sustain all the life forms extant, some members of the species will go off in search of more land, more room to grow. Many colonists are seeking religious freedom and a chance to live life on their own terms. Some, like your own, seek to escape intolerable conditions. But no exploration is possible without adequate technology."

"So the settlers left Eleison looking for a place they could design to suit them," she said. "Why did they choose Samaria?"

"Because it was compatible with their life form. It had the right oxygen mix and a soil base they were comfortable with and a specific gravity that was similar to the one on Eleison. Its only real drawback was the violent weather, but once I was modified to create shifts in the air masses, upon request, that was easily controlled."

"And once the angels were created to communicate with you," she added softly.

"Yes, that, too. I can hear the angels most clearly when they are aloft, but in fact my satellite receptors are sensitive enough to pick up the general prayers of ground-based citizens as well."

"So. The angels. How were they created?"

"Biological alterations. One of the scientists on board, Dr. Hoyt Freecastle, had been an expert in artificial limbs and tissue regeneration back on Eleison, and he had long been interested in the theory of creating a human being that could fly under its own power. Once the colonists realized how essential it would be to communicate with the ship on a regular basis, they allowed Dr. Freecastle to experiment on a few volunteers to see if he could graft wings to their backs. When the operation was successful, he created a whole host of angels and, indeed, altered their genetic makeup so the wings would be passed on biologically to future generations."

"I wonder if they knew," she said, more to herself than to the ship, "what would happen next. That we would forget how the angels came about. That we would forget how we came to Samaria. That we would forget . . . everything. Even who Jehovah was."

"Oh, they knew," the ship replied, startling her somewhat. She had not been expecting an answer. "At least, they theorized. As you know, the colonists deliberately withheld technology from future generations. They cut almost every direct link with me, and they destroyed what few technological marvels they had brought with them planetside. They sought a simpler, more primitive, perhaps more innocent lifestyle for themselves and their children. But more than one sociologist in the group speculated that ritualistic observance of such events as the Gloria, and the creation of superior beings you call angels, would lead to a theistic belief in the existence of an all-powerful being. In effect, a personalized god."

"And that's what they wanted?"

"No. They had their own religion, of course, which had nothing to do with spaceships, and most of them believed that this was the religion that would persist after colonization. In fact, it died out within two generations."

Alleya felt her interest sharply revive. "And what was their religion? Was it the true one?"

"The true one?" Jehovah repeated. "I do not understand."

She made another impatient gesture. "My whole life, I have believed that Jovah is a god, a supreme being that watched over me and heard my prayers. And now I learn that Jovah is a machine, built by men, a thing, a—a computer. But I cannot erase from my heart the belief that somewhere there *is* a god who watches over me, who hears my prayers, who knows my name. Perhaps the colonists knew who he was. Perhaps he is the one who sent them safely from Eleison to Samaria."

"Perhaps, but even on Eleison there was more than one religion, and fealty to more than one god. Those you call the Edori, who believe in a nameless god who oversees the universe, have a religion that is relatively close to the basic tenets of the faith the Christers brought with them from Eleison. But that is not to say their religion is the true one. And throughout the universe, from planet to planet, there exists such a diversity of divinity that to set one aside and call it the true religion is a task no sage or philosopher has been wise enough to achieve."

Alleya felt herself sag against one of the pristine white consoles. "But then—no one knows who the god is, and if there is one? Everywhere—in the whole universe—there are people who *believe* they worship the correct god, but have no proof—people who may not even know that their god is false, or one of many?"

"That is correct," Jovah said.

"But that is—that is disastrous!" she cried. "I thought you would know—I thought you would be able to tell me—who the god was we had forgotten and how we could reach him after so many centuries of neglect. But if there is no god, or no god that anyone can identify—then what holds the world together? What binds the stars and the suns, what turns the seasons, what gives any of us the will to live?"

"These are questions that, over the millennia, have concerned a great number of men and women," the ship replied. "People with far more education than you in far more advanced societies have despaired when uttering those same queries. And like you, they believed there was an answer somewhere—that there was a god, whose wisdom knew no boundary and whose strength could not be measured. They believed he was an infinite being and their own abilities were finite, and so they could never know him, or define him, or limit him.

"If it comforts you," he continued, while Alleya listened intently, "in every society, on every planet, whether humanoid or alien, some form of religion exists. Some members of every sentient species believe that there is a divine being, who, as you say, guards them and listens to them and knows their names. They have different names for these gods—and some of them have more than one god, and some have gods who are cruel and some have gods who are benign. But they believe their fates are not entirely in their own hands, and they believe their souls do not go wandering undefended after they die."

"It comforts me. A little," she said slowly. "But perhaps they have been as deluded as we have. Perhaps there were forces directing them that were just as bizarre and inexplicable as—as a spaceship so complex they would not be able to comprehend it if they saw it. Perhaps they just *wanted* to believe that someone cared for them, and believing made it so. Perhaps they have all created their own gods."

"Indeed, you will find essayists and scientists on every planet who make exactly those same arguments. One of them has said that religion is the soothing opiate of the common people. Another has said that god is an advanced form of desire. Men have always, through the centuries, found ways to create what they did not find in the natural order. And men have always, through the centuries, sought to put themselves in the context of the universe. The universe has remained too vast for them to quantify. Thus they hypothesize an entity even more vast as a vessel to contain it. Men are, in the final analysis, agoraphobic. They want a roof and a fence and a definable boundary. Otherwise, they are too afraid of what lurks outside."

Much of what he said made no sense to Alleya; she wasn't sure if that was because he used too many unfamiliar words from that foreign language or if her brain just refused to accept too many new concepts at once. But one statement she clung to, as if it were the only truth in a sea of lies: Everywhere in the universe, men and women believed in a god. It was not the same god, or at least, not a god in the same contours; he bent to amazing molds, took on radically different identities. But from planet to planet, star to star, he extended; and his fingers touched every believer's heart.

"I wish I knew more," she said aloud. "I wish I knew all the names the god went by, and all the ways he was worshiped."

"I have all that information, if you wish me to download it," Jovah said. "It is all in the Eleison tongue, but you have mastered that, have you not?"

"You mean, the language the oracles use to speak with you? Oh, yes."

"In fact, you can call up the files from the interface on Sinai, if you wish. It is more material than you could read in a lifetime, but I can guide you to the texts you might find most interesting."

She felt a spurt of gratitude toward him, much akin to the warm glow of fellowship she had used to feel toward Jovah, back when he listened to her voice alone, back when she had thought he was a god. It would be hard to remember that this voice belonged to a machine, that every act she had considered divine had been programmed into a computer by human hands. And yet, perhaps it would not be wrong to consider this electronic brain, in some sense, a friend. He had in many ways befriended her over the years—as she had befriended him.

"Tell me," she demanded. "Why is it you could hear my voice and no other before Caleb repaired your circuit board?"

"The pitch was specific and singular, and could still be read by my receptors," was the immediate answer. Which, again, made no sense. And was not what she had wanted to hear.

She smiled a little sadly. "Oh. I thought it was because I had some special place in your heart."

"I am not constructed with emotions such as humans have. I do not have what you would consider a 'heart.' I thought you understood that."

She sighed. "I understood. It was a stupid question."

"But you are, if it makes you feel more appreciated, unique. At least, your voice is unique. It resonates at a particular level that I have not seen replicated, and I have heard every singer on Samaria for the past six hundred and fifty years."

"Yes, that does make me feel better," she said, smiling more brightly. "Although I would not have expected it to."

"Every Kiss has a unique electronic pattern as well," he continued. "Which is how I am able to track and identify everyone who has been, as you call it, dedicated. But that is a different thing entirely from voice identification."

"And do you really cause Kisses to flare when true lovers meet for the first time?"

"In a manner of speaking. I am usually able to calculate, almost from birth, which offspring bear gene clusters that I think would be valuably combined with another person's gene clusters. For instance, your friend Caleb Augustus inherited remarkable abilities from the first genetic combination of angels—"

"Nathaniel and Magdalena," she supplied.

"Yes. And it was inevitable that, several generations later, a man with a predisposition to scientific discovery would be created from that gene pool. It could have been the generation before or the next generation. These things are not exact."

"And you thought that would be valuable? To facilitate the birth of a man who was a natural engineer?"

"It seemed likely that some of my mechanical functions would begin to fail sometime in this century, and I thought it would be beneficial if someone on Samaria had been bred to correct those problems."

"Do you always—breed people like that? With a specific goal in mind?"

"Not always. Sometimes."

"For what goals?"

"They vary."

"But is there—some kind of overall plan? For the development of the entire race on Samaria?"

"Nothing so grandiose. Sometimes I want to pair men and women of obvious intelligence merely to ensure that some genius is still produced in this world. Other times I seek to strengthen failing bloodlines or eradicate inherent diseases. But men and women are too unpredictable and contrary to mate and reproduce according to some great scheme of mine. They do what they will. Now and then I urge them along."

"So if—for instance—the Archangel did not marry the man or woman you selected, what would be the consequences?"

"Merely, offspring that were not as vital and gifted as they might otherwise have been."

"But you would not—again, for instance—display your wrath by sending down thunderbolts if the wrong angelico sang at the Gloria?"

"Is that what the angels believe?"

"Oh, yes. It is what motivated Gabriel to search all over Samaria to find Rachel, a hundred and fifty years ago."

"I did not realize the dictum carried such weight, although I believe your world is better served if angels heed my words. In any case, only one Archangel has not sought and followed my advice about who to marry."

"Delilah," Alleya guessed.

"Precisely."

"And she sang with Levi at her side, and the world did not end, so his voice must have pleased you," she added. "And her voice must have pleased you as well, if you selected her."

"I expected a difficult decade or so, for I knew my circuits were burning," he said. "I believed Delilah had the strength of will to shepherd fractious contingents through a great trial. I still believe I was right, though she had physical disabilities that eventually rendered her unfit for the position."

"Would you know," Alleya asked, "if she suddenly regained the ability to fly?"

"Is that likely?" he returned.

"It's possible," she amended.

"If she takes wing again, yes, I will know. I will be able to judge by the variances in the pressure on her Kiss."

"Watch for it, then," Alleya said. "It may occur."

There was a moment of silence while Alleya brooded over all the things the computer had told her in a few short minutes. Almost too much to take in; and yet, in some strange, unforeseen way, deeply exciting. In a few sentences, her world had expanded to the size of a universe, densely populated and unimaginably diverse.

And, for her, largely theoretical.

"Caleb said this ship was fantastical," she said suddenly. "May I look around? Will you tell me what everything means and does?"

"Certainly," Jovah replied. "Just ask me about anything that seems unclear to you."

Alleya laughed. "Everything will seem unclear."

She started with the rest of the consoles in the chamber she was in (the communications bridge, he told her), which he explained to her item by item. They moved on to the next room, which appeared to be a kind of casual anteroom to the bridge, and then outward to the other corridors and levels of the ship.

There was too much to take in; soon enough, Alleya felt her mind begin to haze over, to resist more marvels, and she merely nodded as the disembodied voice bid her look at this special feature and that compact invention. In the central levels, where most of the living had been done, she viewed room after room designed for sleeping or washing or play, until the walls and the furniture began to blend in her head and she wondered how anyone could find his way to the proper suite if he journeyed too far from his own door.

About half of the lower levels had been turned into vast greenhouses, farm fields sown with standard crops like corn, wheat, barley and oats in all stages of growth and maturity. From a hallway window, she watched a slim mechanical arm harvest row after row of ripe yellow corn which, the computer told her, would be processed and dried and stored for seed against the time Samarians might request it. "And then an angel prays for grain, and you release this over our farmland," she said. "Precisely," Jovah replied.

She glanced in only the most cursory way at the locks and storage holds located in the very bottom of the ship, and felt she was better off not attempting to examine the crystal core that powered the ship and that could be found behind a locked door which, Jovah assured her, he could open at will. But it was not something she needed to see. Her head was stuffed full of wonders.

Surely it was her imagination, but the civil voice sounded a little disappointed when she requested directions back to the communications bridge. Hard to believe that a ship could feel loneliness; but Jovah had had very few visitors in the past six and a half centuries.

Back on the bridge, where she felt almost at home by now, Alleya did one last slow pivot to look around. She had told Caleb he could never return here, and she had sworn that she herself would never come back, but now she was not so sure. There was so much knowledge here, more than she would ever think to ask about. *Could* she just allow the ship to orbit austerely overhead, rich with gifts, but untouched and unremembered? True, that had been the colonists' original intention, to separate themselves and their children from every taint of technology; but hundreds of years had passed since that decision had been made. The world was a different place, inhabited by personalities not even Jovah had been able to predict. Was it right to assume that this society could not be trusted with advanced scientific knowledge? Was it fair to withhold that information if it was available? Eleison had destroyed itself using sophisticated weaponry, but did that mean Samaria would do the same thing if the same tools were available?

She remembered again the angry meetings with the Manadavvi councilors, the sly conspiracy between the merchants and the Jansai and the Manadavvi elect. If they were not forced by their belief in a vengeful god to act in harmony with angels, with all peoples of Samaria, would they do so? If they believed there was a way to circumvent Jovah's wrath, would they not instantly attempt it? If any kind of weapon were to be put in their hands, would they not use it?

She thought of the factories in Breven, dreary and desolate and worked by exhausted, hopeless wraiths. Who would reap the benefits of any technology she was able to translate from the ship's circuitry to Samarian electronics? Not the independent farmers, not the Manadavvi serfs, not the Jansai work force.

She had been suspicious of technology all her life, resentful of its displacements, horrified at its outright ugliness. Jovah was not frightful nor usurping nor homely; it was tempting to allow his very existence to seduce her into changing her lifelong beliefs. And yet, even Jovah was a product of a world gone to war, and his efficient beauty had been fertilized in a noxious bed.

Perhaps all science bloomed amid such dismal waste; perhaps all progress was founded in squalor and gradually reshaped itself into something sleek or even beautiful. She was looking at both ends of the spectrum now. It was hard to determine if what was beginning as a Breven factory would be transmogrified into something as elegant and breathtaking as the spaceship *Jehovah*.

Or merely into the last fierce war on Eleison.

They were a different people on Samaria now, but their fathers were the same, or their fathers' fathers. They were guided, no doubt, by the same primeval impulses and led by the same fears and desires. She had no proof that the centuries had changed them. She had no reason to believe they could maintain harmony on their own.

"Jovah," she said aloud, her words slow, "when you were combining gene clusters and breeding for intelligence, did you ever think to breed for something better? Gentleness, for instance, or at least an aversion to violence. Did you seek to create men and women who would be less and less likely, with each generation, to want to kill each other or destroy their entire planet?"

"I did not know a way to breed aggression from the human race," he said, and his voice sounded almost regretful. "There does not seem to be a gene for pacifism, even a recessive one."

"Then perhaps I would do best not to hurry this along," she said at last. "Soon enough, as Caleb says, we will reach the point where you will be a mystery no longer. And then—farewell the ordered life on Samaria. No more god, no more Gloria, no more harmony among all peoples. I hope I do not live long enough to see it."

"It's doubtful," the ship said. "Given the current level of technology your generation has achieved, I would expect a hundred years or more to pass before men of science are able to build or even theorize the existence of an object like myself. You will be dead long before that."

She laughed faintly. "As always, you offer grim comfort."

"It is no more than the truth."

So—decision made. Another incredibly difficult one. She grimaced, remembering her arrogant words to Caleb: *That is why the god named me Archangel.* Although in fact he had named her Archangel merely because of the way her voice resonated on his . . . receptors. It had nothing to do with her ability to reason, or control the fate of an entire nation. She sighed.

"Is there something else you would like to know?" the ship inquired after she had been silent for more than ten minutes.

"Not at the moment. Anything else I wish to ask you I presume I can ask through the interface at Sinai?"

"Yes, although at times it is more difficult for me to communicate through the written word. That programming was left deliberately primitive so that oracles did not accidentally stumble upon knowledge too vast for them to bear, and so my range of responses is limited."

"I'll remember that. And if I need to know something that you cannot answer over the interface—well, perhaps I will come back. But perhaps I won't. It would be an addictive pleasure, I think, and I should not indulge myself where I refuse to admit others."

"Then we will communicate as best we can. Be sure to remember to tell me how the Edori fare on their migration."

She sighed again. "I wish—I wish there would be some way to know if they arrived safely. I wish there was some way to know if Ysral exists so I could know if they have a chance to actually find it."

"Ysral," Jovah repeated. "I assume you mean the small continent on the far side of the planet?"

"You are aware of it?"

"Oh, yes. This world has only two principal land masses,

and the settlers originally considered colonizing the other one—Ysral, as you call it. But it was significantly smaller than the one they chose, and had much less diversity of terrain, and they felt that Samaria would better answer their needs in the long run."

"Can you—do you know—is there some kind of map you could give me, showing where Ysral is in relation to this continent? We have nothing but legends to tell us that Ysral even exists."

"Certainly, I can print out detailed navigational charts for you. The scientists mapped out the entire world when they were first exploring. There will have been some geological shifts, you understand, which will have affected ocean currents and even some submerged land masses, but in general, these charts should give the voyagers a fairly comprehensive guide to their destination."

She was lit by a wild elation and shaken by a sense of relief so great it made her momentarily faint. "And will there be any way to let me know if they make it safely to Ysral?"

"Only if one of them is dedicated. I can roughly track the physical location of that person's Kiss and relay the information to you."

She thought hard. At the moment, she could remember no Edori who wore a Kiss in his arm, but there must be one or two in that assortment of people who had been, long ago, dedicated to the god. If not, surely she could persuade Thomas or one of the others to submit to having a Kiss implanted, if she explained why she asked for the favor.

"Thank you, Jovah," she whispered. "You are very good."

"I exist to do your will," he said.

She smiled a little. "And all this time, I thought angels existed to do yours. The world is not at all as I had believed it."

"Yet the world is the same as it always was. It is merely that you see with new eyes."

"And might I live long enough to see the world yet again as a place completely different, through eyes that see another truth not yet revealed?"

"I have given you the truth as I know it," Jovah replied. "I cannot predict what else you might learn."

"I will try not to be afraid of it, whatever it is," she said, moving slowly to the center of the bridge. She did not want to think too closely about how soon, if ever, she would return to this place, and she did not want to linger too long, memorizing details against the possibility that she would never come back. "Have you finished my map yet?"

"The navigational charts? Yes, they have been deposited in the silver basket by the power reactor gauge."

She looked quickly for the silver basket and found a neat pile of papers that carried an impressive array of numbers and diagrams. "I wonder if these will make sense to my Edori," she murmured.

"I have included a simple map, drawn to scale, which anyone should be able to read," he told her. "There are also star charts taken from a land-based position, which any navigator should be able to decipher. They will do some good, I believe. You will have to translate the words, of course, before you pass them along."

"That I believe I can do," she said, moving back to the middle of the room. "And now, one final request, Jehovah."

"And what is that, Alleluia?"

"Teleport."

Alleya spent the whole next day seated before the Sinai interface, typing in names of the Edori and anything she could remember about individuals and families. When she looked away from the sapphire screen, her eyes saw pink rectangles on the cool stone walls. Twice, she took long breaks, rubbing away the soreness in her neck and her fingers, shaking the stiffness from her knees. She should have dictated all this information while she was still aboard the ship; it would have been much faster and at least as accurate.

She had thought she would feel impatience at this slow, awkward method of speaking to Jovah, now that she knew how easy it was to ask a question and have him respond; but in fact, she rather liked the distance created by the flat screen and the buttons on the keyboard. This gave her time to think, helped her reassess her own place in the order of the world. This was a task, no matter how specialized, that seemed right and familiar. This was how Samarians were supposed to communicate with Jovah.

When she had told him all she knew, she asked if he had any

questions for her, and he did not. He then asked if she had any questions for him, and she did, but only one.

"Who should be angelico to the Archangel?" she typed in.

His response was immediate, the name she had most hoped to see. She smiled and turned away from the screen. She must be on her way to Breven in the morning. And after that, to the Eyrie.

Where Caleb would be waiting.

Chapter Twenty-One

Later, Caleb heard the story told with much embellishment, some of it ridiculous, but all of it eerily catching the flavor of the event. For he was there, and it did seem a momentous occasion, and he was not surprised to hear it described as if it were an event from the Librera itself.

"And there was a crowd that day on the main plateau of the Eyrie, right where the grand staircase empties. For word had spread throughout Velora, throughout the three realms, that Delilah was whole again and claimed her right to be Archangel. And there had been much anger and much speculation, for there were many who had never cared for Alleluia and would be glad to see her gone, and just as many who felt Delilah had lost her place and had no right to try to take it back.

"And just past noon, as the crowd milled about waiting to hear what the angels might have to say, a wild shout went out from the throats of the people gathered there, and many hands began pointing to the sky overhead. And above them, her arms outstretched and her wings perfectly still, seeming to merely float down to the earth, was the angel Alleluia. The sun made a halo of her golden hair and the air around her seemed to sizzle with a burning light. Closer and closer she came, so slowly she seemed not to move at all. Angels poured from every door in the Eyrie to see what had caused the commotion, but soon enough the howling crowd grew still, waiting for the angel to arrive.

"At last she came to a halt, her feet just inches above the stone, hovering in the air though not a single feather of her wings fluttered. And from her spread hands, sunlight dripped in a jeweled display, and she was too bright to look upon.

"And she spoke in a voice so soft it would not have wakened a babe in arms, and yet so clear that everyone in the hold could hear. And she said, 'Behold, I bring glad tidings. Who was lost is found. Who was broken is mended. The angel Delilah is among us again, and she soars on her glorious wings. Jovah, who has long loved her, has claimed her as his own again. Let the word go out to all men and all angels, that Archangel Delilah once again rules over Samaria.'

"And then there was such a clamor that no single word, no single voice could be heard, and not even Alleluia herself could persuade the crowd to listen. And then, while the bright angel still hovered above the plateau, a second shape, a dark angel, separated itself from the crowd and rose to Alleluia's side. Those two embraced as they soared above mankind, and it was as if the glory of the bright angel enveloped the dark angel, and soon they were both aglow with a light too fierce to bear."

Close enough, Caleb thought, the first time he heard the story; close enough, for he had been there. He was among the hundreds, the thousands, of people packed into the Eyrie, awaiting Alleya's return with an impatience so great it almost amounted to a fever.

He had been unable to get close enough to Delilah to speak with her, to upbraid her for her treachery and tell her to her face that, had he suspected what she would do with her restored wings, he would have left her in pieces till the day she died. Delilah, after her one dramatic announcement, had disappeared into the maze of the Eyrie and had not re-emerged. And, not surprisingly, no one who did not live there was allowed past the gateways on the great plateau.

Caleb had managed one quick, impassioned conversation with old Samuel, who took his turn guarding the entrances to the labyrinth. "How could she? How could she do such a thing?" he demanded, but Samuel merely shrugged.

"She is Delilah. Of course she would reclaim her own."

"And you will accept it? You will deny Alleya her place?"

"Delilah's claim is by no means certain," Samuel said somewhat bleakly. "There are those here, and in the other holds, who will refuse to acknowledge her. Asher is livid—we have had to restrain him, for he swears he will accost the angel Delilah and make her a cripple again."

"It is what I would do," Caleb said fiercely, though he knew he would not. But he might use words in an effect almost as wounding.

Samuel smiled sadly. "Thus do angels lead men in harmony," he said. "I cannot see to the end of this bitter day."

But the old angel (for to him Caleb attributed whatever amenities continued to exist) was able to keep the throng under control and the Eyrie itself peaceable. All through that tense morning, soothing music poured from above, angels and mortals singing their incessant duets, choosing (or so it seemed) the most calming melodies in their repertoires. Refreshments were passed among the crowd, and there were always at least three angels available to answer questions. Though they had no real answers, and there were only two questions: *Where is Alleluia? What will the angels decide?*

When, late that day, the small winged form took shape overhead, the response was immediate and verbal. Caleb, staring desperately upward like all the others, felt his heart contract with a new spasm of worry. He wished he had a minute to warn her, to give her a chance to brace herself. But perhaps she did have some kind of advance knowledge. Certainly, she made her descent in the most leisurely fashion, as if to draw attention, as if to make sure no one missed her arrival. And indeed, she seemed bathed in a divine light, as if she had been dipped in opal, and it was hard to look at her for too long.

By the time she finally made her landing (and her feet did touch the ground, albeit on a small pile of stones that put her about a yard above the crowd), there was dead silence and an almost palpable aura of waiting. Even the angels, who had poured out of the Eyrie in response to the uproar—even Delilah—stood motionless, speechless, waiting to hear what the angel had come to proclaim.

Alleluia spread her hands as if in benediction; and she smiled. "Good news," she said in that fey voice that everyone, even the god, could always hear. "Jovah tells me that the angel Delilah has been made whole again and that she once again takes wing to offer him her prayers. Celebrate with me, good people of Samaria, for the Archangel Delilah is returned to us! Glad tidings on this day of great joy."

Everyone around Caleb surged forward with a roar of exultation. Caleb himself fell backward, stupid with surprise. Could she mean it? Or was she simply feigning her pleasure, yielding gracefully to Delilah to avoid the ugliest battle imaginable? She had never wanted to be Archangel, after all, but surely even Alleya would feel some resentment at giving up a position of such power and adulation.

He was forced from his musings at the next unexpected sight: Delilah throwing herself over the crowd and into Alleya's arms. It was impossible to hear what the two angels said as the dark head burrowed under those golden tresses, but surely Alleya lifted Delilah's chin and kissed her on the cheek. Then Alleya said something else privately to Delilah, and she smiled; and Delilah, who now appeared to be crying, smiled back.

Alleya turned her attention back to the clamoring crowd and flung one hand out for silence. Which she was instantly accorded. "Jovah has entrusted me to tell you of two more appointments," she said, "which I hope you will like as well. For Delilah's angelico—"

And the instant before she said it, Caleb knew what the name would be.

"Jovah has selected the Edori called Noah, a good man with a clear eye and a sweet voice. He will arrive in a day or two, and I want all of you to welcome him, for Jovah's sake, and the Archangel's and his own."

A polite smattering of applause went up while people leaned toward their neighbors and whispered their disbelief. An Edori? It had not happened since Jovah chose Rachel for Gabriel, and even then she had not been true Edori, only adopted by that indiscriminate tribe. Nonetheless, they would do their best, they seemed to say; and for his own part, Caleb could not repress a grin. How far this particular Edori had traveled! Almost as far, in a way, as he would have journeyed from Samaria to Ysral, though the borders were invisible and the hazards less chancy. Still, there would be plenty of both.

"Jovah also asked me to inform you that a new oracle has stepped forward to fill the vacant post at Mount Sinai," Alleya was saying, and the crowd quieted to hear her last pronouncement. "And that oracle is me. I hope this appointment pleases you as well."

And now the response was thunderous for, although most ordinary men and women had only a hazy idea of an oracle's duties, they knew the position was one of power and responsibility—certainly a respectable post for a displaced Archangel. For his part, Caleb saw the incredulity he felt mirrored on Delilah's face, on the faces of the other angels and a few of the mortals who stood nearby. An angel as oracle? It had never happened before. Could such a thing be fitting? And yet, an oracle merely conferred with the god. Surely an angel was well-suited for that task.

Well enough, Caleb thought as his initial astonishment wore off. *In fact, good—excellent—the best thing of all. She alone knows Jovah as he truly is. And she alone can keep us all safe.* And he lifted his hands over his head and pounded them together, loosing three wild whistles of approbation. A faint smile crossed Alleya's face, and he knew she had spotted him in the crowd, and was pleased that he understood her.

This time, the assembly was quieted by Delilah's hand held out in a gesture of supplication. But when, silence achieved, Delilah turned to Alleya, her tone and her stance still bespoke entreaty.

"The Gloria is in five weeks," said the Archangel. "And my angelico and I must sing to the glory of Jovah. Will you sing at my side on the Plain of Sharon? For the god loves your voice—and so do I."

For a split second Alleya hesitated—clearly this had caught her by surprise—and then she smiled and nodded. "I will be glad to sing with you, angela," she said. "For the harmony of the angels is what pleases Jovah the most."

At that, the crowd went mad, and there was nothing to do but submit to the tide of joyous furor. Caleb fought his way to a back wall, out of harm's way, to wait out the tempest. He was still recovering from the multiple shocks of the afternoon, but it seemed to him that Alleya had orchestrated the event pretty much as she had wanted. And if she was happy, then he had no quarrels.

He smiled broadly and then he laughed, not with mirth but joy. For this brief moment, at least, everything in his world was in perfect harmony. Which was just as Jovah desired.

Five weeks later, a crowd of nearly ten thousand gathered on the Plain of Sharon. It was the largest group ever assembled to hear or perform the Gloria, though there had been very few of the problems usually associated with setting up a substantial if temporary city. Days in advance, vendors from all three provinces had unpacked their booths; enterprising hoteliers had arranged rows of tents to be rented out by private parties; the angels from all three holds had arrived with their own well-constructed pavilions.

It seemed the whole world was here. Caleb, strolling through the makeshift streets, watched a parade of people pass by, from rich young merchants' sons to the veiled Jansai women to the mischievous brown Edori children who played running games up and down these crowded avenues. Despite the volatile mix of classes—rich Manadavvi landowners brushing elbows with farmers' daughters—everyone seemed to co-exist in smiling good humor. For the weather was fine and the Archangel was restored and all was right with the world; what was left to quarrel over?

Caleb was glad to see the Gloria finally arrive, for the last five weeks had passed in a blur of motion that somehow left him on the outside. The two people he cared about most, Noah and Alleya, had had only moments here and there to spare for him, and he had tried nobly to refrain from demanding more of their attention. Noah, of course, had been closeted in the music rooms, learning a mass with Delilah's help; Alleya had been half the time in Velora and half the time away, consulting with the other oracles. Caleb had entertained himself by visiting with the Edori engineer Daniel, working with him to try to find new uses for the marvelous batteries.

He had managed to snag a few precious hours with Alleya, who was in high spirits. He had been dumbstruck when she told him about her visit to the spaceship—dumbstruck and jealous.

"I can't believe it," he said, "after the promise you extracted from me—"

"I know. I realize it was unfair."

"So now must I force a similar vow from you? That you will not return without me? Notice I do not demand that you never return."

"I don't think I will, though. I don't think I should."

"But if you do—"

"But if I do. Yes. I will inform you, and we will go hand in hand. Does that satisfy you?"

He smiled down at her. "Nothing will satisfy me until I have you to myself for a day or two."

She actually took the time to blush, although, even as they spoke, she was restlessly moving around the room packing items for the Gloria. It had seemed to scandalize no one when he essentially moved into her quarters at the Eyrie, and so he stayed there whether she was present or not. "Hard to imagine when that might be," she said.

"After the Gloria?"

"After that. But then, of course, there is all the work of making Mount Sinai a functioning sanctuary again. Some renovations must be done, and I will need acolytes, and to find them I will have to woo the likely parents—mostly the merchants and the landowners, but I want to reach some of the independent farmers, as well, and perhaps some of the factory workers. And there is a child in Chahiela—I think she would make an excellent acolyte. Perhaps even a priestess, if she shows a bent for it, though she's a little young to know—"

He stopped her with a hand laid gently across her mouth. "Time for that later," he said. "Surely we will have a day or two of rest before you must completely overhaul Mount Sinai."

She pulled his hand away after kissing his palm. "And what will the famous engineer Caleb Augustus do while I am getting Mount Sinai in shape?"

"I will build a workshop at the foot of the mountain and conduct strange scientific experiments. I want to figure out how these batteries are made and see if I can make my own. I've already talked to your friend Daniel here in Velora—he says he might want to come spend a couple months with me working on some projects of his own. Who knows, maybe we'll open a school to teach engineering. There has to be a better way to learn it than the way he and I did."

"That would please me, to have you so close," she said. "I have been picturing you back in Luminaux or perhaps at Velora, a long flight for me and a longer ride for you. But if you were right there at the edge of my mountain—"

"I could see you every day," he finished. "Yes. That was my thought as well."

She kissed him on the mouth, then turned away. "A good thought. But we first have the Gloria to get through, and much to do before that. Work before dreaming."

But with those dreams he had been forced to content himself these past few weeks. Those dreams, and what diversions he could find. Once or twice he was able to pry Noah from his music lessons, and they made their way down the grand staircase to a friendly Velora bar. Noah seemed dazed but happy, a man whose fortunes had veered so often and so rapidly in the past few weeks that he was not entirely sure now which direction he faced.

"Once I get through the Gloria, then I'll start trying to reconstruct it," the Edori told Caleb as they shared a pitcher of beer one night. "A few weeks ago, I'd expected to be halfway to Ysral at this point. And now I'm in Velora preparing to sing an unfamiliar mass before thousands of people, side by side with the Archangel Delilah. Jovah moves with great mysteriousness to bring us to a state of wonder."

"And how well have you learned your piece?" Caleb asked.

"Not well enough! We've chosen the simplest one in the repertoire, but it runs nearly two hours. My solos are only about fifteen or twenty minutes' worth of that, but it's formal music. Not campfire songs. I don't know how well I'll master the technique."

"Jovah chose you," Caleb said. "He must admire your voice."

"Well, he has listened to my voice often enough these past months," the Edori answered quietly. "For I prayed every day to see Delilah restored, and I prayed every day to keep her from those ships bound to Ysral. And he has answered my prayers. So he must love me even better than I had hoped."

How to respond to that? Caleb thought about it while he lifted his beer to his mouth and swallowed half the glass. "I think Jovah loves us all equally," Caleb said at last. "If he answers a prayer, he has his reasons for doing so—reasons that may seem obscure to us but which, in ten or fifty or a hundred years, make perfect sense. It is hard for us to think in those terms, but for Jovah, time is immaterial. He sees all life as one continuous whole, no beginning, no end. And the prayers that move him are the prayers that will restore the world."

Noah was laughing. "Why, Caleb, you old atheist!" he exclaimed. "What philosophers have you been reading? I didn't think you believed in a god, let alone a god with a purpose—such as it is."

Caleb smiled. "I am revising my thoughts somewhat," he said. "I'll let you know when I've worked out all the details."

"Do," Noah invited. "I would be interested to hear *your* treatise on the divine principles. Though I doubt if I will agree with them."

"But then, when did we ever agree?" Caleb mocked, and they settled into a friendly argument on engineering theories that had divided them in the past.

That was rare enough; even rarer was the chance to speak to the Archangel, who was never surrounded by fewer than fifteen people. Feeling as though he was lurking in the glowing hallways of the Eyrie, Caleb occasionally watched her from afar. She seemed alive, vibrant as he had never seen her; it was as if she had long languished on a sickbed and, suddenly cured, had been restored to full exuberant health. Her dark hair was sleeker, blacker; her skin was pearlescent and flawless.

But there was, in addition, some subtle magnetism at work in her that was even more compelling than her physical beauty. Caleb saw how she could, with a twist of her hand or a sideways look, unfailingly draw people to her side. There was something about her joyousness and her intensity that was irresistible. More than once Caleb saw petitioners standing near her lift their hands as if they wanted nothing so much as to stroke her feathers or her skin. Most of them dropped their hands before they committed the sacrilege, but one or two simply could not stop themselves—and they touched her, and she turned immediately, and she smiled. And they forever after adored her.

Even Caleb, who had considered himself inured to her charms, now and then found himself longing for a brief moment of her recognition, a chance to stand within her radiant circle. It amused him, but it also discomposed him, and he thought it was just as well that she was too busy to notice him.

But late one night, as he read himself to a solitary sleep, he was surprised by the chime at the door. When he answered the summons, he was struck into incoherence by the sight of Delilah standing there alone.

"Ah—angela—she is—that is," he stammered, "Alleya is not here. She's in Monteverde."

Delilah gave him that familiar wicked grin. "I know she is. It is you I have come to talk to."

"Me?" he said. "Well! Then—yes, come in." And he stepped aside to allow her entry.

She strolled a few feet into the room, but her stance made it clear that she was here for only the briefest of visits. Still, she stalled for a moment or two, looking around the room as if to examine its few adornments. "You must think me rude beyond description," she said at last, not quite facing him, "to have delayed so long in thanking you."

"But you did thank me," he said, "back in Velora."

"Then I thank you again, this time as Archangel," she said. "Whose prayers carry more weight with Jovah."

He hesitated, then shook his head and spoke the truth. "Had Alleya not been willing to cede you that title," he said, "it would have been hard for me to rejoice with you now."

"Oh, you would have hated me forever!" she exclaimed. "Just as Noah hated poor Alleya! Don't worry—I don't hold it against you. It is one of your few virtues, in fact."

"What, that I can muster resentment?"

She laughed. "No, that you have the wit to love the angel Alleluia. Though you are the last man I would have expected to win her staid heart."

"Oh, and my friend Noah is just the man I had thought to see in your arms," he retorted.

She laughed aloud. "True. We have mismatched ourselves, have we not? Still, I cannot find it in me to be sorry."

Soon after that she turned to go, then paused at the doorway and turned back. Despite her gaiety throughout this visit, he sensed a seriousness in her, a familiarity with melancholy that would never completely evaporate. It led her, now, to give him a smile that was tinged with sadness, and to hold her hand out in farewell. "Thank you again," she said. "I do not feel I can ever say it enough."

"It was an honor," he said, and took her in his arms.

"Stay well. Be happy," he whispered in her ear. She kissed him on the cheek and disappeared into the corridor. He never had a chance to speak alone with her again.

And now he waited on the Plain of Sharon with ten thousand others to prove to Jovah one more time that harmony reigned on Samaria. From where he stood, in the inner circle with the angels, he could not see all the massed attendants, but he knew they were there: scores of Manadavvi, Jansai, rivermen, farmers, miners. Of Edori there were only a few, maybe a hundred, for Edori did not consider the Gloria a sacred event, and in any case, more than a thousand were gone from the continent already. Those who were present seemed happy and friendly as all Edori did, but Caleb thought he caught an uneasy bewilderment in their eyes from time to time. Maybe they missed their departed brethren, or wished they had not stayed behind, or wondered what the rest of Samaria had to offer them that would make up for the loss of so many.

Caleb glanced around once more, wondering how quickly the music would start, and forced himself to swallow a yawn. They had all risen quite early, since the Gloria was scheduled to begin an hour past dawn, and it was no easy task to arrange ten thousand people in their appropriate stations. Morning still seemed to have barely begun; the sky had a fresh-washed look to it and even the air seemed to have wandered down, new-minted, from one of the encircling mountains. Only in one place was the Plain of Sharon unguarded by a high peak, and that was at its southernmost point, where once the mighty Galo Mountain had stood. One and a half centuries ago, when the Gloria did not proceed as planned, Jovah had leveled that mountain with a single bolt, and even now the ground around it was blackened and disordered from the heat and force of that blow.

But there would be no such theatrics today. Even now a sigh of anticipation rippled through the crowd, for Noah, Delilah and Alleya had finally moved forward to take their position in the center of the angels. What conversation there had been came to a halt; nothing but the wind moved or breathed.

Into that utter stillness a low, clear voice sang the opening notes of a prayer of jubilation. Even Caleb recognized this piece, and he saw the angels around him exchange silent looks of surprise, uncertainty and then approbation. It was the simplest of the holy masses, the one taught to schoolchildren, and it was almost never used in any formal ceremony. Yet it was a joyous piece, celebrating the common delights of life and praising Jovah for his many goodnesses, and everyone knew the words to it. And it seemed, under the circumstances, appropriate, as Samaria prepared itself for a spell of calm contentment after a long season of storm.

Noah's voice rose and fell liltingly through the playful intervals of the melody, and it was plain that this uncomplicated mass was perfectly suited to his style. He seemed neither nervous nor afraid; he stood as he might stand at an Edori campfire, hands clasped before him, face upturned so that his words might flow directly from his mouth to the god's ear.

When Delilah joined with Noah for the first duet of the mass, Caleb initially thought the angel's magnificent voice would overpower the Edori's. But it was not so; hers soared and raved above his, but his full, steady tones seemed to tether her sublime ones to the earth. It was as if, without his voice in counterpart, hers would have disappeared in a celestial transport; he made a place for her to exist here on the Plain of Sharon.

The close of that first duet was the signal to the assembled crowd. They came in on cue with their choral response, a deep, rumbling sound issuing from so many throats. Even Caleb, who had not planned to sing, found himself joining in with the traditional, familiar words, the music that graced every mass no matter how formal or complex: "Yes, there is love. . .yes, there is beauty . . . yes, we believe in the wisdom of our god . . ." Affirmation, exultation, absolute faith in the rightness of the divine.

And why not? Caleb thought as he intoned the stately, majestic words. *Why not believe with your whole heart, never for a moment doubt the goodness of the god?* Jehovah the spaceship was not at all loving, though in its way it was beautiful and it was certainly wise; but that did not mean there was not, somewhere, as the Edori believed, a greater god who informed the entire universe and held all the stars and planets in place. The universe was grander than Caleb had ever thought to consider, and there might very well be room in it for a god. It was hard to know, but there might be no harm in scraping out a small foothold for belief.

The brief choral interlude ended, and now it was Delilah's turn to show off her ability. But she had amended this part of the mass; it was no longer her solo. Twining around the Archangel's voice like ivy around a flowering vine, Alleya's voice rose with Delilah's in such perfect harmony that it was hard to separate the bright voices one from the other. Clearly there was a dominant and a subordinate note, but they seemed indivisible, as if neither could be sounded unless both were. And the gorgeousness of that music! The sky seemed painted with it, the air was scented with it; Caleb felt himself inhaling it a breathless stanza at a time. This was true prayer, then; hearing this was what had made a machine divine. Caleb thought such music would have deified anything.

He completely missed the next choral entrance, so enraptured was he with the duet, and he was not the only one in the crowd who fumbled for the note. This time, though, he sang out more heartily; this time he was nearly won over. *Let there be a god, then,* he thought, *if this is the devotion he commands.*

It was more than an hour later before the last note of the mass was sung, a long, achingly beautiful "Amen" which Delilah had reserved entirely for her own. No one spoke or breathed or rustled for a full five minutes after her last note died away, and then the crowd of ten thousand erupted into pounding, whistling, ecstatic applause. Archangel and angelico held hands and bowed to their well-wishers; Alleya merely raised one arm and waved, though she smiled broadly. A tangible wave of euphoria swept through the crowd, moving people to spontaneous embraces and moments of giddy laughter. Another Gloria gloriously concluded;

the wrath of the god averted, the friendship between men and angels reaffirmed. Truly, it was a day made for celebration.

And the following morning, Caleb left with the oracle for Sinai.

He had thought the morning would never come, for the day of the Gloria was endless, filled with music, filled with feasting. The formal mass was only the first of a long series of musical offerings—anyone from the highest angel to the humblest mortal could perform to the god's glory this day, and hundreds of people did. City choirs, Edori troubadours, angel trios—all took their turn before the appreciative crowd, lifting their voices to the god. Meanwhile, minor festivities went on around them, as people paused to eat, gossip, and play games at booths and tents across the plain.

Eventually Caleb tired of it and retreated to the Eyrie pavilion and the curtained room that had been set aside for his and Alleya's use. He was sleeping when, well past midnight, Alleya slipped onto the cot beside him. He felt her feathers slide with a foreign silkiness against his exposed skin; it was a sensation that never failed to make him shiver with a shocked desire. The bed was small for two people—especially when one was an angel—but it was manageable for a night or so. Certainly preferable to two separate cots.

"Are you happy?" he asked her drowsily, and heard her laugh in the dark.

"Yes," she said. "Are you?"

"I will be tomorrow," he said, and heard her laugh again. She resettled herself once and was soon asleep in his arms. He kissed the top of her head, and followed her down the shadowy avenue of dreams.

In the morning, there were endless details to attend to, and Caleb thought they would never get away. But while Alleya made her farewells, he pared down their belongings and rounded up enough provisions for a week. He packed as lightly as he could, but still he wondered if he might be expecting one angel to transport too much.

"Can you carry all this?" he asked Alleya anxiously as she finally joined him.

She laughed. "I've flown farther with more. I can carry all this, and you besides."

"But how far?"

She reached her hands up, placing one very carefully on either side of his face. "To Ysral, if need be," she said softly. "To *Jehovah* and back. Trust me. We will be safe together."

After that, there was no need for protests. They loaded up, and she put her arms around him. "Are you ready?" the angel asked.

"I have waited my whole life for this," he replied.

It was like nothing he had ever known and everything he had dreamed of. The great wings rose and fell around him; the angel's slim body tensed and sprang forward. The world hurtled backward; the sky stooped low. Beneath him, the landscape was a dizzy blur of green and slate and blue, but if he concentrated very closely he could make out individual features—trees, mountains, lakes. The air felt winter-cool, snow-damp, and yet it glittered around his face with sunshine that had not yet fallen all the way to the earth. There was a perpetual wind against his cheek and a pleasant sense of vertigo, and with delight he realized that this forward rushing movement might not come to an end for hours.

He threw back his head and laughed, for the world was a wondrous place. At this moment, he believed in everything, science, religion, and the melding of the two. He loved an angel and she loved him. And he was flying.